Chosen

Chosen

Jerry Ibbotson

© Jerry Ibbotson, 2008

Published by Media Mill

www.jerryibbotson.co.uk

November 2008

ISBN 978-0-9560635-0-2

A CIP catalogue record for this book is available from the British Library.

Cover design Paul Moss

Prepared and printed by:
York Publishing Services Ltd
64 Hallfield Road
Layerthorpe
York YO31 7ZQ
Tel: 01904 431213
Website: www.yps-publishing.co.uk

Acknowledgements

Thanks to all the people who helped me make this book a reality.

To my long suffering wife Louise who goaded me into getting started. Without your support, patience and good ideas *Chosen* would have gone nowhere.

To my proofreaders: Matt, Tracy and my dad. Thanks for spotting all my stupid mistakes.

And to Ellie, Lottie and Daniel. Thanks for showing me what magic really is.

Jerry Ibbotson
York, 2008

Jerry Ibbotson was born in 1969 in London but spent his childhood in various parts of the UK thanks to his dad's job. Who would guess that being a weather man would mean so much moving around?

He was a BBC radio journalist for nearly ten years, finally ending up reading the news for the likes of John Peel and Chris Moyles on Radio One. He left the BBC in 2000 to try 'different things' and has been running his own sound company since then, making strange noises for a living. He lives in York with his wife and family.

If you want to tell him what you thought of *Chosen*, feel free to email him. Don't let all the pain and effort it took to get the thing into print put you off being honest.

jerry@jerryibbotson.co.uk

Chapter One

Weird Things

He always hated train journeys at night. By day they could be quite inspiring because he could stare out at the passing scenery. The sideways scrolling backdrop of houses, factories and fields fired his imagination like mental rocket fuel. Every aspect of human life was being played out just beyond the glass and he feasted on the possibilities. He only had to catch a glimpse of someone at a window to begin constructing a life for them: a family, a past, a secret. He created all this in his mind for just long enough for the next distraction to arrive.

That was the thing with Alex Preston. His imagination was what kept him going in a world of mental static and white noise. Half his life was spent drifting off into a place of his own. It could happen anywhere: on his way home from work, alone with his wife or even in the middle of a conversation. A switch would flick inside his head and he would begin spiralling away from everything around him, conjuring up scenarios in which his life was whatever he wanted it to be. He could be a hero or a victim, a legend or a history maker. There were more things that Alex had done in his imagination than were possible in a hundred lifetimes.

But at that moment the only thing he could see was his own reflection against the pitch black of an October night. That did nothing to distract him from the cold and discomfort of his journey. Whatever the time of year, railway carriages always seemed to him to be colder and noisier after dark. This particular train rocked back and forth as it wound its way down the track. The clatter from the wheels seemed so much louder than it had twelve hours ago that it drove itself into his head. There was no escape from the din.

He glanced at his watch and wished he had not stayed so late. He could have been at home kissing the baby goodnight instead of being squeezed into a broken, stained seat on a godforsaken train. He closed his eyes and tried to doze away the journey. Alex had learned from years of commuting that it was possible to sleep on public transport by locking his neck and balancing himself in his seat. There was a film he had seen as a child about a medieval king called El Cid. The man had died on the eve of a huge battle and his generals knew that this could prove disastrous for morale. So they had nailed him to his saddle and sent him onto the field of battle on his horse, bolt upright, to lead his men to victory. Alex had adapted this technique to allow him to nod off on the late train without flopping back against the window like a drooling fool. He just had to position himself properly then...

"Is this taken?"

He jerked upright at the sound of the voice. The carriage was half empty but still a middle aged man was pointing expectantly at the vacant seat beside him. "Oh. Er. Yeah," Alex mumbled, hoping to put the man off. But the stranger simply smiled and sat down. He looked in his fifties and was wearing a dark pin-striped suit and was carrying a raincoat folded in the crook of one arm. After settling himself into the seat and placing the coat over his lap he pulled a newspaper from a leather holdall. He started reading the front page as Alex shifted towards the window and closed his eyes again.

He began to conjure up another daydream. On his way to the station that evening he had seen a newspaper headline about a soldier being decorated for bravery. He could imagine himself in that position: a tough yet sensitive fighting man who is sent to war in a far off land. He comes under attack and, despite overwhelming odds, drives the enemy away then risks his own life to save his comrades from a burning vehicle. Alex knew that he would run away screaming if he ever had to go to war but he liked the idea of being a hero. Besides which, there was nothing he could actually do to stop his imagination from running amok. It happened mostly of its own accord and was getting worse as he grew older. In the past, dreams had been excusable but a responsible adult life had its limits.

"It's been a hell of a day hasn't it?"

Alex's mental meanderings were cut short and he opened his eyes. "Sorry?" He sounded annoyed.

"The weather. I got soaked twice this afternoon. They say it'll last all week."

Alex looked at the man's neatly folded raincoat. It was bone dry. "I don't mind a bit of rain," he said and he closed his eyes again. The picture in his mind now was of him being attacked on the last train home by a nutty man with a dry raincoat. He imagined Sarah weeping and the children being brought in to kiss him as he lay in a coma. He wondered which celebrity his family might ask to record a message of encouragement to be played at his bedside. The nurses on the ward would keep a solemn watch over him and everyone who had ever been bad to him would feel...

"Travelling at night is never fun is it?"

"Oh for..." Alex opened his eyes for the third time and turned to his unwanted companion. He was relieved to see that the old man did not appear to be a threat. There was a kind of softness to his face and creases around his mouth that looked like he spent a lot of time smiling. But he was still being annoying. "You don't like it?" Alex asked.

"Oh I don't mind," the man said, "I meant you."

At that moment the train began to make a loud grinding sound, like nails being dragged slowly down a blackboard. It grew louder and louder until it filled the carriage like a scream. The wail of metal on metal made other passengers raise their heads above the line of seats like frightened animals. At the other end of the carriage a woman holding a baby looked back towards Alex with tears in her eyes. The train lurched

3

to the side, as if it was about to flip over, then righted itself. The metallic screeching stopped. The disturbance seemed to have passed but then there was a tremendous bang and all the seats juddered. A deep roaring sound started from the front of the train and everything around Alex began moving in slow motion. There was an intense vibration from the floor and the lights flickered as the roaring grew louder. Alex looked over the top of the seat in front and saw the fear on the faces of an elderly couple. The young mother was holding her baby and crying even more loudly than the child. And then he saw it: tearing its way towards them through the other carriages and devouring everything in its path with a hellish bellow.

Another train.

"Crap." He sank back into his seat.

"Just do the right thing when the time comes." The man barely whispered, yet the words carried over the insane racket. In the final moment he laid his hand on Alex's and leaned in close. Alex was paralysed by the enormous dark shape that was about to swallow them up but then he felt the coolness of the stranger's palm and his fear left him. He breathed out slowly as a huge shard of metal twisted through the air and flew at him down the length of the carriage. The lights went out.

"It's too bloody dark."

The metal felt cold between Alex's fingers and his grip was so weak that he struggled not to drop it. He gritted his teeth and tried again.

"Bullseye."

The key slid into the lock and with a quick twist the door sprung open. Then he was in the hallway fumbling for the light switch. The house was in darkness and the sounds of his sleeping family drifted from the landing. Alex Preston was home.

* * *

"Biscuit."

Alex opened one eye and closed it again.

"Biscuit."

4

He felt a chubby finger poking him as the little boy grew more insistent. Matthew was standing by the side of the bed trying to wake his Daddy up. A quick look at the clock on the bedside table and Alex realised it was pointless trying to resist his son's pestering. He slid out from under the covers and stumbled downstairs to make Sarah her morning tea. When he returned to the bedroom, Matthew and Katie were both curled up with their mother, who was watching the news.

"Have you seen this?" she said, pointing at the screen. There were images of firemen sifting through a huge pile of wreckage, an unrecognisable mass of dark metal that looked like it had been through a blender. There were bright red patches dotted around the heap of blackened steel that Alex realised were blankets covering bodies. "That must have been the train after yours. Those people…"

Alex sipped his tea and said nothing. He had a head full of confusing thoughts. The pictures on the television evoked vague memories of a train journey through the dark, screaming metal and a sense of terror. But the news report was about a crash with no survivors. He looked at his hands for any cuts or scratches; any sign that he might have been involved. They were unblemished. He was convinced that this was just one of his daydreams. Then he heard the reporter begin the roll call of the dead. A mother and her young child were among the victims, along with an older couple who had been celebrating their wedding anniversary. "Oh my God that's awful," said Sarah, but Alex was not listening. He felt unsteady and his heart began to beat frantically, not out of sorrow for the deaths of strangers but because his body was buzzing with the news that he was still alive.

As he buttoned his shirt he considered telling his wife what he was thinking, but he could not imagine hearing the words, "Darling I think I was on that train with all those people who died but I survived without a scratch and I can't remember how I got home." They sounded absurd enough in his head. Miracles did not happen, not to him anyway. It was like he had the ghost of a memory about trains and strangers. Then the moment passed as a mental numbness swept over him like morphine pouring through his veins. There were no more thoughts of miraculous survival, only of getting dressed and going to work. After grabbing a mouthful of coffee he snatched up his keys and left the house. The railway line was still closed so he had no choice but to drive. He pulled out of the end of the road and slid through the suburbs.

On the main road leading down towards the office there was a bridge across the carriageway. It was made of grey concrete, with ominous brown stains leaking through its stony skin. As Alex's car approached through the nose to tail traffic, he noticed some graffiti scrawled across the side. He wondered how anyone managed to write anything upside down on a bridge. "B… e… r…" He slowed the car down to study the white letters. "Be ready."

"Ready for what?" he wondered. It was bound to be something religious; these things usually were. "Nutters," he muttered as he accelerated away. It was then that he glanced up at his rear view mirror and saw the graffiti on the other side of the bridge, written backwards like the words on an ambulance.

"Alex. Do the right thing."

* * *

He spent the first hour at the office phoning his insurance company, explaining his broken front bumper and dented bonnet. This was done while he should have been working. Alex had mastered the art of making personal calls with the facial expression of someone dealing with vital business matters. It was the skiver's version of the poker face; straight and serious with a steely gaze. He used it now as he explained to the woman in the call centre how he had driven up the back of a delivery lorry on his way in to work. He left out the detail about seeing a bizarre message on the side of a bridge. He doubted that it would help his claim.

As the call wound up he opened his email and saw a stack of messages demanding his attention. This was not what he wanted to be doing. He would much rather be sitting on a beach, somewhere remote, watching the wind from the sea whipping over the grass topped dunes of white sand. He would have his coat pulled up around his chin and Sarah and the kids would be there with him, feeling relaxed and happy. He could hear the children's laughter as they ran over the sand. His head would be clear of the noise and nonsense and he would be able to enjoy life for what it was.

But to get to that beach he would have to quit first. He could imagine walking into Peter Jones's office and telling him where to stick his stupid job. Just the thought of it was enough to get his pulse racing. He could see it now: the man's drooping jaw and look of shock as Alex announced his departure. It would be only at this point that the idiot Jones would realise how it was Alex who kept the place running. He would really feel it once he had gone and things started to fall apart. But by then...

"Heard you smacked your car up mate."

Alex looked up from an invisible point in space, just above his coffee cup, to see Andrew Marshall grinning down at him. It was to Marshall's credit that Alex only resented him half as much as he did Jones. But at least his boss had the excuse of being a manager who made life hell for others; Marshall was just plain annoying. Nothing ever bothered him. He never admitted to any kind of weakness or failing and it was clear that he had absolutely no doubt about his own abilities. He would also refer to his male colleagues as "mate" at every opportunity and was forever shaking hands with them, in the most insincere way possible.

"Yeah, just a knock. I don't even drive in normally." Alex's voice trailed away. The mental painkiller had begun to wear off and he started to shiver but Marshall did not notice. He had already switched his attention to the stack of papers he was cradling.

"Oh, why's that then?" he asked distantly.

It was a mark of how little Marshall knew about his

colleagues that Alex had to explain that he usually commuted by train, as he lived so far out of town. "There was a crash on the line last night. It's still shut so I had to drive in."

Marshall snorted. "That was unlucky." There was something ugly about the way he said it. He went on, "Are you coming to Phil's leaving do tonight?"

Alex grimaced. He had forgotten all about the party that evening, in honour of a colleague who was moving abroad. Faced with a drive home he would not be able to drink so it hardly seemed worth it. It was not even being held anywhere decent; just beers in the office followed by more at the pub down the road. But he lacked the will to argue and agreed to stay for one drink. That was enough to send Marshall away and allow Alex to get on with some work. For the rest of the day he put all thoughts of trains, graffiti and car accidents out of his mind. At five o'clock Peter Jones appeared from his office pushing a trolley loaded with bottles and plastic cups. Though most of Alex's colleagues shared his sentiments about their boss, they all crowded around to get some free alcohol and toast their friend who was leaving.

Alex sat on the edge of his desk and sipped orange juice while the rest of the office attacked the pile of beers with gusto. He just wanted to be at home. At least if he had been drinking he would not have felt guilty at leaving Sarah alone with the kids for the second night in a row. His mind began to wander away from the banter and gossip of his inebriated colleagues and off into his own world yet again. This time it was not a day dream but one of his personal petty rants.

There were many things that got on Alex's nerves and every day he seemed to find a new one to add to the list. Now it was people who did not have kids and could drink themselves dumb without worrying about getting home before a toddler's bed time. Then there were the people who were married or in long term relationships but who spent so much time away from their partners that they may as well be single. Alex's office was full of those. They were the ones who went on every business trip going, would spend all weekend playing golf or football and see their partners at some point in between. And yet they were the same people who would go on pretentious foreign holidays as the perfect loving couple. When he walked into their houses he would see them grinning down from photos on the wall: Mr and Mrs Perfect standing by a waterfall in Thailand.

"You look miserable Alex. Had some bad news?" Marshall's sweaty, drunken form was swaying about in front of him. He had a beer bottle in each hand and was bobbing and weaving around with a ridiculous grin on his flushed face. Alex resisted the temptation to give him a kick just to see if he would bounce back up again.

"No, just planning on heading home. I'm driving."

Marshall steadied himself against the edge of the desk. "So why did you drive in to work today then? Bit stupid wasn't it?" He was leaning in towards Alex's face, the fruity smell of beer pouring off him. "You must have known we were on for a session."

"I said before. I had no choice," said Alex, "there were no trains running. Not after the crash on the line last night."

"Bad news. I saw that on the telly. You didn't get caught up in it did you?"

Alex paused. He had the same feeling as earlier in the day: of a kind of ghost memory appearing in his head. "Nah, but the line was closed." He felt his face reddening but Marshall had drunk too much to notice. The man leaned in again with a smirk, as if he was struggling to contain himself.

"I've got a secret Alex. If you knew what it was it would blow you away. Blow your mind." Alex leaned away and moved to slide off the desk but Marshall blocked him. He moved even closer to Alex and lowered his voice. "I've got a ticket to the ride of your life. It's like nothing you've ever seen or done. And if you're really nice to me I might share it with you." He giggled childishly and pulled back.

Alex got to his feet and frowned at him. "You're a nutter Andrew. A bladdered one. Too many beers."

The other man laughed so loudly that some of the others in the room looked around for a second before returning to their friends and their drinks. "You can say what you like Alex. I'm the one with the key to ..." he stopped mid sentence and his head went back slightly as he straightened up. The expression on his face had changed from a loose grin to an intense stare. "I could show you my secret."

"So where is it then, in your sock drawer?" Alex's sarcasm bounced off Marshall like he was armour plated.

"Nah, somewhere much better than that. I can show you right now if you want. If you can handle it. Which I doubt."

Alex was bored with Marshall's drunkenness but he quite fancied seeing his colleague make a fool of himself. "Yeah go on then," he said. Marshall backed away and smiled again. He turned and walked towards the main office door, looking back just once as he weaved and swayed his way across the carpet. With each hand still clutching a bottle, he shouldered his way through the door and disappeared into the corridor.

Sometimes the biggest of decisions can depend on the smallest of things. Sometimes events so massive that they fill the pages of history books are formed and shaped by the most inconsequential of objects, places or even people. Like the silver face on the wall above Alex. Behind it, a tiny motor drove small plastic gears that hauled three spindly arms over its smooth metal surface. Second after second, minute after minute, hour after hour. Until then it had signalled nothing more crucial than the time to get a smoke or a coffee, or when to grab a coat or handbag and head out the door. But now it held the power to turn his life upside down. If it had been just five minutes fast it might have sent him down a different route but instead it told Alex Preston that he had time to spare before driving home. So he put his drink down on the edge of the desk and followed Marshall through the office door.

Chapter Two

Tunnel Vision

The padlock was brown with rust, which made it look fossilised and out of place next to the fresh layer of green paint on the door. The hinges had also been recently painted and shone black and glossy under the light from Marshall's tiny pocket torch. "This is where it is," he slurred. Now that he was away from the office party he seemed even more inebriated, as if he had been using the other drinkers for camouflage.

"Bloody hell. You dragged me down here to look at a door?" Alex was not impressed and was more convinced than ever that Marshall was the most annoying man alive.

"Don't be so stupid," Marshall replied. "It's what's behind it that'll blow you away."

He rummaged in his pocket and fished out his keys: there was the one for his expensive black hatchback, the one to his neat little flat in an upmarket part of town and a small one for his locker at the gym. Then there was one that caught Alex's eye, even in the poorly lit shadows of the basement to the office building. It was long and slender and made of highly polished steel. It glinted in the weak flickering beam of the miniature torch that was being waved about in Marshall's drunken hand.

"Where did you get that?" asked Alex.

"I just found it here on the floor."

Alex frowned with disbelief but Marshall already had his back to him while he worked the lock. "What were you doing down here in the first place?" Alex asked, but the question went unanswered. There was the sound of the thin shiny key being jiggled frantically back and forth in the rusty padlock before finally a crisp click rang out and Marshall gave a chuckle. With more jiggling the lock was free from the clasp and he placed it on the floor.

"Okay. You ready?"

"I'm ready," Alex humoured. He really could not wait to get back upstairs and go home instead of being in the dark, cluttered basement surrounded by cardboard boxes full of old personnel files and broken desk lamps. There was a heavy damp smell in the air down here, which was not surprising given the age of the building, and it made the place feel dark and unhealthy. He nodded at Marshall to get on with things, "Show me then."

The pair of them faced the door together and Marshall took hold of the green handle and gave a quick tug. The door moved back a little and then stuck, with an ugly, dirty sound of scraping metal. There was a grunt and he tried again, this time with a longer, more powerful pull on the handle. Now the door flew open and the two men fell backwards over each other. Alex righted himself and peered through the doorway as something cool and welcoming hit him in the face. Fresh air.

Through the doorway there was nothing but darkness. Then gradually, as his eyes adjusted to the lack of light, he could make out the shape of a tunnel stretching backwards into the wall. There was a soft breeze drifting out and as it blew across his face he tried to place the scent that was being carried with it.

"It's the smell of trees," said Marshall, enjoying his companion's look of confusion.

Alex squinted into the dark, as if his eyes might be able to see the smell. "How can it be trees? Does it come up in a park somewhere?"

Marshall laughed and stepped into the mouth of the tunnel. "Why don't you come and see for yourself?" he asked over his shoulder, before walking a few feet into the passageway. "I said it would blow your mind and it will."

A moment ago Alex had been on the verge of leaving but

now he had to admit to being extremely curious. The tunnel probably went nowhere out of the ordinary but still he felt a huge buzz of excitement. It filled his body and made his fingers tingle and his heart beat in his chest. It was a familiar feeling; like the one he had experienced at home that morning.

That reminded him of Sarah. He really ought to be leaving. He was nice and sober and ready to go. He just had to walk...

Now he was in the tunnel. Its walls were made of white bricks and the floor was of hard stone. He moved a little further along and tried to see into the darkness but could only make out the shape of Marshall standing a few feet away. "Why don't you use that little torch of yours?" he shouted.

"Because it won't work in here," came a voice out of the dark. "Just walk forwards and keep moving. It's not far."

"What do you mean it won't work?" shouted back Alex, but he could hear Marshall already walking further away. He put one foot out in front of himself hesitantly and began to edge carefully down the tunnel. Marshall was moving slowly but Alex still struggled to keep up. He had taken just a few steps when he looked back and realised that he could no longer see the light from the office basement. Now he was in pitch darkness and had to stretch out his fingers to find the walls on either side. He walked like a man on a tightrope, using the brickwork on the left and right to balance himself as he edged down the passageway.

The darkness was so complete, so utterly enveloping, that he began to panic. He could see shapes moving around him; forms that were even darker than the blackness, if that were possible. Like black paint on a black canvas. They moved around the floor then rose up in the air in front of him, shapeless masses that appeared and disappeared at random. He knew it was just his eyes working overtime in the dark, trying to wring anything at all out of the lack of light. But then he swore he felt something brush past him and stopped in his tracks. Now not only was he standing in the pitch dark but in total silence as well. Like the grave, he thought.

That did not help. He felt his fear rising up inside him and the panic started again. There was nowhere to run, nowhere he could turn. He just stood in the middle of the silent, black tunnel and froze. Then he smelt it again: the clean, clear smell that he had picked up when Marshall had opened the green door. The smell of trees and leaves and rainwater. A forest smell that was coming from a little way down the tunnel. It drove out the panic and the fear and pushed back the swirling dark demons that were taunting him. It reached out a cool, calm hand and led him forward. He began to walk, not with faltering, frightened steps but with confident strides that took him on through a darkness that was powerless to stop him.

The smell grew stronger and stronger. The scent filled his lungs and made him dizzy with its sweetness and power. Now he could see the wood in his head. There were trees of every shape and size; those nearest him were small and slender with silvery white bark, while the ones further away were tall and stout and had moss growing up their trunks. On the floor beneath his feet, instead of cold dead stone, was a carpet of bluebells. They stretched away beneath the trees like a blue tide.

Then he was in the wood for real. The tunnel had ended and the darkness was gone and he was standing under the branches of one of the silver trees looking at the sunlight being filtered through the green canopy above him. It gathered into a pool where it hit the ground and made the blue flowers shine and glisten in their sparkling coat of dew. All around him were similar puddles of fallen sunlight where the bluebells nodded their little heads in a delicate breeze that moved through the wood. It stirred the branches of the trees and set up a chorus of gently rustling leaves that moved back and forth on its current.

He saw a shape moving through the forest: a tall, dark shape that hopped and skipped through the rock pools of sunlight as it made its way towards him.

"It's amazing," shouted Marshall as he got near. "I told you didn't I?" For once there was no smugness in his voice. There was no need for it. A place like this went beyond all personal pride.

14

"Where the bloody hell are we?" asked Alex.

"Somewhere amazing," said Marshall.

Alex was not about to disagree with him. He walked out from under the branches of the tree and stepped into a shaft of sunlight that warmed his face and made him raise one hand to shield his eyes. It was the most incredible thing he had ever seen and yet so simple; a woody glen with a carpet of bluebells. He stood in silence and breathed it all in for minute after magical minute.

There were fallen logs, growing thick with moss and lichen a few feet away. A butterfly was resting on one of them and it nervously took flight, rising and dipping through the air. Several large green bushes with bright pink flowers were dotted around the glen and he could see a pathway of bare earth leading away to the right. A small brown bird bounced from branch to branch and a squirrel hopped along the forest floor and scampered up the crusty grey trunk of one of the larger trees. And all the while he was breathing in that sweet, luscious air.

"Look behind you," said Marshall, who was now sitting on one the logs. He pointed past Alex, who turned to follow his gaze. There was nothing there. No tunnel entrance. No door. Nothing. Alex began looking for some sign of it but Marshall reassured him that the door would appear when it was good and ready. "It knows when it's time for us to go home," he said calmly, "I freaked out when I first came here. But while I was sitting down wondering what to do it just popped up."

"What is this place?" Alex asked again. He began to walk along the path and heard Marshall come up behind him.

"I really, really don't know. It's like something out of a fairytale. But you know what?"

Alex looked back at him.

"I really don't care. Don't you feel that too? I should be doing my nut but I'm not bothered."

Alex felt the same. When he had realised the tunnel had vanished he had felt no more panic than if he had missed a bus or lost his way in traffic. There was a sense of reason about this place, he thought. He took a huge breath of the rich forest air and let it fill his lungs and pour into his blood. What he was inhaling tasted pure and uncut, heavy with oxygen from so many trees. It made him feel incredibly awake and alive while at the same time calm and at peace. This was a world away from the semi coma in which he spent most of his life: dozing through each day with a head full of chatter and panic. For the first time in ages there was no noise inside him, no angry buzzing filling his thoughts.

He went further along the path until he came to a bend, where he noticed something on the ground where the earth was muddy. It was the first sign that there were more than butterflies and squirrels living here. A set of footprints, large enough to be a man's, led away from the glen along the track.

"Are, are there people here?" he asked.

"Oh yes," Marshall said. "You didn't think I'd bring you here just to look at trees did you?" He walked past Alex and rounded the bend. The path stretched away in a straight line between the trees as far as the eyes could see. The ground rose and fell in giant crests and dips. In places the path was hidden from view where the forest floor dropped away into shadow before rising up again to another peak. The track here was wide enough for the two of them to walk together side by side, Marshall swinging a stick he had picked up off the ground and Alex turning his head from left to right in wonder at the sights all around him. They looked like a pair of very large schoolboys up to no good.

At the sound of wings flapping above him, Alex looked up and caught a single beam of light coming down through the leaves of an oak tree. He followed the shaft up into the highest branches and for the first time saw the sky, a vast dome of brilliant blue stretching over the tree tops. He drew another deep breath and blinked slowly. This was a special place.

After a while the ground levelled out and they began to hear another sound mixing with the birdsong and high dry whispering of the wind in the trees. It was like soft laughter, coming from the forest to the right.

As the wall of trees thinned they caught sight of something glistening through the lower branches. A wide silver stream was running away between shallow banks lined with even more bluebells. It gurgled noisily over rocks and around fallen logs and spun in pools in the shadows.

The stream kept them company as they walked along. Alex began to think about the place they had left behind: the basement, the office, home, Sarah, the kids. His watch told him they had been away for more than half an hour and he knew he was already going to be late back. But he just did not care. And as each extra minute passed he found that thinking of home became harder and harder. Every time it entered his mind something else, some new sight or sound, would nudge it away to one side.

Now the stream had matured into a small river. The chuckling and gurgling had vanished as the body of water flattened and widened, stretching itself from grassy bank to grassy bank. The trail keeled to the right and a wooden bridge appeared. The rough, unpainted timber creaked and sagged as they clattered over. Once on the other side the path looked much more worn, with many more footprints and ruts formed by narrow wheels.

Then Alex saw it for the first time: the village of Hambledon. This would always be the first place they came to when they made the crossing of the boundary between the two places. They would refer to it simply as The Village and in the end, when something magic and marvellous happened, this would be the first spot to be reached and touched by its power.

It was a collection of small wooden houses formed in a tidy circle around a well. To Alex they resembled the kind of expensive Wendy Houses that spoilt rich children had in their gardens; like miniature versions of full size cottages. They had small doorways and shuttered windows, many of which were folded closed. There were some other buildings behind the houses that looked like barns or storage sheds.

As the two men walked into the centre of the circle Alex

noticed that many of the houses had broken doors that had been poorly patched up. There were shattered barrels and containers outside some, while others had scorch marks creeping viciously up their walls. Only one house of the twenty or so that Alex counted appeared undamaged or unmolested in any way. Marshall walked up to this one and knocked on the door.

There was the sound of someone moving inside the house, slowly shuffling towards the door. It was an uncomfortable, painful sound as if one foot was being dragged across the floor. Then the door opened a few inches and an old man peered out. He recognised Marshall immediately. "Good morning Andrew," he said, with soft wrinkles deepening around his mouth as his lips drew back in a smile. His voice wobbled slightly as he spoke and he moved stiffly to haul the door open and beckon the two inside. Marshall led the way.

The interior of the house was full of shadows as the sunlight struggled to fight its way through the small windows. But Alex could make out a table and two chairs in the middle of a single room. A small wood burner stood in a corner, there was a dark wooden dresser to the rear and to the right was a bed, covered in a patterned woollen blanket. A ladder stood on the left, reaching up to a small hole in the ceiling. It all reminded him of something he had seen in the local museum at home, where they had reconstructed an old drover's cottage.

"It's nice to see you once again Andrew," the old man said, as he gestured for them to sit on the chairs, while he went and perched on the edge of the bed. He wore a dark robe, like a monk, and there were a few stubborn strands of grey hair across the top of his head.

"You know me, I can't keep away," said Marshall. The tiny house stank of wood smoke and the old man's bedding looked like it had not been washed in weeks. Alex wondered how uncomfortable his neat and tidy work colleague must be feeling in a place like this but Marshall seemed determined to put on a brace face. "I've brought a friend of mine along. This is Alex."

"Pleased to meet you Alex, my name is Nicholas," said the

old man, extending his right hand. Alex noticed the joints on his fingers were swollen and hard and he pitied the man, living in this tiny house all alone. At that point the door to the cottage flew open and a young boy appeared.

"Grandpa, grandpa…" He stopped short when he saw the two men at the table. Then he recognised Marshall and ran over to climb onto his lap. Alex could not believe his eyes at the transformation in his colleague: his arrogance and overpowering self-confidence had turned into something resembling warmth and even kindness.

The boy introduced himself as Edward and told Alex he was eight years old. He was slightly built with dark hair that was uncut and drooped over his eyes so that he had to constantly sweep it back with one hand. He wore a pale cotton shirt and rough brown trousers and had bare feet. He spoke quite nervously to Alex, his fingers often playing with the heavy fringe and his eyes shifting constantly back to his grandfather for reassurance.

Alex began to think of his own children. They would be asleep in their beds and Sarah would probably have tried calling his mobile. He reached down to his pocket to feel for his phone but once again something interrupted, moving in front of his mental line of vision to block out thoughts of home.

"Tell him about this place," Marshall said to Nicholas. "Tell him what you've told me."

The old man smiled and began to explain a little about the land that Alex had stumbled into. The country was called Theland and the forest was called King's Wood. It was a holy place and Hambledon was the only place of human habitation for miles. The path that Alex and Marshall had been following led east. It was called the Great Track and was a trading route between towns and cities across the country.

"Cities?" Alex liked the sound of that.

"Oh yes. There are many fine cities in Theland. The greatest of all is Middleton. At the eastern end of the Great Track. I went there once as a young man. A truly magical place…" His eyes glazed over slightly and he gazed at Alex and through him at the same time.

Alex waited for the old man to snap out of his daydream but eventually gave up. "So," he said, "what do people here know of our, er, country?" He gestured at himself and Marshall.

That was enough to bring Nicholas back to reality with a thump. He smiled but his eyes narrowed at the same time, as if he was balancing his good humour with something much darker. He drew in a heavy breath and held it for a moment before it hissed out from between his lips. "You'd do well, if you're to travel here, to keep talk of your own place to yourselves," he said. "There are few here who know of the Other Place and those that do may not take kindly to your presence in their land."

The words were spoken so impassively but with such power that it was if a cold shadow passed through the tiny house. Then the old man rose to his feet and moved to the dresser. He pulled out a jug and three cups and sent Edward scurrying up the ladder into the upper room to bring down a plate covered with a piece of white cloth. When they were all on the table he pulled back the cloth to reveal a small loaf of bread and a large chunk of cheese. Two rough knives came from the dresser drawer and he waved at his guests to begin eating while he poured from the jug into the three cups.

The food tasted, to Alex's surprise, delicious. The bread was soft and white and the cheese had a salty tang that he liked. He lifted one of the cups to his lips and sipped from the beer coloured drink inside. It ran sweetly and warmly over his tongue to the back of his throat. Then he noticed that neither Nicholas nor Edward was sharing the food, though the old man sipped from a cup and both were watching him eat. He looked down at the small loaf on the table. "I won't have anymore," he said, "unless you join me."

The old man and his grandson looked shocked and Alex presumed he had committed a terrible faux pas. But then the old man leaned forward and tore off a piece of the bread, which

20

he ripped in half and shared with Edward. The four of them ate the rest of the food together. When they had finished, Alex brought up a subject that had been dogging him since they first arrived. He wanted to know where the other villagers were. Nicholas looked away from him for a moment then back with a distant stare. "They're out in the fields," he said softly, "there's work to be done." He got up and cleared the table, moving the things to the dresser.

Alex wanted to ask more questions but the old man moved back to the bed and sank heavily on to it. Edward moved to his side and put a hand on his shoulder. "My grandpa is tired," he said. "Maybe you can come back soon?" Alex and Marshall rose from their chairs and offered their thanks and farewells.

As he crossed the threshold, Alex looked back at the old man on the bed, sitting in the shadows. He looked so weak and frail, it was painful to watch. His skin was grey and his gnarled hands were crossed on his lap but this was more than old age or weariness. Sorrow seemed to hang from his frame like a coat. He was heartbroken.

The door closed.

Walking back through the forest the dark feelings lifted. Alex realised why this place was regarded so highly by the locals. When he had first stepped from the tunnel into the green glen he had felt so many troubles and petty aggravations dissolve from his system. Now the sense of despair that had been overwhelming a moment ago was fading as quickly as The Village disappeared from sight behind the wall of trees.

The pair of them retraced their steps through the wood. Just as the river beside them had begun with a stream, so this narrow path was just the beginning of the Great Track. He wondered what lay at the other end of it, once it had grown from bare earth worn down by a few feet to a trading route between magical sounding towns and cities.

Soon they were back on the section of the path where the ground rose and fell in giant sweeps through the forest. As they walked he began to feel a sense of urgency come over him; that they should hurry back to the glen as quickly as they could in case...

It was coming. Oh God it was coming up behind them through the wood. Alex could hear something stamping its feet as it rushed along the path behind them. He felt his own heart suddenly start to race, painful hammer beats that crashed through his chest. There was the ferrous smell of blood in his nostrils and his ears rang. It was getting nearer.

He exploded into a sprint, leaving Marshall shouting after him in confusion. The forest track flew under his feet as he tore down each dip and up the other side, floating over ruts and roots. It was getting nearer now and he could feel it. He risked a glance over his shoulder and saw only Marshall running after him down the track. But then he felt it move in the corner of his vision: a dark shape coming through the trees. It was lunging through the bushes and gaining on him with every stride. So he ran on and on, pushing harder and harder, grabbing huge lungfuls of burning air until...

He burst into the clearing and stopped. As quickly as the feeling had come over him it had gone. Now he just stood there panting, his hands resting on his knees and his back arched as he struggled to recover. He had no explanation for what had happened, other than his imagination running riot. Then Marshall sprinted into the glen, his face purple with effort and anger. "What the hell is wrong with you," he screamed furiously, veins pulsing on his neck like snakes. "You bloody idiot."

Alex raised one hand weakly and tried to explain but whatever words he could think of never made it past his gasps for air. He just shook his head and finally managed a feeble, "I panicked." Marshall looked at him with disgust and walked past.

There at the back of the clearing was a large, arched wooden door set into a mossy stone wall. Marshall reached into his pocket and pulled out his set of keys. He thumbed through them for the thin steel one, slid it into the lock and turned it clockwise. There was a loud clunk and he pulled the key back out. A heavy black metal ring hung from the door and he used this to pull it open.

When they were inside the tunnel Marshall dragged the door shut behind them and at once they were in darkness, with just a thin halo of light leaking around the edges of the heavy wooden frame. "Keep going that way," he said, his words echoing off the walls. A hand landed on one of Alex's shoulders and gently nudged him in the right direction. This time he led the way, walking slowly down into the darkness. He stumbled once or twice but each time recovered and started walking again; his hands stretching out in front.

There was the feeling that they were walking downwards. He had not noticed any incline when he had been walking the other way but now there was a definite slope to the floor. In the pitch black of the tunnel it was disorientating, he felt as if his body was going to topple forwards at any minute. His sense of balance was out of control, trying to keep him upright while being sucked down into the dark. It was like gravity was trying to bury him in the floor, beneath the cold stone.

He gritted his teeth and focused on a tiny patch of light that was up ahead. It was gradually growing bigger and he could begin to see the pattern of the bricks on the walls and the silhouette of his own arms reaching out for balance. Then he could make out the open doorway into the office basement and the harsh yellow glow of an electric light bulb. They were back.

The building was empty as they left. Marshall locked the big green door with his special key and switched off the basement lights before they went upstairs. In the lobby there were a few empty beer bottles left on the reception desk but no sign of any straggling party goers. The two men hardly spoke as they left the office complex. It was all shockingly normal.

The journey home passed in a flash. The clock on Alex's dashboard said it was only midnight but the roads seemed empty. He passed through green light after green light and was out of town in record time. When he got to the house he let himself in and crept upstairs like a thief. He kissed the children goodnight and padded across the landing. There was a light on in the bedroom and Sarah lay asleep on her side of the bed, her hand draped around a paperback. He bent slowly to kiss the tip of her nose, then slipped into bed and turned off the light.

For a while he just lay there, listening to the sound of his wife's breathing. Gradually his eyes closed and he sank back into the pillow. Sleep had warm arms that wrapped themselves around him in a comforting embrace and he made no attempt to resist. In the half way state between awake and proper sleep he began to dream. He could see Nicholas in The Village. He was pottering about his little house while Edward slept upstairs in the loft space on a tiny wooden bed. Then the old man pulled on a coat and left the cottage. But he did not head in either way along the Great Track. Instead he walked into the trees on a tiny narrow path, where he had to brush away branches of thorns that barred his way.

He was walking by the river, downstream of the wooden bridge. He came into a clearing when the ground was bare. There he fell to his knees and raised his cupped palms to cover his face and his shoulders began to shake. He wept and wept. Then, as Nicholas knelt over the rough earth, he was joined by a chorus of muffled weeping from beneath the ground. Dozens of voices cried out from under the dark soil and while the old man shed tears of grief, they wailed in pain and fear.

Alex slept with the light on for the rest of the night.

Chapter Three

Running Away

"Oh gross."

Sarah pulled her hands out of the soapy dishwater and grimaced at the bits of rinsed off spaghetti hoops that clung to her skin, making it look like she had the pox.

"These hands were not made for this!" she shouted, punching the water in frustration and sending up a fountain of foam that hit her in the face.

Sarah Preston's life was hectic. Her two young children kept her busy from the minute they woke up to the moment when they finally surrendered to sleep, at the opposite end of the day. And even when they were snoring gently in their beds, she still had to wash their clothes, prepare meals and attempt to stem the tide of untidiness that threatened to engulf the entire house.

Engulf. That was a good word. It could so easily describe the way she felt about her life: a never ending cycle that allowed no room for personal freedom or self interest. She felt engulfed every day. She was following other people's rules, chiefly four year old Katie and two year old Matthew. And Alex of course. It often felt like she had three children to look after; her husband having failed to grow up into a proper adult.

As she wiped the bubbles from her nose, she tried to work out where it had all gone wrong. She had earned straights As in her exams at school and ended up at a good university. That had led on to teacher training college and a job teaching English at an above average comprehensive. She had settled in to her profession and was heading up the career ladder, with the prospect of reaching department head one day soon, when it all came to a grinding halt in a landslide of nappies and plastic feeder cups. Now life was about responsibilities and routine; a mortgage, bills and proper grown up behaviour. It was also about rarely leaving the house. There were days when she felt like a prisoner in a semi-detached cell.

Her best friend Annie was still living the kind of life that Sarah longed for. She had just come back from yet another holiday; this time to Thailand with her boyfriend Simon. Though Sarah thought the world of Annie, she could not help feeling jealous when she listened to her talking about all the places she had been to and the things she had seen. Annie believed that travelling the world helped her to "find herself". Sarah knew the only place she was likely to find herself was under a pile of ironing in the kitchen. As others had grown dependent on her, so she had watched her own independence drift away.

Looking after Alex was almost as demanding as caring for the kids. She had met him ten years ago at a party in Bristol. He had been a shy young man, chatting in a corner, who had been introduced to her by a mutual friend. They had started going out almost by accident, after a group outing to the cinema had seen every other member of the party cancel, one by one. So if it had not been for one friend having a cold, another losing her car keys and a third getting food poisoning from some left over chicken, they might not be together at all.

What attracted her to Alex was the way he kept making her laugh and never seemed to get angry. He would just roll his eyes if something went wrong and make a joke about it. She remembered one night in a restaurant when the fire alarm went off and the customers were forced to leave their meals and stand outside in the rain. While others were furiously shouting at the staff, Alex was the one making wisecracks about food critics getting their revenge and chefs burning one steak too many. He was not really all that funny but he had made her laugh. But at some point over the last couple of years Alex had stopped making jokes and instead went quiet if things took a wrong turn. She had watched him change, as a dark cloud formed over him and cast its shadow over his moods.

As time rolled on, the little oddities about her husband that she had once found so endearing began to blossom into annoying idiosyncrasies. Top of the list was his daydreaming, although to her it was more like he became lost in himself. If they were out together and he saw something that triggered his imagination then off he would go: building scenarios about people he had never met and inserting himself mentally in other people's lives.

At first he would share these with her and she would laugh and burst his bubble. But all too often these days he would keep the thoughts to himself which made things worse. She could tell what he was thinking by the way he went quiet and blanked out everything and everyone around him. This had once been something she could accept as part of his character but now it felt like he was building a wall between the two of them.

Recently he had become even more distant. He would not answer his phone and was coming home from work later and later. She would have guessed he was having an affair but he looked in such a state she knew nobody else would have him. But with the children screaming next door she did not have time to dwell on it any further. The treadmill was not going to stop for her to figure out what was happening inside Alex's head. So she finished the dishes and got on with making lunch.

When Alex came in that night, grumbling about feeling tired, her patience was wearing thin. He had missed the kids' bedtime again and she was hunched over the kitchen worktop, planning a meal for the following evening. He asked her what she was doing. "You do remember that Annie and Simon are coming for dinner, don't you?" she said, as Alex collapsed into the sofa.

He rolled his eyes and cursed. "Do we have to?"

"Yes we do," she snapped, tearing a page from her notebook, "and as a special treat, you can do the shopping."

The next morning he disappeared out of the house with Katie

and Matthew. The supermarket was a short drive from their house so he strapped the children into their seats and headed off. As he swung into the car park he saw a lone driver pulling into the last available parent and child space, the slots that were nearest the door and extra wide to make lifting a small infant out of the car a bit easier. This was one of his increasing number of pet hates: selfish idiots who just had to ignore basic rules and make others' lives more difficult.

He slowed his own car to get a good look at the other driver. He was a younger man, in his mid twenties, with short hair and a pair of sunglasses perched on top of his head. Now Alex detested him even more: a pretentious, arrogant fool who wore sunglasses on a cloudy day. The man turned in his direction and Alex got a brief glimpse of his face. He was gloating. The guy knew he was being a pig and was proud of it. With his anger now roaring inside him like a furnace Alex drove off to find a space elsewhere.

Once inside the store, he put Matthew in a trolley seat and let Katie hang off the side. They grazed up and down the aisles, gradually filling the trolley with food. It took longer than it might have, as Alex tried to clear his head of as many thoughts as possible, before the dinner party.

It had been a mad fortnight. After that first trip through the tunnel he had hardly spoken to Marshall for three days, as if they were both embarrassed by their shared experience. But then the two of them had been making coffee in the small staff kitchen and it came up in conversation. He could not remember who had mentioned it first, but once the subject was raised they both sighed in relief that the ice had been broken. They talked about what they had seen and Marshall explained how he had been there several times before, after finding the key to the door on a trip down to the basement to look for an old file.

They agreed to rendezvous in the basement after work that night, once their colleagues had left the building. Marshall had the thin, shiny key with him and together they heaved the door open and went back into the tunnel. This time Alex knew what to expect and the dark moving shapes did little to bother him. When they were out the other side they made their way quickly to The Village and went to Nicholas and Edward's house. Alex made no mention of his disturbing dream and tried not to think about what might lie under the ground in the woods. Instead, he spent a few minutes chatting before walking a little further out of the forest.

Marshall pointed out the way the fields were lined with dry stone walls like they might see at home; if they ever ventured out into the countryside. The Great Track was bordered on both sides by fields of corn and in the distance Alex could make out cows grazing in distant pastures. After an hour or so walking in the open countryside they turned back and went home.

This had been repeated every day for the last two weeks and each time they went further and further into Theland. They started passing through The Village without knocking on Nicholas's door, as the old man and his grandson would want to chat and hold them up. Eventually they were walking for hours at a time and Alex was not returning home until early morning.

They had met a few other travellers along the way. Once they had been invited to share a cup of something hot and steaming with a hunter out snaring rabbits. He told them how much the skins would fetch at market, as the fur was fashionable amongst the ladies of Middleton. "Proper posh," he said, as he gnawed on a piece of meat cooked over a campfire. Another time, they were given a lift by a trader with a horse and cart. He was heading east to buy spices from the sea port of Armouth. He told them how wild it was and how he had once gambled away two months' profits playing cards with a group of sailors.

Now, standing in the supermarket weighing up the price of breakfast cereal, Alex was undecided about whether to go back to Theland at all. It was like he was having an affair: every night he lied to Sarah about where he had been but he could not tell her the truth. It was his secret; his place to explore. But the burden of that secret was getting too heavy to carry and he decided the best way out was to forget about it. He could write it off as a weird dream and go back to normal life.

He finished paying for the shopping and drifted towards the exit. Sarah had asked him to buy her something to read, so he wheeled Matthew and Katie in to the newsagent section near the door. There were racks and racks of glossy magazines about nothing in particular, with the faces of minor celebrities beaming from the front covers. But his tolerance levels were at an all time low. As he stood surrounded by headlines about new diets and failed marriages he felt a cold anger begin to rise up inside him. He threw down a magazine and left the store.

This had been happening over and over since he had been to Theland. Like a religious convert, he could see nothing around him but greed and selfishness. From arrogant passengers on the train who forced everyone else to listen to their appalling choice of music, to grinning millionaires on the television; he was sick of them. When he was in Theland he felt calm and focused and for the first time in years his head was empty of pointless daydreams. But each time he came back that quickly vanished and he was left drowning in the horrid white noise of everyday life.

He hurried back to the car. As he did, a teenage lad on a bike cycled directly towards him on the footpath. Alex had to quickly sidestep out of the way to avoid a collision. Now he felt his anger glowing white hot and he cursed the boy under his breath. As he bent to open the car door he heard a crash and turned to see the cyclist lying in a heap on the ground, with blood pouring from his mouth and nose. The lad looked shocked and confused as if his tumble had been a bolt from the blue. Alex just laughed.

As he drove home the raging inside him grew a voice. It cursed old drivers and young ones, those in expensive flash cars and those too poor to afford anything better than a clapped out old heap. As he approached a roundabout he saw that a car had left the road up ahead and was stuck on the grassy verge by the side of the carriageway. The front of it was crumpled and the remains of a buckled road sign lay beside it. The driver was standing by the side of the car, looking slightly traumatised and talking into his mobile phone. His sunglasses were pushed up high on his head.

Alex was grinning as his car slowed. He caught the man's eye and beamed at him with satisfaction. "Stupid fool," he thought, glancing in his rear view mirror as he drove away, "serves him right for stealing the parent and – "

He threw his head round to look at the empty child seats behind him.

"Shit!"

At the supermarket it took nearly twenty minutes of persuasion and grovelling to the manager for him not to call the police. Katie and Matthew had been taken into a backroom and fed on juice and biscuits after it had become obvious that they and the trolley had been abandoned. Both the children had been in tears and as Alex finally wheeled them out of the shop everyone glared at him with disgust and anger. Now the one person he cursed as he drove home was himself. His hands were shaking on the wheel and his voice was weak and unsteady as he tried over and over to calm the children.

Sarah was not happy. He saw no point in trying to hide it from her because one of the children would have blabbed eventually anyway. But he tried to play it down as much as possible, not going into the detail of how far home he had actually driven before realising he had left them behind. She was incandescent. She asked him over and over, "What planet are you on?" and "How stupid can you be?" His feeble attempts at apologies only made things worse.

Eventually she said it might be a good idea if he went for a walk to let her calm down. Her exact words involved him getting out of her sight. He left the house and walked to the end of the road where there was a park with rolling lawns and a small lake where old men sailed model boats. He sat on a bench and stared out at the people walking dogs, at the parents with children and at the gaggle of ducks making its way across the grass towards the water.

He occasionally brought the kids here and today there was a woman he recognised from previous park outings. He did not remember her name but she always looked terribly sad. Today she had dark rings around her eyes and her hair hung in straggles down either side of her face. As he watched her making her lonely way across the park he started wondering what might have caused her sadness. But she disappeared from sight behind the trees and was gone. He sighed. Surely there was more than just this.

He knew the answer immediately. In the past he had sought refuge from the pain of everyday life by escaping into his daydreams. But now he had the chance to experience something that even he could never have imagined. His dreams had been all there was to cling to at times but he did not need them any more.

He drew another slow breath. It was time to go. He got up from the bench and began a slow walk home. On the way he took out his phone and rang Marshall's mobile. It went straight to his voicemail and Alex considered whether or not to leave a message. There was a long tone.

"Oh, er, it's Alex. Listen, I'm er, on my way in to work and was wondering if you wanted to help me catch up on some extra stuff. I know it's Saturday but it's important and it might take us a while. If you get this, meet me at work." He was not sure if Marshall would understand the garbled message but he could not risk saying anything too obvious.

Standing outside the house, he hesitated for a moment with the car keys in his hand. He suddenly felt a twinge of guilt; not for planning to disappear for several days, maybe even weeks, but for leaving Sarah without any transport. He stood on the pavement and peered in through the lounge window. He could see Katie and Matthew playing on the carpet, none the worse for their earlier ordeal.

Sensibly he should go in and pack a bag but that would lead to questions and more shouting. He stared at his children through the glass and bit his lip. He could imagine what the dinner party would be like: Sarah would make an unconvincing excuse for his absence and probably cry to herself in the kitchen. He swallowed hard.

It would not be forever. He would just go to Middleton, the city at the end of the Great Track, and come home. Then he would be the perfect husband and father. He promised. He would come back a changed man, with all his petty grievances lost forever.

If he had taken a moment to really think about it, he would have realised how impossible it was going to be to immerse himself in the magic of Theland and ever be the same again. But he did not. Instead, he put his car keys on the wall at the end of the drive and walked to the bus stop.

Chapter Four

Appledore

He looked out over the balcony at his car, way below in the fenced off parking area, and tried again to decide whether to drive or take a taxi. It was the top of the range, with the best engine in its class and had received rave reviews in the press. He loved that car and did not fancy leaving it outside the office for several days and nights, if not longer.

Andrew Marshall was having doubts about what he was about to do. He could think of no way to explain a sudden absence from work for a week or more. He knew that was what Alex was planning and it scared him. But Andrew Marshall always hid his fear well, even though he spent half his life scared out of his wits. He was frightened of failure, terrified of success and just plain petrified that some day soon they would all realise that he did not have a clue what he was doing. Then they would come for him.

He had joined the department straight off the graduate training scheme and was one of the youngest junior managers in the company. That meant a healthy salary every month but looking around at his flat he just wished he had something more to spend it on. Apart from the huge television and expensive hi fi system there was only the leather sofa that was worth anything. And the car outside. He looked at it once more and decided it would be best left where it was.

In the cab across town to the office he began to feel scared again. He practised his exercises for helping to bring the fear under control, most of which involved pulling a weak grin and holding it. His heart was thumping as he thought of what they were about to do: seriously explore Theland. So many things could go wrong. They might not find their way back. They could become ill or be attacked. It was all so scary. But Alex would take care of it. Alex Preston was the one person at work he really admired. He was always so calm and controlled. With Alex around Andrew knew things would be all right, which is why he had shown him the door and the tunnel in the first place. He knew that Alex would cope with it better than he could.

And he had. Andrew Marshall had been violently sick the first time he had been through the tunnel and had been so nervous when he entered The Village that he had almost been in tears when Nicholas found him wandering around the houses. Alex had dealt with it so much better and he felt the two were finally becoming friends.

As the cab pulled up at the offices there was no sign of his travelling companion. He found him in the basement sitting on a box of old invoices with a brand new rucksack at his feet. It made his own look rather tatty in comparison.

"You made it then?" they said in unison.

They closed the door fully behind them as they stepped through. One short stumble through the dark later and they stepped out into weak sunshine and the familiar clean smell of the woods. This time, because they were travelling at a more moderate pace, they stopped in The Village. Nicholas greeted them at his door but his smile was a lot weaker than the last time they had visited. When they stepped in to the house, Edward was lying asleep on his grandfather's bed.

"He's resting," the old man whispered.

"He doesn't look well," said Alex, looking over at the boy who seemed pale and drawn. "What's wrong?"

Nicholas sighed for a moment before speaking. "It's just tiredness I'm sure. This place. It – "

Alex turned to him and saw there were red rings around the old man's eyes. He remembered the dream he had had about the place in the trees. "The others are all dead aren't they?" he blurted out.

Nicholas stepped back in shock, as if Alex had read his mind. "Yes. Yes, they're all dead." Then he invited them to sit down at the table. He spoke again as he fetched drinks from the dresser. "It's been a few months now; just me and Edward here on our own. We do what we can with the few animals there are left and what we can grow in the back field."

"What happened to the others?" asked Alex, still not mentioning what he had seen buried beneath the ground behind The Village.

Nicholas sat on the very edge of the bed and reached over to gently pull back Edward's hair from his face. As he spoke he kept his eyes fixed on the sleeping boy, who stirred restlessly but did not wake.

"There was a sickness. It started with just a few of the older ones falling ill. A handful died and we all mourned but we had no idea how bad it would be. Then it began to afflict the young people as well. Gradually more and more of us grew sick and we began to see it for what it was: a curse. It drove them mad and turned neighbour upon neighbour. Then a physician came here from up country and told us to dig up those we had already buried and put them in a pit full of lime. Their bodies were…"

He broke off and turned to stare into Alex's face. "Their bodies were untouched by death. It was as if they were sleeping. The doctor said it was the nature of the sickness that had claimed them. He said moving them away from the village was the only chance of saving the rest of us."

"And did it?" Marshall asked

"It did nothing." The old man raised a hand to his mouth and wiped a line of sweat from his top lip. "The sickness kept coming until just two of us were left. And then it stopped."

The three men sat without speaking for a while. The only sound in the tiny room was the uneven breathing of Edward on the bed. Eventually Alex spoke. He said the first thing that came into his head. The truth.

"I dreamed about you. After my first visit. I dreamed about you going in to the trees. I knew what was there."

Nicholas looked at him as if a great burden had been lifted from his shoulders. His eyes again welled with tears and he answered quietly, "And I dreamed of you. I dreamed you would come," and as he spoke he pointed at the jug and cups on the table. Three cups. He always had a jug of drink and three cups ready when they came to his door.

"What did you dream would happen when I came?" Alex asked.

Nicholas poured from the jug, his hands shaking as he tipped the golden liquid into the cups. "Nothing," he said, "I just dreamed I would meet you here." There was a pause. Alex waited for him to say more. "But there is something that you can do for me." Alex and Marshall put down their cups and listened. "Some travellers who have passed this way have talked of a prophet, a wise man who moves on the Great Track east of here. They say he promises to cure the sick and even raise the dead. Perhaps..." he stopped.

"You think he might do something here?" asked Marshall, with a laugh of derision.

Nicholas turned to him and spoke firmly. "Not for those who've passed but for my grandson. He's growing weak." He gestured to the boy on the bed whose forehead was shiny with sweat. Then he laid a hand on Alex's forearm and spoke softly, "Perhaps if you see him on your travels you might ask him to come here. Only if you happen to meet him of course."

Alex had heard that kind of voice before. It was used by someone who desperately needed a favour but whose pride stopped them from asking for it directly. "I'll do what I can," he said.

That seemed to lift Nicholas's spirits and he sat back in his chair and drained his cup. Marshall huffed quietly; feeling left out of a private conversation. His eyes moved from Alex to Nicholas and back again in a suspicious way before he broke the quiet in the room. "We should be going."

They said goodbye outside the little house. Nicholas pressed both his hands over Alex's and kept thanking him. Marshall threw in a loud goodbye to remind them that he was still present and walked on ahead in a sulk. As Alex pulled away he realised that a small bag had been slipped into his palm. It jingled with coins but as he tried to hand it back Nicholas shook his head and smiled at him.

As they left The Village, the pair looked back one final time and saw the old man waving from his doorway. Alex waved back but Marshall turned to face the path ahead and muttered, "Old fool," under his breath.

It was late afternoon as they headed up the Great Track and they wanted to clear as much ground as possible before nightfall. It was hard to tell what season it was here in Theland but it was certainly warmer and milder than back home. Neither of them had brought a tent so they were faced with sleeping out under the stars. They hoped the weather would be kind to them.

By sunset they felt they had made good progress. They reached a pile of giant grey rocks and unrolled their sleeping bags in a spot where the boulders would hide them from the view of anyone walking the main path. Alex opened his rucksack to reveal a supply of fruit, crisps and energy bars, along with bottles of water that he had bought on his way to the office. Marshall opened his small rucksack to reveal... nothing.

"I... I forgot about food," he stammered. Alex just rolled his eyes and threw him an apple and a packet of crisps which he devoured noisily. As they settled down in their sleeping bags a warm breeze was drifting across the moor land. The night sky was cloudless and Alex was amazed at the number and brightness of the stars above them. There seemed to be thousands of tiny burning dots in the sky. At home they were obscured by the reflected glow of a million street lamps, but here they beamed down at him undisturbed. Across the open moor he could hear the sounds of animals. He was no expert on wildlife but a fox seemed to be barking and howling in the distance while closer to hand there were the sounds of something snuffling about in the undergrowth. Eventually a badger emerged and sniffed the air downwind of the two men before disappearing into the night.

Alex thought of Sarah, back home with the children. He wondered how the dinner party had gone and whether she had got his message. He began to worry about Katie and Matthew but then the usual thing happened: his thoughts were interrupted, as if his mind did not want him to think of home. Instead he began to picture the great city of Middleton that lay at the eastern end of the Great Track. The images came thick and fast: streets lit by lanterns and torches, the silhouettes of tall stone buildings. He could even imagine the aroma of wood fires burning and the noise of music and laughter wafting from busy taverns. The day was over but the city was still awake as people ate and drank, mothers tried to sooth their crying babies and lovers quarrelled by open windows. The sights, smells and sounds in his mind grew stronger and then dimmed. He was asleep.

When he woke up, it was just starting to get light. He checked his watch but it had stopped working before midnight. He looked over at Marshall who was curled up uncomfortably in his sleeping bag. He roused him and they shared some more apples before packing their bags and getting back on to the Great Track. They hardly spoke for the first mile or so, each man lost in his own thoughts. Marshall was feeling scared again and wondering why Alex had not told him about his weird dream, while Alex was thinking about what Nicholas had said and was wondering why Marshall seemed to be sulking.

As the sun finally rose over the horizon the dark moods lifted and they began to chat again. The path zigged and zagged down the side of a hill and was cut deep into the incline. Each turn was like a hairpin and they wondered how a horse and cart would fare on the downward slope, although they saw no one on the route.

By the time the sun was directly above them they were back on level ground. The path crossed a river by a wooden bridge and continued across the floor of a wooded valley towards a group of houses. These were different to those in The Village; they were larger and built of stone and many were painted white. They formed an oval around a large building with a tower at one end and large windows running along each side. Even here, Alex could recognise a church when he saw one.

As they came nearer they saw a tall metal fence running around the perimeter of the village, with high posts set at regular intervals. Marshall led the way towards a gate that was held shut by a large bolt. There was a bell hanging from one of the gate posts and a small hammer dangled from a length of rope beside it. Marshall lifted it up and tapped it against the bell. As the sound rang out several doors flew open and faces appeared. A man of a similar age to Alex and two younger women approached them looking worried. They were dressed in the kind of clothes that Alex had seen in old paintings: the man wore a pale coloured shirt under a brown jacket, dark trousers tucked into knee high boots and a wide brimmed black hat. The women wore plain brown dresses with white bonnets over their heads.

"Can I help you gentlemen?" the man asked through a slightly nervous smile. All three of the villagers studied Alex and Marshall closely.

Alex answered, "We're travelling along this road and are running low on food. We were wondering if you could spare us some."

The three villagers looked at each other as if a silent message was passing between them. "I have money," said Alex and he shook the bag of coins in his coat pocket.

The man laughed. "Oh we don't want your money." He nodded to the women, then reached and pulled back the gate. "Please come in," he said and gestured them forwards. "Welcome to Appledore." Alex and Marshall followed him as he led the way towards the houses. The women walked behind, their hands crossed in front of themselves and their heads slightly bowed. Alex kept looking at them over his shoulder and at one point tripped over his own feet as he gazed backwards. One of the women reached down to help him up and he looked into her face as he staggered to his feet. She had fair skin and a fringe of dark hair was hanging from beneath the front of her bonnet. Her brown eyes sparkled as she smiled at him, awkwardly picking himself up off the grass, and he noticed small laughter lines at the corners of her mouth. She looked away as she met his gaze.

"M- my name is Alex," he said.

"I am Rebecca," she replied, "and this is my brother Peter and sister Anna."

Her brother laughed at Alex as he dusted himself off. "Please gentlemen, come to my house," he said, "you look like you're in need of refreshment." He led them towards one of the houses and up to an open wooden door. Inside was a square room with a stone floor, a large fireplace to one side and two other doors. In the centre of the room a heavy wooden staircase rose from the floor and disappeared into the ceiling. There was a table near the fire place with wooden benches alongside and Peter suggested they sit there.

"Where are you two gentlemen from?" he asked Alex, as the two women left the room.

"We're from – "

"The west," interrupted Marshall, "a long way west. It's our first visit here."

Peter looked at them both with curiosity. "And where are you heading?" he asked, watching closely as the two strangers glanced at each other before either would answer.

"Well er..." began Alex.

"We're heading for... the big city," said Marshall.

"Yes that's right," said Alex, "Middleton isn't it?"

Peter looked from one to the other, "What a funny pair of travelling gentlemen you are sirs," he said with a chuckle. "I'm not sure you really know where you want to go at all."

A door opened and the women returned carrying trays with plates of bread, cheese and cold meats, along with a jug and some cups. These were laid on the table and Rebecca served the plates to the three men before pouring drinks. Alex caught her eye again and smirked up at her and a smile slipped across her face. It was not flirting, he told himself. But there was something about her that seemed quite special, a kind of brightness that shone from her eyes.

The two women left the room again and the three men began to eat. The bread, cheese and meats all tasted good and Alex and Marshall tucked in eagerly while Peter tried to find out more about them, to discover where exactly they were from and where they were heading. With Nicholas's warning still fresh in their minds they dodged the questions about their homeland with vague answers but Peter was persistent in his probing about their destination. Eventually Alex gave a version of the truth that might satisfy him.

"We've been asked to find a wise man. A travelling prophet somewhere east of here. A friend needs his help and we've said we'll find him."

Peter put down his knife and regarded them both coldly. "We'll have no talk of this man at our table. He is unholy. Let those who choose to follow his false words do so, but they shall pay the price. Here we follow the word of our Lord."

Alex and Marshal flicked their eyes to each other as they chewed their food in silence. Marshall swallowed first and answered for them both, "We meant no harm sir. We have merely agreed to ask him to visit our friend's village if we should ever meet him on our travels." Alex, still busy with a mouthful of bread, nodded in agreement.

Peter huffed and picked up his knife again. "I shall accept your apology," he said rather pompously. "The man your friend seeks passed this way three weeks ago and stayed a while here. He made promises which no man can keep. He..." Alex and Marshall looked up from their plates. Peter had stopped and was staring off into space, his mouth moving slowly as he toyed with a piece of food between his teeth.

"He what?" asked Alex. But there was no answer and the silence hung in the air over the table. At that point the two women appeared again and began clearing the plates away.

Peter behaved as if nothing had happened and drained his cup of water. He then surprised them with another question.

"Would you gentlemen care to rest here for a while?"

The two travellers happily accepted the invitation. Alex was particularly keen to find out more about the church in the middle of the village and while Marshall sat back in a chair and rested his eyes, he asked Peter if he could pay it a visit.

"Minister Toms will be there this afternoon," Peter replied, "One of my sisters shall take you across the way."

Alex could not help himself hoping that Rebecca was the sister in question and he was quietly pleased when she came to escort him out of the house. They left Marshall dozing and crossed the open space in the centre of the village. The building they were heading for was a large white single storey structure with leaded windows and a bell tower at one end. They went in through the large wooden doors beneath the tower. Inside it was empty; the Minister was out tending to his flock.

Rebecca acted as a guide and pointed out the architecture of the building: the large stone arches that held up the roof, the wooden pews and highly carved pulpit. She spoke with real excitement about the way the church had been put together and the workmanship that had gone into it. Considering she had barely spoken a word when they had been in her brother's company she talked now with real confidence and warmth, as if she had known him for years and years.

Along the walls beneath the large stained glass windows were two long shelves filled with unlit candles. When Alex stopped to look at them Rebecca walked quickly to his side. "What are these for?" he asked.

She hesitated before answering. "These are to keep out... to keep away evil."

Alex laughed. He could not help himself. "But from the way your brother spoke I wouldn't imagine he'd believe in stuff like that!" He immediately wished he had kept his mouth shut.

"My brother is a man of faith," she said in a voice that was calm and matter of fact. "We are all people of faith in

Appledore. But we must do what we can to protect ourselves."

"Protect you from what?"

"From evil itself," said a voice behind him.

He turned to see a middle-aged man with a tidy beard, wearing a black robe and large floppy hat. "My name is Minister Toms," he said, "Rebecca's brother told me you were here. I hope you've found our place of worship interesting."

"I do. It reminds me of places at home."

"And where is home?" asked the Minister.

"Oh, a long way from here. A long way west." Alex said. He saw the older man's eyebrows rise and he tried to divert him from any more questions, "I was interested in these candles."

Minister Toms's eyebrows dropped and his mouth tightened. "They're a protection from things that might harm us," he said. There was an uneasy silence which signalled that the matter was closed. Then the Minister broke into a smile and offered to show Alex round the rest of the church.

At one point they stopped under one of the stained glass windows and looked up. There were strange letters beneath an image of a large white cloud with a span of blue light rising over it like a rainbow. "That's the day when evil is driven back from the earth," said the Minister.

"And what does that say?" asked Alex, pointing at the letters.

"It's in our old language," said Rebecca and she reached out her hand to follow the line with her finger. "When love is stronger than fear, marvellous things will happen."

As they walked around the church, Alex asked Rebecca and the Minister questions about the village which they answered happily, as if few who passed this way ever took such an interest. Appledore was the largest settlement on the western end of the Great Track. Its inhabitants were mainly farmers who followed a religion based on a God similar to the one Alex had left behind many years ago.

Rebecca was twenty five and had lived in Appledore all her life. Her parents were both dead and so Peter looked after her and the younger sister Anna. It meant she had to follow his rules but in return he took care of them both. Most women of her age in Appledore were married and she described herself as being "old fruit". She said that with a raucous laugh that echoed up into the rafters. A couple of times she began to ask Alex about where he came from, about what kind of people lived there and how far away it was. He would have answered her but each time she changed the subject herself, as if she felt out of place being so direct.

In such warm company Alex barely noticed the passage of time. It was late afternoon when he remembered Marshall. "It's time we were back on the road," he said, nodding towards the low hanging sun that was pouring light through the church windows. At this, his two new friends looked at each other and Minister Toms drew Rebecca to one side and spoke to her in a low whisper. They returned with smiles and the Minister said, "We would be most grateful if you would accept my invitation to stay here for the evening. I have plenty to eat and drink and we'd love to talk some more."

Alex said yes without hesitation. An evening meal with Minister Toms plus a night in a warm bed seemed a better prospect that a bag of crisps and a sleeping bag on the ground. The great outdoors would keep until the morning.

Chapter Five

Tavistock

As the setting sun put on a light show in the evening sky, they walked across the village to Minister Tom's house for dinner: Alex, Marshall and Rebecca. She had been included in the invitation, although her brother had to give his permission first. The Minister seated them all at a large oak table in a galleried room on the ground floor. After he had poured red wine into each of their wooden cups, a door opened and a short middle-aged woman appeared, carrying a tray. "This is my wife Margaret, the finest cook in Appledore," he said, making her blush.

"Don't be silly dear, it's just a chicken," she laughed and placed the tray on the table in front of them. There was a large plate piled high with carved roast chicken, bowls of vegetables and five wooden plates. "Now help yourselves my dears," she said and sat down to join them.

Throughout the meal Rebecca and Mrs Toms laughed and joked and shared in the conversation as well as the food. It was a world away from Peter's house and as the wine flowed Alex found it harder and harder not to talk about home. He had to keep reminding himself of Nicholas's words of warning, but it was beginning to feel like paranoia.

After their main course, while his wife was in the kitchen with Rebecca, Minister Toms leaned across the table to Alex and Marshall. "Peter told me how you're looking for Thomas Peters, the one who claims to be the Messiah. You do know he was here, don't you?"

"Yes," said Marshall, "Peter didn't seem very taken with him."

"Well," began the Minister, "he made certain promises." He took another sip of wine then stared into the rich red liquid at the bottom of his cup. "He claimed that when he reaches Middleton he will realise a prophecy and have the power to solve all of mankind's ills."

The Minister sounded wistful and distant, as if he wished such a thing to be true but was prepared for disappointment. "So what did he promise to do here?" Marshall asked.

Toms looked at him coldly over the top of his wine. "He promised to stop the demons that come from the woods to torment us and steal our souls."

Marshall choked on his drink.

As the evening drew on, the Minister lit a fire in the large stone hearth and they lifted the table to one side and drew in five high backed chairs. One by one they began to nod off until just Alex and Rebecca were left awake, sitting in opposite chairs in front of the quietly crackling flames. The only other sounds in the room were the clock in the corner and Mrs Toms's quiet snoring. Then Rebecca spoke.

"I want to leave this place," she whispered to Alex, "I want to travel the Great Track like you. I want to see places that you'll see, maybe even see your home."

"Oh that's nothing special, believe me," he laughed quietly. "I couldn't wait to get away."

"But it's somewhere I've never been. And I want to go east like you, maybe to Middleton. I've only ever been a day's journey from here in my life. Everything I know is from this village or what I've read in books."

"Then why don't you go?" he said, and felt guilty almost immediately. It must have sounded like he was mocking her.

"My brother would never allow it. People here are afraid to leave the valley."

He took a different approach, hoping to reassure her. "But why would you want to leave this place anyway? It seems a good life to me."

"Because there is so much more out there than this life; trapped in a..." she stopped. Her face was pale, even in the glow from the fire, and her eyes were wide and staring. There was the sound of a bell ringing in the dark: the bell at the gate to the village. With a shout she leapt to her feet and roused the others from their chairs. The ringing bell was now much louder and the Minister grabbed his coat and hat and a lamp from the table and ran to the door, followed by the two women. Alex and Marshall exchanged confused looks, then threw on their coats and went out too.

Outside, more villagers were gathering in front of Peter's house. Many of the men carried lanterns and some had burning torches of the kind that Alex thought only existed in films. The crowd seemed frightened and many of the women ran back to their houses to slam the doors and hurriedly pull shutters across the windows. All the while the bell kept ringing.

Peter was taking charge. He was a tall man and stood above the crowd in a clear position of authority. He spoke quietly to one or two of the other men and they in turn led small groups off to various points around the village's perimeter fence. After a few minutes Peter raised a lantern high above his head and began to stride down towards the main gate. The other villagers followed him and as Alex joined the back of the group he felt a hand slip into his. Rebecca squeezed his palm and whispered to him, "You don't have to do this. Go back to the house. Or to the church."

Alex looked at her, puzzled. "Why? What's happening?"

There was no time for an answer; they were at the gate and Alex could see a figure in the same spot where he and Marshall had stood twelve hours earlier. He was wearing a long coat and a similar hat to the one that Peter wore. One hand rested on the gate, while the other struck the bell at regular intervals. Then Alex saw his face.

For a moment he thought the man was wearing a mask. His skin was pale grey and his lips were black, he had a fine pointed nose and his eyes were hidden by shadows. But as he moved forwards closer to the gate it was clear this was no disguise. There were dark veins visible on his neck and as one of the villagers moved a lantern it shone across the man's face. There were two gasps from the crowd; one from Alex and one from Marshall. The light that should have filled in the shadows around the man's eyes had no effect. There were two dark holes beneath his mop of black hair. Then he spoke, "Good evening again my friends, are you not going to douse the lights and let us in?"

Peter stepped forwards, a light in one hand, "Get yourself back to hell Avery," he spat.

The figure by the gate laughed, "Oh Peter, you should try and find some different words."

Then there came another voice. "I have a few choice words for you Avery," shouted Minister Toms. "Take your evil disciples and leave this village alone." He strode up to within a few feet of the gate and raised a lantern in the air.

The figure stepped back and raised a hand to block the light. The limb was thin and bony and the skin was the same colour as his face. He had no fingernails. "Your lights won't work forever Minister," Avery spat, "The flames grow weak as I grow strong. Soon we'll be able to cross this threshold and take what's ours. So why not just send one out now for us to enjoy? It's easier to be merciful if you're not so hungry."

"Over my dead body," swore the Minister.

Avery just laughed.

Now for the first time, Alex noticed there were other figures in the shadows beyond the fence. A rotten band of men and women with the same grey, dead skin and empty faces was standing behind the stranger at the gate.

"Oh look. This is interesting. We have a traveller staying do we Minister? How very generous of you." With a flush of terror, Alex realised that Avery was pointing at him. He felt his hands shaking and his skin began to prickle and burn. He should have been staring into a man's eyes but instead he was being drawn into two dark, deep pools where shadows seemed to shift and swell. He felt an urge to walk to the gate.

Then there was a stabbing pain in his hand and he heard a voice close by. "Don't look at him," Rebecca whispered as she squeezed his hand tightly, digging her nails into the skin. "Look at me instead."

Alex turned to her and saw fear drawing tight lines across her face. But when he looked in her eyes he saw a spark of something far greater moving within; like a candle burning in the dark, driving back the shadows. Her courage. The spell was broken. Then he heard Avery's voice again, "Oh and there's another one. An odd couple of fellows aren't they?"

He had found Marshall in the crowd. Alex looked over at his companion who was staring at Avery in terror. He noticed that Marshall was wearing his coat and looked down at himself to see that he was wearing Marshall's. In the confusion they had grabbed each other's jackets. "For God's sake..." he scolded himself for noticing such trivia.

Avery had stepped forward and was gripping the top of the gate with both bony hands. "Why not send these two gentlemen through the gate Minister? I promise I won't tell. Just pass them over to us and we'll leave you be for a month or so. One would be good but two would be better." His voice had a greater urgency to it, a hunger. He sensed a crack in the villagers' united front and could almost taste the flesh he wanted; he craved.

A small number of villagers had gathered around the Minister and Peter, speaking with muffled voices and giving sideways looks at the two strangers in their midst. Alex turned back to Rebecca. "What's going on?"

"The man you see is Avery Tavistock. Some say he made a pact with devil. Others say that he was a Minister himself once."

"Doesn't anyone know?"

Rebecca looked Alex in the eye. "He's over a hundred years old. No one knows the truth about what made him like he is. He used to come once a year to take a soul. Those are the ones you see behind him. They're his devils. Now he comes almost every month just to taunt us. He tries to scare us into offering him a sacrifice. He won't give up till he gets one. And our lights are dimming." She caught Alex's baffled look. "The lights you see around the village are what keep him out. But they have less effect as each month goes by. Soon he..."

Peter had turned to address Avery again. "Thank you for your kind offer." As he spoke, Alex held his breath. "However, our message is unchanged. Take your evil back into the woods with you."

Avery's mouth opened but the shout that rang out came from further round the fence. There was movement in the shadows. A few of the villagers began screaming as their lights fell on the scene. Some of Avery's followers had hold of a man who looked terrified beyond all reckoning. His eyes were stretched wide and he was whimpering and moaning as he fought to break free. His captors all had the same pale, fleshless faces with black holes where their eyes had once been and as their captive struggled he tore at one of their shirts, revealing skin that hung off in dead strips.

"Oh, it seems we don't need to bargain after all," shouted Avery, playing to his audience of the living and the undead. "One of your flock wasn't quick enough to light his torch. We'll just lead him away to the woods and have our fun. Sorry if his screams keep you awake but these things do drag on."

The villagers were in uproar. Alex saw Marshall back away. Marshall wearing his coat. Alex wearing Marshall's. Which meant...

His mind was working fast, buzzing on an energy that had been hiding somewhere deep within him. He ran his hand down the side of the jacket, feeling for something. He heard a clink of metal and put his hand into the pocket.

"Mr Tavistock." He shouted and walked forward through a crowd that parted before him. It had gone very quiet but for the sounds of terror from the captured villager. "Mr Tavistock, we haven't been introduced." Avery had turned towards him but this time the eyeless face had no power over Alex. Something was driving him on. "My name's Alex Preston and I want to show you something." He pulled a small black object out of his pocket and held it up. He bellowed, "Remember my name Mr Tavistock. I want you to let that man go. Now please." His blood was roaring through his veins. Even some of the villagers were backing away from him.

Avery laughed at the same moment that Alex pressed the small button under his thumb. A shaft of light burst from the end of the torch and with a sweep of his hand Alex swung it to point in Avery's face. For a split second the darkness there was pushed back and Alex caught a glimpse of the man's true face; twisted in torment. Then a scream exploded across the village. It was a noise that came from everywhere; from beneath the ground and way up in the night sky. A scream of pain and terror. Avery Tavistock, the first Minister of Appledore, who had fed on the flesh and souls of the living for so long, was afraid.

He fell backwards into the cool arms of the darkness, where he was safe, and held his undead hands to his face. Alex walked up to the gate, holding the torch at eye level and keeping it pointed at Avery and his devils. He flicked it to one side, causing those holding the villager to release their grip as they fought to protect themselves from its beam. A smile broke on his lips as he marvelled at the effect that two small batteries and a bulb could have. They should see the one he kept at home under the sink, he thought.

The devils were backing away now, leaving their captive sobbing on the ground. They disappeared into the darkness, one by one, until Avery was alone. "I will remember your name Alex Preston. If you and I never meet again then I shall still take my revenge for this, but it will be paid in the flesh of others. I'll carve your name in their skin Mr Preston, so they know who to blame."

Avery stepped back into the dark and was gone. Immediately many of the lanterns and torches seemed to burn more brightly.

Three of the villagers ran through the gate and dragged the man on the floor to his feet and hauled him back through. All eyes were on Alex. Having faced down Avery it was only now that he was growing afraid. The men and women in front of him were staring. There were some looks of gratitude among them but many were suspicious, as if he were in league with the dark creatures he had just sent scuttling away. He turned off the torch and started to back away. He had no idea where to run but flight seemed the best idea. Then there was a familiar voice by his side.

"Don't worry. They won't hurt you." Minister Toms laid a hand on Alex's shoulder and spoke to the crowd in the voice he normally reserved for the pulpit. "This man deserves our thanks. He and his... device... have saved young Robert and possibly the rest of us from Avery Tavistock. He rests at my house tonight."

While some of the villagers lit fresh lanterns around the fence, in case Avery and his unholy followers thought of returning, the Minister led Alex and Marshall away. Alex looked over to Rebecca, heading home in the coat tails of her brother. "If she looks at me like they did," he thought, "I'll go home tomorrow and never come back here." She glanced back at him and smiled.

* * *

Alex and Marshall were woken by the smell of baking bread and the sound of Mrs Toms clattering about her kitchen. The pair came downstairs from the guest room and feasted on a breakfast of boiled eggs, cheese and ham. When it was time to leave, Margaret Toms gave them each a bag of food that surpassed anything they had eaten on the road so far. She kissed them each on the cheek and wiped away a tear as she hugged them on the doorstep. "You're both special boys," she said and disappeared inside.

The Minister led them down through the village towards the gate. It was still early and there were no signs of life. Shutters were drawn across windows and thin wisps of smoke could be seen rising from some of the lanterns that had only recently burned themselves out. When they reached the gate they stood in the same spot where they had faced Avery and his devils the night before. "You have my eternal gratitude," the Minister said as he shook them by the hand, "but I would ask one other favour of you. If you do catch up with Thomas Peters, then perhaps you could remind him of his promise."

"But I thought no one believed him?" asked Marshall.

"That's possibly true," said the Minister, "but as you saw last night, these are desperate times." Alex swore to do what he could and then turned to open the gate.

"Wait! Hold on!" They turned back at the sound of a woman's voice. Rebecca was running towards them, struggling under the weight of a large canvas bag that was slung over her shoulder. She reached them at the gate and drew breath. "I'm coming too."

The Minister looked shocked. "But your brother..." he spluttered. "I take it you've not asked him?"

"I already know what he'd say so there's no point," she said, "Oh please Minister, don't stop me from going. You know how life here drives me mad." She reached out and touched his arm. "I just want to see what lies outside this valley. When I've done that I'll come back and never leave again. I promise. Please let me go."

Minister Toms regarded her for a moment. Then he turned to Alex and Marshall. "If I do agree to let her come with you, you must promise to take care of her at every step. I would rather face Avery Tavistock and all his demons than to allow this young woman to come to any harm." Alex swore his agreement. Marshall frowned.

After Rebecca had hugged and kissed the Minister goodbye and he had promised to help placate her brother, the three of them headed onto the Great Track. As they walked up the valley they kept looking back at the figure of Toms, waving at them from the gate. He grew smaller each time they turned, until he was just a dot in the distance. Rebecca took one last look and felt a pang of guilt for leaving. Then she followed the others up the path and Appledore was lost from sight.

Chapter Six

A Parcel Arrives

"These ducks must be the fattest in the world."

Sarah tore off another piece of bread and threw it at the birds on the pond. They splashed forwards hungrily, beaks open and wings flapping as they scrabbled for the tiny chunks of week old loaf. She threw another and another, each time trying to get the bread further and further out into the murky green water.

"Are you trying to feed them or kill them with each throw?" said the woman sitting next to her.

Sarah laughed and passed Annie a large handful of the hard white loaf. "I'm just trying to add some excitement to their day. See if you can do any better."

Her friend tore off a chunk and hurled it at a haughty looking mallard, which caught the piece in mid air and swallowed it whole. "So you've still heard nothing then?" she asked.

"Nope. Two weeks now and not a peep. I thought about calling the police."

"But he left a message didn't he?"

"He did, yeah. That's why I didn't call them in the end. I think it's a case of him choosing to disappear, not one of him going missing." Sarah sighed and paused in her bread bombardment for a moment. Every time she directly mentioned Alex's disappearance the sadness hit her again. It was like a weight dragging her down into the park bench.

Annie looked across at Matthew, asleep in his pushchair, and sighed. "I'm so sorry this has happened to you," she said,

"I never saw it coming."

"I know," said Sarah, "None of us did. I knew he wasn't happy but I never thought he'd just take off. I thought he…"

Annie, her friend for so many years, knew how to properly finish the sentence. "He did, I mean, he *does* love you. All of you. I'm sure it's just some man thing and he'll come back soon enough." She sounded unconvinced by her own words.

"But what if he doesn't?" Sarah said, her voice rising in tone and wobbling uncomfortably. "I've put everything on hold over the last few years. If he doesn't come back to us soon then I'll have to go back to work. But I've not even set foot in a classroom in five years."

"It might not come to that," said Annie flatly, trying to disguise the worry she felt for her friend. "And you will cope. That's who you are. You've always been the one to deal with whatever gets thrown at you. And you were always a better teacher than me."

"That's not true," snapped Sarah, "and it's not fair either." Now her voice cracked completely and she began to cry. "I've handed my life over to other people for years and now I'm repaid like this." She used the back of one hand to wipe away her tears and she smiled weakly at Katie who was standing by the edge of the pond, feeding the ducks. "It's just not him Annie. It's just not him. I can't even sleep at night for worrying."

The flowing tears washed away some of the tension that had been building in both of them and Annie was much more upbeat when she spoke again. "People do get over things," she said. "Look at her over there." She pointed at a woman of about their age who was walking a dog on the grass. "She knows my friend Carol. Her husband died a few months ago and she was totally destroyed by it. Well you would be really…"

"Would I?" asked Sarah edgily.

"I didn't mean Alex is…" Annie grimaced at her own clumsiness. "I just meant… well, see what she's like now…" They both looked across the water to the other side of the pond where the woman was standing. She had a smile on her face and even from this distance there was something about her; the way she walked and the way she carried herself, that let the world know that she was happy. As Annie and Sarah watched, a man approached her and the two began talking. They did not touch, not even a shake of hands or a peck on the cheek, but it was obvious that there was some kind of bond between them. Their eye contact was constant and they leaned into each other as they spoke. Eventually the two walked off across the park together, talking as they went.

"What was all that about?" said Sarah.

"No idea," said Annie, "but I'll have some!" Their laughter was so loud that a few of the other park visitors turned to stare at them for a moment. Sarah looked at her watch and readied herself to go.

"I've got stuff to do at home," she said, "it's been good to talk". She hugged her friend goodbye and after Katie had thrown the very last chunk of bread at the ducks she wheeled Matthew's pushchair down the path beside the pond and away through the park gates.

Sharing a laugh with Annie had lightened Sarah's mood but the effect did not last long and the trio wound their sad way home. It was a typical Wednesday morning and the pavements were busy but Sarah spoke to no one as she pushed the buggy with Katie in tow. Instead she kept her head down and narrowed her gaze to the thin path she had to tread from the park to her front door. When she turned the last corner the street was virtually empty. The only other people she saw were the window cleaner at number thirty and an older man carrying a raincoat who stepped off the pavement to let her past with the pushchair. These would be the last adult faces she was likely to see for the next few hours. The rest of the day would now be spent within the four walls of the house with two fractious children and a television.

As she walked up the drive she could see the outline of a parcel through the frosted glass of the front door. Someone had dropped it through the letterbox while she had been at the park.

She let herself in, woke Matthew and released him from the buggy before she paid any attention to the small package lying on the mat. It was wrapped in brown paper and addressed by hand with the words, "Care Of Mr Alex Preston" in neat black writing. She lifted it from the floor and carried it to the kitchen worktop. Next came tea making and the fetching of juice for two thirsty mouths, before she had another chance to inspect the parcel. There was no stamp on it, no postmark and no return address. The folds in the paper had been made perfectly and the whole thing seemed to have been wrapped with loving care.

Loving care: maybe there was someone else. That made her grab at the parcel with both hands and tear the brown paper away. Now she held in her hands a book. Its hard cover was strangely patterned and the corners were protected by brown leather. She turned it over and over as she examined it more closely. It looked quite old but at the same time well cared for: the cover was gently creased but there were no tears or signs of damage. It was kept shut by a small brass clasp on the front, which she quickly released.

"A book of love poems?" she wondered.

When she opened it she found something far less interesting. It was a text book of some kind, written in a foreign language. Not just normal foreign, as Alex himself would have said, but odd foreign with symbols for letters and nothing she could even begin to translate into English. She flicked through the pages, feeling quite disappointed. She was not really sure what she had been expecting but it was not this. "But then, what the hell *is* this?" she muttered. As well as pages and pages of unintelligible writing there were maps and drawings of all shapes and sizes. She skimmed through at random. On one page was an illustration of some kind of giant monster; on another were pictures of a huge cloud and then there was a map. This showed a path or passageway, surrounded by yet more obscure symbols and dark writing. At one end of the path was a poor drawing of a tree and a castle, while at the other end was a vaguely familiar boxy shape.

A child's cry from the living room rescued her from the puzzle. She closed the book and laid it down in the worktop while she went to see what was wrong with the kids. It turned out to be Matthew, who was wailing at the piece of biscuit he had trodden into the carpet. Her heart ached as he broke from his crying to call "Daddy", over and over, while staring at the crumbs.

Sarah slipped another biscuit into his chubby fingers before ducking back into the kitchen to finish her tea and return to the book which lay open at the curious map. She sat back on her stool and puzzled over it once more. The left side of the page was very badly drawn but it definitely rang a bell. There was some kind of tower, a word in the funny foreign language and a square shaped squiggle below it.

"God this is so annoying."

She reached over for her mug and her sleeve caught the edge of the book. It flipped upwards and before she could react had landed on the kitchen floor. Cursing her own clumsiness, she bent to scoop it up and saw a slip of white paper fall out from between the pages. It was folded neatly in half three times over.

"Let this be your guide and protector."

At least the small blue writing was in English, although it made scarcely any more sense than the book. She moved it between her fingers, hoping it might shed some light on who had left the parcel at her door and where in God's name her husband was. She looked down at her fingers and saw they were shaking. Then a whisper slipped loose from her lips, one she normally saved for the last minute of the day.

"Where are you Alex Preston? I need you."

There were things she had not told Annie; things she had kept to herself. Like the bad dreams about Alex where she saw him in pain a long way from home; the ache in her stomach that left her feeling cold and sick and the growing fear that she would never see him again. She dropped her head into her hands and wept for the second time that day. Now there was no one around to comfort her.

Eventually she went upstairs to fetch a change of clothes for Matthew, who had covered himself in yet more pieces of half chewed biscuit. As she passed the bedroom window she glanced out into the street: the window cleaner had moved on to number thirty four and there was no one else about. But then the same middle aged man she had seen earlier walked back up the pavement on the opposite side of the street, still carrying his coat in one arm. He had dark hair and was wearing a suit, which made him stand out in this neighbourhood. As he passed, he looked up at the window and smiled.

She stepped back from the glass, as if she had been caught spying. It was only when she was halfway down the stairs that she realised what had happened. The sensation in her stomach had gone. The sense of deep dark cold had vanished completely. Several hours later, as she was preparing for bed, she was still enjoying the feeling. She could not help pulling back the curtain and peeking out, just to see if there was anyone on the street. But apart from the teenage lad from number twenty eight sitting on a wall with his girlfriend there was no one about. She felt slightly disappointed as she climbed under the covers.

The book lay on her bedside table and she stared at it as she laid her head on the pillow. It was obviously something precious and special. She just hoped that one day soon Alex would be here to tell her exactly what. She thought she was going to start crying again, but her eyes were weighted and she just managed to turn off the lamp before her closing lids drew her down into a well of calm, dreamless, restful sleep.

On the bedside table, like a child's night light, the little book shimmered in the dark.

Chapter Seven

Archangel

The day was almost over by the time they reached the top of the ridge. The sun was forming a red haze on the horizon and the temperature was dropping as the light faded. Marshall gathered wood while the others pitched camp and then they lit the fire. They had been walking all day and Alex was glad to take off his rucksack and drop to the ground. He rubbed his aching legs.

"That village was very strange," said Marshall, as he unpacked some bread and cheese. "They looked at us like we were about to eat their children."

Rebecca laughed. "That would have been unlikely; did you see how ugly they were?"

They had passed through a village earlier that day where the reception had been less than welcoming. It had been an odd place, even by the standards of Theland. The villagers were ugly, down to the last man, woman and child, and had stared and squinted at the strangers who came asking to trade with them. In the end they abandoned any plans to buy food or supplies and hurried away.

"I guess not everyone is used to seeing strangers around here," said Marshall, "it's quite pitiful at times."

A look of hurt and annoyance spread across Rebecca's face. "Not everyone is as well travelled as you two," she said coldly.

Alex saw the way her eyes had narrowed with quiet rage at Marshall's arrogance. "We're a strange looking bunch though," he joked. "I think I'd probably slam a few shutters closed if I saw us coming down the path."

They sat around the campfire eating their supper, which was the last of the food that they had taken out of Appledore. In the days since they had become a threesome they had crossed miles of open countryside, passed through dense woodland and along a steeply sloping valley that stretched upwards as far as the eye could see. One thing they had picked up on their journey was an earthenware jug containing a kind of cider. They bought it in a small village a day's walk from Appledore, handing over a few of the coins in Alex's bag in return for a container of sweet, warming liquid. It was surprisingly strong and they had learned to enjoy it in small doses.

"A cup of grog mate?" asked Marshall as he passed a cup across the flickering fire.

"Don't mind if I do," Alex said, taking the cup with a grin.

Rebecca shared in the ritual, raising her cup in a toast. "To ugly children everywhere," she said, to an echo from the two men. They flicked back their drinks and there was a short pause before they began coughing and wheezing in unison.

"I never quite figured it out," said Alex as he cleared his throat, "how you come from such God-fearing folk and yet you like a drink so much. You're nearly as bad as the Minister."

"I think it was left off the end of our religion," said Rebecca, "there's plenty of behaviour that is frowned up, certainly compared to what you've told me of your culture. But drinking with friends is not a problem. The grape and the grain are all part of nature in our eyes."

"Oh I don't know," piped up Marshall in a high, strained voice as he peered into his cup, "there's definitely something unnatural about this."

They shared some more of the jug and began swapping stories about themselves, encouraged by the alcohol. On an earlier evening like this Rebecca had learned where the two men really came from. It had made her eyes widen with shock and she had responded with a flurry of questions about what 'the other place' was like. The morning after, Alex had been afraid that she would see him in a different light and perhaps even ask to go back home to Appledore. But she had not. Instead, she asked more questions: about his family, his house and his life at home. Her desire for knowledge was able to leap the enormous gap between their two worlds in a single bound. He was impressed and amazed.

As the campfire burned, sending tiny red fairies of flame into the air, they lay back on the grass and stared either into the fire or up at the stars. "What do you want to be?" Marshall asked after a few minutes studying the heavens.

"I've always just wanted to be somewhere else," answered Rebecca, "somewhere away from the village. I used to talk to the traders who passed through Appledore. I'd ask them about where they came from and even buy books and newspapers from them. I'd do anything to learn about the world outside."

"Weren't you happy there?" asked Marshall.

"No one is truly happy there. Not with the shadows hanging over the place, but most are too afraid to leave." She went quiet for a moment. Then she spoke again, with a harsh edge to her voice. "I've left Appledore before but each time I knew it wouldn't be more than a few days before I was back."

"And this is different is it?" Marshall asked again.

"Yes. Something tells me that this will be very different. I don't know why, but it does. I don't think I'll be going back for a while." She sounded determined.

"So where do you want to end up?" asked Marshall.

"I used to picture myself pottering around a garden," laughed Rebecca. "It's not the most exciting thing but I'd love to find somewhere with a beautiful garden full of flowers. Maybe near the sea."

Alex poked at the fire with a stick, stirring it up again and sending another cloud of tiny red dots buzzing up into the air like insects. "I've never been bothered about travelling until now. With me it's about doing something with my life."

Marshall stopped his stargazing and looked over the fire at Alex. "Do what exactly?"

"Have you ever seen old photos of famous people, someone like a writer or politician?" He caught Rebecca looking at him blankly and he addressed her directly. "A photo's a kind of picture. Imagine a picture or painting of someone really famous."

"And you want to be that person?" she asked.

"No, that's not what I mean. If you look at a picture like that there are nearly always people in the background, people who were there when the picture was taken. But no one ever remembers who they were. The people in the foreground are the ones who are remembered while the others disappear into history. That's what I worry about: ending up as a forgotten nobody in someone else's picture."

"That's a bit deep," Marshall muttered and went back to his astronomy. Rebecca stared at Alex over the flickering orange flames and tiny dancing sprites of fire.

"That isn't going to happen to you Alex. I really don't think that will happen."

"Oh but it might," answered Alex, "I mean it does for most people. I just don't want to slip into nothing. But I'm too lazy most of the time to do anything about it; to do something worth remembering. Whatever that might be."

He was gazing hard into the burning pile of wood and did not notice the way Rebecca was still staring at him, as if she was reading something written across his face. Her pupils scanned slowly from side to side and at one point she opened her mouth to speak. But then he looked up at her and smiled and she blushed and turned away.

"I'm different." Marshall spoke now, without moving his gaze from the stars. "I just want to be in control. I hate the idea of others having power over me. I want to decide my own destiny, not to have it controlled by others. I'll never let that happen."

"And I thought I was insecure," said Alex. He had meant it as a joke but Marshall sniffed painfully, wounded by the comment, and turned onto his side with his back to the fire and his companions. Alex's eyes met Rebecca's and his eyebrows arched in comic pain and weary resignation. Marshall could be cruelly barbed and critical towards others but he displayed a very tender hide when it came to his own life. There was nothing that Rebecca and Alex could say now that would make the uncomfortable atmosphere any better so they opted for silence instead. It lasted long enough for all three to fall asleep beside the crackling fire.

The sun was clawing its way up over the hills when they awoke and there were blue pockets of mist lying in the shallow dips in the ground. Rebecca had brought with her a small iron kettle which they filled with stream water and boiled over the fire. She also had a battered metal casket of tea. It had a sweet fruity flavour and they sipped it slowly as they rubbed the night from their eyes and packed up the camp.

They dropped down off the ridge and followed the path out across open meadows. The fields were full of tall, scented grass and Rebecca plucked several blades from the ground and wove them together into a lush green ribbon which she put in her hair. Eventually they headed towards a line of oak trees on the horizon. The Great Track cut through the wood in an arc and once out the other side they were standing on the edge of a flat, open plain. In the distance a mass of buildings rose up out of the ground. There were white painted houses with open roofs covered in striped fabric; others were topped with polished domes that glinted in the sun, while standing above them were buildings made of dark timber that rose to narrow gables with tiny windows beneath the eaves.

"The city of Archangel," said Rebecca, as they stopped and stared. "I've heard of it but never been there."

"Then how do you know what it is?" asked Alex.

"That." Rebecca pointed to a large tower that rose above the huddle of squat buildings in the centre of the city. It had several large windows around its upper section and a flat roof that overhung in all directions like a lighthouse. "The Tower of Archangel is often mentioned in books," she said, "I've seen its likeness many times."

"Why is it so special?" asked Marshall, "Apart from being quite ugly?"

"It has a history to it. When I was growing up they used to say the city was guarded by a giant who lived on the top of the tower."

"A giant?" Alex tried to stop his voice rising childishly in pitch.

"It's just a story," said Rebecca with a smirk on her lips. She strode out towards a large stone archway at the edge of the city. "And you don't have to sound like such a girl Alex Preston. Where's your sense of adventure?"

Inside the city the narrow cobbled streets were teeming with life. The first area they walked through was a giant outdoor market, with covered wooden stalls selling everything from food and clothing to pottery and furniture. There were men cooking meat over large metal drums full of burning wood and the smoke drifted into Alex's path. On either side came the sound of voices calling out to the crowds. Some were in English and what sounded like French, others in languages he had never heard before. Those he could understand were trying to entice would be customers into stopping for a while to inspect their goods and part with some money. Drawn by the smell of cooking meat, they stopped at one of the giant barbecues and immediately a short haired girl stepped forward and spoke. "Would you like to try some of the finest food in Archangel?"

Alex peered over at the sizzling flesh on the large metal griddle. He wondered what kind of bizarre animals the locals fed on. The meat certainly smelled good. "What exactly is that?" he asked the girl.

"Er… pork." She said, with a tone of voice that suggested Alex might be less than a genius.

"Oh right. Um, I'll have three please." He pulled the bag of coins from his pocket and opened it up. Immediately the girl's eyes widened and she stepped forward.

"Sir, you must be more careful with your money. The streets of the market are full of people who'd part you from your coins, but not all of them are offering you something in return, except maybe a sharp knife in your ribs."

That made Alex smile and the girl grinned back. He guessed she was about eleven or twelve and her hair was cut in a neat bob around her fair skinned face. Her dress was not too dissimilar to Rebecca's but she had a bright red skirt. "Are you a visitor to Archangel?" she asked.

"I think it shows, don't you?" he laughed back, "My name is Alex. What's yours?"

"It's Elisabeth." The girl smiled even more and giggled. "Don't worry. Most people who pass through here have just arrived. If it's three you want just give me one shilling."

Alex opened his fist and peered down at the coins, not knowing which to pick. The girl giggled again at the look of confusion on his face and reached out to take one. "He doesn't travel much," said Rebecca, peering over his shoulder. Her cheek was so close to his that he could smell the scent of the grass in her hair.

"I'd be lost without you," he said.

"Then it's a good job I'm here, isn't it?" she smiled, tilting her face slightly so that he caught the smile on her lips.

The girl reappeared with three large green leaves, piled with slices of sizzling pork that were smoking and spitting. The travelling trio took them from her and began to gingerly lift the hot pork to their lips. The meat was crispy on the outside but surprisingly soft on the inside and had a spicy taste that made each of them cough in turn. The girl laughed again before going back to check on the rest of the cooking meat.

Carrying their leaves, the three wandered further down into the market. They passed several stalls where a type of tea was being brewed in enormous decorated urns. Men were sitting in wicker chairs sipping from cups of the steaming liquid and leaning forward in conversation. Others were drawing on pipes and watching the crowds. One of these winked at Rebecca as she walked by and raised his pipe in a kind of salute. She turned away and hurried on.

The streets grew wider and now stone buildings replaced the wooden market stalls. Through small, darkened windows they could see into shops selling glass bottles full of coloured liquids, piles of patterned fabrics and even fancy coats and hats. Those made Alex look down at his own clothing. When he had brought his breathable, all weather jacket he had never imagined he would be wearing it in a place like this. But the fact that no one gave him or Marshall a second glance suggested that the people of Archangel were used to seeing visitors dressed strangely.

There was a shop with a window full of jars containing coffee beans and a handwritten note that said ominously, "Closed due to unforeseen demonic events". Next to this was a building that they recognised as an inn or tavern. Above the door hung a painted sign of a large misshapen figure with the words "The Messenger Inn" written beneath it.

As they approached, they saw another sign in a window that said simply "Rooms". The three exchanged glances. Sleeping under the stars may well have been a romantic way to travel but the prospect of at least one night in a proper bed under a roof, with cooked food and maybe even a chance to wash, was definitely appealing. The only thing that stopped Alex getting to the door first was Marshall. The only thing that stopped Marshall getting through it first was Rebecca's elbow in his ribs.

On the other side of the door was a large room with a bar along the far wall and rough tables of dark oak dotted around the bare wooden floor. Square pillars supported a low ceiling. People were sitting at the tables: gangs of men with heavy tankards of frothy beer, whole families with children and dogs and, to Rebecca's surprise, groups of women sharing jugs of wine. A cloud of rich, fruity pipe smoke hung at ceiling height as if suspended from the rafters.

Alex, Marshall and Rebecca drew the attention of the drinkers in the inn for a moment as they walked across the room but the interest quickly evaporated. Alex led the way to the bar where a grey haired man was hanging empty tankards on hooks above his head. He looked up as the trio approached.

"Drink sir? What'll it be?"

"Actually, we wanted rooms for the night," said Alex.

The man frowned and ran his fingers over his chin. "It's our busiest week of the year so I'll have to see. You do know it's the rededication of the tower tomorrow, don't you? That and every lost cause for miles around is here to see that lunatic preacher."

Alex could hardly believe his ears. "Thomas Peters? He's here? Now?"

"I think that's his name. The one who claims he's the Messiah. Yes, he's been here for two days." The man now eyed him suspiciously from under a raised eyebrow, "You're not one of his lot are you?"

"No, no. Not at all," said Alex, trying to shrug off his interest in the man whose name had been mentioned in every village they had passed through. "We've just heard a lot about him."

"I'm not surprised," said the landlord, as he began looking at the pages of a scruffy ledger that he had fished out of a drawer, "He reckons he's here to save us all from ourselves. Lunatic." He paused for a moment as he squinted at the book. "Ah, here we are." He peered up at the trio in front of him. "You'll want how many rooms?"

"Two please," said Alex. He gestured first at himself and Marshall and then at Rebecca. "One for us and one for our friend."

The barman murmured something just out of earshot before fishing out two keys and handing them over the counter. "You gentlemen are up the stairs and first right. The lady is two doors down. No animals in the rooms and no noise after midnight. You can pay me now for the first night." He held out a wrinkled hand.

After paying the man, the three went up the flight of stairs and found their rooms. Alex and Marshall's contained two single wooden beds, a small wardrobe and a chair. On a table was a large jug of water and a white bowl. There was a small fireplace with an iron hearth and a pile of logs in a battered bucket. They threw their bags on to the floor and flopped down on to their beds. They might have been expecting a feeling of luxury compared to bedding down out in the open but in fact the mattresses were hard and lumpy, as if they were stuffed with wood for the fire. After a few minutes Alex got up and went down the corridor to Rebecca's room. He tapped gently on the door and said softly, "It's just me."

"Come in just you."

She was sitting on a double bed, brushing her hair. Sunlight streaming through a window caught her face and made it glow. He said nothing and just looked at her as she ran the brush through her long brown hair. Eventually she spoke. "Are we heading back out? I want to find Thomas Peters, if he's really here."

"I reckon so," said Alex. "Knock on our door when you're ready." He left the room. His heart had begun its familiar race, beating out a fast rhythm against the inside of his chest. It was a relief to shut the door behind him and walk down the corridor.

A short while later they were back out on the crowded streets of Archangel. The landlord at the tavern had no idea where they would find Thomas Peters so they began asking passers-by. Most shook their heads but eventually one very tall and well built man smiled and said, "I'm heading that way now, let me take you to the Master and you may enjoy his company."

It all sounded rather grand to Alex but he smiled back and the three of them tucked in behind the enormous, muscular stranger as he cut his way through the crowds, towering over the people on either side. He had short hair and a beard and was wearing a heavy sheepskin coat and leather trousers. People seemed so intimidated by him that they moved out of his way as he weaved through the narrow streets.

Eventually they came into a large square, ringed by narrow

townhouses with tall windows and covered balconies. There were people everywhere: in the square itself, on steps leading up to the houses and hanging from the terraces. Men and women were craning their necks for a glimpse of the activity on a stage at one side of the square. As Alex followed their gaze he saw that the stage was in fact a wooden cart, parked sideways on to the crowd. A man in his late twenties, with pale skin and neatly cut blond hair, was standing on it. He was wearing a long blue coat and was waving his arms about excitedly as he spoke to the crowd, his voice echoing around the confines of the square.

"People of Archangel, I promise you that day draws near. When I am able to reveal to you the nature of my powers and the source of my miracles you will have the veil lifted. I will travel to the city of Middleton where it's my destiny to be revealed to you all as the one true saviour. I implore you to come with me, to follow me and join with me in this celebration of our joint destinies. For as I am revealed to you, so you all will find new life."

He drew his hands up into the air then spread his arms wide to greet the cheers of the crowd. "But I will leave you now with more than words my friends. Let me show you that I am a man of action." As he spoke, two men lifted a large wooden barrel up onto the stage. It was tipped on to its side so that the crowd could see that it was empty before being stood upright again. Thomas Peters then spread his hands over the top of it and closed his eyes. The crowd went silent as he muttered quietly under his breath. Then he curled his hands closed and opened his eyes again, shouting, "Believe in me people of Archangel! For I alone can show you the way!"

One of his helpers drove a wooden tap into the base of the barrel with a hammer and instantly wine sprayed out into the faces of those at the front of his audience. They in turn began dancing under the red shower, cupping their hands to drink in the liquid. "Praise Thomas Peters! Praise him!" cried the tall man who had led Alex and the others through the streets. He raised his hands in the air as he shouted, "He is the true path.

He is the one true path!"

The words were taken up by some in the crowd who began chanting "True Path, True Path," over and over, while others shouted Thomas Peters's name at the tops of their voices. Alex looked around. People were jumping up and down with excitement; their faces alight with a kind of joyous fervour.

The messy chorus of voices grew in volume until Alex could not even hear himself speak as he leaned in to talk to Marshall; his words were swept away by the shouts and cries of the human swell all around them. On the homemade stage Thomas Peters was smiling cheerfully at the crowd with his arms stretched out. Then he stepped back off the cart and disappeared from sight.

That triggered a massive and sudden rush from the crowd, as a hundred or more people tried to push forward to follow Thomas Peters out of the square. Alex held back, seeing that it would be impossible to try and fight through the wall of bodies, pressed together like sardines in a tin. Marshall did try on two occasions but both times failed to even get past the first layer of people. He and Alex glanced at each other with resignation on their faces.

Already there were cries of alarm coming from within the crowd, as the front rows slowed down and began to be crushed by those behind. A mood of panic had suddenly descended on the square and Alex realised that he had lost sight of Rebecca. Then Marshall shouted her name and pointed into the moving mass of people.

Like a piece of wood being carried by a strong current, the top of her head was just visible in the sea of flailing arms. As Alex and Marshall watched, her face turned towards them. Her skin was paler than ever and there was fear and panic in her eyes, wide with terror. She was trying to shout something but the words were lost. And so was she.

Alex felt his own vision go dark, as if the human walls were closing in on him too. He felt a rushing sensation, his heart began to hammer and he could sense air pouring into dark spaces in his head. And then he was moving. Into the enormous, crushing crowd. Bodies moved past him without touching. People turned and looked with shock and then fell back away from him. There was a feeling inside him which seemed to force its way out through every tiny pore in his body. Energy. Anger. Passion. It drove a mighty wedge in the wall and forced people backwards. He was moving faster now, as Rebecca's head disappeared from sight beneath the deadly tide. She had just seconds before the air would be squeezed from her lungs and her ribs would crack in the vice of people so desperate for a closer look at the man on the stage.

Alex was hemmed in by bodies. The rushing noise was deafening and his heart was racing out of control in his chest. He drew a slow, noisy breath and made a final lunge between two men and caught hold of her hand. He drew her back towards him and held her close to his chest. Her skin was as pale as paper, her eyes were closed and her hair was wet and matted on her face. Alex turned to face the way he had come and saw that the wedge he had driven into the wall of people had closed in around them.

He lifted Rebecca over his shoulder and pushed forward again. Just like before, through the crowd. But now the anger had left him. The moment he felt his hand touch hers it had dissolved and now they were both trapped in the middle of the deadly, thrashing human sea. He felt hands pushing into him from all sides and tried as hard as he could not to stumble. He knew they would both be dead if he did. But it was bound to happen soon.

Then he could see something large moving towards them. A tall figure in a heavy sheepskin coat was steaming through the crowd like a giant ship. One very big and hairy hand reached down and scooped Rebecca from Alex's shoulder while a voice he had heard before said, "Hold on to my belt and follow me." He did as he was told and was almost dragged off his feet as the enormous man stormed his way back to the rear of the square. Alex hung on to the man's thick leather belt and just prayed it would soon be over. He saw Rebecca's lifeless face hanging over the stranger's shoulder and feared he had reached her too late.

As they broke free from the crowd, whistles were sounding and men in green uniforms had appeared from two alleyways and were attempting to pull people out. Marshall looked nearly as white as Rebecca when he saw them emerge and came rushing to Alex's side. "Is she..?" he asked, looking between his two friends.

Alex shrugged open mouthed before he heard the stranger's voice again. "Follow me quickly. I can get help for your friend."

They tucked in behind him once more as he darted out of the square, down one of the alleyways. He still held Rebecca over his shoulder and her body seemed like a toy against his enormous frame. Marshall whispered breathlessly in Alex's ear. "What went on back there? You looked like you'd gone mad. It freaked me out."

"I don't know," said Alex. "I think I just panicked when I saw her in that crowd."

"It looked like much more than that," said Marshall as they turned left into a side alley. "You looked like you were having a fit. It was frightening." They turned left again into a passageway that dropped down a flight of steps. Then the tall man stopped at a closed door and tapped three times. The door opened and he stooped through the doorway and vanished. A moment later he reappeared and beckoned them to follow.

Inside was a square room lit by candles; heavy with the smell of perfume or incense. A single window was shuttered and more candlelight came from a hallway at the back. The room was full of people; men and women were sitting on the floor or on cushions while others leant against the walls. Rebecca was laid on a rug in the middle of the stone floor. Her face was still stony white and there was a quite rattle each time she let out a breath.

The tall man was kneeling beside her, holding one of her hands. His voice trembled as he spoke. "My name's Anthony.

I'm sorry your friend was hurt like this. Everywhere we go the hysteria gets worse. If I'd known this would happen I would never had shouted out like I did." The big man's eyes glinted tearfully.

"Be calm brother," came a voice from the rear hallway. The blond haired figure of Thomas Peters entered the room and all the occupants, save Alex and Marshall, clasped their hands in reverence. He walked over and knelt beside Rebecca, studied her face for a moment and rubbed at his chin. "This woman is very ill," he said and sat back with his hands on his knees.

"Oh for God's sake, we can see that." Alex spat his impatience across the room. Even his tiny amount of medical knowledge gleaned from an office first aid course and watching television was more than anyone's here. The reality had hit home: he was stuck in a medieval fantasy world with a friend who was gravely ill. He wanted to run across and punch the man kneeling by Rebecca, then snatch her up and away from this madness but his legs felt like lead. "I thought you were a miracle worker," he said. "Or can you only do tricks with barrels of wine?"

Through steel blue eyes, Thomas Peters regarded him for the first time. "I don't believe we've met before, my friend. But you will learn that I do have the power to help those who have faith in me." Then he turned away and spoke to the man beside him on the floor, "Anthony, fetch the book please."

There was a table in one corner of the room, where a purple cloth was covering a flat, square object. The big man went across to it, removed the cloth and lifted the object with both hands. He passed it to his master.

It was a large book with a leather cover that was held shut with a clasp. Peters unclipped it and began flicking through the hand-written pages. He stopped at one and scanned a paragraph before moving on. Eventually he settled on another page and pressed it flat with his hand.

"Friends," he called out, "join with me in praying for this young woman. That she may recover from the injuries caused by the passion of our followers. I will now call upon the powers within me to guide her back to health."

Around the room people were bowing their heads in prayer as the man on the floor spread his hands above Rebecca's body. Alex could see that her breathing was now becoming shallower and was much noisier than before. Her face was raked with lines of sweat that ran down her cheeks to the floor. Thomas Peters muttered under his breath as Alex and Marshall stood and stared. When his muttering stopped, the only noise to break the solemn silence was the painful sound of Rebecca's strained breathing. Each slow rise of her chest was accompanied by a dry, rasping rattle and her exhalations sounded like gas escaping from a pipe. And still Thomas Peters held his hands over her body as his followers kept their eyes to the floor.

Nothing happened. There was no change in Rebecca's breathing and no sign of life on her face. Her eyes stayed shut and her hands lay limply by her side. But now Alex's anger burst through his body. Like a drug, it poured through his veins and brought nerve endings and muscles to life with a roar. He tore his feet from the floor and lunged forward. Shoving past Thomas Peters he fell upon Rebecca's body just as her life was being expelled in one long final breath. As Peters and the followers looked on in confusion, he lifted her head from the floor and cradled her face in his hands. Tears of frustration and terror were raining down his cheeks as he bent and kissed her, his eyes blurred and his fingers trembling. Then he heard a voice.

"Alex."

The room erupted into cries and cheers as Thomas Peters' followers threw themselves at their leader, clapping him on the back and praising him at the tops of their voices. In the midst of the celebrations, Alex brushed Rebecca's damp hair from her face. "I thought we'd lost you," he whispered.

"I was lost at first," she answered, "but then you came and got me. I remember. You came and got me." He held her closely as the voices around him cried out a miracle. Then with

Marshall's help he lifted her to her feet.

The big man approached them and held out a hand. "Though my master has proven himself yet again, I'm still eternally sorry for what happened. I hope you can forgive me."

Although he towered over them all, he had such a kind face that Alex could not help but reach out and shake his hand. Then he saw Thomas Peters regarding them from across the room. The followers were pouring him wine and celebrating noisily but he was just staring at Rebecca. Alex expected to see a look of quiet pride on his face, even smugness. But there was only confusion.

Chapter Eight

The Guardian

"I've grown used to weird over the last few weeks," said Marshall over the top of his beer tankard, "but today was strange in a totally new way." They were in the bar of the Messenger Inn, enjoying the delights of the tavern's kitchen: plates of hot sliced beef and fresh bread covered in thick gravy. Marshall was giving Alex and Rebecca his opinion of the events of the day. "What was it all about?" he barked, between mouthfuls of food and drink. "The crowd in that square went mad after a few words and a party trick with some wine. Then I've no idea how you got Rebecca out of there." He glanced at Alex. "And as for Thomas Peters and his mumbo jumbo..."

He leaned forward as he spoke, in case any of the followers might be lurking around the corner. "It was like they were all on drugs," he whispered, "and that's how I felt in that room with all the incense. I felt like I was dreaming or under sedation. I'd no idea what was going on. At least with flesh eating zombie vampire things you know where you are."

They all laughed nervously. "But he is letting us go with him to Middleton tomorrow," said Rebecca. "That's good isn't it? He's not sent us on our way just yet."

Alex looked at her as she tucked into her food with a voracious appetite. It was hard to believe that just a few hours earlier she had been at death's door. Her cheeks were full of colour and there was a sparkle in her eyes that he had never seen before. "If it means we can persuade him to help us, then yes it is good. Although I've no idea if he can really do anything useful."

After they had cleared their plates and drained their tankards they retired to their rooms. Marshall fell into a beer induced sleep almost immediately and his snores filled the room. Alex lay awake on his bed and stared up into the darkness. He kept replaying the day's events in his head, trying to rid himself of the image of a dying Rebecca on the floor on the candlelit room. Her face was so pale and soaked with sweat as she fought to fill her crushed lungs with air. He could hear the sound she made, the breath of the dying. He imagined he could see her life force drifting upwards out of her body as he just stood back and watched.

He rose from the bed and let himself out of the room. Down the corridor he pressed his hand gently to Rebecca's door. It moved open silently and there she was: asleep on her bed with her face caught in a beam of light from the window and her brown hair spread across the pillow. He stood over her for a moment and watched as she breathed normally, the only sound a gentle whisper of air on her lips. He so wanted to kiss her but was afraid she would wake. So he went to the chair in the corner and sat, as the night hours slid by, and watched over her. Then just as dawn was breaking he went back to his room.

* * *

The party of Thomas Peters and his followers was due to leave Archangel in the early afternoon and Alex, Marshall and Rebecca were going to join them on their journey to Middleton. That meant they had a few hours to spare. They had heard people talking in the bar of the Messenger about an event that morning to mark the rededication of Archangel's odd looking tower. Many believed it would bring the city good fortune, so the trio decided to tag along and see what all the fuss was about. "It'll kill time," said Alex, "and you never know, it might bring us some luck."

After the three had handed back the keys to their rooms and sought directions from the landlord, they left the inn behind and disappeared into the city once more. It was still early and the streets were quiet. But as they neared the site of the tower the size of the crowd grew sharply. Alex felt Rebecca's hand press into his anxiously.

The Tower of Archangel was a circular column of white painted brick. It rose fifty feet into the air from one end of a diamond shaped arena. Open walkways ran around the arena's high walls and at the end nearest the tower there were two vast wooden doors that were bolted shut. As the trio walked into the plaza, the voice of Anthony bellowed warmly over the heads of the swelling crowd, "Friends! I thought you would be here! The others are preparing for the journey but I couldn't resist coming to see what's happening."

The group climbed a set of steps to the walkway on the walls. Below them the city of Archangel rolled out in all directions. They could see the tops of roofs and the messy networks of streets and alleyways. Alex thought he could make out the city square where they had first met Thomas Peters and he shuddered. But there were far more pleasant sights: buildings with tiny blue minarets, houses with roof gardens full of flowering plants and others with striped awnings that flapped like deckchairs in the breeze.

The sightseeing was interrupted by the sound of a horn. A group of four men in long blue coats and tall hats was making its way through the throng. They walked in a square, with a much smaller figure wearing a hooded cloak in the middle. They reached the tower and disappeared inside.

For a minute nothing happened and some in the crowd began to chatter impatiently. Then the figures appeared on the flat roof of the building. Two were now carrying incense burners and one was holding a silver staff with a gold star at the top. The horn blew a second time. As it did, there was a deep, animal moaning from behind the giant doors in the side of the plaza walls. Before this could create a distraction, a human voice rang out from the roof. "Citizens of the city, it is a day for celebration," shouted the staff bearer. He moved close to the front edge of the roof. "The emptiness of the tower has been a shadow over us all for too long. Today that shadow is lifted. The one thing that guarantees our future prosperity will be returned to its rightful place."

He raised the staff into the air above his head and for the third time there was the sound of a horn. Then there was a slow, creaking noise and the enormous doors began opening inwards, pulled by men dragging on heavy ropes. Something edged into view: a large object, as tall as the doors themselves, which was hidden under an enormous shroud. The fabric reached to the ground and was dragging in the dust as the object moved to the threshold and stopped.

There were men on all sides of it, some of them holding on to ropes attached to the cloth and others carrying spears, swords and shields. They looked nervous and were glancing from side to side and then back to the huge moving mass beside them. Then one of the spear carriers, wearing armour on his chest and arms, stepped forward and approached the object. "Move on!" he screamed, but nothing happened. So he lifted his spear and jabbed at the cloth with considerable force.

There was a sound that reminded Alex of an animal in a zoo. A low, beast like groan floated out from under the sheet. The shape seemed to grow in height. The bottom of the shroud lifted off the ground and from beneath it two giant shackled feet emerged. The crowd let out a cry of shock and some began clapping. Then one of the feet lifted and took a step forward and the giant shape began moving again, into the plaza with the crowd parting before it. Eventually it stopped in front of the tower and the armed guard formed a semi-circle around it.

The man with the staff shouted down from the roof. "As Bishop of Archangel I thank the Mercenaries of Brampton for returning our most treasured trophy after two decades of emptiness. For this act they shall be rewarded and so shall we, as the good fortune that left us once will now return."

"He's a windbag isn't he?" whispered Rebecca with a giggle.

She was right, thought Alex. And as he looked around the city from his vantage point on the walls he could not see much sign of bad fortune. No one seemed in rags or to be starving and most of the buildings beneath him were in a good state of repair. But the Bishop had more to say.

"For two centuries the city of Archangel was guarded over by a sentinel. A creature of such immense size and strength that none dared to challenged or threaten our city. And so our wealth grew. But in a moment of weakness the city's leaders allowed the Guardian of Archangel to leave its post. Now we have seen our prosperity wither and have lived with the threat of attack from our enemies. Until today. The Guardian is returned and never again shall leave us. No more shall the name of the city of Archangel be taken in vain. No more shall we be humiliated. Our standing is restored."

"Vanity," Alex thought to himself, "That's what this is all about. Vanity." He had begun to understand what was happening.

"Now let us begin," went on the Bishop. "Uncover the beast." He shouted down at the armed men, who pulled on the ropes holding the enormous shroud. As it slid to the ground the crowd let out a collective breath. Then there was silence.

Standing before the Tower of Archangel was a massive two legged creature. It was roughly man shaped, with legs and arms like tree trunks and huge hands and feet. Its skin was dark and scaly and marked with cuts and cruel bruises. On its back were two diamond shaped wings that were folded inward but still stretched from the base of its spine to just below its shoulders. The animal had a massive neck, ringed with muscle, that led to a head at least four or five feet in diameter. As it gazed upwards at the Bishop, Alex caught a glimpse of the animal's face. It had hard, bony features with a single enormous eye that was sparkling in the sunlight and a mouth that stretched from one side of its vast skull to the other.

Then Alex realised that the twinkle in the creature's eye was not caused by the sun but by welling tears. The animal that was standing at the base of the tower, with huge chains around its ankles and blood running down its back, was crying. Then the beast spoke. "But they said I could go free," it said in a soft human tone. "They said I could go home." There was some laughter from the crowd in the plaza at the pitiful sound of the Guardian pleading for its freedom. And as the people laughed, the animal lowered its head again and more tears ran down the enormous face.

"Why doesn't it just break the chains?" asked Anthony. "It looks like it could snap them like twigs."

"It's afraid of something," said Rebecca. She was staring at the Guardian with tears in her own eyes and she stepped so close to the unprotected edge of the walkway that Marshall had to hold her arm to stop her tumbling off. "Look at it," she implored them. "It's terrified of something."

The Guardian of Archangel, a beast powerful enough to keep a city's enemies at bay, stood at the foot of the tower and sobbed. But this meant nothing to the Bishop, who shouted, "To the roof. You know the penalty for disobedience." The men with swords and spears stepped back, creating a space around the creature. It stood alone and unmoving with its head bowed and its arms at its side. The mercenaries were unsure what to do. Eventually one of them stepped forward and prodded it with a spear. But it still did nothing.

Then a noise from above made it raise its head again. It was the sound of a child's voice crying out in shock. Up on the roof the Bishop was holding the hand of the small figure in the cloak, which had dropped its hood and was peering down at the Guardian in disbelief.

Alex let out a cry of "Oh my God!" as he recognised her. "It's the girl from the street market, the one who sold us that hot meat."

"Elisabeth," said Rebecca. "I remember her. What are they doing with her up there?" She slid her hand back into Alex's and felt him squeeze it hard. At the base of the tower something was happening. The Guardian was shaking its head slowly and

84

its crying had stopped. Then it took a step backwards, which alarmed the Mercenaries, and raised its head again. The wings on its back opened outwards and stretched halfway across the plaza. With two giant flaps, the creature's feet left the ground and it took to the air, its arms by its side. To an accompaniment of excited shouts from the crowd it rose to the top of the tower.

Only now could its real size be appreciated. The vast wings were spread even wider as it hovered over the top of the tower and with its legs suspended beneath its body it looked far taller than it had on the ground. Alex was sure he was not the only one who was willing the enormous beast to turn tail and fly away from Archangel and whatever fate lay ahead of it. But it did not. The Guardian simply lowered itself on to the roof and sat back on its haunches in a sad crouch. Its eyes closed and it dropped its head to its chest. It looked asleep.

Then the Bishop came forward once more, still holding the girl's hand. "This child was chosen to be the new Attendant at the Tower of Archangel," he shouted, "and she will ensure that the Guardian does not leave us again." The Bishop smiled coldly as he called out to the crowd beneath him and to his audience on the walls. "The Guardian sees this child as sacred and to be obeyed."

As the Bishop spoke, Alex felt a throbbing in his ears. It was a slow pulse, like a heartbeat, that stabbed against the back of his skull. The sound of the Priest's voice had become muffled and distant and he strained to read the words on the man's lips. Then he heard someone speaking close by. At first it was just a whisper but as he looked around for the source, he heard the words, "They said I could go free. They said I could go free." He turned to the tower, where the Guardian was hunched over with its head touching the roof surface.

"Do you know what they will do if I leave this tower?"

He stared at the creature's slumped body in silence.

"I know you can't answer me. I know how men think. I've known men for too long. But you can hear me. You have to tell them. You have to tell the people that I am being forced to do this. Because if I…"

Alex leaned forwards, dangerously close to the edge of the walkway. He could hear the voice so clearly, it was like the Guardian was whispering in his ear.

"If I leave this tower they will kill the child. They will cut her throat if I break my bonds. They have told this to no one. But you must tell. You must help me, I cannot help myself. I am held to ancient promises that bind me more tightly than these shackles. They may break their oaths but I cannot."

Alex felt sick. He looked at the girl, who was standing beside one of the incense burners. "I need to shout," his conscience was screaming, "I need to shout out the truth before it's too late." But his mouth stayed shut and he did nothing but watch.

The Bishop had turned to face the creature. "You bear the name you were given by the builders of this tower. You are The Guardian. You are the servant of the city."

It lifted its face and its gentle voice rang out from the roof, "My name is Samuel. My name is Samuel. They set me free."

The Bishop was angry at this defiance. "You are The Guardian of the Tower," he shouted. "If you are not that then you are nothing."

"I am Samuel," wailed the humiliated beast, with its head still just a few feet from the floor. "My name is Samuel."

The Bishop raised his staff in the air. In a swift, precise movement he brought it down on the Guardian's head, striking it full in the face with a crack. It let out a single, piercing shriek and pulled its head back and upwards out of reach. Blood ran from a large gash on its face. From their vantage point on the walkway Alex and the others had a clear view of the attack. Rebecca and Marshall let out cries of disgust and even the giant Anthony raised his hands to cover his face in horror.

The Bishop was laughing. They could hear it from across the plaza. He was standing in front of the Guardian and laughing. Alex wondered why on earth the enormous beast did not simply knock the man off the roof. Then he heard the Guardian's voice again, crying inside his head.

"I'm blind. He's made me blind."

A feeling of terrible pain and panic swept over Alex and he rocked on his feet. It was only the quick reactions of Anthony that stopped him from crashing from the walkway to the floor of the plaza.

The Guardian moaned and cried, with one of its enormous hands now covering the wound on its face. The Bishop turned to the crowd and a smirk was drawn across his face. "The Tower of Archangel is empty no more!" he shouted and waved the staff in the air, its star stained bright red. Down in the plaza, whistles began to blow. Men in uniform were moving through the crowd, ordering people to leave. One of them pointed up to the walkway where the group of friends stood and waved them down.

Alex took a final look at the Tower. The Guardian was being chained to the roof, blood still running down its face. He could hear its moans of pain. He was not sure if the sound was in his ears or in his head but he heard it nonetheless; a terrible lonely, scared groan. Elisabeth was being ushered from the roof in a state of shock. As she was being led away he caught sight of her pale face and frightened eyes. He looked from the creature to the girl and back again. Then he turned and left.

Chapter Nine

The Lezard

The twenty five men, women and children who made up Thomas Peters' group left Archangel and headed east. Ahead of them lay miles of flat, desolate grassland where the wind whined and moaned and cut through their clothing like a knife. As the city disappeared from sight and the air grew even colder, Alex lent his jacket to a young woman called Alice who was carrying a baby in a sling. She was wearing a flimsy woollen shawl and her skin was already turning blue as he draped the weatherproof coat over her shoulders. "I'm very grateful," she said. "When I joined our Master I didn't think we'd be travelling so far from home."

"And where is home?" Alex asked. She told him it was a village called Meridian, to the north west of Archangel. Thomas Peters had preached there, not long after her husband had died of an illness that sounded a lot like TB.

"When I heard him, I felt my heart fill with joy," she said with unashamed emotion. "It was as if my Jacob himself was telling me to stop mourning and live my life. When the Master said he wanted people to follow him I had to say yes. My family thought I was mad but they didn't feel what I felt."

"What did you feel?" Alex studied the young woman's face. For a religious convert she looked surprisingly normal.

"Joy," she said and she beamed at him.

As the party wound its way further and further east, Alex learned more about those who were accompanying Thomas

Peters on his mission. They came from all walks of life. The tall man called Anthony, who had saved Alex and Rebecca from the crowd in Archangel, had been a shepherd in the northern hills. An older man called Steven had been a lawyer and seemed to know everything that was worth knowing about Theland and its traditions. And a young man called Jason had been training as a musician and would encourage the group to sing with him as they marched eastwards. The one thing they had in common was their love for the man in the blue cloak. Each time they mentioned Thomas Peters, they spoke with such a sense of awe and wonder that Alex had to restrain himself from giggling out loud. Peters was charismatic, he had to admit, but not enough to explain why Alice and the others worshipped the ground he walked on.

Alex, Marshall and Rebecca had joined the group on the last leg of Thomas Peters' great trek. In each village and town he had passed through, he had performed a few minor miracles and had promised to deliver much more once his true powers were revealed. Now just one destination lay ahead: the city of Middleton. This was where he hoped to meet his destiny and become the people's Messiah and it was also where he expected to face his greatest challenge: a monstrous beast that was terrifying the city. When he first heard this, Alex snorted with laughter. But as he learned more about the creature, he realised that not taking it seriously had already cost many people their lives.

* * *

Four hundred years ago, when the city of Middleton was just a hamlet in the Arwent Valley, a legend was born. It was said that the small cluster of homes was built beside the seasonal nesting site of a giant creature called the Lezard. The story went that it had a dozen heads at the end of a dozen long scaly necks. It flew on enormous silver wings and could swoop from the skies to devour cows or horses with a single gulp.

At first the Lezard was disturbed by the constant noise

of hammering blacksmiths and wailing babies and found a new place to live in the north. But after a great frost it was driven back to its old home, which was now buried beneath the expanding village. So it fell upon the collection of wooden houses and reduced them to little more than match wood with the enormous teeth set into each of its dozen mighty heads.

The people fled into the woods in terror and wondered who would save them from the beast, which was now busily building a new nest from the remains of their homes. Then a warrior called Jeremiah Darkwind set out on his white stallion. He did battle with the Lezard and one by one sliced off its many heads until just one remained. With a final swing of his blade, he slew the mighty beast and threw its body into the River Arwent. The Lezard would never bother the people of Middleton again.

All of which made a fabulous story to tell the children when they refused to go to sleep, or to act out in theatres as cheap entertainment for the people of the growing city. The brave hero on his mighty steed vanquished the evil monster and set the poor people of Middleton free from terror. The people thought it was a marvellous tale but the truth was quite different. Jeremiah Darkwind did set forth to battle the Lezard but he only got as far as hacking off the smallest of its heads while it slept. This annoyed the monster considerably and it woke up with a jolt and devoured the brave Darkwind with a single gulp of its fifth biggest mouth. Two days later it flew away of its own accord after a flash flood washed away its nest; even a many headed monster knew better than to pick a fight with the River Arwent. Instead it headed back north to find a deep, dark cave in which to hide from the world and brood over its hatred of men.

Most legends grow from a few cobbled together half truths without causing any great harm and the same applied to the tale of the Lezard for century after century. A handful of people, mainly scholars and archivists, knew the reality behind the myth but none was prepared to publicly discredit it. They were worried it might spoil an enjoyable evening's entertainment.

Then one morning, at about the same time that Alex and

Marshall were first exploring Theland, a party of traders on their way in to Middleton saw a large bird in the sky. They did not give it a second thought until one in the group noted that all the other birds seemed to be flying beneath it, even the eagles that were soaring on the tallest of currents. Being clever sorts they deduced that the bird was not only a lot further away that they had first thought, but also considerably bigger. The principles of perspective and scale never had a more interesting though ultimately tragic illustration.

Several of the men were keen ornithologists and stopped to watch the unusual specimen circling so high above them. Its wings were silver in colour and there was something striking about its beak: the way it seemed to be moving about like a snake. And then the strange bird went into a nose dive.

The screams of the traders could be heard from inside the city walls as they ran for whatever cover they could find, abandoning their wagons for the safety of the nearest tree or bush. Two horses were devoured first as the Lezard swooped upon its prey like a cat leaps upon a surprised mouse. A cloud of dust rose into the air from the downdraft as it beat its wings to hover over the trading party and enjoy the midday feast. It stretched out two long necks and sunk very many teeth into an enormous ox that was pulling a cargo of the finest cotton and silk. With such a heavy load to haul the unfortunate beast was never going to escape the death that came from the sky.

Two of the traders went a similar way as the flying monster uprooted entire trees, using its great strength to shake loose the juicy human fruit hiding in the branches. The men were swallowed whole. One escaping merchant, who had only come to Middleton to buy some coffee beans for his shop in Archangel, managed to ride a hundred yards before one head caught him and another his horse.

The Lezard finally had eaten enough and with a single massive beat of its wings rose up into the sky and disappeared. Half an hour passed before the terrified survivors dared to crawl from their hiding places to survey the scene. Upturned wagons littered the road and a stream of blood, human mixed with animal, stained the Great Track. There were no bodies left but the odd limb could be seeing lying on the grass, which had been pressed flat by the force of the attack. In the middle of the carnage stood an old donkey, untouched and unmolested, chewing on a nettle. With such rich and tender pickings the Lezard had not even bothered to snap at the animal with its very smallest head.

This was the day when the folk of Middleton and the Lezard each learned a valuable lesson. The people living inside the city realised the importance of historical fact. The giant flying beast discovered that the traffic heading in and out of the high, arched gateways provided a rich source of food. For those who were determined to get through, or who had no choice, it meant the last mile of their journey now had a worrying edge to it.

***

Thomas Peters' party approached the outskirts of Middleton with all eyes raised to the skies. They had no time to marvel at the sight of the vast walled city lying at the side of the sparkling River Arwent, no time to draw breath at the splendour of the delicate spires and steeples that rose from within or to enjoy the hundreds of flags that flapped in the breeze from every available window and ledge. Middleton was a city at the very pinnacle of its wealth and power but all this was lost on them as they scanned the heavens for a giant flying nightmare.

There were four main entrances to the city walls, facing to each of the points on a compass. These stone gateways, known as bars, looked like miniature castles with tiny towers and turrets that allowed the guards to peer down on whoever approached the vast wooden gates. The bars were kept open during the day and that was especially prudent now that the Lezard was paying frequent visits to prey on the unwary or just plain slow. The beast only fed out in the open and once through the bars travellers would consider themselves safe.

As the group reached within a couple of hundred yards of

the West Bar a small dust cloud could be seen approaching them out of the city. As it drew near the cloud dissolved to reveal a party of riders on horseback. At the front was a man in a suit of armour, carrying an upright lance with a triangular flag at the end. On his head he wore a gleaming metal helmet with the visor raised to reveal a rugged looking face with heavy, stubbled jaw and piercing blue eyes. An enormous broadsword hung at his side. Immediately behind him was a man in a pale blue cloak that floated above the back of his horse. Beneath it he wore a gold waistcoat and dark blue trousers tucked into leather riding boots. The rest of the horse party were dressed in purple tunics except for the last two: a boy and girl sharing a tired old mare. They wore the traditional Theland servant's uniform of dark hooded cloaks and black trousers.

The lead rider slowed his horse as he approached Thomas Peters' group and the rest pulled in behind him. "Good day people, I trust you are heading for the safety of the city?" he said. It sounded like more of a command than a question.

"We are indeed sir," said Thomas Peters' undisturbed by the arrogant edge to the man's voice, "although there's been no sign of the Lezard today."

The rider looked down at the group and snorted. "That is because she prefers to attack after noon, as anyone here would tell you. Only the foolish or the brave remain out in the open after midday."

Alex's voice cut across from the back of the group. "And which are you?" he asked.

The horseman's cheeks flushed red. "I sir, am Nathaniel Arbiter of Aberwell, a Knight in the army of Lord Mawwhinney of Brigstock. I set forth to do battle with the Lezard and finish what Jeremiah Darkwind began. You may stay and watch as I kill the beast. The Archbishop is here to assist me with whatever magic may be necessary to dispense with such a foul creature."

The figure on the second horse had a cheery round face and rosy cheeks and waved a hand in greeting. "Hello friends," he said quietly, "My name is Boniface, Archbishop of Middleton."

As the horse party dismounted and unpacked their saddlebags, Rebecca whispered to Alex. "Is it safe to stay here? If he's come out to face this monster, shouldn't we be getting away?"

Alex agreed, but Thomas Peters was harder to convince. "I must see what the beast is like," he said. "If the knight fails, then it will be my duty to return and defeat it. My powers may be all there is to stop it."

Alex sighed. This was Peters at his most arrogant and annoying. "But can't you just watch from inside the city? Isn't that good enough?"

"No, no," he insisted, "I must stay here. This is part of my destiny. But the rest of you must make for the city bar, especially the children. I'll be quite safe here."

Alex rolled his eyes at Rebecca. "Someone's got to stay with him," he whispered to her. "If nothing else, he's likely to annoy the knight and end up on the wrong end of his sword." He was sorely tempted to leave Peters to his own devices but he seemed so unworldly that it would be like abandoning a kitten. A handful of the others, among them Marshall and Anthony, agreed to stay with him and Rebecca led the rest of the group into the city. She departed with a plea for Alex to take care and he watched her disappear towards the western bar.

Nathaniel Arbiter was busy checking his sword and practising a few swings as the men in tunics erected a square patterned tent that carried his coat of arms. Then he and the Archbishop disappeared inside, leaving the others to lounge on the grass and amuse themselves. Alex noticed the two children were staring at the way that he and Marshall were dressed. He waved over at them, "Come and sit with us." They dropped on to the grass next to him and introduced themselves as Gillan and Levine. Gillan was a squire boy to Nathaniel Arbiter and was ten years old. His job was to polish the Knight's sword and make sure his wine flask was filled. Levine was eleven and Gillan's best friend. She was a serving girl and would attend the Knight's chambers with the older women, lighting the candles and laying out his wardrobe each day.

It is a powerful spell that makes a man forget his own children but the magic of Theland had woven itself deep into Alex's heart and mind. Although he was sure the two reminded him of someone, he could not remember who. Instead he chatted to them about their lives in the service of the Knight. Nathaniel Arbiter lived in comfort in one of the wealthier districts of Middleton, although much of his time was spent travelling on his Lordship's business. The children had already been working for him for over a year and were likely to remain in his employment for years to come. They looked happy and healthy enough but both seemed too weary for children of their age.

After they had spent a while in conversation the tent flap flew open and the Knight strode out, helmet in one hand and sword at his side. The Archbishop followed behind wearing an embroidered cape fastened with gold braid and a matching mitre that made him look a foot or two taller. He walked with a decorated crook in his right hand. Jewels shone on its curved head and a green pattern wound its way down the shaft.

"We're ready to face the beast," boomed Nathaniel Arbiter. He was a handsome fellow and without his helmet his long dark hair was able to flow down over his collar. He ran one hand through it slowly and theatrically as he realised that all eyes were once more on him. "The Archbishop will say prayers as necessary while I wield my sword against the Lezard." He drew his broadsword from its sheath and planted its tip in the soil so that it stood unaided. With both hands he then raised his helmet over his head and gently lowered it into place.

Some of the Knight's servants began to clap and cheer. Nathaniel responded with a regal wave of a gloved hand. Alex, sitting on the grass, said nothing. He was staring at the fighting man's left foot. It was trembling fearfully, even as he was accepting the applause. No one else seemed to have noticed but as Alex watched the tremble became more pronounced until Nathaniel lifted his foot and stamped in to the ground. While the others mistook this for a mark of his readiness to fight, it made Alex shiver. Suddenly this did not feel like such a good idea; watching men do battle with a monster had lost any element of entertainment or spectacle and seemed a foolish notion.

He shivered again as the once warm air around him took on an unpleasant chill. As a feeling of dread crawled over him like a wraith, the sky grew darker and heavy clouds began to gather overhead. All life had drained from his arms and legs and he sat spellbound as events unfolded before him.

First came a cry that the Lezard had been spotted. One of the tunic wearers pointed at the sky, where a dark shape was fast approaching the city. Nathaniel dropped his visor, lifted his mighty sword and walked out across the grass, his confident strides betraying no sign of his trepidation. Archbishop Boniface was a few paces behind, one hand steadying his mitre and the other holding his crook. He began to pray under his breath.

The shadow in the sky was drawing nearer and drifting towards the earth. The Lezard had its enormous steely wings stretched out lazily on either side and appeared to be gliding on the currents like a bird. From where he was sitting, Alex could make out only a shapeless, writhing mass where the head should be. But then it snapped into focus and everyone on the ground let out a cry.

Like crazed eels, the necks tumbled and slid over each other as they moved to their own rhythm and calling. Jaws snapped hungrily at the air as the creature caught the scent of prey and hurried its descent to the feeding ground. The biggest head of all peered down at the tiny specks on the earth far below. The narrow eyes set into the hard bony skull fixed on the two figures that stood apart from the rest. One of these glinted like silver, even in the dull light of the afternoon. The Lezard's wings drew in towards its body and it lifted its tail and dropped like a stone.

Nathaniel Arbiter could see little through the narrow slit in his visor and he could hear nothing but his own breathing, which was coming in rapid gasps. The trembling in his foot had returned but now his muscles were frozen in terror and he was unable to raise it again to stamp out the fear. He checked and rechecked his grip on the huge silver sword that his squire Gillan had spent all morning polishing until he could admire his own face in it. It had been given to him by his father when he was first appointed a Knight.

Ah, his father. He so much wanted to be like him. Torquin Arbiter had also been a Knight and had fought in many battles alongside Lords and Kings. He had pushed his son into following in his own footsteps even though the young Nathaniel had dreamed of a life in the arts. He had also persuaded Lord Mawwhinney to take his son on board as a favour for saving his life many years before. But whatever Nathaniel did, wherever he went, he was always in his father's shadow. When he had heard of the Lezard he knew it was his chance to prove himself to the whole world. To show what he was made of.

At that moment he was having trouble keeping hold of his weapon as his fingers began to twitch nervously inside the enormous plated gloves. He could see the grass around him being blown flat by a heavy wind that made even standing up an ordeal. Now his breathing was being drowned out by a sound like a roaring waterfall and the sun must have slipped behind a cloud because he was suddenly standing in shadow. The wind and the roaring grew stronger and he saw the Archbishop's mitre tumble past him on the gale. He knew this was his moment and that he would not fail. With the weight of the helmet bearing down on him he finally managed to raise his head and...

Pandemonium broke out as the Lezard swooped down and swallowed Nathaniel and Archbishop Boniface whole. The cleric went down first. Two of the smaller heads snapped at him, sending his hat rolling across the grass into the distance. They fought over their prey for a moment before a much bigger rival leapt in and devoured the poor man in an instant. Then the jaws on the mightiest head of all opened wide and engulfed the Knight with a roar and a snap. All that remained of the men were the gleaming sword and jewel encrusted crook that stood upright in the soft earth, moving in the breeze with a darkly comic wobble. Then the Lezard looked around for more meat.

Alex was still sitting on the grass in a trance. It was only Marshall tugging at his shoulders and yelling, "Get up man, get up and run" that snapped him out of it. He scrambled to his feet and they began to race towards the city, tucking in behind Anthony and Thomas Peters. Then, after just a few yards, the faces of the two children flashed in his head. He stopped running and looked back. The Lezard hung in the air about twenty feet from the ground. Its huge wings generated a whirlwind of raging air and flying dust as it floated over the heads of the dead Knight's servants who were vainly trying to fend it off with pikes and staffs.

Alex froze again at the sight of the creature. This must have come from hell, he thought to himself. When he had heard the story of it returning after centuries to wreak havoc it had felt like a joke but now it was here and it terrified him. He stood half hypnotised and began counting the lizard-like heads that teased and toyed with the men who were fighting for their lives. Then he almost sank to his knees and prayed for the end to come quickly. "Oh my God. There are so many of them." The words escaped from his lips with a cry of despair. His travelling companion Stephen had told him the Lezard had grown more heads in its time in exile; that they now numbered more than twenty. But that was pitifully out of date: Nathaniel Arbiter's footmen were fighting for their lives against a dragon with at least thirty heads.

When the Lezard had first troubled the people of Middleton so many years ago a mere dozen necks grew out of the creature's scaly body, although Jeremiah Darkwind did at least manage to reduce that to eleven. What no one had realised was that this was a creature in its infancy and that as time rolled on, the army of writhing spines would increase. With so much fresh meat to prey on since its return to the Arwent Valley, the dragon had found that it was sprouting new heads almost daily. With each one its hunger grew and grew.

For the second time Alex was snapped out of his daze by a voice calling to him. He heard Gillan screaming for help as he cowered by the side of the tent, which was being torn from the ground by the Lezard's downdraft. He was trying to cover Levine with his cloak, as if that would protect her from the dragon's vast appetite. Around them blew a whirlwind of the dead Knight's paraphernalia.

Alex covered the ground in seconds. He threw Levine over his shoulder and grabbed Gillan's hand. "Run as fast as you can and don't look back," he shouted over the din of human screams and monstrous roars. They took off towards the city bar, which seemed a very long way off. Alex gripped the boy's hand tightly as he sprinted over the grass. He was terrified he would drag the child off his feet but he knew that speed was all that could save them now.

As the Lezard prepared to finish with the last of the fighting men, one head noticed the figures fleeing towards the city and reached out to snap at them. But its neck was too short and it screeched loudly, drawing the attention of several of its siblings and Her: the one they all obeyed. Now the body twisted to the side and the wings changed their rhythm to shift the massive bulk through the air. A chorus of synchronised shrieking echoed across the valley as it gave chase.

Alex heard the noise but kept his eyes focused on the city bar up ahead. He tried to block out all thoughts of the dragon bearing down on them and of what the mean, spiteful heads would do to their bodies if they fell within reach. He had one hand locked over Levine's body on his shoulder and the other gripped Gillan's fingers for dear life. His legs pumped like pistons as he pushed forwards with every shred of strength he had in his body.

The grass on all sides began to flatten outwards as a great wind caught up with them. Alex could feel the huge cushion of air fall upon him like a cold breath on his neck. The world grew dark under a vast shadow and a great liquid roaring was the only sound he could hear, blotting out the screams of the terrified children. He knew he had to run faster, to protect Katie and Matthew.

He remembered who Gillan and Levine reminded him of. It was like a cloud moving away from the sun for a moment, letting the warm rays shine through to touch his skin. In his mind he saw the faces of his own son and daughter and was filled with a sudden desperate desire to see them again. It charged his tired muscles with new energy and he felt himself rise up from the ground as he raced the final few yards for the gateway. The grass flew beneath him in a blur and the child on his shoulder felt as light a feather while the boy in his grip was swept along with him.

Then the cloud blew across the face of the sun again and the thoughts that had filled him with new hope drifted away as quickly as they had come. The air froze as the shadow swelled and engulfed the three figures. Alex could hear a dry whistling sound in the air above his head and he began to stumble as he made a last sprint to safety. He imagined he could see tiny shapes moving past him from the direction of the city walls. The whistling, the roaring and the sound of the wind blended into a terrifying cacophony that made him want to cry out.

The Lezard was surprised at the pace of its prey. The man seemed blessed with incredible speed, as if lifted on invisible wings. But then he slowed again and it was time to bring the chase to an end. Only a dimly familiar whistling noise distracted it from the swift kill. A wave of arrows shot up from the walls of the city and a dozen of the steel tips managed to pierce its scales. It used its teeth to pull them from the flesh but the race was already lost.

Alex's lungs were about to burst as he fell into the arms of Marshall, who stood beneath the city bar waving him on with terror in his eyes. Once Levine had been lifted from his shoulder he slumped to the ground and screwed up his face. Burning tears flowed down his cheeks and he rocked back and forth as he wept with relief. Beyond the high stone walls of Middleton, the Lezard shrieked indignantly and flew in a slow circle around the Arwent Valley before lifting into the sky and disappearing for another day.

Chapter Ten

A Final Gathering

Several hours later, Alex's hands were still shaking as he raised a cup of wine to his lips. Around him the rest of the group were enjoying the food that filled the long table before them. But all he could manage was to swallow back the drink and pour another refill with trembling fingers.

They were staying in a large house close to the heart of the city. It was owned by a wealthy retired tailor who spent most of his time at the coast. He was a family friend of one of the followers, a young man called Jason who had grown up in Middleton, and he had lent him the keys as a favour. The four storey house was built around a central courtyard with a fountain. Heavily scented plants and lush vines grew up the walls and scrambled over the covered wooden landings that hung out from each floor.

They had reached their lodgings after a meandering walk through the city streets. Middleton was bigger in every way than Archangel; the stone and brick buildings were much taller and leant forward awkwardly, as if they were trying to look down on the people walking below. Tall chimneys smoked above red tiled roofs and balconies clung bravely to the sides of houses. They passed through one open market and it was several times bigger than anything they had seen in Archangel. But many of the stalls were empty and there was talk of the effect the Lezard was having on trade. "That thing's the work of the devil," one man was saying to another, "and it's killing my business too."

The group came in to a large cobbled square and to one side was an imposing white-faced building. Jason frowned when he saw it. "That is the home of the Commissioners," he said and volleyed Alex and Marshall's blank looks. "They're the religious rulers of Theland."

"They're much more than that," said Thomas Peters as they walked across the square in front of the enormous shuttered windows.

Jason looked at his leader for a moment, choosing his words carefully. "Master," he said quietly, "I think it best that we hold our tongues while we're out in the open." He looked around and lowered his voice further. "It would be unwise to be overheard and there may be spies close by." They hurried on to their lodgings.

When they had entered the courtyard an old woman came out of a doorway, threw her arms around Jason and kissed him on both cheeks. "This is Henrietta," he said. "She is the housekeeper and will take care of us." At the same time, the faces of the other group members appeared over the edge of the balcony.

"You've lost the best rooms boys," shouted Rebecca. Although the house had many bedrooms most of the group still had to share. Alex, Marshall and Anthony squeezed into one room, while Rebecca shared with Alice and her baby. Thomas Peters was the only one with a chamber to himself but no one seemed to begrudge him that.

Night time was a few hours off so they went out into the city to explore. Street after street was full of similar courtyard houses, fronted by stone walls and metal gates. Then there were the five or six storey tenement buildings with lines of washing strung across the road between them. At ground level there were inns, drinking houses and coffee shops on nearly every corner. Rebecca was in shock at the fine dresses worn by many of the women and she was sure they were looking at her as if she was a peasant girl. "You were stupid to stay and watch the Knight try to kill that monster," she said, when Alex told her what happened outside the city bar. "I could have..." she stopped abruptly and her cheeks flushed red. "*We* could have lost you." Alex just laughed and gave her a hug, aware that they were under the gaze of Marshall and Anthony.

That had been earlier in the afternoon. Now they were enjoying a communal dinner in the main hall of the house, where Henrietta had laid out a table full of food. They tucked into chicken, bread, cheese and fruit and Jason opened bottles of wine from the cellar. Despite his unsteady hands, Alex had managed to refill his cup at least twice. The feeling of the wine hitting his stomach was the only thing to blur the memory of the Lezard bearing down on him.

The children had left him at the city bar. By custom in Theland if a Knight died in combat then his heirs must allow his servants to continue in the family's employ. But as Gillan had explained, "Master Nathaniel has no wife or children." Alex had been too afraid to ask what that would mean for them. He simply hugged them close and promised not to forget them before watching as they disappeared into the city throng.

Now he felt like crying. Rebecca came to sit next to him and rested a hand on his arm but it did little to revive his spirits. Around them the rest of the group were celebrating their escape from death. "It's another miracle that we are all here tonight," Anthony said.

Marshall was determined to pick up on the conversation that had been abruptly halted earlier. "So tell me about the Commissioners," he said to Thomas Peters.

"Some people think they have spies everywhere but I am sure we're safe here." Peters said, waving a hand of reassurance at Jason. He took another swig of wine and leaned on the table with his elbows. "They're high priests, police and judges in one. They outrank even the Archbishop we saw earlier, God rest his soul. They decide how people worship and when and they can arrest anyone they see as unfit or ungodly." He held his cup in the air as he spoke. "The only reason they've not had the Militia arrest me is that they're too afraid of a revolt."

There was an approving murmur from around the table as he went on. "When I've had my day they'll be nothing but a spent force. Their years of bullying and torture will be over."

"Torture?" said Marshall in disbelief, "You make them sound like secret police."

Now Jason spoke. "They are like secret police," he said. "Over the years many people have simply disappeared after they've spoken out against the Commissioners. That's why I urged you to be careful outside earlier. There are graves around this city and beyond, filled with those who've challenged them."

There was an uncomfortable silence after his words. Then Anthony lifted the mood by asking, "So tell us, Master, what you plan for tomorrow. It's the day we've all been waiting for."

Thomas Peters put down his cup and wiped his mouth on a serving cloth. "Friends, this is indeed the day we have waited for. Tomorrow I will lead you to the Place of the Elders, to the Courthouse, where I will reveal to you and the world the nature of my destiny."

Alex and Marshall looked at each other across the table. Since their first meeting with Thomas Peters they had listened to the same words used over and again to describe how he would show himself to be the next Messiah for Theland on a certain day. They used to find the little speech annoying but now it just made them chuckle to themselves. They felt the same about Thomas Peters himself. They had grown to like him, despite his quirks and his taste for stage magic. Marshall raised one eyebrow and Alex giggled into his wine as the man at the head of the table continued.

"Not all of you know how I came to be in this place or why I have chosen to lead you to the new dawn. I feel it's the right time to share it with you all. So many have joined us on this journey and this time tomorrow things will be so very different. Until a year ago I was a man of the law. I did nothing each day but sign papers and count money. Then one day I received a gift that changed my life."

He nodded at Anthony who reached to the large leather bag than hung from the back of his chair. He slipped a hand inside and drew out the hard covered book that they had seen in the scented room in Archangel. It was placed on the table in front of Thomas Peters, who laid one hand on it. "This is why we're all here," he said. "I discovered it one day among the private possessions of a client who had passed away. His family didn't want it and they gave it to me in thanks for my kindness to their father."

He ran both hands around the edges of the book and let his fingertips creep up over the cover. "At first I thought it was a journal or diary. Then I wondered if it was some kind of holy encyclopaedia. It's written in a language I didn't understand at first. But then as I studied it each evening I found I could begin to make out its true meaning."

He opened the front cover and laid his hands on the first page, on which were written lines of delicate, almost decorative, black text. He rang a finger over the words and read out loud. "Let he who reads these pages be wise and most holy. For the one who shall bring these words to life shall lead man into the new dawn. He shall be called Saviour and Messiah and the words of God shall flow through him and bring forth miracles."

Those gathered around the table began to whisper excitedly to each other as Thomas Peters read the words from the book. He saw this from the corner of his eye and smiled. "Within the pages of this book are prophecies, miracles and magic," he said, "but they can only be read by one who is the Messiah. I am that one."

At that, a round of applause broke out and he smiled even more. Alex was sitting a few spaces down the table but he could still see the open book and squinted to see if any of the writing made sense. There was nothing but dark lines and patterns. Thomas Peters caught his glance. "The book has proved itself already Alex. The miraculous acts I've performed; curing the blind, allowing the deaf to hear and of course healing Rebecca," he smiled down the table at her, "all these things came from this book that I alone can read."

There was more excited chatter amongst the group. Some already knew about the book and its prophecies but the more recent recruits were hearing it for the first time. Marshall frowned, as a thought sparked in his mind. "But why have you performed some miracles and not others?" he asked. "What about the creatures that haunt Rebecca's home, or the disease we told you about; the one that's wiped out most of a village at the west end of the Great Track. Why haven't you dealt with them?"

The chatter died down and all eyes fixed on the top end of the table. "I understand your feelings Andrew, I do. But the truth is that until tomorrow I can only perform the acts that are held within these pages. That is why tomorrow is such an important day. Once I have read the final page, in the place and at the time specified, all magic and wisdom will be known to me. It says so here..." He flipped through the book to find a page marked with a torn piece of paper. "And when the final chapter is said and done, the worlds of man and God will be known to you and you will have the power of the Universe within."

He looked around the table and then settled on Marshall. "This is what will happen tomorrow. I've followed the writings in this book to the letter and in a few hours we will all see..." He sat back in his seat and raised his cup to his mouth. His hand was shaking.

Alex did not know what to think or say next. There were plenty of questions he could ask, not least why a legal clerk from a small town should be chosen as a Messiah. Instead he chose to take a wine bottle from the table and adjourn to the steps of the house. He sat listening to the noises of the city, carried across the wall of the courtyard by a warm breeze. There were raised voices coming from one of the tenement windows opposite and a baby crying in the distance. Then came a rustle and the sound of soft footsteps and Rebecca appeared beside him. "What are you thinking?" she asked, stealing a sip of his wine.

"Actually," he said, "I was thinking that this place seems oddly familiar."

"How?" said Rebecca.

"It sounds weird but I dreamed of somewhere like this when we were right at the start of our journey. Even the smells were there." They lifted their noses to taste the scent of wood smoke. "I must be mad."

"Then you're in fine company," she said and looked down at the floor. "I must have been crazy to think that someone could end the nightmare at home. My brother is right..." she sighed heavily and Alex put his arm around her.

"You never know," he said, "Miracles do happen."

They sat together on the steps surrounded by the sounds of the evening and shared the last of the wine.

* * *

As the candles and lanterns burned down to their wicks a figure skipped from shadow to shadow. There was not the slightest sound as it crossed the yard and scaled the steps before making its way from landing to landing until it reached the very top of the house. There, it hugged the wall until it came to the third door along. There was only the tiniest of clicks before the lock was sprung and the door swung inwards.

Inside the room someone was asleep on the bed but they did not stir as the figure moved from the doorway to a tall dresser by the far wall. The top drawer was slowly pulled open and an object was gently lifted out and placed on the dresser top. The figure then drew something from the bag that hung at its belt and lowered it into the drawer, which slid closed. Finally, as the occupant of the bed snored gently, the object on the dresser was dropped into the bag and the figure retraced its steps down to the courtyard.

* * *

Across the city three men sat at a table. "The job is done," said a tall man with glasses on his nose. "The last chapter of this charade will be acted out tomorrow and we can breathe a little easier."

"I still wonder if all this is worthwhile," said a large framed man with a tidy dark beard, sitting opposite. "This seems like such an elaborate scheme. And for what? There's nothing to say he is here."

"But that's our aim isn't it?" said a third voice. A man with a purple hood around his shoulders leaned forward and lit a small cigar from one of the candles on the table. "No one likes being made a fool of. When people realise they've been hoodwinked and humiliated we know how they'll react. No one will dare whisper his name after this."

"But why use our powers in such a way?" the bearded man said. "Why not be open and proud of who we are: the rightful heirs to this world and the other?"

"Oh Mallory, my friend, it was you who first suggested this scheme, so don't go cold on me now." The smoker dragged on his cigar. "The people must be the ones who're making the decision, or at least believe that they are. Otherwise we'd appear as bullies and even our own police might not be enough to handle the consequences. Far better to let things take their own course, guided by us in the background. The time for us to step out of these shadows will come later."

"But need so much blood be spilled?" the bearded man went on. "Johan; it only had to prove a point."

"But that's exactly it," his companion answered with a puff of rich, scented smoke. "Only the sight of blood upon the streets of Middleton will bring people to their senses and stop any thoughts of a second coming or a visit from their gentle stranger. This nonsense will die with the fool tomorrow."

He looked at a clock on the wall, where both hands were past twelve. "I really should say today." He laughed and got to his feet. "Gentlemen, be brave and we will be rewarded with the future we all deserve. Now I will take a few hours sleep and be ready for the spectacle. I suggest you do the same." The three departed and with a snuff of candles the room was in darkness.

Chapter Eleven

Blood on the Road

Even as the sun rose over the chimneys and spires of Middleton, people began to gather. Whole families left their homes with pets in tow to pick the best spots to watch the miraculous events unfold and traders began erecting their stalls around the edge of the square. The city people were used to festivals and galas but word had spread that this was the show to see and to be seen at. Rumours flying around the inns and taverns ranged from it being the end of the world to the beginning of a new age and all things in between. For one day at least, their fears over the Lezard would be forgotten. No one wanted to miss this.

The house woke to the sound of footsteps running along the landings and knuckles rapping on doors. One by one, bleary heads appeared from rooms and made their way downstairs where a hearty breakfast had been prepared in the large hall. A pot of steaming coffee was laid at the centre of the table and bread was passed around, then torn into chunks and forced into mouths still lined with the wine of the night before. Alex sipped his coffee and blinked repeatedly, concerned that his eyeballs were about to escape from his head in disgust at the hangover he had inflicted on them. Thomas Peters alone seemed to be suffering no ill effects of Jason's raid on the wine cellar. He breezed into the room with a cheery smile for everyone. "Good morning Alex," he said and slapped him on the back.

"Is it?" Alex muttered back across the rim of his coffee cup.

"Oh yes," Thomas Peters said, "Can't you feel the excitement in the air?"

If Alex's mind had not been clogged by the wine he had consumed the night before, he might have noticed that on this occasion the other man was not exaggerating. Across the city there was a sense of expectation and the feeling was present among the group of followers. They tidied away their breakfast things and prepared to leave for the Place of the Elders. The group set off en masse: twenty five men, women and children, headed by Thomas Peters in his blue coat. They quickly drew the attention of the crowds. Even those not heading in the same direction stopped to clap and wave at them as they passed. There was no one on the street that morning without a smile on their face and a kind word to offer.

They entered the Place of the Elders and gasped at the sight before them. It was an open arena at least two hundred yards across and was filled with people. As word of their arrival spread, a ripple passed through the sea of bodies and hundreds of faces turned towards them. Alex felt uncomfortable as so many eyes focused on the group. The vast wall of smiling people parted as Thomas Peters led the way across the arena to a grey building with pillars. In front of it, stone steps led up to a raised dais. As they crossed, more hands were extended to touch them and offer greetings. They felt like royalty or returning heroes. Even their leader was taken aback. "I passed on word of our arrival," he said, "but in my wildest dreams..." He drifted off for a moment as he took in the size of the crowd.

They reached the steps and were on the dais. Thomas Peters arranged his followers behind him and turned to the crowd. He raised his arms and shouted at the top of his voice. "People of Middleton, hear me. That so many of you are with me today shows that you feel as I do. I am the ray of light to herald our new dawn. Darkness and fear shall be driven out. I make that promise."

The crowd roared back its approval. Hands were raised in the air and people held their children aloft for a glimpse of the man they had heard so much about. This was a moment in history and just by being here they hoped to be touched by his magic. Thomas Peters pulled the book from his bag and held it open in the upturned palm of one hand. He read the first page aloud, as he had the night before, and again the crowd cheered madly. Then he turned the pages to find the last chapter. Panic gripped him for a moment as he failed to find the scrap of paper that marked its place. He flicked back and forth with shaking fingers until he found the page and breathed a heavy sign of relief.

"At these words shall all secrets be known," he read, "Light of Day. Breath of Life. Let he who is with God, be with mankind." He closed his eyes, lowered his chin to his chest and raised his free hand to the sky. "Father fill me with your magic." The crowd went silent as every eye was fixed on the figure on the dais. The shouting and clapping, the cheering and singing had all stopped. They held their breath as they waited for the magic to happen, for the clouds to part and the face of God to appear as they had been told.

Then Thomas Peters opened his eyes and looked at the book. An expression of utter astonishment slowly spread across his face, becoming one of terror as his eyes moved across the page. Mysterious dark lines covered the paper where before were words promising the universe and all its mysteries. He could no longer read the book. In his shock he dropped it to the floor and it was like a spell had been broken. The silent crowd of excited, expectant people roared in fury. They had been misled. They felt cheated and betrayed. They were humiliated. They wanted blood.

As the followers edged backwards, Thomas Peters stared at the crowd and began to sway from side to side. Then he saw his way out: in the faces of the blind and crippled who filled the steps before him. They had come to be cured and he could at least do that, he had spoken the words so many times they were like a child's nursery rhyme. He could cure the sick and please the crowd until he had time to work out what was wrong with the book. This was just a hiccup.

He ran down to an old blind woman who knelt on one of the upper steps. He pressed one hand to her head and whispered the sacred words under his breath. The crowd seemed to pull back for a moment as he had intended them to; they were giving him his second chance. He skipped from the old woman to a man with a crippled leg lying a few feet away. The same hand was now pressed to the twisted limb and more words were uttered to conjure the holy magic.

Then a terrible scream rang out, to be joined by another and another. People were pointing at the old woman who was wailing and clutching the side of her head. As she turned towards him Thomas Peters saw dark streams of blood pouring from her eyes. There was nothing in the sockets but the thick fluid that was already forming a pool on the steps. Then the crippled man let out a cry and he arched his back in agony as a great spasm travelled up his frame. His buckled leg began to smoke and smoulder and then flames burst through the fabric of his trousers. They spread upwards until his entire body was engulfed by the fire. His screams grew louder and more frantic as he rolled back and forth on the ground, trying pathetically to douse the flames that ate his flesh. Thomas Peters fell back. The crowd roared once more and several people began advancing up the steps. He felt a hand grab his shoulder and yelped with fear.

"It's only me," Alex said and he hauled him to his feet. "Get inside or we're both dead." He dragged him backwards a split second before the crowd began to run at them. They made it into the Courthouse just in time and bolted the door behind them. Hands began beating against it and it buckled in its frame but held.

They were in a long hallway with a set of doors at the far end. "Where are the others?" asked Thomas Peters.

"They're just ahead of us, with Anthony. He reckoned I was faster on my feet than he is. We need to join them."

"But they're killing each other out there." They both looked at the door. They could hear screams and cries from

113

the other side, as the crowd turned on itself in a fury. "If only I could…"

"You really believed what you were saying didn't you?" asked Alex, "I mean you really felt you were here to save people."

"I did," the man sighed, "I believed in the book." He looked again at the door, where the banging had stopped as the mob fought each other.

"Well it's gone for good," said Alex, "and we should go too. Now come on."

"No," said Thomas Peters, "You leave. I must make amends. This is my fault, it is my responsibility. I cannot run."

"What do you mean?" said Alex. He was already a few feet down the hallway. He looked at Thomas Peters and saw tears running down his face. There was none of the self belief and over flowing confidence that was his trademark. Instead he saw resignation and a strange sense of calm in the man's eyes. On the day when he had expected to fulfil his destiny he was instead accepting his fate.

Thomas Peters walked to the door and reached for the bolt. He turned to Alex and looked him straight in the eye. "Promise me one thing Alex Preston."

"What's that?" he answered, his heart thumping up into his throat as he prepared to run.

"That you'll do the right thing when the time comes."

He felt himself nodding. It was like he was floating out of his body and looking down at them both. He saw himself turn and start running. At the same time Thomas Peters opened the door and stepped through. It took a moment before anyone noticed he was there but then a cry went up and like dogs they fell upon him. He reached out his hands and tried to calm them, offering his regrets and asking for forgiveness, pleading for the violence to stop. But they tore at him, some using their fists while others kicked at his legs and body. They circled round him and rained down blows from all sides. Then someone lunged forward with a knife and blood stained the blue coat. The crowd closed in and he was lost from sight.

Alex got to the end of the hallway with panic filling his veins. He burst out through the doors and saw he was on a wide street with several routes leading off. He flicked left and right but saw no sign of the group. Then he heard a familiar voice. "Quickly, down here."

Gillan and Levine were standing at the entrance to one of the side streets, waving at him to join them. He sprinted across and they hurried him down towards a large house with a wide gateway that stood open. "We saw your friends run from the back of the Courthouse," said Levine, "and we sent them down here while we looked for you."

Now it was the two children who took him by the hand and ran with him as fast as they could. "This is Nathaniel Arbiter's house," said Gillan, "there's no one here at the moment but a few servants. You can't stay long though as his parents may be calling soon to collect some possessions." Once through the gateway they dragged him to a large brick outbuilding where the frightened faces of the group greeted him.

Anthony was the first to embrace him. Then he stepped back and asked the question that Alex was dreading. "Our Master?"

Alex just shook his head and looked away from Anthony's desperately pleading eyes. "He chose to stay. He blamed himself." Crying broke out among several members of the group and Rebecca came up to put her arms around him and hold him close.

"I'm just glad it wasn't you," she sighed in his ear.

Gillan and Levine tugged on Alex's jacket. "We have a way for you to escape," said the boy. He pointed at two large covered wagons that stood at one end of the outbuilding. They had the Arbiter crest painted on either side. "You can take those and leave the city. No one will check as they will see our Master's coat of arms. It would be disrespectful. There are horses in the stable you can use."

It did not take long to hitch up two animals to each of the

wagons and for everyone to climb aboard. They pulled out of the gateway with Gillan sitting at the front of the first wagon alongside Anthony, while Levine sat in the second with Jason. The others cowered in the back as the horses' hooves clip clopped over the cobbles. Across the city an angry mob was on the rampage driven by anger, hatred and secret magic. The group could only hear the muffled roar of the crowd as they wound through the narrow backstreets but it was enough to fill them with terror.

Eventually they came to the East Bar. Beyond it was the road to the port of Armouth, where the River Arwent reached the sea. This would be two days' journey or more but would at least provide them with a safer place to stay.

Farmers' oxen and traders' carts mixed with regal carriages of the gentry as they all fed into the bottleneck under the stone archway with its precarious iron portcullis. At either side were men in blue uniforms armed with swords and tall staffs with curved blades at the top. Anthony whispered just loud enough for those in the wagon to hear, "It's all right, if the Militia are here then at least we'll be safe from the crowd. Best not to draw their attention though."

He nudged the horses forward past the men, who looked at the insignia on the side of the wagons and nodded approvingly. With a twitch of the reins the first one slid beneath the archway and was out of the city. Then Jason pulled forward and followed him through. Middleton was behind them.

They trotted away from the bar with relief bursting out all over. Tears flowed and there was nervous laughter as they counted their blessings and thought of poor Thomas Peters. The road ahead was straight for a few hundred yards before bending to the left at a large tree and disappearing from view. They would stop there to let Gillan and Levine jump down and walk back home. There would be questions to answer regarding the missing wagons and horses but they were sure no one would suspect two young servants of such grand theft. With madness on the streets there were far more likely explanations.

As they passed the tree the wagons slowed to a stop. The children jumped down and Alex walked with them back down the road. He hugged them for a second time and watched them walk away, past a group of men approaching from the city. Gillan turned and waved as he shrank from sight.

"Hoy there! What are you about?" Alex realised the men approaching him were wearing the clothes of the Militia and carrying bladed staffs. He looked back at the tree for a moment, seeing it was too far to the wagons to make a simple dash for it. If he stayed put then at least the others would be out of sight while he talked his way out of this. "Didn't you hear me?" shouted the lead figure in the group, "I asked you what you were doing."

He looked the man in the face. He was taller than Alex and had dark spots on his skin that marked his complexion. There was a cold hardness to his eyes and Alex began to feel afraid. This time there was no feeling of being adrift from his own body, instead he felt every nerve twitch and tingle with fear. "I, I was just heading into the city. I am here on business."

"Oh and what business would that be then sir?" toyed the man, looking Alex up and down and studying his clothes. The four Militiamen walked around him in a circle. He had seen this before. It was how bullies teased their victims before they attacked. He moved his gaze from one man to the next, trying to catch an eye and find some spark of common ground that he could work on; a foothold of decent humanity. But he found none.

"I, I, just business," he stammered. His fear burned like acid in his stomach. The men were on all sides of him now.

"So are you going to tell us then sir? " The lead man asked.
"Tell you what?"
"Where the others are? If you do that then we'll let you walk away. Seems fair to me."

Alex drew his breath for a moment and held it. He forced himself not to look back at the tall tree, where the shadow of one of the wagons might just be visible. He hoped that none of the horses made a sound as they grew impatient of waiting and he prayed with all his might that no one chose to jump down and come to find him. Like Rebecca. His sudden thought of her loosened his breath. He had to do the right thing. "I've no idea what you're talking about," he said, "please just let me go about my business."

The Militia Captain laughed meanly. He stepped up to Alex and stared him in the eyes. "None of you will get away from this," he said, "I have my orders. Now lie on the floor."

Alex did as he was told and lay face down in the mud. "What are you doing?" he managed to gasp as his terror finally engulfed him. He closed his eyes just as the Militiamen raised their bladed staffs above their heads. There were four clicks as a short curved spike sprung outwards from the tip of each weapon.

"I'm doing my duty," said the Captain and the blades fell.

In the rear wagon Rebecca heard the first scream and turned. As the sound of Alex's agony cut through the air she scrambled to escape from the back of the carriage. Then his voice, laced with pain and fear, rang out. "Go! Go now!"

At the sound, the horses lunged forward and hauled their load away down the road. It was as if a whip had been cracked above their heads. No one tried to rein them in. They simply sat in the wagons like they were dreaming. All except Marshall, who pulled his knees up to his chest and began shivering, and Rebecca who stared from the back of the carriage and wept, "I love you Alex. I love you."

In the shadow of the tall tree, as blood mixed with the dirt, Alex Preston died.

Chapter Twelve

Secrets Revealed

The world was covered in a shiny wet coat. Water ran off rooftops and down leaky drainpipes, gathered into pools in the potholes in the road and hung in the air as a fine mist. The bush below the window was weighed down by the rain droplets that lingered stubbornly on every leaf and stem. Sarah ran a fingertip down the pane to draw a face in the condensation. After the round outline of a head she doodled in two eyes, then a button nose and ears. When she came to the mouth she hesitated, her fingertip lingering over the glass as she weighed up the possibilities. Then in one flick she drew in an upturned frown and sat back from the window.

It had been raining since three in the morning and Sarah had listened to every drop fall from the sky. The darkness amplified the sound of the water hammering down from the heavens and dripping noisily from every gutter and ledge. The chorus rose and fell as wave after wave of rain clouds swept in across the rooftops and spiralled round over the town.

It would soon be time to wake the children and start another day. She sorely wanted to crawl back into bed and disappear beneath the covers but that would just delay the inevitable. So she wiped the face from the glass and went to the shower, where the water was at least warm.

Today was playgroup day, when Katie got to be with other children her age and Sarah could retreat to a café for strong coffee. She would have Matthew with her but he was much less trouble without his sister to egg him on. "Divide and rule," she called it. Trying to enjoy a moment of sanity with the pair of them in tow would always be doomed to failure: they would end up fighting over who got to eat the last biscuit or who was Mummy's favourite.

She gave them their breakfast and walked to the church hall at St Andrew's near the park, where she dropped Katie off for a two hour session of chasing boys and playing with dolls. Or vice versa. Then she wheeled Matthew straight into town and headed for her favourite café.

It did not serve the best tea or coffee in the world but it had a relaxed, shabby atmosphere where no one complained about the pushchair blocking the way or piles of rain soaked coats hanging off the backs of chairs. And the waiters were gorgeous. Today the windows were misted up so she could not tell how busy the café was as she approached. She always sat in the seat by the window where she could watch the world go by, though on a day like this it was doubtful she would be seeing anything. As she nudged her way in through the door it was clear they were having a quiet morning. Richard, the waiter she liked the most, looked relieved and pleased to see her. "Wet out?" he asked sarcastically as she stood in a puddle at the doorway.

"A touch damp," she said and flicked water at him from her jacket sleeve. It was then that she noticed her table by the window; or rather the man who was sitting at it.

"He's been there since we opened," said Richard, "I think he's waiting for someone."

"Bugger," said Sarah under her breath, cursing the bad karma that made someone pick her favourite spot when they had an entire café to choose from. The man was middle aged and was wearing a dark suit. He had a raincoat folded on the seat beside him and was studying one of the serious newspapers the café provided for customers. They kept the tabloids under the counter for Sarah and her friends to read.

The man looked up and smiled. He had warm, twinkling eyes and she immediately smiled back. "Have I taken your favourite seat?" he asked intuitively. Sarah looked at Richard who shrugged, as if to say, "I didn't tell him."

"Oh no it's fine," she said, in her best "Actually yes, you are sitting in my seat" kind of voice.

"Well there's room for two at least," he said, "so why not join me?" At any other time she would have sat somewhere else but on this day things were different. Maybe the rain keeping her awake had made her less able to argue or perhaps there was something about the man that was just so welcoming. Either way, she was soon sitting in the seat opposite him with a coffee in her hand. He put down his newspaper and sipped his tea, which she noticed was in one of the few proper cups and saucers the café owned. You had to ask for one specifically or put up with one of their chipped mugs.

"I do like a nice cup of tea on a cold day, don't you?" the man said, smiling over the rim of his cup. "It's one of the few real pleasures left." His face was lined and his cheeks were marked with tiny red veins just beneath the skin. She tried to think where she had seen him before. There was something very gentlemanly and respectful about him that stood out from the ordinary. But while he looked so dapper and neat, she could see that he was also a little frayed at the edges; his collar was beginning to look worn and the knot in his blue tie hung slightly to one side. She was aware that she was staring at him so she went back to her coffee just as he spoke again. "This is your favourite place isn't it?"

Sarah stopped drinking and looked up again. "Pardon?" she said. She was a frequent visitor to the café but did not like the idea of being so predictable that even a stranger knew her movements.

"This window seat. I saw it in your face when you spotted me here. I'm sitting in your favourite place."

"Oh it's all right. I shouldn't be so sad really."

"There's nothing wrong with having favourite places. There's a coffee shop I know in..." he drifted off, his words lost somewhere between his thoughts and lips. "Somewhere I go on business." He seemed to have recovered himself. "Charming little place near the Arwent..." Now he stopped again and looked uncomfortable. Sarah cut in.

"The Arwent... isn't that somewhere down south? Oxford or somewhere?"

"Yes, that's right," the man answered, smiling again. "Anyway, this place is charming isn't it?" Sarah muttered in agreement as she inspected the chips round the edge of her mug. Matthew was asleep in his buggy and there was no sign of Richard to ask for a tabloid so she looked around for something to read. She did not fancy the stranger's newspaper so she reached into the basket of the pushchair for the plastic bag she had brought from home. She opened it and took out the leather bound book that had been posted through her letter box a few weeks ago. It was better than reading the menu again.

Since the book had arrived she had been thumbing through it, trying to grasp what it was about. For the first few days it was just page after page of unintelligible scribbling. But as she persisted something odd happened. Bit by bit she had begun to understand what some of the pages meant. She figured that it was a puzzle book that Alex had ordered before he disappeared and which was designed to slowly reveal the English words from the gobbledegook. It was cleverly rewarding her persistence by unscrambling itself like a magic eye puzzle, where a picture appears from a messy pattern once you have stared at it long enough.

"Interesting reading?" The man had finished his tea and was peering across the table.

"This? Oh, it's a puzzle thing; some sort of make believe about magic. I think it's a competition actually but there don't seem to be any instructions. I'm making some sense of it though."

"Really?" He sounded surprised. "What does it say?"

Sarah flicked backwards through the pages. "This bit here," she said, pointing at the very first sheet in the book, "says 'Believe in the magic of love and the darkness will slip from the earth.'"

"Sounds a bit churchy to me," said the man.

"I'm sure it's taken from a song," Sarah replied.

"Oh really?" the man across the table seemed to find that amusing. "I suppose it might be. I'm a bit out of touch with modern music. What else is in there?"

"This for a start," she said and turned a few pages. "To the One who pledges all to the King of Men. To the One who protects and guards over his estate. Let no harm befall or evil hold sway." She read from a line of text that danced before her eyes on the crisp, heavy paper. "It's a puzzle of some kind," she said.

"What's the answer?" the man asked.

"I'm not even sure what the question is," said Sarah, "so I've no idea what the answer is."

"I'm sure it'll come to you before the end," he said.

"End of what?" she asked. There was a funny tone in the man's voice that made her shiver.

"Oh," he seemed to be searching for his next word. "Of the world of course."

She flipped the book shut and laid her hand across the cover. At the same time the stranger moved his own hand and laid it over hers. Instantly she felt something pull at her stomach, tugging her in towards the table edge. Her breath caught in her throat and she felt faint. Darkness moved in from the edge of her vision until she was looking at the world through a shadowy tunnel. All she could focus on was the middle-aged man sitting opposite.

"You must listen to me Sarah. You have to listen to what I say."

His voice was the only sound her ears could detect. The cappuccino machine had fallen silent and the quiet murmur of voices had stopped. Even Richard's radio, tucked behind the bar, was no longer audible.

"I'm a friend Sarah, a very good friend." His voice was calm and reassuring. "I've been looking after you since he left. I gave you the book and I need you to keep reading it. You'll have it cracked sooner that you think and when that happens, it will tell you everything you need to know." The rest of the world had dissolved into nothing and the only things left were within a few feet of this table. She was entwined in a dream and tried to rouse herself. "Don't worry Sarah, it won't make any sense right now but you need to believe. You must have faith or we are all lost."

She could see herself from outside her body, as she did in dreams. She was sitting at the table and seemed to be reaching out to the strange man. When she looked closer she saw that his hand was resting on hers, with the book underneath. She felt a warm glow under her palm and at the same time the coolness from the man's fingers on the back of her hand. "There are dark times ahead Sarah and those who understand must be ready. You must be brave and stay true. You feel lost and betrayed but you must understand that shadows are moving in. Everything that is most precious will be stolen from us and locked away for ever. They will take everything from us unless we can hold fast. Can you do that?"

She saw her mouth move but no words came out; none that she could hear. The coolness of the stranger's hand was the only thing her senses could detect as the tunnel closed in completely. Then a voice cut through the darkness.

"Are you okay Sarah? Are you okay?" Richard leant over her with a fresh cup of coffee in his hand. Sarah raised her head from the table and wiped away the thin line of spittle that ran from her mouth on to the woodwork. She did a quick double check: Matthew was still asleep in his pushchair, the book was under her right hand and the seat opposite was empty.

"Here," said Richard, putting the cup down in front of her, "the old bloke bought this for you as he left. He said you might need it."

***

It was dark and cold. Damp earth pressed against hard skin and the black void closed in from all sides. There was no sound, not even the gentlest of breathing disturbed the silent space beneath the ground. There was nothing, nothing at all. She was all alone.

Sarah's body jumped and she kicked out instinctively as she woke, her legs caught up in the knotted bed clothes. She sat up in bed and looked around with her heart thumping like a drum. The same darkness blanketed the room as when she had switched out the light and laid down to sleep. But now it was mean and threatening, reminding her that she slept alone in the big double bed, with no one at hand to keep the nightmares at bay. A monster squatted in the corner where the small chest of drawers normally stood, waiting until she lay back down so that it could creep out and attack. Instead of her dressing gown dangling from the back of the door there was the body of a hanged man suspended on the cruel metal hook.

She brought her hand down on the switch and the bedside light burst into life. Instantly the darkness was chased back into the corners. The chest sat where it always did and her blue gown hung innocently on the door. There were no monsters here, at least while the lamp stayed on. Beyond the curtains the streetlights poured their familiar orange glow down on to the pavement. She looked out expectantly but was disappointed by what she saw. There was nothing there but parked cars.

She perched on the edge of the bed with her head in her hands and rocked back and forth. "God, if it's not rain it's the bloody nightmares," she cried and staggered to the bathroom. There was an odd taste in her mouth, a dark heavy scent of earth that she had to rinse away.

She returned to the bedroom but could not face switching the light off so she started rummaging about in her bedside drawers for something to read. Then she remembered the book, resting in the bottom of the pushchair down in the hallway. For the first time in a week she had gone to bed without it.

Her feet seemed to float over the carpet as she skipped down the stairs to retrieve it from the buggy. As she pulled it free, a slip of card fell from between the pages. It was an unused train ticket for one adult and two children. Both the destination and the date of the journey were unreadable; just a haze of badly printed black ink. She studied it as she climbed the stairs once more and then dropped it into her top drawer.

Now she had the book back in her hands she felt the stain of her nightmare dissolve. Something flowed through Sarah, purging her veins of the fear and trembling that she had woken with. The same warmth she had felt in the café spread from its covers and seeped into her skin. She turned off the bedside light and sat in the dark. There were no shadows that could touch her now, not while it was here to protect her. She remembered the words of the man in the café. "Be brave and stay true." At once a brilliant blue light filled the room, pouring from the pages of the little book and bathing everything in its glow. She gazed into the source of the light and the last shred of her fear was gone.

Chapter Thirteen

Escape and Capture

The fishing boats sat four deep in the harbour; a floating, creaking island that stretched from the base of the lighthouse to the foot of the stone bridge. The boats were of a uniform design; small vessels with a cabin to the rear and a single mast. Piles of faded and stained sail cloth sat on the decks as the crews made repairs. To get to the jetty, those working on the furthest boats had to climb over their neighbours' bobbing craft. They were so well practised that they could skip from one to another like a child on stepping stones. On the quayside, nets and lobster pots were heaped together and small carts loaded with a day's catch stood ready to be hauled by hand up to the fish market.

On the hill above the quay a scented cloud hung over the flat roofs of the smoking houses. The aroma of smouldering woodchips and drying fish drifted down the slope into the town and slipped through every loose window and under every door. On a busy working day every lungful of breath carried the odour of gently smoking kipper or mackerel.

In the room three floors above the Crab Inn, Rebecca peered out of the tiny leaded window and studied the clouds on the horizon. This was no wistful daydreaming. She had heard that a storm could be moving up from the south and that might mean a delay to the voyage. The plan was for the ship to sail at ten thirty that night from one of the piers down in the Old Harbour, away from prying eyes and unwanted attention. It had taken a hefty bribe to get a guarantee from the skipper that no questions would be asked about the passengers. Captain Weller had eyed her curiously when she and Anthony had first approached him downstairs in the Inn, asking if he would carry a ship load of travellers away from Theland and then westwards to the New Lands. But once the bag of coins was laid on the table, with a promise of more to come, his face lit up and he swallowed his questions along with his beer.

But Weller's ship, *The Eagle*, would not be carrying the entire group that had fled Middleton in the Knight's wagons. Rebecca, Anthony, Marshall and Jason had chosen to stay behind. Jason claimed to be more afraid of the sea than he was of the Militia while Marshall was intent on finding his way back to The Village and then home. Rebecca could see from his eyes how terrified he was of being alone in Theland now that Alex was gone. He had swapped his old clothes for something less conspicuous but he still felt out of place and confessed to her one evening that he was close to losing his mind with fear. So partly out of pity and partly out of respect for Alex, Rebecca said she would stay and help Marshall get home. Anthony insisted he would stay with her to repay Alex's debt in helping them escape. In truth he could not bear to leave her unprotected. Word had spread of the events in Middleton and the local guard were on the look out for suspicious strangers.

Wisely the group had chosen to split up and stay in separate lodgings around the town. Through the chatter in the inns and ale houses they had learned that the Commissioners were in pursuit of the followers of the False Prophet. It was painful for Rebecca to hear them describe Thomas Peters in that way; she had not been one of his devotees but she had judged the man to be honest and to truly believe what he was saying. No one now had a good word to say about him; some claimed he was a trickster and conman while others boasted that he was in league with the devil.

It was even more painful to hear the drinkers talk of how the Militia had already killed one member of the group who had disobeyed them while trying to flee. The Commissioners' private police force had never been popular in this part of the country but the tale was told with glee by old men with froth stained beards. They would cackle merrily at the story of the misguided fool who was cut down where he stood and left to rot at the side of the road as a lesson to others. For those who knew the truth about Alex's murder it would have been suicide to speak out, so the lies went unchallenged and were allowed to fester and infect all who heard them.

In the top room of the Crab Inn, Rebecca drank tea and rehearsed the evening's events in her mind. The members of the group would rendezvous on the quayside when the clock on the Harbour Master's office struck ten. They would have a window of just half an hour to get on to *The Eagle* and prepare to sail. At that hour the fishermen would all be enjoying the warmth of the drinking houses and the quay should be empty but they dare not wait any longer. Those who arrived late would be left to find their own way out of Armouth.

Since the death of Thomas Peters she had become the new leader of the group. She had found a new strength within her; an energy and purpose that had not existed before. While Marshall was sick with fear and Anthony looked pale and lost she had shouldered the responsibility of ensuring the safety of the party of followers. Food had to be bought, shelter had to be found and transport arranged. At times she felt herself inspired; guided by an unseen hand. She wondered if a guardian angel was looking over her shoulder, helping her to make the right decisions upon which so many lives depended. She did not know what would happen if the Militia caught up with them but she could guess: she was still haunted by Alex's screams on the dirt road out of Middleton.

It was Alex, she knew, who was her driving force. Meeting him had sown seeds within her that were only now coming to life. The day the stranger from The Other Place rang the bell at the main gate at Appledore her life had begun to change and now there was no going back. He had inspired her to do so much and she knew that she must not let him down. Alex's great fear was of becoming a forgotten figure in the background of other people's lives and she was determined to stop that from happening.

Marshall was asleep on one of the room's two beds. He slept a lot these days. The fear inside him ate away at his energy until he was a walking ghost. While Rebecca and Anthony might go downstairs in the evenings he would lie on a bed and press a pillow over his face to drown out the sound from the bar or the rattle of the rigging on the trawlers in the harbour. Sleep was his only escape from the living hell he was in.

She let him doze while she mapped out the timetable for the escape. This would be the first time they had gathered as a group since their arrival in Armouth five days ago. The members of the group were staying in lodgings around the town and would come together at a precise moment to rendezvous with the ship. It was fraught with danger; they had to be sure the Old Harbour was clear of the town guards and Militia before they could emerge from the shadows. She drummed her fingers on the window sill and scanned the heavens for signs of rain.

As Rebecca studied the skies, Anthony was walking back towards the Crab Inn along one of the narrow alleyways that threaded like veins through Armouth. He had been down to the New Port where the trading vessels loaded and offloaded their cargo. There he had seen a three-masted ship arrive, carrying silks from one of the ports in the western lands. As soon as it was tied up a team of dockers had begun crawling across the decks like ants, lifting cases and trunks to the quayside as if they weighed nothing. Meanwhile another ship was preparing to leave, carrying a hold full of bleating sheep to a destination in the east.

The noise of the animals reminded Anthony of home. He had grown up on a farm north of Mickleborough, away to the west of Theland, and had worked with sheep all his life. He grew sad as he remembered how simple and honest life had been then. He had nothing to worry about but the care of his herd and the price of wool. Now he was hiding out like a thief in an attic and looking over his shoulder every minute of the day. He wished more than anything to turn the clock back and return to his shepherd's life on the moors. People like him did not get mixed up in riot and murder, he kept telling himself.

He had followed Thomas Peters out of his own free will. He had heard the man speaking in the market place at Mickleborough one morning and felt something happen. It was like a candle being lit in his heart. The man's words reached into him and for the first time in his life he had a sense of something other than the solid world around him. All he had ever known were the hills above his cottage, the changing of the seasons and the importance of keeping the herd safe. Now there was something else that crept into his head and his heart and led him to hand the care of his sheep to a neighbour while he set off to follow the man in the blue coat.

"And a lot of good it did," he cursed to himself as he weaved through the back alleys. He had seen the miracles fail and watched as a mob had torn Thomas Peters limb from limb. Then to know that Alex had died while they escaped made him weak with sorrow. He might be a strong man but he carried a big heart and right now it was broken. Anthony had few friends in life and the loss of two of them had stolen something from him. He stopped for a moment and leaned against the back wall of a house. Tears welled in his eyes and he fought and failed to keep them from bursting forth and rolling down his cheeks. A shepherd was supposed to guard his flock and he had failed twice. He raised his hands to his face and wept as the sadness finally overcame him. He had remained solid and brave while in the group's company but now, in this dark backstreet, he felt the tap open and his sorrow flow in a warm torrent of salty tears. He stood like that for a minute or two, his hands spread across his face as he gave in to the emotions he had tried to bury since that day in Middleton. He did not notice the twitch of curtains above him as he stood in the lonely alley and cried.

* * *

The single candle in the top room struggled to light anything but a tiny patch of floor as the flame flickered back and forth in the draught. The three figures by the door looked at the one standing by the table and nodded. With a single, sharp puff the room was in total darkness but for the arm of moonlight that came in through the tiny window. The four descended the narrow winding stairs and went straight to the street. As they crossed the cobbles outside the Crab they heard the ringing of the Harbour Master's bell, away in the dark. The soft chimes carried above the masts of the fishing boats and urged them to hurry onwards. They went over the stone bridge without looking back and walked around to the quayside. There, behind the line of boats, were more figures huddled together in the shadows. At the sound of a baby crying Rebecca whispered, "Alice, is that you?"

"Yes, we're all here," the woman answered. "But the baby's unsettled and needs to feed."

"I know," said Rebecca, "but we've got to be quick. All of you follow me." The storm had never arrived and the sky was lit by a bright half moon that threatened to reveal them to the guards unless they moved quickly. She led the way along the quay and then right, towards one of the piers that extended along the far side of the harbour directly into the West Bay. They could already see the lights of *The Eagle* up ahead. The ship was ready to sail and men were silhouetted against the stars as they worked the rigging. The group hurried along the pier to the foot of a wooden gangplank where a burly man stood in the lamplight, a short sword tucked in one side of his belt and a musket in another.

"Who approaches *The Eagle*?" he barked at the pack of shadows.

"We're here to see Captain Weller," said Rebecca. "These are your passengers." The man snorted and told them to stay at the foot of the gangplank while he fetched the Captain. He returned a moment later with Weller, a slim man who wore a three-peaked hat and leather boots that squeaked on the walkway.

"Miss Wilde", he said with a flirtatious chuckle, "how delightful to see you. I hope everything's in order for the voyage?"

"If you mean your money Captain, then yes we have the rest. Once you've left port they'll give it to you." Rebecca nodded at the party behind her.

"And you're positive that you won't be joining them on their little trip?" the Captain asked with his lips drawn in a mock frown. He gestured at his subordinate to let them on board.

"Not tonight Captain Weller," Rebecca said. "It's just the numbers we discussed." She stepped back to let the men and women up the gangplank. As her friend Alice came past, the two women hugged and said their goodbyes. "Look after the baby won't you?" Rebecca said, "I'll be imagining him growing up."

"Why not come with us and see for yourself?" Alice said, "It's so dangerous here."

"There are things I need to do," said Rebecca. She had not risked telling anyone where Marshall and Alex really came from. Even now she had to keep the truth to herself. "I will try and join you when I have sorted a few things out." They hugged once more and Alice pulled herself away and disappeared onto the ship. Finally the Captain turned and skipped up the plank himself. He turned and waved from the deck as the crew cast off. The sails billowed about the masts and *The Eagle* inched away from the pier.

They watched as she nudged her way into the bay. The ship's lanterns become dots of light above the silver water and then, as she sailed in view of the Harbour Tower, they were swiftly extinguished. Now there was nothing but a faint shadow and a foaming wake to give away *The Eagle's* position. Within a minute those too had melted into the dark and the ship had vanished. Even the noise she made as she moved over the water was carried out to sea by the breeze.

The four were in sombre mood as they climbed the stairs to the room. Anthony, lost in his thoughts, dawdled at the rear.

He was still wondering if they had done the right thing in letting the others sail away on their own. He was not sure they could trust the sea captain who could so easily be setting a course for the nearest port with a gaol. But at the same time he wondered if staying behind was a stupid idea, what with the guards and the Militia on the prowl.

As they neared the top floor he looked up at the small wooden door to their room. He hated being cooped up in such a cramped, cold space. The sooner they were away from Armouth and back out on the open road the better. He gritted his teeth at the prospect of another night spent jammed in behind that door. And then, a moment before Jason pushed it open, Anthony noticed the sliver of candlelight that crept beneath it. He sprinted up the last few stairs as shouts rang out from inside the room. He heard a man's voice followed by the sounds of a struggle and Rebecca calling out his name.

As he burst through the open door there was the crack of a weapon being fired and a body slumped to the floor. Three Militiamen stood at either side of the room, one of them holding a smoking musket and another pinning Marshall to the wall. Rebecca knelt over Jason who lay on his back with his legs twisted beneath him. A cloud of blood spread across his chest and his eyes were staring upwards, unblinking. A crude choking sound came from his red stained lips. Then it stopped.

Anthony prepared to reach out and grab Rebecca and make a dash for the door. But as he made his first move there was the sound of heavy footsteps on the stairs and he saw Rebecca glance past him in fear. He felt a sudden, intense pain in the back of his head and then he was in darkness.

Chapter Fourteen

From the Earth

He got to the bend in the road and stopped. There was a fine layer of dust on the toe of one of his polished shoes which he bent and wiped with a piece of tissue from his pocket. Over the years he had travelled more miles than he cared to remember and he always hated arriving poorly presented. Looking around for somewhere to deposit the soiled tissue, he settled for tucking it into one end of the rolled up newspaper that stuck from his bag.

He walked past the tall tree and stopped again. This time it was to look at the road stretching away towards the city and, just within sight, the outline of the gateway with its stone arch and castle like towers. He had always thought the bars were far too grand and pompous. If someone had come this far from the eastern lands then they deserved to be greeted with something more welcoming than a miniature fortress, at least in this day and age.

There was no one else in sight and that was important. He waited for a moment just to make sure that no travellers were heading to or from the city. When he was certain of being alone he moved away from the shadow of the tree. He walked quickly and confidently and after a few yards stepped off the road and down a slight slope that led to an unplanted field. He headed for an untidy pile of earth a few paces away.

The grave diggers had only been called out after travellers had complained about the stench and they had shown little care in the way they had thrown together the earth mound. From one side of it, a trail of dark, sticky drops led back up the slope to the road, accompanied by several sets of heavy footprints. As he stood back and surveyed the scene, he could picture the men heaving the body unceremoniously down into the field before hastily shovelling dirt over it. He shook his head in disgust then stepped over the blood spots and walked to the earth pile, where he crouched down and spoke. "You see Alex, the problem with being immortal but not knowing, is that you can have this annoying habit of dying." His voice sounded tired but there was still a hint of a smile on his lips. "Anyway Alex, there are things to do. So if you wouldn't mind terribly getting up, people are waiting."

He stood up and looked at the ground. The pile of earth lay unmoving at his feet. This was not what he had been expecting and he frowned. "Alex, get up please. I don't have all day." His frown grew more pronounced as still nothing happened. He knew he must be missing something. Looking down at the grizzly trail leading out of the field, he narrowed his eyes and pulled one of his thoughtful faces. Then he walked back up the slope to a spot in the road where a shadow hung beneath the surface of the dirt. He touched four fingers to the ground and, conjuring up the most powerful magic he knew, whispered, "Wake up."

The top layer of earth moved ever so slightly as a single bead of blood rose up through it: dark blood, dead blood. It sat twitching on the surface before rolling away like a ball of mercury. Other drops began bursting through. They were drawn up out of the dirt and bonded together into a pool which trickled down into the field. The blood kept coming. Droplets were being pulled from the ground like filings by a magnet and were merging into a reservoir at his feet. As the red dam burst he stood and watched a stream of dark liquid running down the slope and disappearing under the heap of dirt.

Now all the blood that had been spilled near the tall tree was on the move, even the trail of congealed spots had found new life and was crawling over the surface of the ground until it reached the shallow grave. Before the last of the blood had slid beneath the heaped soil, steam began rising into the air. A heat haze formed over the mound of earth and the man raised one hand across his eyes as he struggled to look without squinting.

Beneath the loose earth a fire raged. Blue flames ran over the flesh that hung to the bones but they did not burn or ravage. The heat grew intense as the inferno took hold but it did the grey skin no harm. The blood boiled but did not waste. Instead the fire reanimated dead cells, mended broken bones and infused the torn body with the greatest power in the worlds of God and man. Life. New skin wrapped itself over open wounds; veins were healed so they ran with fresh, bright blood and a heart that had stopped beating in a moment of pain and fear pulsed again.

The man smiled as he heard a muffled cough. A hand reached out from beneath the earth, followed by an arm and a bruised shoulder. Then a head appeared, the eyes blinking away the dirt and the mouth spitting and spluttering angrily. The other arm came out next and both hands began rubbing at a face that was smeared with earth. "Welcome back Alex," the man said.

The figure appearing from beneath the blanket of soil rolled to one side and lay face down on the ground. A series of dry, animal coughs came from lungs still heavy with earth and it arched its back and retched. Then slowly and painfully Alex got to his feet. "Steady now," the stranger said, grasping one arm supportively. "It'll take you a while to get your strength back. Death does that to you." Alex stood upright, still blinking, and looked around. "I know you're confused and probably quite frightened", the man said, "but I'm here to help you." Alex peered at him through glazed eyes that were not yet working properly. Then they rolled back up into his head and he collapsed in a heap.

A while later Alex was sitting in the shade of the tree, his head resting in his hands. "I can't believe this is happening," he said, over and over, as he ran his fingers through his hair, pulling out the occasional clump of earth or twig. "I'm just a normal bloke. There must have been some sort of trick."

"Hmm yes," said the other man, who was standing a few feet away, gazing up wistfully through the branches of the tree. "You were tricked into believing you were being hacked to death just so they could leave you rotting at the side of the road for a week or so before finally burying you in a shallow pit in an old turnip field. Ingenious."

Alex groaned and extracted another sod from his scalp. "And your version is any better? That I'm some kind of emissary from God, or an angel or something and can't be killed by man or nature? Fat lot of good that did me." He rubbed at the red scars on his bare back and winced.

"This is the truth Alex," the man said, "Empty your mind of notions about angels. It's something far beyond what has ever been written about in any book by man. You have to do what your friends at home might say and 'think outside the box.'" He caught the painful stare that Alex was throwing him. "Well maybe not. But you carry something inside you that is, well, special. It goes beyond any idea you might have in your head. You would need to recalibrate your brain to fully understand it. And trust me, you will in time."

"Then how come I ended up buried by the side of the road?" Alex said, peering through one open eye at the man who was now examining a broad green leaf in one hand.

"Because you were totally unaware of who and what you are and that meant you could do nothing to avoid being killed. You expected to die and you did. Just like on that train. Do you remember? When it came off the tracks and went into the freight train coming the other way you fully expected to die and you would have, if I'd not been there to shield you."

"This is madness." Alex cupped his hands over his face and breathed slowly and deeply. His whole body tingled as the air was drawn into his lungs. He could feel it burning inside him. Every nerve in his body danced and his muscles tingled with energy but at the same time he felt sick and afraid. His hands were trembling and the only way to stop his blinking was to close his eyes. "I've been dreaming," he said, "I was lost and it was dark and there were voices I didn't understand."

"That's because you weren't dead, even though your body was as cold and grey as any corpse. You thought you were dead but there was nothing those Militiamen could have done to kill Alex Preston. You're immortal and I'm here to be your guide and friend."

Alex's eyes had lost the deathly grey glaze that covered them earlier and he stared hard at the stranger: a man in a dark suit with a newspaper poking from the zip of his battered leather bag. "Who the hell are you?" he said, "I know you're the bloke from the train but who are you?"

The man came and crouched down in front of him. "I'm glad you asked Alex. I'm terrible at introductions. My name's Foxton Scarfe." Alex shakily accepted a handshake.

"Foxton Scarfe?" he asked, "Isn't that a law firm or something?"

Foxton smiled. "I've had many names over a very long time. To be honest I can't quite remember where this current one came from."

"So are you like me then?" said Alex.

The man stopped smiling. "No. I am not. I was asked a long time ago to watch over you, until the time when you were ready to know the truth. That truth would keep you alive forever but in the meantime my task was to protect you from your own idea of mortality. Then I was to help you find your place."

"So this is the moment you've been waiting for is it?"

"Er – no." Foxton frowned and sat down on the grass in front of him. "Things were not meant to happen quite like this. I don't believe you're quite ready to understand who you are."

Alex rested his head in one hand. All of this sounded like nonsense.

But still...

There was something within him, perhaps the part that conjured up daydreams from thin air, that was ready to accept it. A few months ago he would have laughed himself breathless at what he was hearing. But that was before he had found the doorway to Theland and arrived in this magical place. For once in his plain, ordinary life he knew that anything was possible.

"I can see things Alex. I can see events a short way in the future. In return for being your guardian I was given certain abilities. I saw you die on that train before it happened and I was able to save you. I did it once years ago when you were a child. Do you remember your appendix?"

"Not by name," he snapped. Then he said more calmly, "I remember it burst and I had to go to hospital in an ambulance. My mum says I could have died."

"Would have Alex. Would have. I saw it happen and was able to intervene. The doctors weren't going to operate on your swollen stomach and it was going to kill you. So I changed the order of events to make it obvious to the most stubborn of physicians."

Alex tried to remember exactly what had happened when he was six; as if he might be able to recall a stranger with a newspaper standing by his bed. But it felt like so long ago. In another lifetime. He kicked at the ground in frustration. "So what went wrong here?"

Foxton frowned. "To be honest, and most days I find it hard not to be, I don't know. Maybe I'm getting a bit too old for this but somehow I missed seeing it before it happened." He pulled at a few blades of grass distractedly. "That's one of the reasons why I need you to come back with me to your world as quickly as possible."

"Sorry?" Alex sat up straight. "You need me to do what?"

"I think there are reasons why I didn't see your death in time to stop it from happening." Foxton looked Alex in the eye. "I have saved you before because you weren't ready to see yourself as I do. You had to remain an ordinary man until the right time but you also had to remain alive. I think someone may have deliberately stopped me from seeing your death here so that I wouldn't be able to step in and save you. Think of it as

– blocking my radar. There are people in this place who won't be as glad to see you as I am. I think they wanted you to walk into death's arms in ignorance."

"Who?" Alex asked.

Foxton drew his fingers across his grey, stubbled chin. "I can't answer that at this time. But this place has a bond with you, in the same way that I have. There are bound to be some who see you as a threat. But if we can get you back home, there are people to look after you until you're ready to face your enemies. There are people at home who…"

"I'm not going back home," Alex cut in. "I need to find Marshall and Rebecca and the others. They won't be safe."

"Their fortunes are not your concern. We must hurry back before you come to the attention of…"

"I said I'm not going back. Not right now anyway. I'm going to find my friends and make sure they're okay. If half of what you say is true…"

"Don't doubt my words." Now it was Foxton's turn to interrupt. He snapped at Alex, "I've waited years for you. You are what I say you are."

"Then I should have no problems helping my friends should I?"

"You're not ready," protested Foxton. The two men stared at each other for what seemed like a very long time until, to Alex's satisfaction, Foxton looked away and sighed. "But if you're so adamant, then I'll help you as I'm sworn to do. Then we'll go back to your home together."

Alex smiled and looked down at himself. "But can you do one thing first?"

"What's that?" asked Foxton, standing up and dusting himself down.

"Pull some clothes out of that bag of yours. I'm stark naked."

Chapter Fifteen

Friends

With just one tiny window set high on the wall, the air in the cell barely stirred. Every breath felt hot and heavy and filled their lungs with the stench of captivity. Rebecca sat on the edge of an iron bed frame that hung from the wall on chains. The thin mattress had ceased to be of any use a long time ago and the pattern of the metal dug into her skin. She closed her eyes and tried to imagine some way out of the situation.

Anthony stood by the window and raised himself up on his toes to peer through the narrow opening. "We're at basement level," he said, "I can see feet walking past. I think we're under a building on the Place of the Elders. It's probably the courthouse."

They had been brought here in the back of a closed carriage, bucking and jolting over an unfinished road that they guessed was the route back to Middleton. Then there had been the sharp rumble of cobbles under the wheels, which must have been when they entered the city's streets. The carriage doors were eventually flung open in a high walled courtyard. They were bundled out and led down a set of narrow steps and along a claustrophobic passageway to this cell, where their manacles were finally removed.

"Does it help us, knowing where we are?" muttered Marshall. He crouched in one corner, using the walls on either side to support his weight. "We're in a prison cell and that's enough." His voice wavered and he swallowed as he spoke. There was no way to hide his fear. It pulled at his insides, making his stomach burn and his heart feel like lead. He had been sick once in the stinking privy that sat in the alcove behind him and he felt the need to do it again. He just wanted to wake up from this; to open his eyes and be at home in his flat.

It was a cruel trick but the spell that Theland had cast over him, to make him forget about the Other Place, had stopped working. Now he closed his eyes and imagined sitting in front of his TV or taking his car for a drive, standing on his balcony or lying in his king-sized bed. He could picture it all so clearly he was almost there. But when he opened his eyes he was back in this rotten cell in a place that was twinned with hell. He had met vampires, monsters and angry mobs and now he wanted out. There was no fun left in this and he wanted the nightmare to be over and normal life to resume. So he closed his eyes and tried again.

"You! Wake up and snap to." A man's voice broke his thoughts and he opened his eyes. The haggard face of one of the gaolers leered at him through the bars in the door. "Get up and stand in the middle of the room. You others stand back against the walls. No messing or you'll feel my boot." Marshall pulled himself to his feet. His legs ached with cramp and he hobbled painfully into the middle of the floor. Rebecca and Anthony backed away obediently. The door opened and the man beckoned him out.

"Where are you taking me?" Marshall asked in a high, frightened voice.

"One of them upstairs wants to see you. Best not to keep him waiting," the gaoler barked impatiently. He had heavy stubble on his chin and stank of beer and sweat. As Marshall stumbled forward the man reached out a fat, tattooed hand and dragged him through the door.

"It'll be okay Andrew," said Rebecca from inside the cell.

"Course it will lassie, course it will," mocked the gaoler, as he led Marshall up a flight of steps. "I'm sure it won't hurt a bit." At the top of stairs he reached into his belt and pulled out a black hood which he slipped over Marshall's head. It smelled even worse than the gaoler did and he fought back the urge to gag, knowing that he would get no sympathy if he did. "Just to make sure you don't get any ideas o' running away from me laddie," the man whispered through the stinking cloth.

Marshall had no thoughts to escape; his only ambitions were to rein in his impatient breathing and keep his stomach under control. He lost count of how many steps he was led up and down and of how many left or right turns he made. The gaoler's grip on his arm never weakened, even when keys were drawn and locks opened. Eventually he was brought to a halt and he felt the man's fingers slip away. Then there was the sound of footsteps disappearing to the left and a heavy door closing. He considered lifting the hood from his face. But it could be a trick and the consequences of such disobedience might be...

"You can take it off if you want." The voice was soft and unthreatening but still Marshall did not move his hands from his sides. "No really, it's not a trick. Here, let me help." The hood twitched and in a moment was pulled from his head.

Standing in front of him was a man dressed in a purple robe. He smiled and reached out to shake Marshall's hand. "I'm terribly sorry for the way you've been treated," he said, "But I didn't realise quite who you are. Come and sit down." They were standing in a large study. The walls were lined with bookcases that stretched to the ceiling and the floor was covered with woven rugs and carpets. There were statues dotted about the room and standing on tables were scientific instruments and a large globe. Marshall was beckoned to sit in a large leather chair in front of an enormous desk. The man went round the other side and did the same.

"Welcome Andrew, I am Commissioner Banberg but you may call me Johan," the man said politely.

"How do you know my name?" asked Marshall.

"Oh, I have sources in places you wouldn't believe," Johan said with a smile. "I've also discovered that you're not exactly a local boy, are you?"

Marshall shook his head. The man seemed extremely satisfied, quietly congratulating himself for being so clever. It made Marshall's fear start to bubble up again. He blinked nervously.

"There's no need to be so concerned Andrew," Johan said, "I know a lot about you. It's always been my ambition to meet someone from the Other Place." He caught Marshall's glance. "Don't be so surprised that I know about it. Those in positions like mine understand a lot about the world we see and the worlds we cannot." He sat back in his seat with the same self satisfied grin on his face. Then his mouth straightened as he asked coldly, "How did you come here?"

Marshall's mouth opened and closed like a fish out of water. He feared what Johan might do if he knew about the doorway in the woods but at the same time he doubted that silence was the best policy. As the impulse to talk fought with the instinct to say nothing his jaw dropped and rose silently. Johan grew impatient. He leaned forward on one elbow and rested his chin in his palm, staring at Marshall. With his other hand he lifted back the lid on a small wooden box that sat on the desk top and took something out. "You need to trust me Andrew," he said softly. "If you can trust me then there's nothing to fear." As he spoke, he turned the object over in his hand.

It was a rough cut green gem that glinted as he toyed with it. It became harder and harder for Marshall to look away from Johan as the stone moved between the man's fingers. His fear dissolved as he was drawn into the twinkling green of the jewel. His breathing slowed and he could no longer feel the sweat that had been running down the back of his neck since he had left the cell.

"You see?" said Johan, "you know you can trust me."

He extended the hand that held the green stone and opened his palm. Marshall felt his own arm move from his side and his hand reached over the gem. For an instant he thought the gaoler had returned with the hood, as he was plunged into darkness. But the air that brushed his face was cold and sweet.

He felt Johan leading him by the hand. He heard a door open, wood scraping over stone, and felt steps falling away beneath his feet. He walked through the darkness, down and down into the depths of the earth. There was the sound of footsteps far off in the distance.

And then he stopped. His hand fell back to his side and the darkness lifted. They were standing in a stone chamber, with a set of narrow steps leading upwards behind them. There were no windows or decorations but in the centre of the room was a small stone pillar, upon which stood a much larger version of the green gem.

"This is the Monkton Stone," said Johan. "It sees everything within the souls of men, both living and dead. Don't be afraid, look at it." The stone was about a foot high and a tiny flame was moving within. It grew stronger and brighter as Marshall peered closer. The hypnotic state swept over him again. This time there was no darkness, instead he could see images of recent events within the shining green jewel. It was as if time was moving back on itself. He saw his arrest in the room at the Crab Inn, Alex walking away from the wagons on the road near the tall tree and the crowd turning on Thomas Peters.

The images were crystal clear. There was none of the fuzziness of memories; it was like a projection of the actual events within the swirling green flame. He saw the Lezard swooping from the sky, the chaining of the Guardian to the Tower of Archangel and the confrontation with Avery Tavistock. More and more images were drawn from him by the power of the Monkton Stone. He saw the dead emptiness of The Village and then the path through the woods to the spot where the doorway stood in the glen, lined with bluebells.

He so wanted to step into the deep green fire that burned before him and be swept back to the place under the trees where home was just a short walk away. He could see the basement of the office building and the freshly painted door. It was almost within reach. Then it faded and was gone. "I understand how you feel Andrew," said Johan, placing one hand on his shoulder and stepping close to the stone himself.

Now Marshall began to see other images. As Johan leaned closer, faces appeared in the fire. Men in cloaks were sitting in a small room lit by candles. Smoke hung above their heads as one dressed in purple drew on a cigar. Two identical books lay closed on the table in front of them.

Now Marshall understood. There were no voices or written words but in a split second he knew what they had done. Their very thoughts appeared before him like sparks of light in the darkness. The Commissioners had sent Thomas Peters to his death. They had created the book that he had found in the old man's belongings and had given it the power to bewitch and perform petty miracles. But they had also made another that carried within it elements of dark magic that would curse those it touched. Then they had switched the two so that Peters was made to face the crowd and pay the price. Marshall could read the men's minds as they sat at the table. They wanted a sacrifice. But it was not to please a God; it was to scare a population.

"We had to Andrew. We had no choice." Johan was beside him, staring into the green fire. "We knew a time would come when the God the people worshipped would send his gentle prophet. So we had to show what would happen to anyone who claimed to be that man." The voice sounded smooth and seductive. It was trying to win him over. "We had to make an example of someone. Then if he ever came, the people would not believe his words and would turn their back on him. God's time is over Andrew. Science is honoured over religion. Knowledge above belief. That is the way it must be and we have to…"

Johan's words were cut short as the green flame began to spit and spark. At the heart of the Monkton Stone lay an ancient dark magic. It did so much more than read human souls. It corrupted and twisted. And it could follow its own path when it chose. And now it did. It looked beyond the two men and sought the answer to a question.

"Has he come?"

An outline began to appear from inside the stone. A man's

face was shaped from the twisting fire. Alex Preston was walking down a dirt road towards a mighty city. Around him shone a white light that made the Monkton Stone shake and wobble on the pedestal.

Johan ran his fingers through his hair. "Oh Father," he said, as tiny cracks began to appear like frost on the surface of the Monkton Stone. "He was here all along."

* * *

"All right, hold your horses." Gaoler Brent got to his feet from the wooden stool in the corner of the room. His left leg was numb with cramp, and he could straighten it only slowly. He leaned heavily against the wall as he tried to get the blood flowing into the stubborn limb. The knocking came again; three hard raps on the door to the gaoler's chambers, a pair of interlinked rooms with a filthy bed in one and the stool and a table in another. The lack of bars was all that distinguished them from the prisoners' cells.

"I'm coming as fast as I can," he cursed as he shook his leg and scratched himself. He belched loudly, tasting again the beer that he had enjoyed earlier that afternoon. He moved out to the corridor and drew back the bolt. As it slid away the door flew open, knocking Brent to the floor. Two men, one in his thirties and the other a fair bit older, burst through and slammed the door behind them. The younger man stood over him, his eyes wide and staring and his skin pale and dotted with sweat.

"Where are they?" demanded Alex.

Brent was stunned. In all his years of guarding prisoners, he had never known of a rescue attempt in this place. They were in the cells of the Commissioners' Palace, one of the most heavily guarded buildings in Middleton, if not the whole of Theland. He did not know how this mad pair had managed to smuggle their way in but he was sure they would not be leaving so easily. As he lay on the floor he considered his options. There was no reason for him to play the hero. These men and the three inmates would be dead before they crossed the courtyard and

148

he had another jug of beer waiting for him under the bed. There was no decision to take.

"They're in there," he whispered, pointing down the passageway. Alex stepped over him and jumped down the small flight of stairs. He stepped to the door of the cell and pressed his hand to the lock. He cast a nervous glance back to Foxton, who nodded him on. Then he pressed harder against the cell door and closed his eyes. In his mind he could picture the workings of the lock and he tried to imagine them moving. But he found the moaning of the gaoler, rubbing at one leg as he lay on the floor, a distraction and he struggled to focus his mind of the innards of the lock.

"There is another way." Foxton was at his side.

"How?" Alex asked.

"I believe it's called a key," Foxton said, holding up the set he had taken from the gaoler's belt. He slipped one in the lock and turned it. There was a slow clunk and the door moved in the frame and swung open a little. Alex hesitated. He had not considered how he would explain to his friends his return from death. They must have believed, as he himself did, that the Militiamen had cut him down him on the road. How would they react now when he appeared fit and well? He took a breath and reached for the door.

In the cell Anthony was standing by the wall directly opposite. He looked up at Alex and stared, open mouthed. Across the room Rebecca lay on a metal bed frame that hung from the wall. Her eyes were closed and she breathed slowly. Alex studied her in silence. Then he turned to the corner behind the door and saw Marshall squatting there, his head low against his chest. "Is no one going to say anything?" he said in a loud voice.

The minute that followed was full of tearful embraces, cries of disbelief and hands pressed to Alex's face in joy. He tried to answer their questions but fought for space to speak between the kisses that Rebecca planted on him and the giant hugs that Anthony threw around his frame. "It's not something I can explain right now," he managed to say, "But it is me, I can promise you." As he spoke, Rebecca ran her fingers over his face as if to make sure it was not a mask and Anthony stood grinning behind her.

Then Marshall stepped forward. He had shed no tears nor made any cries of joy but had stood quietly in the background while the others had welcomed their friend back from the dead. Now he placed a hand on Alex's shoulder and looked him in the eye. There was something about his gaze that unnerved Alex for a moment; a coldness that went through him. But then Marshall threw his other arm around him and the two men hugged silently.

There was a cough from the doorway. "Oh, I'm sorry," said Alex, "This is Foxton Scarfe. He's... well..." Alex was not sure how to describe him.

"I'm a friend," said Foxton, "and I'd urge you not to stay here any longer. The pleasantries can wait a while. We need to get out quickly." He shot a curious glance at Marshall, his eyes narrowing uneasily, before ushering the four out of the cell. "Keep going to the door," he said with a note of urgency in his voice.

Before they even reached the first flight of steps three men in the uniform of the Militia appeared in the narrow corridor. Behind them, by the open door to the courtyard, stood the gaoler, rubbing his leg and smiling. The lead Militiaman had a sword drawn in front of him. "Stop there," he shouted, "you are prisoners of the Commissioners. All of you."

"We're leaving and you're not going to stop us," said Alex, the sweat rising from his skin again. "Now get back and let us past." He moved forward and put a foot on the first stair.

"I'm warning you," the Militia Captain shouted, "one more step and you'll taste my sword. Now move back and surrender yourself."

"I will not," Alex said slowly, his eyes staring at the Militiamen. "I did that once before and it cost me my life. You kill me once shame on you. If I let you do it twice, shame on me."

Confusion cast a shadow over the Captain's face. He looked from Alex to the others and back again and his fingers moved uneasily on the handle of his sword. He repeated his warning, "One more inch and you'll suffer…" He said it with less conviction than before. Alex smiled and moved to the second stair.

The Captain felt every muscle tense as he brought the sword down with a hefty swing of his arm. He aimed for a point to the left of Alex's head, where it would strike his shoulder hard with the sharp edge of the wide steel blade. He had done this once before and had felled the man with a single blow.

Alex saw the blade coming. His body went light and a pulse of energy raced through him. He wanted to shout with joy at the sensation. He raised one arm and extended his hand, palm forwards, to catch the edge of the weapon in the deep V between his thumb and forefinger. It happened in a split second and then he was standing, one foot on the second step, with the tip of the Captain's sword resting in his hand. "I've had worse paper cuts," he said, looking at the tiny trickle of blood that ran from the point where the blade rested against his skin.

As the Captain let go of the sword and it fell to the floor, Alex withdrew his hand and peered at the tiny wound. As he watched, the blood began to run upwards, back into the small opening in the flesh. There was a tiny flash, like a match being lit, and the injury was healed. Now the Militiamen turned and stormed out of the door, knocking gaoler Brent to the floor for the second time. He struggled to his feet and hobbled after them as quickly as he could.

"We must hurry," said Foxton, stepping past Alex and peering through the doorway. He held his rolled up newspaper in one hand and raised it in the air above his head. "Gather round, all of you." There was a look of confusion from the others. "Just do as I say," he pleaded in frustration. "This isn't the time for lengthy explanations. Hold hands and stand close to me."

They followed his instruction and he began to move the

newspaper in a circle in the air over them. There was a sound like a machine whirring into life and the pages of the paper flew apart, spinning in a vortex that reached up into the stone ceiling. Foxton kept his arm moving round and round as the newsprint tore itself to shreds. Alex and the others felt invisible hands pulling at their clothes, trying to lift them from the floor as the whirlwind grew stronger and stronger and the noise became a scream. Through the open doorway to the courtyard they could see fresh Militiamen running with weapons. They would be upon them in seconds.

As tiny shreds of newspaper began falling to the floor there was a sound like distant thunder. Looking up, Alex saw the ceiling of the corridor had cracked wide open and a bright light was pouring through. He turned to Foxton who was holding what was left of the paper in his hand and smiling at him. "No news is good news Alex," he laughed, "no news is good news."

As the Militiamen reached the door to the cells, it slammed shut in their faces. They caught only a brief glimpse of the huddled group of figures standing in the eye of a tiny tornado. They were left hammering on the woodwork as the four men and one woman were lifted from the ground and disappeared into a ball of light that grew out of the ceiling. By the time they had smashed their way into the gaoler's chambers there was nothing to greet them but a pile of paper rags and the stench of stale beer.

Chapter Sixteen

Home and Alone

Marshall rested his hands on the rail and smiled out over the city. In the evening shadows the buildings seemed to be huddling together for warmth. There was a chill on the breeze that came in across the rooftops but that was a small price to pay for the comfort of being home. After all, there had been times when he had thought he would never enjoy this view again.

He stepped back into the flat and left the door open, not wanting to lose the noise of the cityscape. The sounds of life far below him, the roaring engines, the blaring car horns and the urban hum were music to his ears. He still had moments when he thought he was back in Theland; lying in the cell in Middleton, being arrested at the Crab or watching the lynching of Thomas Peters. These terrors came back to visit him when he was alone in the sealed solitude of the apartment, so he was happy to suffer the draught for the sake of his sanity.

As he flopped back onto the sofa he slid one hand into the pocket of his jeans and pulled out the small piece of green stone that Johan Banberg had given him. He held it up to the light and stared through it, enjoying the way it glimmered in his hand. He knew that keeping it so close was what brought on his flashbacks but at the same time it made him feel so special, so excited to be alive and buzzing with energy. It was worth suffering a few nightmares in return for being filled with its dark power. He was not the same Andrew Marshall who had first ventured into Theland with fear gripping his insides. What happened to him in the Commissioner's dark chapel had changed him forever.

The piece of the Monkton Stone sparked into life. Green flames burst from its tiny heart and made Marshall's hand glow. He was getting used to it now; the way it would lay so still for hours on end and then fire up without warning. He sat it down on the glass coffee table and studied it, as it in turn studied him. It was nowhere near the size of the jewel in the chamber but it held many of the powers of its larger sibling. Johan Banberg had been adamant that he should take it with him, pressing it into his hand with such intensity that it hurt his palm.

Johan had told Marshall that he had often tried to cross over to his world, the place of science and invention, but he had never managed to find a way through. He believed that those who were Theland born were unable to make the crossing. "But now," Johan had said, "you can take a piece of Theland with you when you go home. I'm going to let you return to The Other Place. This little piece of stone will let you do many marvellous things there."

As Marshall remembered the Commissioner, the flame flared again, lighting up the table top like a neon sign. He watched tiny pockets of fire dance over the glass and dissolve into the air. Then, from the middle of the stone, grew a picture. A group of people were standing at a crossroads with open fields around them. He could see himself standing next to Alex's strange new friend, Foxton Scarfe, who had a shabby raincoat slung over one arm. He seemed impatient. Meanwhile Anthony was hugging Alex goodbye. There were tears in the big man's eyes as he held his friend close. "I'm going to miss you," he said, "I feel like I've known you all my life. You take care of yourself now."

"I will," Alex smiled, "and you look after yourself and Rebecca." Anthony, Marshall and Foxton moved away self consciously as Rebecca stepped forward. Alex put his arms around her and the pair looked into each other's eyes. "I have to go back," said Alex, "I made a promise to Foxton."

"But I want you to stay here with me," Rebecca said softly, her voice faltering as she pleaded, "I need you to stay with me."

This is what the stone liked most: to bring sadness and misery to life within the green flame that burned at its wick. "Don't go," she said. The words fell from her mouth with a sob.

"I have to, at least for a while," Alex said, "But I will be back soon. I mean it. I'll be back as soon as I can."

The pair hugged again and as Marshall watched from his sofa he smirked at the sight of them, caught in their miserable embrace by the power of the stone. He wondered what Alex's pretty suburban little wife would make of a scene like this and he contemplated showing it to her one day. Then they pulled apart and as Rebecca drew her hair back from her face it was clear that she was crying. Foxton approached and put something into Rebecca's hand and spoke quickly, "This will protect you," he said, "If you keep it safe then it will do the same for you." She opened her palm and for a moment the images in the stone flickered and blurred.

Marshall leaned closer to see what she was holding but the picture was too distorted to get a clear view. "Why didn't I see this when it happened?" he wondered out loud. Then he saw, standing at the back of the scene, his own figure gazing away into the distance in deep thought. "You idiot." He cursed himself for his lack of attention.

Alex gave Rebecca a final kiss on the cheek and the two stepped away from each other. Then Foxton took hold of Alex's arm and beckoned to Marshall to snap out of his daydreaming and join them. The three men stood close together as Foxton reached into his bag and pulled out yet another newspaper, once again rolled into a short paper rod. As he raised it in the air, Alex lifted a hand to wave slowly at the two figures standing a few feet away from them. Rebecca held her hands to her face to stifle her cries, while Anthony waved back tearfully.

Then the green flame at the centre of the stone grew so fierce that it spilled out of the confines of the jewel. It fizzed and roared until Marshall had to cover his eyes from the brightness of the light. Then it was gone and there was nothing to see but a small green stone on the glass coffee table.

Marshall was disappointed. The stone lived by its own rules and had a habit of showing some events from his memory and ignoring others. He had wanted to see them arrive in the forest glen where the entrance to the tunnel was waiting for them. It had felt like coming home just to have reached that point. It would have been even better to have been able to watch them all reappearing the other end. This time the tunnel had not emerged into the basement of the office building, but in the wall of a railway arch in the centre of town. They had stumbled out of an old metal door set into the crumbling brickwork, much to the alarm of a pair of tramps who were dozing under a pile of boxes.

There was a flicker from within the green gem on the table. Another image was forming. This time the room around him and the distant noise of the city faded away as Marshall was drawn into the light spilling from the Monkton Stone. It was replaying the events down in the Chief Commissioner's secret chamber. He was there, in the small dark room, looking lost and afraid while a tall man in a purple robe smiled and rested a hand on his shoulder.

"I need you Andrew," Johan Banberg said softly. "Your friend's a very dangerous individual. He could spell enormous trouble for all of us and I need you to watch over him for me."

This was the point when Marshall's old life ended and his new existence began. Though he would lose one precious thing, he would gain such power in return.

"I don't know what you're talking about," said Marshall. He was confused and frightened. "Alex is dead. He was killed on the road from Middleton. I heard his screams. We all did."

"But you can see for yourself Andrew." Johan pointed at the large green jewel that stood on a plinth before them. Inside it, two people were walking along a dusty road towards a gateway. "Here he is, alive and well. He tricked you Andrew. He left you to look after yourself while he made new friends and learned what real power is."

"No…" In the chamber, Marshall whimpered as he struggled to understand what he was seeing. Alex was walking towards the walls of Middleton with a middle-aged man. There were deep in conversation but he could not make out what they were saying. He was excluded and he felt tears well in his eyes as the sense of betrayal bit into his heart. His friend had lied to him. "But he died on the road. By the tall tree…"

"He cheated death and he cheated on you," whispered Johan, pressing his hand into Marshall's shoulder. "But I understand how you feel and it doesn't have to be like this. No one need have power over you. Not even him. You can be the master of your own destiny."

Marshall sniffed and blinked away the tears. "How?"

"Just make a promise. Promise to follow my Master. He will take care of you and give you the strength you need."

"But how will God help me?" Marshall said.

"Oh this isn't the God you know. That's their God, not mine." Johan waved at the two men whose images moved in the deep green flame of the Monkton Stone. "Their God lives in damp churches and dry books. That makes him a dead God. Mine is infinitely more powerful because he lives in our flesh and blood. Every man and woman alive carries a piece of my God in them. He doesn't need miracles and visitations. The greatest power he has is the base nature that every man is born with: greed, lust, guilt. What a wonderful gift. We only need to harness that to have power over everything on earth." His fingers dug into Marshall's skin, pressing hard on the bone beneath. "Open your heart to him Andrew. Touch the flame and let our Father into your heart."

Through his tears, Marshall raised an arm and opened his hand to reach for the flickering green light. He wept as he stared at the image of Alex walking along the dusty road and he thrust his hand forwards. His crying became a wail as the flames reached out of the Monkton Stone and scorched his skin. Johan's grip left his shoulder and the Commissioner stepped away into the furthest corner of the room as the green fire engulfed the weeping man. In the time it took for the burning to cover his entire body, Andrew Marshall's soul was gone.

In the flat, Marshall watched this replaying of events impassively. It meant nothing to him now. It was just the price he had paid for the power he now possessed. He lifted the green jewel from the table and held it close to his face. The sliver of the Monkton Stone was indestructible and belonged to him and him alone. It was his link to Johan Banberg on the other side of the void that separated this place from the land of Theland. It bound him to the Commissioner and to the great power that they both obeyed. There was no one alive who could control Marshall's destiny now: no petty bureaucrat or dim witted boss. For the first time in his adult life he would decide his own fate and he had new friends to help him.

* * *

Alex sat on his bed with his head in his hands. The walls of the bedsit closed in on all sides, driving him to curl into a ball with his back to the damp wallpaper. He was starving hungry but lacked the energy even to get to the tiny kitchen and make some toast. The room was cold and filled with shadows but his real discomfort was on the inside, where his mind wandered back to the place where he said goodbye to Rebecca and Anthony. It felt like he had left part of himself behind on the crossroads.

He may have come home but he felt more lost and adrift than he had at any time on his travels through Theland. He had thought before that a spell was being cast over him while he was there, one which made him shake off the anger and bitterness than normally filled his days. Now he was doubly convinced. The grievances he felt at the world around him had disappeared while he was away, along with his desire to escape on pointless daydreams. But since returning, the dark thoughts had begun circling him again, poking and prodding at his mind and spirit in the hope that he would let them in. These were feelings he had been used to before but now he was afraid; afraid of what might happen if they got inside him and made him angry, scared of how he might behave when the deafening roar of his own world became too loud to bear.

So he hid in a tiny, dirty bedsit just off the High Street. Sarah and the children were at home less than a mile away but he had not seen them since his return from Theland. He had come close, when Foxton had led him literally to the front door one evening. But he froze at the last moment and had run down the street with the old man huffing and puffing behind him. He could not explain his reaction but was insistent that he must find his own place to live.

So despite Foxton pleading with him to rejoin his family, he had ended up here. The bedsit was above a laundrette and consisted of a small sleeping and living area, a side room containing a cooker and a fridge and a bathroom with mould growing in every corner. He had seen it advertised in the window of the post office and rang the landlord from a payphone. He had felt the coins appear in his pocket at the exact moment he thought about money and after making the call had reached into his coat and pulled out a wallet filled with notes. At least he was not going to starve.

His new companion had not given up trying to persuade him to return to normal life, patiently reminding him of how pleased his children would be to see him and how relieved Sarah would be to know that he was OK. Alex barely heard the words. Instead he sat on the bed and hid from the world.

It was evening now and he knew what he had to look forward to once night came. There would be more nightmares about Thomas Peters. He would see the man's face as he was swallowed by the mob, knowing that death was just moments away and resigning himself to it. Then the first knife would appear and blood would seep through the blue cloak, turning it a shade of dark purple as the stains spread. The colour would hang before his eyes even as the image of Thomas Peters' slaughter faded from view. Purple. Purple in a dark room.

He would see the same colour on another man's clothes, in a small dimly lit space with smoke in the air. Then he would feel what the man felt: fear, anger and hatred. Fear for something that threatened him. Anger that a promise had not been kept.

Hatred for a man he had never met.

There was a knock at the bedsit door. "Who's there?" Alex asked, his voice dry and rough.

"It's just me. I've brought you some supper," a familiar voice called from the landing. Alex rose and opened the door before retreating to the bed. Foxton went straight to the table, carrying two parcels. He had brought fish and chips. "They're wrapped in newspaper," he said with a grin, "I like them like that but they're devilishly hard to find these days. It's all plastic boxes. You've no idea how far I had to go to get these."

The smell of salt and vinegar drifted the short distance from the table to the bed and was enough to tempt Alex to move to a chair and share the food. As he unwrapped one of the parcels he noticed the paper it was wrapped in. The newsprint seemed dated and the stories were of union strikes and foreign conflicts he could only vaguely remember. Then he noticed the date: March 12, 1978. Before he could mention it, Foxton spoke. "I've been thinking."

"You don't say," answered Alex, with a mouthful of chips.

Foxton either did not hear or was ignoring him. "About what happened in Theland. What went on with your friend Mr Peters."

"He wasn't my friend," Alex said loudly, making sure that this time Foxton definitely would hear him.

"Well anyway, I've been thinking about what went on there and I'm more convinced than ever that something underhand was going on. Something was happening that meant I couldn't see what was going to take place in Middleton."

"Do you think I'm to blame for his death?" Alex asked. He had stopped eating.

"No," said Foxton, "But *you* do, don't you? Isn't that why you have those dreams? Because you feel somehow responsible?" Alex poked at a chip in silence and Foxton went on. "Well you're not. Whatever happened to Thomas Peters was not about you." They ate the rest of the meal without speaking.

As Foxton washed the plates in the sink he asked Alex about

Sarah and the children. "Are you sure you won't go home?" He kept his eyes on the dishes and let the question find its own way across the room.

"I can't," said Alex. He went to the window that looked out on to the street and peered through the grimy net curtain. "I just can't go back there yet. If I do then I could lose them forever."

"How do you work that out?"

"Because I know that before I go home I have to first face up to what I am. Well, what you say I am. But then things would never be the same again. I'd be... different. Everything would change."

"And this is better?"

"At least here I can wait and hope it'll all go away. I can dream..." He pulled the curtain back a little and studied the people moving on the pavement. At this time of day many of them would be heading back to their families, to the warmth and comfort of homes filled with the special magic that not even Theland could provide. "When you took me there the other day, to the front door, there was something in my head. Like an alarm bell. If I went home then I'd be hurting them."

"You didn't say this." Foxton was wiping his hands on a towel. His eyes had narrowed and he was focused on Alex. "I don't know what it was you were feeling at the house but you've got nothing to worry about. You won't lose them or hurt them. Honestly."

Alex turned from the window. Foxton had become a very close friend in such a short space of time, a protector, teacher and confidant rolled into one. But there were still times when he felt that he was keeping something hidden; concealing some element of the truth that he did not believe Alex could be trusted with. This was one of those times. There was a second or two of silence that hung between them. Then Alex spoke. "I'm going for a walk. Maybe I'll feel better in the morning."

Foxton accepted that he would not be changing Alex's mind and left. Alex watched him head up the road, then grabbed his coat and went out. He pulled his collar up under his chin and thrust his hands into his pockets away from the chill evening air. The pavements already seemed dark, even though the sun had another hour above the horizon. He turned into St Thomas's Road.

This was not the place he wanted to be. This was a hard, cold place of strangers and menace. He saw young men standing by a car stare at him as he passed. He looked away and kept moving. As he turned the corner he bumped into an old man carrying two plastic bags filled with shopping. The food fell onto the floor and Alex bent to help pick up the tins and packets that scattered over the pavement. "I'm sorry about that," he said, as he put them back into the bags. "I should look where I'm going."

"Oh that's all right," the old man said with a laugh. "I'm a clumsy bugger." Alex looked at him. He had skin so pale that veins were clearly visible through it. His face was criss-crossed with wrinkles but his grey eyes could have been those of a much younger man. They were lit by a gentle twinkle that radiated outwards and when he smiled a tiny spark danced across them. This was a good soul. Alex could see it move within him. A soul that drove back the circling shadows for a moment. Alex touched his hand.

"Don't forget your peaches." He handed him the last tin and helped him to his feet. He watched the old man disappear round the corner, then stuck his hands back into his pockets and carried on walking.

On St Thomas's Road, Arthur Thompson shuffled along. He was nearly home now and would just have time to feed the cat and make a cup of tea before the news came on. He liked to keep up to date with what was happening in the world and it looked like a war was brewing in the Middle East. He had served there in the army and he always remembered it. He laughed at the thought of all the time he had spent trying to keep the sand out of his lovely black hair.

"Something funny, you freak?" The young man spat the words at him as Arthur walked past the parked car where the gang stood.

"No, no young man. I'm just on my way home."

"Anything tasty in them bags old guy?" asked another of them. All four moved away from the car and approached Arthur on the pavement. One of them, wearing a blue baseball cap, made a grab for his bags but he moved them away just in time.

"If I want to look in those bags you'll let me," the younger man cursed. "Now give 'em 'ere." He snatched at the plastic carriers and spilled the contents onto the floor. "It's just cat food and peaches," he said, kicking at the tins as they rolled away. "What a waste of time." He took at swing at Arthur. The blow caught him on the side of his head and sent him spinning backwards to the floor. He could hear the young men laughing as he hit the pavement and he tasted blood on his lips. The light seemed to dim for moment. Then he stood up.

The laughter stopped as he got to his feet. Staff Sergeant Arthur 'Tommo' Thompson pulled himself up to his full height of six feet two. His muscles stood out from beneath his dark green army shirt and on one forearm was a tattoo of a snake on a shield. His dark hair was neatly trimmed and shone under the streetlight.

"What..?" was all the lad with the blue cap could manage before he was felled by a single, strong blow to the stomach. As he went down a regulation army boot came up to meet him, just to finish the job. Then one of the others came in from the side. Arthur twisted on one heel and used the youth's own inertia to send him spinning to the floor. He punched him in the back, square beneath the shoulder blades, and heard the air rush out of his lungs. Now there were two left.

The first of them reached into the loose pocket of his tracksuit bottoms and pulled out something that glinted in his hands. "Oh silly boy," said Arthur as he looked at the knife. He was starting to enjoy being Tommo Thompson again: twice decorated for bravery before being recommended for Special Forces. He still had his beret somewhere at home. "You really shouldn't carry something like that around," he said, just as the knifeman made his move.

It was like a ballet; the way the weapon came forward and Arthur's arm came up and across to knock it out of the young man's grasp. Tommo had been taught well. Never try to grab the knife or you'll end up with a hand full of cold steel. Instead knock it away. Then turn, grab and twist. And finish off with…

There was a thump as the knifeman dropped to the floor.

That left just one very frightened looking teenager in a tracksuit who tried to back away. "I haven't finished yet," said Arthur, "I've got something special for you my lad."

When he got to the house the cat was at the window, calling for his supper. Arthur put his key in the door and twisted it in the lock. He had enjoyed being Tommo again for a while but he quite liked this life. His daughter would be by tomorrow to take him over to her house for supper. She cooked a great beef stew and he would sit and listen to his grandchildren talking about their day at school. He loved all that. He might even tell them a little about his time in the army. Perhaps he would dig out that beret before he went to bed.

As the door opened he picked up his bags. "Thank you young man, you've been very kind to carry these for me," he said to the trembling, tracksuit clad figure behind him. Arthur smiled as he went indoors. He could hear the sound of running disappearing up the street.

* * *

The house was dark and silent. Not even the slightest trace of light showed from behind the curtains that hung across every window and the lamp that hung in the porch was dead and cold. On the doorstep Alex stood in the cover of a shadow and pricked his ears for any noise from within: a voice or even the comforting chatter of the television. There was nothing. The only sound was the dry rustle of the wind teasing the branches of the trees and the hushed rumble of an occasional car sweeping down the road.

It had taken all the strength he had to come this far. He felt drained. Something was pulling at his insides, a dark fear that dragged him down. It was the same every night when he came here. It had become a kind of ritual. He would leave the flat full of purpose, determined to return home to the family he knew he loved. But as he got nearer he felt the same angry shadows descend on him. Every night it happened. Every night.

He leaned against the wall of the house and let the darkness envelop him. Now he felt safer. When the pure dark of the night was around him he felt at peace. He stayed like that for a while, huddled in the porch with the cold, hard bricks against his back. When he felt some strength return he stepped up to the door once more and raised his hand to knock. But his knuckle froze an inch from the wood. He held it there for a second before dropping it back to his side. He knew it was not the right time for a reunion but that did not stop him wanting to see them again, to check they were OK.

He chose another way. As he pressed his forehead to the woodwork he closed his eyes and felt something stir inside him. It was as if he was standing still and the rest of the world shifted beneath his feet. Then he was in the hallway. The door was still closed but Alex was on the other side of it. A single word left his lips.

"Home."

The children's coats hung on the set of low hooks that he had fixed to the wall last summer. On the floor beneath were their shoes and Wellington boots. Even in the darkness he could make out the fairy pattern on Katie's and he smiled. She loved anything to do with fairies and magic. He wished he could take her to Theland and show her them for real.

The stairs beckoned. He moved silently up to the landing. On the right was Matthew's room and he paused for a moment by the open door, where he could hear his son's breathing. He almost cried with joy at the sound. Inside, he moved to the tiny bed in the corner where the little boy lay asleep. His legs were wrapped untidily in the duvet, his fair hair was strewn across the pillow and he was snoring gently. Alex knelt on the floor and watched him sleep. The glow of moonlight leaked through a crack in the curtains and gave just enough illumination for him to study Matthew's face.

The little boy had his mother's mouth and small pert nose but the general shape of his face was so like his father's that complete strangers had in the past commented on it. To Alex, he seemed to look so much older than when he had last seen him that he felt a spasm of guilt. He leaned forward. "I can't give you me right now," he whispered, "but I can give you sweet dreams," and he placed a kiss on his forehead. He went into Katie's room and did the same, brushing away the locks of yellow hair that hung over her face and planting a delicate kiss on her soft pale skin. During his time in Theland he had all but forgotten about the people he had left behind. He had allowed the magic of the place to sweep over him and push away any thoughts of home. Now, looking at his eldest child asleep in her bed, he wondered how he could have been so foolish as to ever leave in the first place.

When Katie was born he had enjoyed a moment of mental clarity and calm as great as anything he had felt in Theland. All his doubts and fears had vanished the moment he held her in his arms for the first time. No daydreams. No anger. He just knew that he would love her until the day he died. He had joked at the time that it had been like an emotional enema, letting the true feelings inside him come through. But it had not taken long for the clouds to form again and his head to fill back up with all its usual nonsense and clutter. He wished now that he could have found a way back to that sense of purity without having to run away from the ones he loved.

He went into Sarah's room. He felt he did not have the right to think of it as theirs anymore. He moved in perfect silence around the side of the bed and looked down at where his wife lay sleeping. His breath caught in his chest as he saw her. She lay on her side, with her face tilted slightly upwards across the pillow. He wanted to fall down and throw his arms around her but he held back. He had never doubted he loved her but now he felt that love flow through his body, putting to shame any of the rushes he had felt in Theland. This, he knew, was real magic. It made every inch of his body tingle and pulse.

She moved in the bed and for a moment he thought she would wake. Part of him hoped that her eyes would open and see him standing over her but she twisted over and settled back into her sleep. He went back to watching her. It was then that he noticed the book on her bedside table. It was small and square and bore a hard leather cover. Alex reached to take it from the table. As he brought his hand close, the book ignited with a brilliant blue light that filled the room and he heard a voice fill his head. "I am here to protect. Let the one who guards his estate be kept from the darkness."

"Foxton…" Alex said his name out loud and smiled. The man had everything covered. His heart was warmed by the thought of his friend keeping watch over his family in his absence.

It was time to go. He took another look at Sarah, sleeping peacefully on the bed and he bent to kiss her. His lips hesitated for a moment above hers. It felt wrong to kiss her like this, when she was unaware of his presence. That would have to wait until he had been able to make amends for leaving her alone. Until he knew that all this was over. He moved from her mouth and placed the most delicate of kisses on the tip of her nose instead. Then he was downstairs in the shadows of the hallway. He closed his eyes and was back outside the front door, his head touching the cold paintwork. He stepped away from the porch and looked up at Sarah's bedroom window. He swore he could see the blue light of the book flickering from beneath the curtain. With its magic to protect her, he knew she would be safe.

He turned and walked away. As he moved further from the house, away from the magic that his family's love had conjured up, he felt the dark shadows race in from all sides. Now they had voices, high shrill voices that whispered in his ears as he pulled his collar back up under his chin. He could not tell if they meant to tease or to warn him. "Dark forces are gathering. Dark forces. When the fire burns he will come again."

Chapter Seventeen

Bad News

The men were angry and cursing their enemies, while at the same time praising God. They came closer and began waving rifles in the air. One of them, who seemed little more than a teenager, had eyes that stared like a dead man's: hard and cold. Alex wondered why he was so angry. "Revenge, revenge," was all the man could say. Then he pointed his weapon straight ahead and fired.

The image on the screen cut back to the newsreader who continued his explanation of the conflict that was developing in the Middle East. This was, he said, on top of the fighting that had broken out in North Africa, Central America and parts of Eastern Europe.

Alex sipped from his coffee as he sat in the battered green chair in the corner of the bedsit. The gunmen had all been shouting in a foreign language but it had only taken one thought to enter his head for their words to become comprehensible; just one moment to wonder what they were saying for a connection to be made somewhere in his brain. He wished he had kept his thoughts better hidden. The world was unravelling at an alarming pace and he did not want to know what every guerrilla fighter on the planet was thinking.

He tried changing channels to watch a game show instead but was soon drawn back to the news. Maybe this was why he had been 'gifted', as Foxton put it. Perhaps, Alex wondered, he was supposed to be trying to stop these wars from breaking out. But looking at the map of the various conflict zones that the news reporter was pointing to, he had no idea how to start. And anyway, that would mean leaving the flat.

The truth was that he probably had no way of stopping people from killing each other and if he tried he was setting himself up to suffer the same fate as Thomas Peters. The man may have seemed a crackpot but he had genuinely wanted to do good for people. In the end the very ones he had wanted to help had murdered him with their bare hands. Alex did not intend to let that happen to him.

The news was still focused on the conflicts that were building up around the world. There were reports of the most horrific atrocities being committed, of children being butchered by armed gangs, of mass graves containing the bodies of entire families and of neighbour turning on neighbour.

There was a knock at the door. It was a blessed relief. Alex got up from the chair and lifted the latch. "Oh it's you," he said in surprise.

"You don't have to sound so pleased to see me mate," said Marshall as he walked past Alex into the room. He looked around in disgust at the faded wallpaper and dirty carpet. "You've settled in well I see," he mocked.

"How did you know where to find me?" asked Alex.

"Oh I did some ringing around," his visitor said with a smile. "Is this really the best you can do?"

Alex explained that it was a temporary move and that he would be returning home soon. "I'm having a few problems adjusting," he added.

"Really...?" muttered Marshall under his breath. He sat in the tired green chair in the corner near the television. "Terrible things are happening aren't they?" he said, gesturing at the screen. Alex pulled up one of the chairs from the table and grunted in agreement as he sat down.

He felt ill at ease. He had not told Marshall much of what had happened to him after he had been stopped by the Militia on the road out of Middleton. He had certainly not mentioned how Foxton had raised him from a shallow grave and told him he was immortal. Back in Theland it had been easy to be vague about his return from the dead; the place was so brim full of magic that such details barely mattered, but it was harder to ignore when they were sitting in his crummy bedsit just off the High Street. He felt Marshall's gaze upon him and he looked down at the floor.

"What's that?" he said, pointing at his visitor's feet. There was a yellow powder stuck to the soles of his boots.

"Oh, that's just sand," said Marshall, knocking it off on to the carpet. "I've been doing a bit of travelling."

Alex looked at his friend's tanned skin and sun bleached hair and shook his head in disbelief. "Good to see *you're* back to normal. You always were one for your holidays. Anywhere nice?"

"Nowhere special. I just got away from it all. You know; mingled with the locals. Picked up a few souvenirs." Alex's gaze lingered over Marshall. This was one language he could not translate. His former companion seemed to be from another planet: while Alex was living through hell, Marshall was full of the joys of life and duty free.

He sought refuge in the kitchen while he brewed some tea. When he returned to the living room Marshall was looking around the bedsit with cruel delight on his face. "This place is ... er... interesting," he said with a smirk, before turning to Alex and asking, "How are you doing? You don't seem your usual self." Alex handed him his mug of tea and said nothing. Marshall went on. "Look, I know you've been having a rough time of it but I can help, you know."

Alex brushed aside his offer with an excuse about feeling tired. "I just need to get my strength back, then everything will be all right," he said, but Marshall was not taking any notice. He came to sit at the table and put one hand on Alex's arm. His other hand slid into his jacket pocket. As he spoke he seemed overcome with sympathy for his friend: his face twisted uncomfortably, as if he were in pain.

"You know you can call me whenever you want to, don't you?" he said, pressing down on Alex's arm with his fingers. "I'm here to help you through this. I can only imagine what you went through in Theland. We all thought you were dead back there on the road. But if you need to talk to anyone then I'm ready to listen." Alex pulled his arm away and sat back, now utterly convinced that the man he used to share an office with had gone completely mad. He was talking like a cheap chat show host or tacky therapist.

The television was still on in the corner and Marshall was distracted by the latest reports from the various conflicts that were erupting around the world. There were images of bodies discovered in a forest. "You don't think...?" he began, before his words tailed off.

"What?" asked Alex.

"Well, you don't suppose this has anything to do with us, do you?"

"How do you mean?" Alex said.

"I just wonder if us going to Theland triggered all of this. You had that funny attack in the woods on the first trip. And we saw plenty of dark things over there. Maybe something followed us back"

Alex shook his head. "This is about men fighting men. There are no demons or dragons here. There's no magic."

"Are you sure?" Marshall asked, raising an eyebrow. "There might be something we don't know about. It's like a disease is spreading and no one can stop it." Alex looked away from his visitor and back to the news. He had been imagining that solving the various crises around the world might be his destiny. It had never occurred to him that he could be responsible for them in the first place.

"Dark Forces are gathering." He remembered the words from the shadows. There was a dark side to his own nature, he knew that. Maybe it was spilling over into this.

"Anyway, I have to go." Marshall rose from the chair, one hand still tucked in his jacket pocket. "I meant what I said mate, just get in touch if you need anything. Thanks for the tea." Alex showed him out with a quiet goodbye. When the door was closed he sank back into the old armchair and put his head in his hands, as the violent images on his television kept on coming.

Outside on the street, Marshall hurried away with a satisfied grin on his face. When he got to his car he drew his hand from his pocket. The small piece of the Monkton Stone sat in his palm, ringed by a halo of red marks on his skin. When he had touched Alex's arm the gem had grown so hot that he had almost cried out with the pain. But he had held on and now it was done. The first seed had been planted and now it was a matter of watching it grow. Alex was such fertile ground, so full of dark moods and hidden anger, that it would not be difficult. "Father," he whispered to the jewel that had burned his flesh. "You're another step closer."

Back in the bedsit, Alex lay on the bed with his arms drawn up about his head. The television was dark and silent in the corner. Its taunting had become too much for him to bear. He needed to escape from the terrible truth that was confronting him every time he looked at the screen: that something within him was igniting such terrible bloodshed. As his breathing grew slower and slower the quiet hum of the traffic below his window faded to nothing. His eyes dropped shut. He was away from the flat now and walking along a road. It looked familiar. There was a tall tree up ahead that he recognised but further along, where he might have expected to see a great walled city rising from the ground, there was nothing but the dusty path disappearing to the horizon.

A man was standing in the shadow of the tree. He was tall and thin with piercing brown eyes and was dressed in a dark suit with a collarless jacket. He looked like a preacher without his bible. "Nice of you to come Alex," he said with a soft voice, "I've been waiting a while."

"I'm sorry I kept you," Alex replied, "I've been having trouble finding my way."

"I know that," the man said, "I've been watching. You do seem a little lost. That's rather unlike you."

"So what do you want?" Alex asked, sitting cross legged at the man's feet.

"I want you to say that you'll join me Alex. I want you to put what's inside you to good use. I know why it was put there but it would be a terrible shame to waste such potential. You're above party tricks with cripples and conjuring barrels of wine."

"But the road I'm on isn't yours is it? You're the one who's wasting his time, not me." Alex answered. At that, the man flew into a rage. He dropped on Alex like an animal and dragged him onto the road. He pinned him to the dusty surface with immense force, the grit and gravel digging into Alex's cheek. Then he whispered in his ear, his soft tones replaced with coarse venom.

"Use that old dead magic on earth my boy and they'll tear you apart like they do all their idols. Can you face that? Or can you face a lifetime of hiding yourself from the world? Only it won't be a single lifetime will it? It'll be a hundred, maybe even a thousand. All those years spent hiding in corners. Either that or living under a microscope as mankind's favourite novelty."

The man's grip never weakened, even as Alex fought to push him away. "But I don't need magic to show them the truth," he pleaded, "That's what faith is about."

"Wake up you silly boy," the stranger cursed through gritted teeth. "Can't you see what's happening in the world? If all you have are words, how many of them will want to believe in you? Science has killed belief. Knowledge is more important than faith. The clever know, Alex; only the stupid or timid believe." He pushed Alex harder into the dirt and laughed. "He made such a mistake when he picked you. One so muddled and filled with empty rage. That's because there's too much of me in you."

Alex's vision began to blur. The fields on either side of the road were burning. The flames formed walls of fire and he could feel the heat scorching his face. The man released him and stood up. "I'll be seeing you again soon. Have your mind made up by then. I think you're half way there already." He turned and walked through the flames.

Coughing, Alex rolled onto his back and he looked up at a sky filled with black smoke. Even the tall tree was burning, fire eating its branches with a dry crackle.

He woke to the sound of traffic on the High Street. As he rubbed at his eyes he felt something on the palm of his hands. It was grit. He got off the bed and went to the bathroom to wash the smell of wood smoke out of his hair.

* * *

Marshall sipped his beer and grinned at the Monkton Stone's latest picture show. This was better than any holiday video on earth. Here he was now, coming out of one of the faction leaders' houses. Men with machine guns slung casually over their shoulders stood around smoking while he shook hands with the man in charge, a stocky fellow with a dark beard. The gunmen all nodded respectfully at him as he was escorted to a large four wheel drive car that would take him to the border. The information he had given them would prove most useful and they had rewarded him with hard currency, stuffed into two casual bags. He did not really need it as his true reward would come much later, but he could not resist. As he climbed into the car he gestured to one of the armed group, who slipped off his weapon and passed it to him through the open window. This would make a great souvenir. The car sped away in a cloud of yellow dust.

Next, he was sitting at a table under an awning, drinking tea. The men around him were dressed in a mixture of faded combat fatigues and t-shirts. One of them was studying a book that had just been slid across the table towards him. He was earnestly flicking through the pages, lost in thought. The others were listening to their visitor talk, regarding him with a mixture of awe, respect and fear.

He liked that. They had no idea of the power that was at work while he talked. None of them dared move, giving the dark magic a chance to flow over them, find the tiniest gaps in their defences and work its way inside. It was not a difficult thing to do, not when they were already so full of hate. But soon they would feel that hatred grow a thousand times and burst out into full blown rage. It would be a beautiful thing to watch but a terrifying thing to suffer.

But he would not be there to see it. He had a plane to catch that evening and another meeting to attend the next day. Before he left he would take another keepsake, this time a small black pistol, and would put it with the others. This had already been a fruitful trip. Small pockets of violence had broken out in the region at the start of the week and would soon ignite into a bloody conflict of genocidal proportions. A small party of international peacekeepers had been murdered that morning in a small town west of here and there was an expectant air of tension.

He did not need to worry. With the Monkton Stone in his pocket, quietly doing its work, he was perfectly safe from whatever came his way. That was more than could be said for the other men drinking tea at this table. As he looked around, he saw each of their faces in turn dissolve into a grinning white skull. It was an illusion that only he could see, a premonition of the way death would come to each of them before the month was out. The sight of their bleached bony faces and dead eyes reminded him of Avery Tavistock and his band of sad vampires. That made him laugh and the men nervously joined in. Then he was shaking hands and climbing into another four wheel drive. The last image projected from the piece of the Monkton Stone was of yet more dust clouds as he disappeared through the gates of the compound.

The show was over and Marshall picked the jewel up from the table. Watching it replay the highlights of his travels was even more fun than taunting Alex. He made more trips planned but he had not fully unpacked from this one. He went to the bedroom and unzipped the dusty green bag that sat on the chair. On top of the pile of bank notes were the weapons he had been given. They would look great above the fireplace.

* * *

Lucy Mitchell left the house as usual at eight fifteen. Her walk to work took twenty minutes: down along the river bank and over the old footbridge into town. It was a good way to start the day; watching boats on the water and getting some fresh air into her lungs before arriving at the firm of accountants where she worked. As she stepped outside there were dark clouds gathering overhead so she ducked back indoors to grab her umbrella. It was usually kept in the hallway but there was no sign of it today. She began to hunt everywhere; under the sofa, in the kitchen and even in her wardrobe. "I don't have time for this!" she shouted at the empty house after a fruitless and frantic five minutes.

It looked like it was about to pour down, so with reluctance she locked the house and slid behind the wheel of her car. She did not like driving much and only did so when absolutely necessary. She headed into the city centre, glancing occasionally upwards to check for any sign of the rain. As she turned into Taggart Road there was no still no sign of it and she felt cheated. Then, as she waited at the traffic lights on the corner of Terry Street, she saw a drop of water hit her windscreen and felt vindicated. She slid into gear and moved off.

The lorry appeared from nowhere. There was a squeal of brakes and the sound of rubber dragging over tarmac and then it hit Lucy's small red car, shunting it sideways down the road with an awful tearing noise. The lorry came to a halt in a cloud of tyre smoke but the car kept moving and slowly tipped over on to its roof.

That was when Alex came round the corner with his hands stuck in his pockets, on his way to buy a pint of milk. He heard the bang and saw a red hatchback with fluffy animals on the rear parcel shelf being flung down the road. He had been in a car accident once himself and remembered that everything had seemed to happen very slowly. But this was over in an instant. There was the noise of metal hitting metal and by the time he looked up the car was sliding across the tarmac and turning over. He could see a blond haired woman inside trying to shield her face with her arms.

People began to gather around the upturned car, trying to get her out. The door that Alex could see was badly dented and clearly would not open. Several men grabbed the handle and pulled hard but nothing happened. The woman's hands could be seen at the window, hammering desperately on the glass. More people arrived and then one man went to the boot of his own vehicle, took out a car jack and went to smash his way in. But just as he stepped forward to take a swing at the glass the crowd suddenly backed away. A puddle had appeared from beneath the wrecked car and there was a smell that everyone recognised. Then someone cried out, "Fire. It's on fire!"

A couple of the men went back to the door and tried to pull it open again, this time with greater urgency. But as the flames began licking at their feet they were forced back once more. Someone began crying while several others scrambled for mobile phones and began frantically calling for a fire engine. Across the road Alex watched. He could see the fire begin to take hold and he watched as panic set in. But he did nothing.

The shadows watched with him. They circled above him and repeated another man's words; over and over like demonic caged birds. "They'll tear you apart, they'll tear you apart." He sunk his chin further into his collar and walked on.

Inside the car, death was creeping over Lucy Mitchell, sneaking inside with the black smoke. She could sense it through the heat of the fire and the bitter, poisonous stench of burning rubber and plastic. She would be next, she knew, and part of her hoped it would happen quickly. The other part cried out for help, again and again, but she knew that no one was coming.

"Oh God no. No!" She was kneeling on what had once been the inside of the roof and the plastic had begun to melt. The fire had worked its way right inside. Death was around her now and it spread its arms for the final embrace. She was bathed in a shaft of light that made her yellow hair glow and she heard a voice. It was not the one she expected.

"Bloody hell it's hot in there. Quick, take my hand or we're buggered." A man's arm reached through a gaping hole torn in the underside of the car. She thought for a mad moment that it was an angel but then she noticed he was wearing a watch. She grabbed hold of the hand and felt herself being lifted up and through the hole. As she looked back down into the smoke filled wreck she swore she saw a shadow looking up at her with outstretched arms. Its two glinting eyes started at her angrily but at the sight of the man who held her in his grasp it recoiled into the inferno and was gone.

Alex had got as far as the corner before he had seen something reflected in a shop window. It was a face he recognised; one he thought had gone for good. Not an angel or a demon but an ordinary man. One who knew when to do the right thing. He stood on top of the burning car with the flames afraid to touch him and he looked around at the stunned faces of the crowd. There was no going back now.

* * *

Beneath the tall tree the figure stood in the shade and waited. And waited. Time moved on and he grew bored. He looked along the road in both directions, hoping for a glimpse of the figure he so expected. He saw only a gentle haze. "We needn't worry," he said to the souls standing out of sight behind him, "our little seed may yet sprout. He'll fall into my hands sooner or later."

Chapter Eighteen

The Captain Returns

Captain Daniel Weller sat on the edge of the bed and rubbed at his aching temples. When he had first opened his eyes he had wondered if the events of the night before were just a dream. But then he saw the two glasses and the empty bottle on the table. And felt the pounding in his head.

His visitor had called on him just as he was about to retire for the night. There had been a knock at the door and the man standing there had seemed so damn familiar that Daniel had welcomed him in and poured them both a shot of rum. Then they struck up a conversation. The words had flowed so easily that it had been like talking to an old friend or long lost relation. The man had felt like a brother.

On the table beside the bottle was the piece of paper that Daniel had written on. His guest had so much to say that he had reached for his pen and begun making notes, in case the rum robbed him of it all in the morning. But in the cold and sober light of day he could recall every word of their conversation unaided. As he held the paper in his trembling fingers he could even remember the look in the man's eyes as they shared a glass and a joke: there was a warmth that reached out and touched him, even as he knocked back his drink.

When the bottle was empty, Daniel's visitor had got to his feet and thanked him for the time they had shared. The pair shook hands at the door to the cabin and the stranger had promised to see him again soon. Then the man had stepped out into the night and was gone.

**

From the stage it was hard to see more than a few square feet of empty floor space. Men and women stood with their necks craned, listening attentively to the speakers on the platform. More sat on the deep sills by the arched windows while others leant over the rail of the gallery at the far end of the hall.

"They have abused people for too long and it's time we stood up to them," shouted the woman on the stage. "Until I came east I had barely heard of them and their Militia. But now I say enough is enough. We have to put a stop to them."

"And how do you propose we do that?" shouted back a middle-aged man from the floor.

"By refusing to follow their rules. By showing that we are not afraid of them. By disobeying them."

There was a ripple of approval from the crowd but some, including her inquisitor, shook their heads. "They've been running this part of Theland for years," he said, "and we've had to put up with their corruption and lies. Then along you come and tell us we've got to break their rules. Why should we listen to you? You're not even from round here!"

There were nods of agreement and the young woman on the platform paused for thought before she spoke again. "Because all I'm saying is what you daren't say yourself, even though it's what you know to be true. They only have so many Militia and yet people fear them like they are gods. They are nothing of the kind. One month, that's all I ask. One month where we withhold all duty and tax from them. That will hit them where it hurts. In their coffers."

There was laughter and the beginnings of applause but just as the clapping started a volley of whistles rang out, each getting nearer. Instantly the group on the platform jumped down. A half dozen men and woman carrying musical instruments took their place and the crowd dispersed to the edge of the floor.

As the band struck up many began dancing and seconds later the heavy oak doors swung open and a Militia captain led his men through with swords drawn. He regarded the room with suspicion. "Who is in charge here?" he shouted.

A frail voice came from the crowd, "I am sir." A small, elderly man with tufts of white hair gestured for the band to stop playing. He approached the officer. "Can I help you at all Captain? We were just enjoying a spot of dancing."

The officer's eyes surveyed the crowd. "Rather a popular event isn't it?" he said sarcastically, "I had no idea you were such keen dancers in these parts." His eyes dwelled over a tall, muscular man with a sheepskin jacket. "We had information that a meeting was taking place here tonight. One of a seditious nature."

"Seditious?" the old man whispered.

"Yes," the captain said, his gaze moving on around the room, "treason."

The old man laughed with a rattling, chesty cackle. "I know what it means young man. Treason though? That's not likely in these parts is it? Renwick Bay is not nearly exciting enough for that sir. We're just simple folk."

The captain looked him straight in the eye. He clearly did not believe a word he had heard and his fingers toyed with the handle of his sword, which he held upright in front of him. But there was little he could do to contradict a grey haired old man. He tapped his toe on the floor, then slid his weapon into its sheath and ordered his men out of the hall without looking back. When they had left and the doors were closed behind them the old man turned back to the band and shouted, "Well you may as well play on!" His voice was loud and strong.

"I thought we were in trouble there Siegfried," said Rebecca, as the crowd began to dance once more.

"We'll have worse moments than that before this is through. A few hard looks from an ambitious Militia captain are nothing compared to what the Commissioners might throw at us when they find out what we're up to." The old man's eyes twinkled as he spoke, as if he relished the idea. "Now, would you like a dance?" he said and he held out his hands.

Two hours later they were sitting around the heavy oak table in the old man's kitchen: Siegfried, Rebecca, Anthony and two others. Mark was a man in his forties with a tidy beard and short cropped hair. Victoria was slightly older and wore her long hair behind her in a pony tail. "What are we to do next?" she asked. "You've said we should be prepared to face the Militia head on but things have hardly started. There's nowhere near enough of us for a full scale confrontation so soon."

"Perhaps it's true that we can't afford to confront them yet," said Siegfried, "but neither can we afford to watch much longer. We need to start the ball rolling. We've had meetings in every town for thirty miles and we know the level of support we can expect. Tonight was the first so close to home and I propose we hold one more next week before we fix a date for the protest. Then we only need to send word of it to our friends along the coast. Once the rest of Theland hears what we've done it'll be unstoppable."

"But what if the Militia turn up again?" asked Mark. "I don't think they'll believe the same story twice. To be honest I don't think the captain really swallowed it tonight."

"Then we take that chance," said the old man, "we have little choice." He saw the look of concern on his companions' faces and raised a reassuring hand. "But it will not come to that. If we keep our wits about us then all will be fine."

The group dispersed and Rebecca went upstairs to the small room under the eaves of the house. She lit a candle and sat on the bed, suddenly feeling very weary. Since Alex had left, her life had been a series of high and lows. The highs were about organising secret meetings to build support for their fight against the Commissioners, moving from town to town with the others and evading the Militia. The lows were when she thought of the man she had lost twice, once to death and once to his other life in a distant world she would never know. Then she felt alone and pined for home. But that was lost to her as well. She could not go back there now.

The Rebecca Wilde that had walked out of Appledore one morning with a pack over her shoulder was not the one who was sitting in the house of Siegfried Terry of Renwick Bay. She had been an innocent, desperate for new experiences and knowledge of the world outside her little valley. Now she was a political activist and a fugitive. She thought of Appledore at times and hoped her family and friends were safe. She prayed that Avery Tavistock had not returned to haunt the village. Her promise to return home quickly and then never leave again seemed shallow now. But she dare not go back for fear of bringing her current troubles with her.

Her thoughts went back to Alex, the stranger who had rung the bell at the gate and taken her on his adventure. There had been a spark between them the moment they met and she still found it hard to believe that he had gone. She began to cry.

A face poked round the door. "Are you thinking of him?" soothed Anthony as he sat beside her. He always sensed when she was low and was usually able to lift her spirits. She called him her shepherd.

"I am. He's never that far from my thoughts to be honest. It's sad really," she sniffed.

"No it's not," he said, putting a comforting arm around her shoulder. "I think of him too. It's funny; we didn't know each other for that long, but I guess we just…" he struggled to find the right words. "With you it makes more sense. You knew him before I did. That's bound to make it worse."

"We're talking about him like he's dead," sniffed Rebecca.

"Well he was once wasn't he? I never quite figured that one out but I do know we'll see him again. Call it my shepherd's sense. I also know that when we're done here you'll find yourself that house with the garden that you talk about. And I'll end up back on my farm with my sheep."

They were staying in the house of their new friend Siegfried, who was a retired lawyer and one of the main campaigners against the rule of the Commissioners. Before his wife died he had lived in Middleton and witnessed their brutality at close hand. After her death he had moved south to the quiet coastal village of Renwick Bay. But even here, he could not escape them or their Militia and soon after his arrival a local man had been arrested for treason and taken away. He had not been heard of since.

Siegfried had offered Rebecca and Anthony protection when they first arrived in the fishing village. He said he recognised kindred spirits immediately and had taken pity on them. This was not long after Alex had returned to The Other Place and Rebecca was like a walking ghost, with only Anthony to keep her going. In the weeks since, she had become more and more active in the campaign of civil disobedience that was being planned. Just as organising the escape from Armouth had unearthed new strengths, so helping to orchestrate a mass protest had revealed a militant side to her that she had never seen before.

Four days after the meeting in the hall, a crowd gathered in the chapel on the cliff top. It was built of rough local stone and had a tall, thin tower at one end. Inside, the wooden pews were pushed to the sides to accommodate the throng of people who had come to listen to Siegfried and the other protestors. By eight o'clock the chapel was full and the doors were pulled shut. Lookouts had been posted on the main path up from the village and in the adjoining graveyard. They were armed with whistles and would fire off the usual warning at the first sign of any trouble.

The meeting got underway and the speakers outlined the full extent of the Commissioners' abuse of power. Illegal arrests and imprisonment without trial, the disappearance of their opponents, theft and extortion; the list went on. As each point was put there were gasps and knowing nods from the crowd. Then came the call for action.

"We must draw a close to the Commissioners' wicked acts, before it is too late and any chance of a better future is lost," said Rebecca, from the hastily erected stage in front of the altar. "The clock is ticking and we must strike before they have absolute power over all Theland."

As she spoke, a figure at the back of the chapel, with a hat drawn down over his face, scanned the audience. He caught the eye of a man standing beneath one of the stained glass windows and the pair nodded slowly to each other. Then he went back to listening to Rebecca's speech, all the while tapping one foot on the floor.

"We have spoken to crowds as big as this in towns and villages along the coast and each time we hear how angry people are. It's time to put that anger to use…" Her sentence was cut short by the crack of a pistol. At the back of the chapel stood the Militia Captain, smoke rising from the weapon that he held in one hand. "We've heard enough," he shouted, "You're under arrest for treason and disorder."

Throughout the crowd, men were throwing back hoods and cloaks to reveal Militia uniforms and weapons. Some had pistols while others drew short swords and people began to fall back in terror. Two more Militiamen barred the chapel doors and the Captain began to advance on the stage. He raised his weapon again.

"Quickly," said Siegfried, "there's a door behind the altar that leads to the tower. We might be able to make it across the roof." They scrambled down and made it to the doorway just as another shot rang out. Rebecca turned to see the old man crumple to the ground, blood pouring from his neck. She screamed his name but Anthony grabbed her and dragged her through the doorway.

Inside, there was a spiral staircase which they climbed two or more steps at a time. Anthony was forced to stoop to clear his head and the tower became narrower and narrower as they ascended. Eventually they came out under the roof and Rebecca heard Anthony groan. "Siegfried was wrong," he said, "there's no other way down." Through the open arches of the tower they could see beneath them only the flickering lights of the village and the ripples on the moonlit sea. They had no means of escape. At the sound of footsteps on the stairs they backed around behind the bell. Anthony positioned himself in front of

Rebecca and they waited.

There came the sound of raised voices and a single gunshot, followed by a scream. Then more footsteps could be heard coming up the stone stairs, until a tall figure in a hat stepped out into the moonlight.

* * *

After his visitor had left, Daniel had collapsed onto the bed and straight away began to snore loudly. Several hours later he had woken to the sound of drums. Only when he opened his eyes did he realise he was in his cabin and the banging was inside his head. As he dressed hurriedly he squinted down at the piece of paper on the table, next to the empty bottle. The name of the village was spelled out across the top, in writing so poor and shaky that he was ashamed to call it his own. There was also a time and a distance in feet, along with several lines of text. Out of the cabin he squinted painfully in the bright sunlight and steadied himself as *The Eagle* rolled beneath him. "You all right Captain?" asked a crewman with a leer, "Looks like you had a heavy night."

Captain Daniel Weller tucked his pistol into his belt and pulled on his three cornered hat. "Set course for Renwick Bay," he said, "And I'll need a rope ladder from the Quartermaster."

* * *

The old house loomed up out of the dark as they rode up the narrow bridleway, the horses' hooves clattering over the stony ground. The rider on the lead animal reined it in and dismounted, then approached the metal gates and gave them a push. They swung open noisily, the rusted hinges squeaking conspicuously in the quiet night. The others joined him as he walked through into the overgrown courtyard. "What is this place?" Rebecca whispered.

"I'm not entirely sure what it used to be," said Daniel Weller, "but I do know that it's derelict and will offer us a place to lay low. We'd better tie the horses up round the back."

Once the animals were secure, the three of them entered the house through an unlocked rear door. The sea captain seemed to know instinctively which one to try. "I was told exactly how to get in," he said. Once inside, they wandered from room to room and found that each was the same: full of furniture covered in dust sheets. It looked to have been a comfortable country dwelling at some point in the past but had clearly been abandoned and lain forgotten for some time. "Perhaps the owner fell out of favour with the Commissioners and had to make a hasty exit," Daniel Weller said, as he flopped down into a chair in the main living room. They found a pile of wood in the scullery and lit a fire. Then Captain Weller opened one of his saddle bags and produced a piece of linen wrapped around a loaf of bread, some meat and cheese. They ate in silence in front of the hearth.

"Captain Weller, you know I have to ask you," Rebecca said eventually.

"How I came to find you?" he said, "Oh and you are allowed to call me Daniel." He chewed his food and looked into the fire. "I had a visitor. It was on my ship *The Eagle* a few nights ago when we were ten miles offshore, on our way back to Armouth from our trip south with your friends. He looked like a man but I know inside that he was much more than that."

Rebecca and Anthony exchanged glances.

"He knocked on my door and we shared a drink. He told me he needed my help. He said he had friends in trouble and that he could work through me to save them. He asked me to make a choice." He tore off some more bread.

"About what?" asked Anthony.

"About what path I was on. That was how he put it. He said I ought to choose what path I wanted to follow because of what was to come."

"But you hardly know us and you could have been killed," Rebecca said. Daniel looked at her with a smile.

"I know, but he said he'd be with me at every step. He made it clear that it was my choice alone but the moment he left I knew I would not walk away. No man could. No decent man anyway. I can hardly believe I'm saying this but this was no ordinary visitor. I swear."

"Who was he?" Rebecca asked.

"A stranger." Daniel shook his head. "I had never met him before but I swear there was something about him; something familiar. He knew about me and my life." He was not used to language like this and he braced himself for a barrage of mockery.

"I think I know who it was," Rebecca said. She looked knowingly at Anthony, then back at Daniel. "Was he a middle-aged man, dressed in dark stripes? Perhaps with a rolled up paper or journal in his bag?"

The Captain pursued his lips and stared at her, confused. His eyes flicked from side to side as he regarded her fully for the first time since the rescue from the tower. Then he said, "Well actually, no. He was a younger man. He spoke like that nervous fellow you were with in Armouth, only with more charm. He talked about not being forgotten."

Chapter Nineteen

Stolen Souls

"I think I can find my own way after all these years," said Peter Mallory, handing his coat and hat to the maid. Her master was unable to come out and greet him personally so he brushed past her and wandered through to Johan Banberg's outer chambers, where drinks were often served to important visitors and friends.

Mallory qualified on both counts. He was second only in seniority to Commissioner Banberg and the pair had known each other for twenty years. It was to Peter that Johan had first turned when he wanted to discuss how to deal with the prospect of a Messiah arriving in Theland to disturb their peace. They shared a view that the natural order of things should not be disrupted by a new religious fervour. They both believed that such an event was likely to happen at some point soon, their years of study had taught them this. But they also knew that it would do no good for the people's heads to be filled with nonsense about deliverance and freedom.

He pushed open the carved oak door of the lobby and listened for his friend. There was no sound but the ticking of the clock on the mantelpiece. He poured himself a drink and regarded a few papers on the bureau before he became impatient and opened the door into Johan's inner study. It was empty. He had always admired this room, with its shelves lined with some of the rarest books in Theland. As he was reaching for one from a high shelf, he noticed something strange. Part of the bookcase was projecting forwards into the room and when he stuck his fingers into the gap between the uprights he felt a draught. He grasped the edge of the wood and pulled. The section of the shelving moved out on a hinge towards him, revealing a doorway and a set of steps going down. He was stunned. He had been in this study countless times and had never seen this before. There was no sign of Johan and he hesitated at the top of the stairs for a moment. But then his curiosity grew too strong and he edged down the spiral steps into the dark, reaching for the stone walls to steady himself. The light from the study was soon lost but as he wound his way further underground a green glow crept upwards to meet him. Then the stairs ended and he was delivered into a square chamber. In the centre was the stone plinth that supported the Monkton Stone, radiating its green aura.

"My God." He had heard of this jewel, read about it in some of the darker and more obscure texts in Johan's library, but he never expected to see it. It was said to have been an ancient religious artefact, revered by a former civilisation. But it had become corrupted over the years until the power it wielded was dark and twisted. Some scholars believed that it had absorbed the greed and lust of all those who had looked for answers within its flames, while others suggested that it was evil itself.

He stepped closer to it and tiny trickles of light spilled from its core. Looking inside, he saw the faces of his fellow conspirators, the other Commissioners who had gathered in Johan's outer chamber to plot the death of an innocent in order to maintain their grip on power. While they had schemed upstairs, the stone must have been down here in the dark, fuelling their desires.

"What have we done?" he asked the empty chamber. Then, as if to answer his question, the stone sparked to life. A great burning brilliance swelled from its heart and he covered his face from it. When it died back he lowered his hands and cried out. There in the centre of the stone was the face of a man, thin and pale with a haunting smile on his lips. He whispered a name. The name of the power that lay at the heart of the stone. Mallory began to weep. "Oh Johan, why?" Then he gave a short, strangled cry and his mouth fell open. He tried to step forward but his legs buckled and he crumpled to the chamber floor, the handle of a knife protruding from his back.

"You nosy great fool," said Johan Banberg, stepping around the pool of blood that was creeping over the stone flags. "You should have kept out of things that don't concern you." Mallory's breathing was becoming more and more laboured, a noisy rattle escaping from his lips as his life slipped away. His eyes stared upwards, blinking slowly. Tendrils of green vapour reached from the Monkton Stone and teased his body. As they touched his flesh an apparition, the dying man's soul, rose up to the ceiling of the small stone room and hung there.

"You need to understand", said Johan, looking up at the flickering form of his old friend, "this is about so much more than who is in charge. You thought it was about stopping people believing in God, about making them worship us instead. But it's not. It's about making them worship the right God."

The hovering soul of Peter Mallory looked down and pointed at the Monkton Stone. "Yes that's right Peter; I have a new Father now. I grew tired of waiting for our old God to do anything useful for me at all. All those years of obedient service and he never once even showed his face. Then I began reading in my books about one who had so much more to offer so I decided to switch allegiances. He welcomed me with open arms and guided me to this most wonderful stone. And that's just the beginning. When I've ignited the sparks of hate and greed that live in the hearts of men I'll unleash a power that makes any nonsense about a Messiah pale into nothing. When enough of those fires are lit, He will take on human form. He will walk among us Peter. He will rule on Earth as He does in Hell."

The tentacles of green light reached up to Mallory's soul and drew it towards the stone. The phantom tried to scream but no sound came from its dead lips and it was pulled into the jewel on the plinth. "You are part of my Father's Kingdom now

Peter," said Johan with delight. "You have become one of His foot soldiers."

* * *

At the house, Rebecca dozed in a chair near the fire while Anthony and Daniel sat by the window. "What will we do now?" said the big man.

"I was told to lead you here to this house; nothing was said of what would happen after that. I think my visitor thought we'd work that out for ourselves."

"But the Militia aren't likely to give up looking for us are they? Not after you shot their officer."

Daniel Weller grimaced. "That wasn't really part of my plan but I knew he'd kill you if he got to the top of the steps. And he did try to shoot me first." He sounded unconvinced by his own words.

There was a noise from outside the window and the two men jumped to the glass. Shadows could be seen moving up the path towards the gate. They slipped into the courtyard and for a moment passed through a pool of moonlight. "Militiamen," cursed Daniel and his hand went to the pistol at his belt.

"There's too many of them for that," whispered Anthony, "and anyway, they don't even know we're here." As the words left his mouth, one of the horses whinnied noisily at the back of the house. Daniel rolled his eyes and pulled the weapon free. But then there was more movement from outside. "Look!" Anthony pointed through the window. "They're going away."

The Militiamen were moving back out of the courtyard and through the gateway. Daniel was baffled. "They've found out we're here," he said, "so why aren't they coming to get us?" There was now no sign of them in the yard or on the path and the only movement outside was the wind stirring the branches of the trees.

"There," said Anthony, after a minute of staring into the dark. "Coming through the gate." Daniel followed his gaze and saw what looked like a series of tiny lights floating across the ground. As they drew near they formed together into four thin shapes that moved over the courtyard. Anthony and Daniel drew back from the glass as the shapes came nearer and they saw them for what they were; human figures that drifted towards the house like smoke. They came to the wall and stopped.

"What are they?" asked Daniel, his pistol hand limp at his side.

"I think I know," said Anthony, his voice deep and dark. "There was something they used to talk of in the villages round my way when I grew up. They used it to scare the children."

"What?"

"They called them stolen souls. The spirits of those on the very edge of death which are caught by the darkest magic there is. They become trapped like slaves."

"Can they harm us?" asked Daniel, peering at the ghostly shapes outside the window. They were looking at him through the glass, the stolen souls of three men and a woman. He could see right through them if he tried. Their bodies were pale and weightless and they moved on the same breeze that rustled the leaves in the trees. But when he looked at their faces and saw the deep darkness where their eyes had been, he felt a cold terror wash over him. He knew that if Anthony answered yes, then they were all doomed.

"Oh yes," said Anthony, "they'll make us suffer like they do."

The two backed further into the room, towards the fire. Anthony shook Rebecca awake. He half considered leaving her asleep so that at least she would not suffer the fear that was choking him now. But she would want to go down fighting.

She opened her eyes and squinted at him, her dreams still fogging her vision. "Can't you leave me?" she said.

"There's no time," said Anthony, pointing to the window. But there was nothing there. The two men rushed over but they could see no sign of the ghosts. The courtyard was dark.

As they dropped back in relief Rebecca spoke from her place by the hearth, "they're inside." Turning, they found themselves face to face with the stolen souls. The female had hair which flowed over her slender shoulders and she reached out a hand to Daniel's face. The others moved their mouths in a chorus of low, desperate moaning that filled the room. Anthony stood rooted to the spot. It had been a trap. They had been saved from the tower in Renwick Bay and brought to this place to be fed to these monsters. He would rather have died at the hands of the Militia.

By the fire, Rebecca stirred from her seat. She rummaged in her bag, frantically turning it inside out as she searched desperately for something. "It's here," she said, "I know it is. Foxton gave it to me when he left with Alex. He said I had to keep it safe and I did."

Daniel's breath formed tiny clouds of steam as the air around him grew chill. He felt something inside him move up through his flesh and bones as he gazed into the dead, wasted face of the stolen soul. He was about to join her. The stranger had lied and abandoned him.

"Ah, here it is," cried Rebecca, holding out her hand. In her upturned palm lay a small stone. Not a gem or a jewel but a beautiful, smooth, grey pebble with a single vein of white running through it. "I know you brought us here Alex Preston," she called out, "I haven't forgotten you."

The pebble exploded into life. Ribbons of light fired from it in all directions, illuminating the room. Several pierced the bodies of the stolen souls. They reared up like animals, the low moan becoming a high shriek, and they flew at Rebecca. But the light from the stone drove them away. They covered their faces and shrank back, reaching for each other in a pathetic embrace.

Then from the pebble came a figure, indiscernible as either man or a woman, that flew at them with silver wings. It reached out a hand and drew the nearest phantom, one of the men, back towards Rebecca. There was a pulse of light and the two were gone. Then came another and it too led one of the spirits away by the hand. A third figure appeared and did the same, leaving only the stolen soul of the woman remaining.

What made the stolen souls so terrifying were the expressions of desperate torment and loneliness they carried on their faces. The prospect of sharing in that misery was enough to freeze blood in its veins. But now, as another winged creature emerged from the pebble and took the woman by the hand, she looked blissfully calm and at peace. As she too was released from her earthly prison she turned to Rebecca and smiled with joy. Then she was gone.

Even then the light from the pebble grew brighter. It spilled out through the windows and illuminated the courtyard with the power of a thousand lanterns. Down the bridleway the Militiamen were lurking, waiting for the demons their master had sent to finish their work so that they could retrieve the bodies for disposal over the cliff top.

They saw a brilliant light coming from the house at the top of the hill. It flowed down the path and engulfed them, exposing them for what they were: dirty hired assassins skulking in the weeds. When they looked up they saw a flock of beautiful winged creatures hovering above the old mansion, as if keeping watch. By the time the men reached the bottom of the hill it was as if night had turned to day.

Chapter Twenty

Separate Ways

Surveillance was the part of the job they hated most; sitting in a car, staring at buildings for hours on end. On good days it was bearable, on bad days it was torture. This was not a good day. From their position across the road they could see the small window in the front room of the flat, the flickering glow of the television lighting up the grubby net curtain. They had seen the older man go in over an hour earlier, slipping through the faded blue door next to the charity shop. The time of his arrival was noted down in the little book that one of the men held on his lap. "How long do you reckon they'll stay in there?" he asked his colleague, who was sitting in the driver's seat, sipping from a steaming paper cup.

"They'll be out eventually," the coffee drinker said, between mouthfuls. "They're like a pair of lovebirds. The old bloke comes round at the same time every day and after a couple of hours they go out. Normally to the pub. I reckon they'll leave in about ten minutes."

"Who the hell are they anyway?"

"No idea. We've just been told to pick them up."

"Somebody must be pretty keen on the pair of them," said the man with the book, "but they have to be the most boring targets ever. My leg's gone numb sitting here. They don't do anything."

"It's the younger one they're after, I think. I heard someone say there'd been a tip off about him. The older bloke's just incidental."

"So what happens when they come out?"

"Haven't you heard? We got the nod this morning. The minute they're out we take them."

* * *

"Things are getting worse," said Foxton, looking at the television. A multicoloured map was being used to show the positions of different military forces on either side of a dotted border.

"I know," said Alex, bringing two mugs of tea in from the kitchen. "They reckon it'll be all out war by the weekend."

Foxton took his tea and sat in the old armchair, dunking his biscuit in the hot drink. "It's not right," he muttered.

"When is it ever?" Alex said, paying less attention to the news than to the search for a clean spoon.

"No, I mean something here is very wrong," Foxton said, as his biscuit slowly dipped in and out of the tea. "I can sense something dangerous at work. There's some kind of mischief being made here but I can't figure it out."

"You mean someone's stirring things up?" asked Alex.

"It looks that way," Foxton said, "but I don't know how or why. This is covering such a large area that a person would have to be in two places at once and wars seldom benefit the individual. I only know one…" He went quiet as he studied the images on the screen and then jumped back with a cry of alarm and dismay.

"What is it?" shouted Alex. "What have you found?"

"Nothing," said Foxton. "I've just lost my biscuit in my tea."

A while later, with the television muted, the two men were locked in a discussion of a different kind. "You still don't feel ready to go home?" Foxton asked. "Even though you've taken a step towards accepting who you are?"

"Well, for a start I still don't know who or what I am meant to be, so I'm nowhere near accepting anything. And I don't think they'd be safe if I went back. People around here are starting to notice things. The local paper ran a story about a guardian angel saving that girl in the car, even though I ran off before the police arrived. And there was a fire in one of the flats above the arcade last week…"

"That was you, was it?" asked Foxton, feigning surprise, "I read about that."

"Unless you know of any other fool who walks through a blanket of smoke to fish out an old lady, then I guess so. I'm finding it hard to resist but I know that sooner or later someone's going to follow me home."

Foxton was quiet again. He was on the verge of telling Alex something, biting his thumb nail as he wrestled with his thoughts. There was so much that he had not yet shared with his friend; about his destiny and the secret he carried. "There will be greater challenges to face," was all he eventually said, before suggesting that they retire to the Crown and Sceptre.

* * *

"Here we go." Coffee Drinker threw down his empty cup as the blue door opened and Foxton appeared. Notebook Man led the way as the pair got out of the car and stepped into the road. When he was halfway across, he saw two other men approaching the target along the pavement.

"What?" No one had told him that there was another unit on the job. He assumed they were a back up squad but as they drew nearer he changed his mind. The pair had close cropped hair, almost shaven, and wore matching dark jackets. He stopped in his tracks when he spotted the automatic pistol that one of the men produced from a pocket. "Get to the car, he's armed…" he shouted back to Coffee Drinker before a shot rang out. Notebook Man's body was whipped around as the bullet caught him in the chest and exploded out through his back. He spun to the ground, his legs twisting up under his body and a large pool of blood forming around him. His colleague knelt by his side as the light around him dimmed and went out. There was a screech of tyres and a large car with tinted windows pulled up and a door flew open. The men in dark jackets pushed Alex and Foxton inside and the car sped off.

On the street, Coffee Drinker screamed into his mobile phone for an ambulance. It arrived within minutes but by then Notebook Man's skin was already turning grey. The paramedics did what they could at the scene before transferring him to the ambulance. As it sped away with lights flashing, Coffee Drinker stayed behind to await the arrival of his superiors.

In the back of the ambulance, Notebook Man lay on the fringes of death. Then he opened his eyes. "Hello Peter," said a voice. Sitting beside his stretcher, surrounded by a pulsing aura of white light, was Alex Preston, the man he had been sent to pick up. The paramedic, who was busy checking blood pressure levels, seemed not to have noticed her extra passenger. "You're dying Peter. You know that don't you?"

"Yes. I can feel it coming," Notebook Man said through lips caked with blood.

"Were you going to do me harm?" Alex Preston asked.

"No," he said, with a voice that grew weaker with each painful breath. "We were just going to arrest you. They said..." He paused and fought for the strength to carry on. "They told us you were dangerous and needed taking off the streets."

"But I'm not dangerous. I'm not the one who put you here am I?"

"No." His voice was just a whisper and he closed his eyes as the pain grew too strong to continue.

"I can see what kind of a man you are Peter Allen. You're a good one. Inside you there's love for very many people and they don't deserve to be without you just yet. And I reckon the world will need good men before this is all over. Consider this a gift." Then the man that Peter was supposed to have arrested leaned forward and laid a hand on his chest, above the bloodied emergency dressing. At once there was a feeling of warmth that spread through Peter's skin and into his flesh. He arched his back as a wave of ecstasy reached out to ignite the nerve endings at his furthest extremities. The paramedic leapt from her seat as Peter bucked upwards on the stretcher. The readings on the monitoring equipment went haywire as he thrashed about violently. Then just as suddenly he fell back and lay still.

As the ambulance pulled up outside the hospital, staff came running to rush their patient inside. When they opened the doors of the vehicle they fell back in shock and confusion. Peter Allen was sitting up on his stretcher, examining the bullet hole in the front of his shirt.

* * *

Alex was in some sort of old industrial building, maybe a factory or warehouse. The roof was made up of heavily stained glass skylights and steel pillars rose from a concrete floor that was littered with discarded machinery and metal debris. Occasionally a rat would scuttle along beside one of the walls, its feet making a dry scratching sound on the ground.

The chair he was sitting on rocked unsteadily on its worn wooden legs. Alex had his hands tied behind his back and he sat impassively as a man in an expensive looking suit walked back and forth before him. "Alex, I know what you can offer me. I've been told what you can do."

"Really?" said Alex with a smile, "And who have you been talking to?"

"Names aren't important. Let's just say that someone who seems to know a lot about you came to see me and we had..." He paused and stopped his pacing "...a conversation. Certain things were said Alex, that convinced me you'd be very useful to my organisation."

Alex felt something stir within him. It reminded him of the way he had felt when Rebecca had been swallowed by the crowd in Archangel: like energy rushing through spaces inside him. It made a deafening sound, a dark noise in his head. "I know who you are," he said, "You're Michael Petan. You're a multi-millionaire."

"A billionaire actually."

"That's not what you tell the tax man."

"Ouch. That hurt. But you're right," the man said with a smirk. "I'm also an industrialist and investor."

"And a gangster and a crook," said Alex; the sensations inside him were flaring up. Words began to fill his head and spill from his lips. "You run corrupt politicians on three continents and lie and cheat in everything you do. You say it's human nature. You've already been responsible for over a dozen deaths and now you're looking at growing your empire even further."

Petan stared at him. "My visitor said you were something special. He was right. But do you know what I want from you?"

Alex stared back. His abductor was young and clean shaven with perfect looking skin, combined with an expensive haircut and finely tailored suit. He reeked of wealth and power.

"You like what you see, don't you?" Petan said with a grin.

"You couldn't be more wrong,"

As he looked at Petan, Alex saw the faces of the man's victims; not just those he had killed but the many whose lives he had ruined through his unstoppable greed. The dark noise roared inside his head. "And I do know what you want from me. You want me to help you gain even more power and wealth. You think there are talents I possess that would be useful to you." Another rat crept across the floor, sniffing the air as it went. "And you're so twisted inside that you bring me here to try and scare me into doing what you want."

Petan sighed. "This is such a wasted opportunity Alex. But I had half expected this kind of reaction. Still, it's always good to have a fall back plan."

"Like what?"

"Let me show you." Petan waved at his bodyguard, a heavy set man in a black jacket, who went to a door at the far end of the building. He returned moments later with a colleague and between them they were half carrying, half dragging something under a blanket. Then the cloth was thrown back and Foxton's bruised face appeared, his eyes blinking painfully.

"What have they done to you?" Alex said.

"Nothing too bad," Foxton answered, "just a little slap and tickle."

"Your friend is putting on a very brave face you know," Petan said to Alex, "but in a few minutes he won't have such a stiff upper lip. I just wonder how far we'll get before you see sense." He smirked and a small chuckle escaped from his lips as he laughed at a private joke. He could barely contain himself. "I'll let you into a secret. Part of me was hoping you might actually try and stop us playing a few games with your friend here; after all I'd heard about you. Still, you can't have everything I suppose."

"I'm not going to work with you Petan," Alex spat. "The best thing for you is to leave us both alone and walk away." He could feel the dark noise inside him again but now there was something alongside it. It was the fearful shadow that had chased him through the woods so many weeks ago. Now it was moving inside him and mixing with the feeling of power that pulsed in his body. The two were ready to explode.

"You're such a clever man," he said, "I know every thought you've ever had. But you're only happy when you're taking from others. And your own greed blinded you to the dangers of kidnapping me off the street and bringing me to this rat hole. It might work on your rivals, you silly little gangster, but it doesn't work on me. I'm going to make you pay for hurting my friend."

Petan finally gave up on any hope of forcing Alex to work for him. The visitor who had suggested Alex would be a useful tool had also warned that he might refuse to join him. If that happened, he had suggested killing him quickly and burning the body immediately.

"This has been such a waste," he said. "You could have really been part of something. Now I've got to end this." He gestured to his two men, who began to drag Foxton back towards the door, and then he reached into his pocket and brought out a small pistol which he pointed at Alex.

"You know I won't let this happen," said Alex. "Didn't your little birdie tell you who I was?" As he spoke, he tried to read Petan's mind, to discover the identity of the individual who had set him up but the images were blurred. Petan's brain was racing too fast.

"I have to kill you," the man said. "It's something I've done before, as you know."

"But I can bend heaven and earth. I can hold time in the palm of my hand." The words were flowing from Alex's mouth in a torrent and he felt himself losing control completely. "The power in me is older than the sun, than the stars. It runs in every grain of sand and every drop of rain." The knots binding his wrists uncoiled themselves and the rope slipped to the floor. He took a single step forward. "If I want to move whole planets I can. So if I decide that your shiny little gun was never actually made, that the metal in your hand was never even forged, I only have to think it."

Petan made a sound like a strangled whimper and opened his hands. There was nothing in them. "It was never made," said Alex. "Never built and bought by a disgusting little man like you." Petan was staring at his hands in shock, turning them over and over in the hope that the weapon might somehow reappear in his grasp. Then he turned and ran.

Alex ignored him. Instead he turned to the other men, who were dragging Foxton across the floor towards the doorway. One went to reach for the gun concealed in his jacket, but Alex covered the distance to the door too quickly and grabbed his forearm. The man screamed as smoke poured from his sleeve.

The words that Alex had spoken to Petan felt like they belonged to someone else and now his whole body seemed to be acting under the command of another. He pushed the henchman to the floor and held him there by the arm. "How much blood is on your hands?" he spat, as the smoke continued to stream upwards. "Look at them, see how stained they are."

The man turned his hands over as Alex released his grip. He stared at his palms and saw they were running with blood. As he knelt on the concrete floor he held his hands up in front of his face and began sobbing like a child. As the blood flowed across his skin, faces appeared, of those he had despatched at Petan's request. There was his boss's old partner whom he had shot in a hotel room, one of his rivals whom he had drowned with his bare hands and another he had stabbed. The faces reared up out of the blood on the henchman's skin and cried for the justice that had never been brought to bear on their executioner. It was enough to drive him to the edge of insanity.

Henchman Number Two let go of Foxton and began to run towards the main exit from the building. Alex turned to Foxton and said, "Are you okay?"

"I'll survive. I've been through worse. But you must slow down. Stop what you're doing before..." But Alex was not listening. He had begun a slow jog in pursuit of the bodyguard, who was halfway across the open factory floor. As Alex ran, the dark noise and the fearful shadow combusted for a second time, transforming his body. His legs were long and sinewy and his jeans were replaced by scales. His torso was wide and muscular and adorned with the same lizard-like skin as his limbs. His head was large and bony and marked with a ridge of tiny horns. Six small wings sprouted from his back.

Foxton watched as the creature sprinted after its prey. With a dozen yards left it sprang upwards and forwards and vaulted onto the fleeing man's shoulders. Its clawed feet dug into him and its head leaned forwards to grin into the man's face: an upturned nightmare of razor teeth and black eyes.

The henchman screamed with such fear that Foxton winced. He knew there was little he could do to stop Alex now. "Oh, what have you done?" he said softly, as Petan's man crumpled to the floor, brought down by the force of his own terror. Alex jumped away from him and resumed human form.

"Now for the big prize," he shouted and gave a laugh. Immediately, the wooden chair had a new occupant. It was

Michael Petan. He was blinking in surprise and looking around in confusion and fear. A set of keys jingled in one hand.

"I was in my car..." he whined, his voice just a shadow of what it had been before.

"You'll never be far enough away from me," said Alex. The sensation he had felt in the crowded square in Archangel, of being swept along on a tide, had now taken over him completely. But instead of an urge to save he felt a compulsion to punish. He stepped round to stand in front of Petan. "What did you really think I was Michael?" he said.

The terrified man struggled to speak. "Just... just someone who had special gifts. Someone who could help me."

"But that's not what I am Michael. Do you want to know the truth about me?" Petan stared up at Alex and said nothing. He could hear the hysterical moaning of his two men, lying on the rubble strewn floor, and he fought to keep a grip on his own rising swell of fear. "Well I'll let you into a little secret." Alex bent down and brought his lips close to Petan's left ear.

Only one man in the room heard the words. Foxton was too far away and the henchmen were lost in their own worlds of fear and pain. Alex could feel himself whispering something, could sense his lips moving and forming the words, but the only sound he heard was a gentle rush of air. The words were meant for one person alone and when Petan heard them he did something he had not done for twenty years: he began to cry. A torrent of tears burst from his eyes and his body shook as he started to sob.

Alex laughed but he had not finished with Petan. "Do you want to see what you've really become Michael? I can show you something that no mirror ever could." He knelt in the dirt in front of the wobbly wooden chair and placed a hand on Petan's shoulder. "Look up," he said and Petan raised his chin from his chest. "Look at me Michael and see what your own soul looks like."

Alex's face began to glow. Like a flame inside a paper lantern, an orange light leaked through his skin. His veins stood out like lines on a map and then dissolved as the burning light swelled and consumed his face. Petan's weeping stopped. He gaped in wonder at the visions he saw in the brilliant light. The orange flare stretched out to touch him, so that he and Alex were joined as one. Then came the first scream. It carried across the floor of the old factory and up through the broken skylights. "No, please," Petan cried as the light from Alex's face engulfed his head. "Please no, please no!" he begged and then his voice dissolved into a high feminine wail. It hung in the air as he shrieked with the kind of pain that even his own victims never suffered. Then he fell silent.

* * *

Alex and Foxton stepped out into the sunlight just as the first siren could be heard over the rooftops. "I think we deserve to travel in style, don't you?" Alex said, holding up the keys to Petan's car. Foxton smiled weakly. The bruises to his body worried him far less than the change that had come over his friend.

"We need to get away from here and talk," he said.

* * *

When the policemen entered the building they edged cautiously down the narrow corridor leading to the old factory floor. The emergency call had said that someone was being tortured or even killed inside. The cries of terror coming from the old engineering works had been so loud that even the police operator had been able to hear them down the line.

When they got out into the main plant room they saw three men sitting together in the middle of the concrete floor. They looked grateful to see them. The one in the centre, a younger man with a sharp suit and neatly cut hair, sobbed, "We need to be judged. There are things we must confess." He laid a handful of bullets on the ground.

* * *

"There's too much vinegar on these." Alex put a chip in his mouth and chewed.

"You seem remarkably calm," said Foxton, "Considering what happened back there."

"What's not to feel calm about?" said Alex.

"You lost control," his companion said. "You may not even be aware of it but your powers are at work all the time. You've done more than save damsels in distress. There are events that you've triggered in the last few weeks that have come from…"

"From what?"

"From deep inside you; from something you have little conscious knowledge of. But in that factory you lost control of it. You allowed unhelpful and potentially dangerous emotions to creep in. I've been trying to warn you about this all along."

"You mean emotions like anger? Well that's hardly surprising is it? Those men shot someone in cold blood then kidnapped us and beat you up. There were going to kill us both."

"Anger is one thing," Foxton said, putting down his bag of chips and leaning closer to Alex, "rage and hate are another. Anger can make men do great things, like fight injustice and ease the suffering of others. But rage and hate are blind and ignorant emotions that drive us to lash out."

"Us?" Alex asked. "So you've lashed out then have you?"

"This isn't about me, it's about you. You've had plenty of time to 'find yourself' in the last few weeks. Now it's time to go home. Things will only get worse if you don't. I can't help you for much longer."

"No one's asking you to," Alex said, waving one of his chips in the air. "Certainly not me."

Foxton chewed his food slowly and stared at his friend. "But I am bound to you Alex Preston. I told you that when we first met. I have been since you were first born."

"As opposed to second or third born," laughed Alex, attacking his bag of chips with gusto. "If you are bound to me like you say then tell me the truth. Tell me what I really am."

"But I can't. You know I can't."

"No I don't. I only know what you tell me. So now I'm asking you; God no, I'm telling you to give me the answer. What am I? I survived my own death and I've been wrapped up in all kinds of weird magic stuff ever since. So go on Foxton: I order you to tell me who I am."

Foxton's usual calm demeanour was gone and now he was shifting in his seat. Under the oath he had sworn long ago he had to answer, but at the same time he knew that telling the truth might have terrible consequences. He had to make a choice.

"You're an angel," he said, without looking at Alex. Instead he stared out of the car window. "There are only a handful of you left and people like me have to look after you until you're ready to fend for yourself."

Alex sounded disappointed. "But that was the first question I asked you..."

"I lied," said Foxton. "I knew there was too much running through your mind at that moment." He continued to stare out of the car window at passers-by, traffic, shop windows: anything but the man sitting next to him. "But that is what you are. Part of a once great army. Now reduced to just a sad scattering of soldiers dotted around earth and the heavens." There was sadness in his voice and the faintest glint of a tear in the corner of one eye. "I'm sorry it's nothing more exciting but that is all there is. Now, will you please go home? There's... "

Alex took this on board very calmly. "Thanks for filling in the blanks Foxton; at least I have the answer now. And there's a whole world out there that could do with a bit of the old Preston magic. Home will be there when I get back. And if it isn't, I'll just make it so..."

"You mustn't joke like that. And I cannot leave you to do this. We're bonded..."

"Not any more. I officially discharge you Foxton Scarfe. Go forth and raise a family of little Foxtons or something. Find a nice little house somewhere, filled with books, and learn to relax. It must be time you retired."

"But..." Foxton dropped his chips on the floor of the car.

There was panic in his eyes. "I can't."

"Yes you can. You've done your bit. You raised me from the dead after all. Now go." Alex reached past Foxton and opened the car door. The older man stayed in his seat for a moment but then a look of resignation, mixed with relief, came over his face. He had finally given up. The door clunked shut behind him.

It was over. Alex watched his friend disappear into the throng of people on the street before turning the key in the ignition.

Chapter Twenty One

Countdown

The officer checked the lights on the control panel for the third time in a minute. He needed all three to be red before he could twist the large black switch clockwise. At the moment two were still green so he went back to his checklist.

The room he was in was not supposed to exist. Under two international treaties it was not meant to have been built but his government had worked in secret to construct it and now it was about to be put to use; for the first and possibly only time. When the black switch was turned, the rocket engines would fire and the missile in the silo, thirty feet away through a wall of hardened concrete, would haul itself into the air.

Its target was hidden within a programmed code of numbers and letters but it only took an educated guess to work out where it was aimed: at the capital city of his country's arch enemy. The two states were separated by a border that had been prone to shifting back and forth for fifty years. Now that dispute was going to be settled for good.

"Sir, all systems are working fully," said his sergeant over the intercom, from the engineering room on the other side of the silo.

"That's good," he replied, as calmly as his nerves would allow, before checking the panel again. Now just one light remained green. He felt his stomach churning. All morning it had been like this, as the deadline for launch had drawn nearer. An ultimatum had been issued that was based around enemy troops moving back from the border but it looked highly unlikely that they would comply. So unless he received orders to the contrary, he would be firing the missile in under a minute.

They had practised the procedure many times before but then it was just a theory. Now the reality of it all had begun to sink in. He wondered if he would have the nerve to turn the switch when the moment came. He proudly wore the uniform of his country's military but that did not mean he was ignorant of the consequences of what he was about to do.

The final light went red right before his eyes. He reached for the black switch. One half turn: that was all that was required to send the missile on its way. He thought of the cargo that it was carrying and the effects that it would have when it was unleashed on its target. He thought of the lives that would simply disappear from the face of the earth and of the others that would never be the same again. But he told himself that his leaders knew what they were doing: that his country's survival depended on him following their orders.

He turned the switch.

There should have been a low rumble as the missile pushed itself into the air with its massive rocket engines. But there was nothing.

"Sir, we have a problem. You need to come and see this." The voice on speaker was high and excited. That was not the sergeant's normal tone. The officer went straight to the engineering room where a group of men were huddled around a monitor.

"Let me see," he said, pushing past them. They peeled back with confusion plastered across their faces. The officer looked at the screen and blinked several times. His face gradually moved closer and closer to it until it almost touched the surface of the monitor. "Power down the system," he said. A minute later a heavy metal door swung open and he led the group into the missile silo itself. They walked along the gangway that ran around the side of the deep concrete shaft and looked up in disbelief at the shape in front of them. One began giggling like a child before catching a stern look from the sergeant and stifling his chuckles.

The officer had seen one of these before, on a postcard his brother had sent him from his new home in London. He had said that they would both ride on one if he ever came to visit. "As English as a cup of tea", was how his brother had put in on the card. The officer reached out to touch the red paintwork, just to be sure this was not an apparition or a clever trick of the light. He felt cold metal under his fingers and wiped away what looked like raindrops. Standing in the missile silo, in place of the enormous rocket, was a double decker bus. A large number twelve was displayed on the front.

Now he started to laugh.

* * *

Alex sipped his tea and sat back in the tatty armchair. He smiled to himself, like a man laughing at his own joke. The bus idea had been a good one, he thought. He had been watching the news, wondering what exactly to do next, when he had suddenly had the most vivid daydream ever. He had seen a group of men in green uniforms preparing to launch a weapon that could start a world war. At that point he had known just what to do. He had just reached out with part of his mind, part of his soul, and made things happen. It was simple.

He had taken on board the concept of being an angel with ease. It just seemed a perfectly natural thing, like describing someone as left handed or colour blind. He was an angel. There was nothing weird or spooky about it at all. He had never really been a religious person but he was happy to take on the role he had been given.

Slurping his tea, he thought again about that sudden vision of the men with the missile. It made him wonder if his old daydreams had been more than just the work of his imagination. Maybe they had been visions, glimpses of alternative destinies that only one of his kind could see. Perhaps they were part of what made him special, part of what it was to be an angel.

His musings were cut short by the television. The news was on all the time now, as the tensions around the world escalated. There were reports every day of fresh conflicts breaking out; of countries turning on their neighbours and of atrocities, massacres and the slaughter of innocent civilians.

He put down his tea. There was a live report from one of the war zones, where two armies were coming to face each other across the floor of a wide desert valley. A ragged line of white capped mountains could be seen in the distance as a camera in a helicopter panned over the scene. Two enormous dust clouds appeared to be moving across the sand from left and right. Each was being thrown up by a line of military vehicles that was racing over the desert. The television people had cleverly superimposed a dotted white line over the live picture, to represent the border between the two countries that were about to begin bombing and shelling each other out of existence. It was very impressive.

The armies drew up about a half mile from either side of the border. Gun toting helicopters hovered above the lines of tanks, troop carriers and camouflaged vehicles. Slow moving jets circled above like noisy vultures.

"You couldn't make this up," Alex said, half expecting Foxton to answer him. He looked around the empty flat and sighed. His friend had been right; something strange was going on here. The scene was too contrived to be believable. He leaned forward in his seat as if the truth might reveal itself if he was a few inches closer to the screen. The vision of the missile launch had appeared out of nowhere, now he hoped the same might happen with the person or force that was behind all this.

There was nothing. So he clasped his hands together on his lap, hoping that might help. Then at last something happened. It was neither a vision or a daydream; more a sensation, a thought or a feeling. He was standing in front of a barrier, a shadowy curtain that hid from view the answer to his question: who was stirring the pot of hatred around the world? He strained hard to see through it and could just make out the shape of a figure, sitting in a chair. It was nothing more than a vague outline, like a rough pencil sketch, but he sensed that this figure was watching television.

"Why am I looking at myself?" Alex unclasped his hands. This was pointless. As the sensation faded into nothing, he sat back in his armchair. He felt cheated.

* * *

Marshall was enjoying the spectacle. He had invested in a brand new television with an enormous screen, the biggest one he could find, just so he could watch his various plans fall into place. This one was the best. He had lined two armies up against each other like he used to do when he was a boy. Back then they were little green or grey men made of plastic and his mum would usually flatten half a platoon as she did the housework. But he loved to set them up on the floor before knocking them all down in a volley of noisy shots and explosions. By the time he had made the sound of the last bullet being fired there were none left standing.

Now he was about to do it all again, but this time he had real troops to play with and real tanks and helicopters to move around the battlefield. His mum's living room carpet had been replaced by a vast desert but the feeling of anticipation was just the same.

On the coffee table, the piece of the Monkton Stone sat flickering. It had become even more powerful in recent weeks, as the evil it had encouraged in the hearts of so many men and women had strengthened its grip. It flashed and flared constantly these days, as it sensed new buds of hate-fuelled energy bursting forth around the world. It was growing stronger and stronger, getting closer and closer to the point where it could open the door and let Him in.

Everything was working so well. Marshall's little trips had paid off. The seeds of evil he had been busy planting around the world had all taken root. When he had been consumed by the fire of the Monkton Stone, in Johan's chamber, he had seen a vision of what would happen if he helped bring about His return to human form. Marshall had been promised a place at the high table, a chance to decide his own destiny and control his own life. It had been worth the price of his soul.

He opened another can of beer and reached for the bowl of peanuts on the table. The generals he had visited were acting exactly as he had told them to. The two opposing armies were squaring up across the desert and any minute now would begin hurling rockets and bombs at each other. Then the infantry would charge in, just like his little plastic men used to do. It would be carnage. He chewed on a mouthful of nuts and laughed.

But then a movement on the screen caught his eye. The news presenter began shouting excitedly, his voice rising in pitch, "This makes no sense at all...there appears to be a train moving over the sand." Marshall started to choke on his peanuts. A London Underground train was moving along the dotted border line on the screen.

The piece of the Monkton Stone began to hiss and fizz painfully.

* * *

As the train doors slid open a wall of superheated air rushed in off the desert and wrapped itself around Alex's face. He recoiled instinctively before chastising himself, "Why should the heat bother me? I'm not even flesh and blood." He stepped from the carriage onto the sand. He had been expecting the desert to be covered with deep dunes but the surface of the ground was rough and rocky. Looking to the left, he could see the tracks disappearing into the heat haze. To the right they stopped just short of the train but even as he watched a new stretch appeared, reaching for the flickering horizon. At once the doors closed behind him and the train headed off into the distance with a whine and vanished from view.

He looked dead ahead. The first line of army vehicles was easy to see. There were enormous tanks with their barrels pointing upwards, helicopters floating over the sand beneath chattering blades and dozens and dozens of other vehicles of all shapes and sizes. Turning to look across the border in the opposite direction, he saw exactly the same scenario. This looked like two rival gangs squaring up for a fight. "Can you hear me?" he shouted. His voice cut through the dead desert air. He knew they could. "You will not do this thing. Turn around and go home." He felt like a teacher speaking to packs of fighting schoolboys. Across the sand he could hear the distant rumble of engines and the pulsing of helicopter blades. Then came a high buzzing sound, like an insect in flight but with a hard metallic edge, and there was the tiniest movement in the air from the direction of the first army. He stepped to one side and felt a pulse next to his ear as a sniper's bullet went past his head.

"Do not try anything so stupid," he called out, emphasising each word in turn. He had not expected to be shot at; believing that arriving in the desert on a borrowed tube train would prove enough of a shock to persuade the soldiers on both sides to stop in their tracks. But perhaps they thought he was a mind trick or a projection conjured up by the enemy.

There was a deafening roar from the side of the second army as one of their larger military vehicles burst into life. It looked like a truck but had a rectangular box on the back which was tilted upwards over the cab. Rockets were blasting their way from this and heading up into the air. He felt the dark noise rise up inside him and immediately the rockets dropped from the sky like spent fireworks and landed on the desert floor with a harmless thud.

"I said don't do this," Alex boomed. As the echo of his voice died away, he stood in the desert and waited for a response.

* * *

Marshall sat forward on his sofa. It was so like Alex to ruin everything. This was like being a kid again, with his mum treading on his plastic soldiers or sucking them up into her Hoover.

He had been hoping never to see Alex again. He was confident that Michael Petan would have either corrupted him or finished him off, using his considerable expertise in both fields. The Monkton Stone had inspired Marshall to call Petan, just as it had given him the idea to contact the security services as a back up plan in case the gangster failed to get rid of Alex. It was a task that had to be performed in order for Marshall's main duty to be fulfilled: only once Alex was out of the picture would the fire burn properly. He decided it was time to call for help.

* * *

The heat seemed to be increasing. In the short time that Alex had been standing on the sand it had gone from unpleasant to unbearable. But just as he thought he might pass out, he felt the scorching rays of the sun roll away, as if a heat shield had risen up over his body.

He turned first one way and then the other as he checked and double checked the two opposing armies. Beyond the noise of the machinery there was nothing; no sign that anything was about to happen. But suddenly it was like hell itself had opened its doors. Every single weapon on either side fired at once. Rockets and missiles flew, mortars thudded into the sky and bullets tore apart the burning air. And Alex stood in the middle of it all.

He managed to snuff out the first wave of weapons, reaching out with the power of the dark noise to swat them from the sky. They fell to the ground and broke apart on the hard baked earth. But they kept coming: more and more of the rockets and bombs, and he began to struggle to stop them all. The two armies were intent on wiping each other from the face of the planet and he was trapped between them. The air closed in around him and then came the familiar feeling of creeping dread, as the fearful shadow clawed its way inside him once again. He tried to push it away, to concentrate on the erupting battle all around him, but it was too much of a distraction.

Now the earth began to shake as many of the weapons found

their targets. Huge walls of dirt were thrown up as explosions tore apart the ground. Balls of flame ballooned upwards as tanks and trucks were blown to pieces. Shards of metal flew into the air then rained down, as the military machines were turned to blackened scrap. Alex saw one tank in the first army disintegrate before his eyes as it was struck by two missiles at once. One second it was raising its barrel to shoot, the next it had disappeared in a cloud of fire, sand and exploding metal. He was powerless to stop it.

* * *

On the dusty road, the man in the dark suit heard a rumble of thunder. He looked up at the clouds, high above the open fields, and smiled. "Mr Preston feels afraid," he said "He's trying to use the power within him but now he's scared." The man watched as the clouds drifted across the sky, moaning under their heavy burden of rain.

There were figures standing beneath the tall tree at the side of the road and he addressed them again. "My sweet souls," he said, "I can sense the pain he is in. The foolish one who was sworn to guard him had no stomach for the job and now he flounders like a fish. You can hear it in the air." He waved upwards just as the first fork of lightning struck the ground in the distance. "Oh that's so sad," he laughed. "All that potential and he doesn't know how to control it. Well, why don't we give him a little nudge?" The shadows by the tree moved and swayed, excited by the prospect of some afternoon entertainment. He singled one out: "You've had your little fun but I think it's time I stepped in and took over. Let's see what I can do, shall we?"

* * *

Alex was beginning to win back control, just managing to stop any more bombs from falling and nudging several missiles in mid-flight, so they spun off safely into the desert. But then he felt a sharp, stabbing pain in his neck and saw blood running down his shirt. He raised his hand and felt a small piece of metal sticking out of his flesh. He tugged it free and held it in his open palm: a bullet. Now the fearful shadow rose up inside him, furious like never before. It burned through his veins and ignited with the dark noise that had been swirling around inside him. He began to rage. "How dare you strike at me? How dare you even lift a finger against me?" He saw the man who had fired the shot: a soldier standing on a large armoured car, manning a machine gun. He knew the man's name, where he lived and when he was born. He knew everything that was inside his head. If the shadows inside Alex had not been so strong he might have held back, but instead he raised one hand and the soldier vanished. He was not killed; he had just never existed.

* * *

"Oh this is brilliant," the man on the road said. "There's even more of me in him than I imagined. I told him this would happen, that he was not strong enough to defeat me. At least not while he's flesh and bone. He can never deny what's in his blood. None of them can."

His audience of souls moved on the breeze. The thunder was rolling in over the fields. It was the sound of a great power being unleashed above them in the world of men. But here too, a power was at work. It was reaching out to twist and corrupt, to turn a will to save into an urge to destroy. The weakness in one human soul had given it the foothold it needed to cause chaos.

* * *

Alex was screaming. "You will do as I say," he bellowed and the words rang out across the desert, even over the sounds of war. "I can show you what you are, you are nothing compared to me!" The fire inside him was burning beyond control. He could no longer see the desert beneath his feet or the massed ranks of the two armies on either side of him. Instead, he saw stars and planets and a giant burning sun. "You will see who

I am and you will kneel before me." The black void of space seemed to fold in on itself like paper. "I'm in everything you see, in all you touch. You are never to strike me down." He reached out to one small green planet and tore away a piece of the fragile skin of air that surrounded it.

In the desert, the soldiers screamed as one. The sky had gone. There was nothing above them but an endless blackness, punctuated by thousands of twinkling white dots. This was much more than night, it was the view from a dead rock in space, from a planet with no life-giving atmosphere. This was their death. They saw the bottomless black space, where nothing else lived. They saw what they truly were and even as the air around them was drawn away into the vacuum, they cried out.

* * *

The man on the road was laughing hysterically. As the thunder rolled on, as the one in the world above thrashed about in anger, the dark suited stranger lifted his head and roared with mirth. For thousands of years he had been preying on the souls of men. He was drawn to their feelings of guilt, their desire for power and their lust for wealth like a moth to a flame. But he was never the one to be burned. He would merely whisper sweet things as they struggled to make the right choice, offering words of encouragement to those unsure of which path to take. He gave them empowerment; the chance to enjoy life without rules or regulations. He had no commandments or dusty old tablets of stone. He asked for only one thing.

The shadows by the tree were uneasy. The weightless souls huddled together as the thunder burst above them. "Don't be afraid, my little ones," he shouted, "this will all be over soon. I have one last trick to play and then I must ask one of you to deliver a message for me." He looked back to the clouds. The lives of mortals were such easy things to manipulate that he could become bored, but then every thousand years or so he got to make such mischief.

* * *

221

The screams of fear from the soldiers on both sides of the border went unnoticed. Alex was incapable of hearing them. The fearful shadow had wrapped itself around him and would not let go. The great darkness over the battlefield lit up. Flames spread from east and west until they closed in over the heads of the troops who were cowering in terror beneath the fiery sky.

Alex felt like he was being torn apart by the forces that raged inside him. One carried the power that he had used to save Rebecca from death in Archangel and to outrun the Lezard in the fields outside Middleton. The other was what had made him lose control of himself with Michael Petan. Now it was making him rage against the two armies here in the desert and he was powerless to stop it.

He heard himself shouting one last time, urging the men on the battlefield to run as fast as they could and take cover from the burning sky. Then the flames fell upon the earth.

* * *

Alex did not hear the knock at the door, nor the sound of Marshall letting himself in to the flat. He was too busy staring at the television.

"The picture's better if you switch it on," said Marshall, pointing at the black screen.

"I can't. I..." Alex mumbled. He turned to his visitor with eyes red from crying. "People have died. I killed them."

Marshall sat at the table. "I know. I saw most of it on telly, until they lost the picture," he said. "That's why I came over."

"You knew it was me?" Alex asked, his voice trembling.

"I guessed," Marshall lied.

"Oh God no," said Alex. "What do I do now? No one will understand. It wasn't my fault, honestly."

"I think people might believe what they saw," Marshall said. He was enjoying the twist of the knife and savoured Alex's agony.

"Oh God no." Alex slumped forward in the chair and cradled his head in his hands.

222

"Well there is one place you could go where you'd be safe. Somewhere where your magic wouldn't be quite so potent. It would be more contained there…"

Alex looked up at him and whispered, "Theland."

* * *

The man standing on the dusty road was happy. "Well done my friend, you've carried out my wishes perfectly. He'll be safely out of my way in that place, until I choose to deal with him in the flesh." He smiled at the sound of the last word. "Oh, that prospect does excite me. But there is one more thing I need you to do. Summon up some of my old servants and send them to kill his family. I hate loose ends."

Chapter Twenty Two

Cursed

Nicholas lifted the open wooden box by its carved handles and left the house. He hobbled across the ground, carrying the load uncomfortably in front of him. It contained the tools and materials he needed to fix the broken door on one of the homes opposite. He did what he could to keep the houses in a fit state but it was a job that he found increasingly difficult as the effects of old age bore down on him.

He got to the house that needed attention and set down the box. He removed a section of rotten wood from the door, then sawed a new piece to fit and nailed it in place. When that was done he took out a small brush and began daubing pitch over the wood to make it watertight.

It would need to be so, as the weather was on the turn and rain was on its way. He could feel the dampness in the air and had pulled on an extra layer of clothes that morning. He thought of the approaching winter with dread, doubting whether he could survive a season of snow and ice. That would leave Edward to fend for himself, if he did not succumb first. With the boy it was not the winter that posed the real threat but the ailment that was making him sicker by the day. He had held it off for far longer than the old man had expected but now had so little strength that he could barely walk more than a few steps. Nicholas had moved his grandson from the little room up in the loft to the main area of the house, where he slept in the proper bed while the old man dozed in a chair by the fire or on a mattress on the floor.

As he lifted the tool box once more and headed home, he wondered how many months it would be before Hambledon was an empty place. It was a grim and depressing thought but he could not help imagining it once its final human inhabitants were gone. There would be no one left to repair the houses, to tidy the ground and keep the forest at bay. Soon the trees and grass would grow where the homes currently stood. Then there would be little more than a few ruins to suggest that anyone had ever lived here. He shuddered at the thought and felt the beginnings of a tear well in one eye. It had been such a high price to pay.

A high price. The cost of keeping a promise made generations before. The penalty for not revealing the secret behind a passageway to another world. For years it had been nothing more than a legend to outsiders; a myth about a gateway to a place of scientific wonder. Even in a land overrun by magic no one took the story of the door in the forest seriously. Until one man with a burning lust for power had read of it in a book.

Then they had come looking. The Commissioners had arrived in Hambledon one day, demanding to know the location and secret of the doorway. They were led by a cruel faced bully dressed in purple who had met with Nicholas, as village leader, and insisted that he betray the door's magic.

He would not do this. His own grandfather had been one of those who had taken the oath to protect it at all costs, in return for being allowed to build The Village. That was the old name for Hambledon. It was a translation from the most ancient language of Theland, said to be the mother tongue of God, and had been given to this place by the one in the forest. He was the one who had said they could clear some land on the edge of the wood and construct a few simple houses, in return for protecting the doorway from the unworthy.

To break the oath was unthinkable. It had been passed down through two generations and was shared by every man and woman who lived within the green oasis among the trees. This was an ancient, sacred place and the one to whom Nicholas's grandfather had made his promise was spoken of with respect and awe. Some believed he was an ancient king or a knight, while others claimed he was a ghost from the trees.

The man in purple had been furious. He had banged the table and insisted that Nicholas give him the location of the door and the means to open it. Nicholas had responded with the truth: that he could not surrender its whereabouts and could not predict when it would next appear. "Even if you're lucky enough to find it," he had told the man, "the doorway still decides who should be let through. And I don't think it'll pick you."

This had sent The Commissioner into a rage. He had held Nicholas by the throat and, bristling with anger, informed him that within twenty days Hambledon would feel his wrath, unless the answer he wanted was forthcoming. Then he and his men had taken their horses and left.

A meeting of the villagers was held, at which some argued that the oath taken by Nicholas's grandfather had run its course. Others suggested it was a story that had been concocted to stop the forest from being overrun by strangers. They said it would be a simple thing to point the horsemen in the general direction of the doorway and let them find it for themselves. As they spoke they did their best to forget about the sense of precious magic they felt every time they walked in the great forest that surrounded them; the way it made simple daydreams and emotions spring to life. They knew this was a part of the bargain their ancestors had made but they put it to the back of their minds as they argued for their own survival.

At the end of the meeting Nicholas had overruled all dissenters and had sworn that, as the keepers of the forest's secret, they would never betray his grandfather's legacy. No one outside Hambledon would learn the whereabouts of the passageway to The Other Place. It would have been such a simple thing for one of the villagers to slip away and pass a message to the Commissioners; to draw them a quick map of the forest or jot down a few directions. But for some reason or other, no one did. Perhaps they were afraid of Nicholas's anger, or maybe in their hearts they knew which path to take. But in the times to come, even as death swept over them, they each stood by a promise made generations before, to an ancient king they had never met.

Time passed. Nineteen full days went by and there was no sign of the Commissioner's threat bearing any fruit. The villagers believed they had been right to stick to their principles.

But on the twentieth day it began.

Two women began to show signs of the sickness that would eventually engulf the tiny settlement. They complained of sore limbs and an aching head and were unsteady on their feet. No one thought much of it at first, assuming that it was a common ailment that would soon pass. But this was no ordinary illness; it was the work of Johan Banberg, the Commissioner in purple, and his dark magic. By the time the first stages of madness had set in, nearly a week after the women had first grown sick, half a dozen others had already been infected. They had the same aches and pains, then a fever and finally the loss of mind.

The agony for the other villagers was in watching their friends and loved ones suffer, while knowing that they would follow suit. There was no stopping the sickness now and it was developing more rapidly with each new infection. The week it had taken the first two victims to go from a few aches and pains to blind insanity was now just a few days. And the number of cases was spiralling. Every home in the village had been affected and those still untouched by the illness rarely strayed out of doors. Instead they spent every hour tending to their loves ones. While the sun was up it was bad enough; mopping fevered brows and listening to the chattering of the mad, but by night it was far worse. The wailing echoed round the village, as if each victim was trying to out scream the next. When death arrived it was a relief and a release from the suffering.

That was how it had gone on, until in desperation the surviving villagers had called in a physician named Francis

Speake. "If any of you are to survive," he said, "then you must unearth all those you have already laid to rest and rebury them in a single grave. Then pour over them sacks of lime. It's the only way to stop the infection." He said the sickness was most likely to have come from the stream that ran past the village.

So the bodies were dug up. A team of men, their faces covered with cloths, took shovels and began to unearth the remains of their dead relatives and friends. But when they were uncovered the men let out great cries of terror because none of the flesh had decayed, even though some of the bodies had been beneath the ground for weeks. They looked as if they were sleeping. At the moment of death the victims' faces had been twisted in agony but now they looked at peace: calm and serene. At the sight of them, Francis Speake had fled.

But his instructions were still followed through. The cadavers were taken to a place in the forest where a pit had been prepared. There, they were laid together like a family and the lime poured in. Then the soil was shovelled over them. But that was not the last grave to be dug. The remaining villagers had followed suit, one by one, and Nicholas and his grandson had buried them beside the main pit in the wood. The boy's own sister, mother and father were among the last victims and they buried them all. It was something no child should ever have to do.

And that was the price they had paid for protecting the secret in the forest. Nicholas tried to pretend that he never doubted their decision to keep their silence and stand by their oath to an ancient king. But when darkness fell on the forest he would dream of the dead hands reaching for him from beneath the earth and the great wailing would rise out of the soil to stretch his sanity to breaking point. It had been a high price and one that he alone had made them pay.

He and Edward had survived, at least to this point. He had no idea why, other than perhaps it was the Commissioner's way of torturing him for his disobedience. But he was sure that soon they too would succumb and then there were be no witnesses to the curse that had been laid upon The Village. He had once quietly hoped that the one who had made his grandfather swear the oath might return to save them but he knew that moment was long past. He went back inside his house and placed the box on the floor. His chores were done for another day and now he would go back to sitting by the boy's bed, watching him sleep.

* * *

The fire crackled and hissed as the pile of sticks caught light and sent flames up into the night sky. The orange glow created a pool of light in the darkness and the shepherd sat within the comforting ring of flickering amber. He could make out the shapes of his animals grazing in the shadows and felt happy that they were safe. The fire was enough to keep the shadows at bay, as long as he kept it well stocked. He checked the pile of sticks beside him. There were more than enough to see him through the night. He leaned back on his elbows and watched the flames reaching into the air.

In the darkness behind him they gathered. They could see the glow from the fire and it stung their cold, dead flesh. They moved around their prey in a circle but held back, out of the reach of the spiteful, burning light. While the fire burned, they were powerless, trapped between their hunger and the flames. Then their leader moved amongst them and they felt their spirits lift. After so many years in the darkness he was teaching himself how to dim the lights. He had promised them a feast fit for kings once he had gained the power to snuff out the torches that ringed the village. They could hardly wait.

But he was not quite ready for that task. First he needed to hone his skills on something a little simpler. The shepherd, watching dutifully over his flock in the hillside fields above Appledore, would be a perfect opportunity to see how much he had learned. He passed word amongst his followers that it was nearly time to begin.

The shepherd was looking out into the shadows, checking on one of his ewes, when he saw the fire jump in the corner of his eye. The flames seemed to die down for a split second, falling inwards momentarily before leaping up again. He assumed it was a piece of damp wood finally igniting, but then it did it again. The fire went out for a moment before coming back to life with a fizz. But it was far less bright than before and the pool of orange light spread only half as wide.

The shepherd grabbed his pile of wood and moved closer to the fire. He threw two large sticks on to the flames and watched with relief as they caught light. But his comfort was short lived, as once again the strange flickering returned. For a second the darkness came crashing in around him from all sides, before shrinking back to the edges of an even smaller circle of firelight.

He swore he could see shapes moving in the encroaching darkness: tall, lean figures that drifted around him in a circle. Fear chilled his blood, even though he was standing close enough to the fire for the heat to scorch his skin.

Out in the sea of darkness, away from the tiny, shrinking island of light, Avery Tavistock was enjoying himself. He loved to watch the flames die back at his command; the dimming of the fire beckoning him forwards towards his prey. But this was just the beginning. Once he had mastered the art of snuffing out the lights, once his power had grown sufficiently to break the spell that had hampered him for so long, then he would wreak his revenge on the filthy bunch of hypocrites whom he blamed for his years of agony.

The people of Appledore had turned their backs on him, had cast out one of their own like a stray dog. Now he would punish all of them. They were the reason he existed like this, on the edge of their world, sniffing around for scraps of flesh to satisfy an ungodly hunger.

Avery Tavistock had been the first Minister of Appledore, when the village was built by a small group of settlers who had moved west to escape the religious persecution that was rife at the time. He had overseen the construction of the church and had tended to his congregation's spiritual and emotional needs. Every grieving widow turned to Minister Tavistock for comfort; every troubled youngster looking for a purpose in life would knock on his door and every love struck couple needing advice on marriage would seek a quiet moment around his kitchen table.

Then one day he needed comfort of his own. His beloved wife Mary died of scarlet fever. Avery had held Mary's hand as she slipped away and prayed out loud that her life be saved. He swore to follow the word of God to the letter, if only the Lord would heed his call. The prayers became louder and more desperate as Mary's grip on life became weaker and weaker. In the end she let out a single gasp and was gone.

The Minister flashed back and forth between two different emotions: despair at the loss of the woman he loved and rage at being abandoned by the God he worshipped every day. In all his years as a preacher, he had asked for nothing in return. But on the one occasion when he needed his God to show himself, to show how powerful and loving he was, there was nothing but silence and pain and death. In his anger he threw his holy book into the fireplace. As it burned, he swore that never again would he be duped into believing in such an empty, heartless god.

Later that night he had a visitor. As he sat at the table, his fingers wrapped around a bottle of wine, there was a knock at the door. He ignored it at first, assuming that it was another of the old women in the village come to offer sympathy and a cold, bony handshake as a way of showing how they understood his pain. But the knocking persisted and eventually he pulled open the door, ready to fire a barrage of abuse at whoever was disturbing his drinking.

A stranger stood in the doorway; a tall, slim man dressed in dark clothing. He had pale skin and a thin face and smiled coldly as he invited himself in. "You don't mind if I join you, do you?" he said, as he brushed passed Avery and stepped into the room. What happened next became a bit of a blur, his recollections clouded in a haze of high emotion and alcohol. But he did recall pouring out his troubles to the stranger, who responded in the way Avery needed him to: he listened. For the first time in years, someone was providing him with a shoulder to cry on, nodding wisely and without judgement while he unburdened himself.

It was a revelation. Minister Tavistock felt a great weight lift from him. But at the end of the conversation came something even more surprising. An offer.

"I can bring her back to you, if want."

Avery sat with his mouth open, unable to make a sound.

"I realise how that must seem to you Minister, but you know my offer is genuine." Avery forced himself to swallow. He was suddenly feeling very, very cold. But still he could not speak.

"That's right Minister. I understand you must be a little 'challenged' at this moment. But you prayed to your God and he ignored you. I heard you and came round in person. But I don't have long. I can only stay flesh for a very short time. So you need to give me your answer before I finish my wine." He raised his glass to his lips.

Avery knew exactly who this man was and a voice in his head was urging him to run and hide. But then he thought of Mary.

"I want her back," he sobbed.

So a deal was struck. Avery's wife would be returned to him for as long as the stranger deemed fit. And then, when she passed on for a second time, Avery would become the property of his visitor; the one he had preached against so many times. He used to call him the Dark Knight but now he was the Minister's only chance of regaining happiness.

The contract would be completed in three days, when Mary would be brought back to him. That gave Avery enough time to tell the people of Appledore that he was leaving. Not surprisingly, he made no mention of the circumstances surrounding his departure, preferring them to believe he was simply too grief stricken to continue in his post. Once Mary was back they would quickly disappear and set up home far away from the village. He knew how seriously his parishioners took their religion and none would ever accept that Mary had returned from the grave, not even if he told them it was a miracle. They would think it blasphemy. And they would be right.

So he packed his bags and stayed in the house as the days ticked by. On the final night before Mary's return he sat at the table, soberly drinking from a jug of water. As the hours passed he grew weary and eventually his head slumped, he closed his eyes and he began to dream.

He was standing in a garden, filled with sweet scented flowers and plants. Butterflies danced above his head and the sound of birdsong rose above the gentle chuckle of water in a stone fountain.

"Follow the path."

He heard a man's voice, deep and comforting and looked down at the pathway leading further into the garden. He started to walk. "Follow the way you see," the voice said again as he passed under a vine laden with pale fruit. The sweet smell from the flowers grew stronger and he sensed he was approaching the very heart of the garden. Then he saw her.

As the path bent to the right he saw a wooden bench a little way ahead. There was a figure sitting on it and she turned to face him as he approached. A warm, loving smile spread across her face as he drew near. "My Mary," he cried, as he fell into her arms.

They stayed like that for a while, locked in a silent embrace. It was she who spoke first. "I know what you have done, my love, but it must not happen."

"What do you mean?" he asked, pulling back to gaze into her eyes.

"I'm at peace here Avery. There is no pain in this place. If I come back to you, I'll never be as I was. Let me go Avery, my love. Let me be at rest."

"But I only wanted to be with you again. I just…"

She placed a finger to his lips to stem the flow of words. Leaning forwards, she whispered close to his ear, "Don't you see my love? This garden is for us both. One day you shall be with me again. I promise." He began to cry. His tears stung his eyes as he held her close and wept. "You must not do this thing," she said more firmly, "I will not let you. If you lose your soul to Him then we may have a short time together again on earth but an eternity apart. Seek sanctuary in the church and He will not find you. He has other souls to chase and he will pass on."

They held each other for a while longer until Avery, wrapped in his wife's arms, felt his eyes close. Her warmth, her sweet scent and soft touch were like a lullaby. He began to sleep. When he opened his eyes he was at his table. The clock above the fire read five minutes to midnight, the time his visitor was to return to complete the contract.

The church.

Avery rushed from the house to the chapel at the centre of the village. As he reached the door he remembered that he had handed the keys back to William Peeve, the church warden. He sprinted to Peeve's house and began hammering on the door. After an agonising moment, a window above him opened and a head of grey hair poked out.

"What in the name of..?" coughed Peeve.

"There's no time," shouted Avery in a panic. "I must have the keys to the church. Now!"

"I don't much care for your tone Avery. And especially at this time of night. Come back at a more Godly hour."

"But I need those keys or the devil will have my soul. Throw them down!" he called.

"Have you been drinking Avery? You're not the Minister any more, don't you remember? You resigned! And just where are we to find another?"

"I don't have time to argue William, just throw me the keys," he insisted.

"Don't have time to argue? Then the devil can have you!" And with that, Peeve's head withdrew and the window was slammed shut. Avery heard a clock inside the house begin to chime the hour and he started to run from dwelling to dwelling. Few people even acknowledged his cries for help and his frantic knocks, but those that did shouted back for him to go away. The village wanted nothing to do with him. He finally collapsed in a heap on the steps of the church. He lay there, trying to stifle the sound of his own breathing, desperate not to draw any more attention to himself. The church doorway was in partial shadow; the nearest light source was an oil lantern on a fence post that illuminated only the first two steps. If he drew his legs up tight to his chest he could hide in the darkness and the stranger, devil or not, would not see him. He did this and felt safe, pressed in against the church door.

Then a gust of wind made the lantern swing on its mooring and the flickering light flooded his hiding place. "Good evening Avery," said a voice, "I do hate a man who can't keep to a bargain."

It had been a full century and still he was paying the price for his attempt to go back on the deal. If he had never agreed to the offer then he would have been long dead by now and reunited with his beloved Mary in the garden he had seen in his dream. But there would be no tearful reunion in death for Avery Tavistock, only the eternal punishment of being forced to walk in the shadows and prey on human flesh. Mary was lost to him forever.

He stood and watched the shepherd cowering by the fire. Pity and remorse were emotions he had long since forgotten; now he felt only bitter hatred for the descendants of those who had left him to his fate. But once he had learned to control the only thing that kept him at bay, he would make them pay. All of them.

With a wave of one fleshless hand the campfire was out. Now it was time to feed.

Chapter Twenty Three

Monsters

Elisabeth weaved her way through the crowds in the narrow streets that led to the Tower of Archangel. The bowl she held in her arms was covered only by a square piece of cloth and she held it tight to her chest to stop its contents from spilling out. She swerved to avoid a large, round man who was blocking her way and nearly lost her grip. Then she had to sidestep out of the way of two men carrying a large wooden chest out of a doorway. It was like a moving maze of city life.

Eventually she was clear of the winding alleyways and into the plaza. She hugged the wall to avoid being spotted by any of the guards up in the Tower: she was not supposed to leave the building without permission and that was rarely granted, especially for reasons as mundane as fetching some of her mother's special broth. She hid herself behind a moving wall of people and was soon at the foot of the Tower.

To the left of the main door, which was guarded, was a much smaller one that led into a basement level storeroom. She risked letting go of her bowl with one hand to push the door open and duck inside. From the tiny storeroom she went through another door into the main lobby at the foot of the Tower, bypassing another of the guards. Both doors should have been kept locked but one of the senior Tower Attendants, a teenage boy called Matthias, had taken pity on her and left them open. She moved quickly up the staircase. If she was discovered then both she and Matthias would be in a great deal of trouble. She wound her way upwards, constantly checking the stairway above her for signs of guards or Tower officials or even worse, the Bishop.

He was the one she hated and feared the most. Bishop Gerard was a man with not even a shred of kindness or compassion within him. He had imprisoned the Guardian and forbidden him from using his real name of Samuel. The Bishop wanted to convince the people of the city that their future safety and prosperity lay with him and bringing the Guardian back to the Tower was key to that plan. He had even blinded Samuel as a way of ensuring he would not try to escape.

Bishop Gerard had been cruel to her as well. He was the reason she was forced to live in this draughty place, away from her parents and younger brother. Her life consisted of ritual and hard work, instead of play and learning and this was all down to the Bishop. He had sent one of his officers to visit her parents one day, several weeks ago. The man had said that Elisabeth had been chosen to be the Attendant to the Guardian of Archangel, which was being brought back to the city after a gap of many years. He told her parents that she was lucky to have been selected and that this was a most prestigious position. But behind all his flattery and promises there was the shadow of what might happen if Elisabeth's mother and father refused permission.

The Bishop was the most powerful man in Archangel and in recent months he had taken over the running of almost every aspect of life in the city. He decided on the laws that governed the population, he ruled on how much tax should be paid and he controlled the police. But as powerful as he was, he still craved the adoration of the people and the envy of his rivals. Bringing the Guardian back was how he hoped to achieved both of those things and Elisabeth's parents knew that he would not allow them to spoil it. There were people enjoying the comforts of Archangel Prison who had crossed Bishop Gerard.

So Elisabeth's parents had no choice but to accept the "offer" of having their daughter taken from them and installed as Attendant to the Guardian. She still snuck home from time to time, like on this morning when she went to visit her parents in secret and brought back a bowl of her mother's broth. She knew someone who would enjoy it.

She reached the chamber immediately below the roof. Here, there was no escaping the guard but with a little guile she knew she could be past him easily.

"Who passes this way?" he said as she approached out of the shadows. When he saw who it was his tone softened. "Oh hello, where are you going?"

She lowered her head as if in prayer and whispered, "I go to the Guardian. I have duties to perform." She held the bowl a little tighter as the guard peered at it and sniffed.

"What's in there?" he asked.

"Holy water and oil," she said, "to anoint the Guardian's skin."

"Really? It smells nice," the guard said with a smile breaking out at the corners of his mouth. Elisabeth kept her gaze downwards, happy that her ruse was working. She did not see the way the guard, a man in his early forties, smiled kindly at her. "Well, you'd better pass then. I mustn't keep you from your duties." Elisabeth moved up the final staircase to the roof, smiling to herself at the way she had so cleverly duped the watchman. As she disappeared up the steps he laughed quietly, "Definitely smells like chicken soup to me."

The roof was perfectly flat and completely open. The first time she had been up here, at the ceremony to mark the return of the Guardian, she had been terrified of falling off. With no barrier at its perimeter, the roof seemed to tip downwards every time she looked across it. She had felt drawn towards the edge, knowing full well that it was a long drop to the ground below. Now, though, she had grown used to it and felt quite safe coming up here several times a day.

She could see that the Guardian was asleep. She placed the bowl down next to his enormous head and knelt beside him. She laid her hands on his thick, scaly skin and stroked him gently. The scales were dry and cracked but she still got a sense of how they had once been: smooth and polished like steel or silver. The Guardian's skin still held a tiny part of the majesty that had once captivated all those who saw it. The Bishop had brought him back here and had broken his body and his spirit. Fetching him broth was the least she could do.

The creature's single eye moved slightly and the pace of his breathing changed. He was awake. "Elisabeth?"

"I'm here Samuel. I've brought some of my ma's special."

He let out a quiet moan. "You shouldn't take such risks. You know you'll be punished if they catch you leaving the Tower. It's not worth it."

"I don't mind," she said, putting a hand to his face. His eye moved again but she knew he could not see her.

"My brave little soul," he said, "I never expected to find one like you in a place like this."

"I'm just being your friend, like you've been mine. Drink some of the broth. It'll make you feel better." She lifted the bowl to Samuel's mouth and he took a large sip. He made an appreciative groaning noise and smiled as the first mouthful went down. She had to feed him like this because for most of the day he was kept chained to the roof. Whenever he tried to eat from a plate or drink from a bowl he looked pitiful; like a stray dog wolfing down scraps. She preferred to feed him herself.

That was part of her job. As Attendant to the Guardian, she was supposed to look after his every need. It was a role that had been performed by countless girls before her, in the old days when Samuel had first lived here. The Attendant fetched food and drink, brought oils and towels with which he could cleanse himself, and would sit and read to him every evening. It was a tradition going back generations.

But not all traditions are good ones. The Attendants had been, like her, virtual prisoners in the Tower until they were deemed too old and a replacement was found. This was all part of the history of the Guardian of Archangel, which Samuel had shared with her.

He was old. His age went beyond any reference point she

might have; past anything she could fully understand. He was older than anyone she had read about in books or heard about in stories. He was older than anyone or anything she had known in her life. He was also the last of his race. They were magical creatures who could walk like men and fly like birds. In ancient times they were regarded as holy kings and treated with great reverence. He could remember the tribes who first lived on this land honouring them as messengers from God, able to cross the divide between the domains of man and The Almighty. When Elisabeth asked him if he could really do this, Samuel had simply smiled.

"They believed we were angels," was all he said.

But then, within the reach of written history, came a terrible plague that destroyed this race of wonderful creatures. Samuel spared her the worst of the details but he did tell her they perished one by one. Their deaths were so vile that the people who had revered them for so long became convinced that they must have fallen out of favour with God.

Eventually just one of the magic beasts was left. He was close to death and lying alone out on the open ground near one of the larger settlements. A girl who was out walking came across him and went to fetch help. He was carried to the village and nursed back to health, with the girl at his side the entire time.

Maybe he was stronger or luckier than the others of his kind, or perhaps the care he received in the village was what made the difference, but miraculously he survived. Now he was left alone in the world as the sole survivor of his race, with many centuries of life left ahead of him. The villagers, who had once regarded him as angelic, now saw him as a useful tool. These were troubled times and attacks from roaming gangs of brigands were common. Having a creature as large as Samuel to hand would prove a useful deterrent. So they approached him and suggested that, as they had saved his life, he now owed them something in return.

Although he was now physically healed, he was still reeling from the loss of his race. In a moment of weakness he swore an oath to protect the villagers, to become their Guardian. The young girl who had helped to save his life was given the task of looking after him, fetching him food and drink and keeping him company. In return he would fly over the village each day to make his presence known and warn potential attackers to stay away. It worked: the settlement remained undisturbed and grew steadily into a town and then a city.

Archangel. All the time Samuel watched over it, attended to by a succession of girls of a similar age to the first. Once they had grown too old they were sent back to their parents and another took their place.

Then, two decades ago, the city leaders saw how old and weary Samuel had become. Archangel was by then a great and powerful city with no need for a magical protector and they decided to let him free from his ancient oath. He flew from the top of the Tower on his tired and tattered wings and settled in a forest on the northern horizon. He would end his days there.

But when Bishop Gerard was appointed a year ago he immediately began to make plans for the Guardian to be returned. The city had been through hard times and some blamed it on the loss of Archangel's ancient talisman. In the pubs and taverns, drinkers would claim that the city's decline started right about the time Samuel was set free. In fact, it had already begun by the time he left and was mainly down to a collapse in the wool trade, upon which Archangel's economy relied. But when ancient flying creatures are part of an argument, reason is hard to find. Gerard knew all of this, but he also was aware that if he were to reinstall the Guardian in the Tower, then his public standing would rise ten fold.

So he hired a band of private soldiers, the Mercenaries of Brampton, to ride north and bring Samuel back. They found the woods where he lived and nailed a declaration to one of the trees. It said that unless he stood by his original oath of four centuries ago a girl of Attendant age would be punished with death.

Samuel was in many ways a simple creature and found it

hard to discern whether the Bishop was bluffing. But he felt compelled to return to the city, both by the threat of killing an innocent child and by the idea that his old promise still carried some weight. He submitted to the mercenaries' humiliations; their beatings and their shackles and came with them back to Archangel where he was blinded and chained to the roof of the Tower.

He told Elisabeth all of this except the part about the threat to her life. She was the one warm heart he had met since his return and he had no wish to burden her with such nightmarish thoughts.

The broth her mother had made tasted good and it filled him with warmth. He was enjoying another mouthful when there was the sound of footsteps coming up the stairs on to the roof.

"What in God's name is this?"

The familiar sound of the Bishop's voice rang out angrily. "This isn't a pet for you to feed your slops to, you little brat." Elisabeth raised her head as the Bishop drew near. His face was purple with anger and he was striding across the roof in a rage. "Get that disgusting mess away from him," he screamed and kicked the bowl out of her grasp. It spun across the roof, spilling broth as it went, and disappeared over the edge. There was a moment's silence before it could be heard shattering on the ground below. Tears welled in Elisabeth's eyes as she thought of how lovingly her mother had prepared the food. She began to cry.

"Stop snivelling, brat," the Bishop snarled and he raised a hand and struck her across the side of her face. She let out a cry as she fell back, her cheek stinging with pain. Samuel lifted his head and moved it back and forth, struggling to conjure up some vision from his blind eye. He stretched out his neck and found the girl, sobbing in a heap just a few feet away. He placed his face close to her and she leaned in towards him, her tears touching his scaly skin.

"You're pathetic, the pair of you," the Bishop mocked. "She treats you like a puppy and you..." he poked Samuel with a foot, "...you couldn't guard a cage full of chickens. I may as well have you thrown out with the rubbish." He turned and stormed away, leaving the sound of the child's sobbing behind him.

* * *

The voices of the grown ups could barely be heard in the small attic room above the Knight's Chambers. Gillan had to press an ear to the floorboards to make any sense of what they were saying. He could pick out a few words: 'estate' and 'tax' were being used an awful lot and so were some very big numbers.

The conversation had been going on for several minutes already. Gillan recognised the voice of Nathaniel Arbiter's father, Sir Torquin, and the family's adviser, Simon Tregarth. To the Arbiters he was the man who oversaw their accounts, legal affairs and property disputes. To Gillan and Levine he was a rather scary looking figure in a tall hat who attended all Arbiter family functions and would often call at Nathaniel's house to discuss important matters.

He and Sir Torquin Arbiter were raising their voices at different points throughout their conversation. Gillan heard Simon Tregarth say, "But they are your responsibility now."

A short while later Sir Torquin said, "These matters are already in hand, the estate has already been sold."

Levine was standing by the window in the attic room, gazing out over the rooftops of Middleton. "What are they talking about?" she asked. She sounded distant and distracted.

Gillan bit his lip. He had promised to take care of Levine whatever happened, but listening to the voices beneath the floor, he feared the worst. It sounded as though they were being sold on to another household, possibly to pay off some of Nathaniel's debts. Upon his death at the hands of the Lezard, they had become the responsibility of Sir Torquin. In theory, it was their positions that were passed over: page boy and chamber maid. But in practice it meant that they were now personally the property of the dead knight's parents.

They had enjoyed working for Nathaniel Arbiter. He could be strict and formal whenever other grown ups were around but there were times when he would sit with them and read stories from his old books. Even though he hated being a knight himself, he still loved tales of heroism and bravery and as time passed, Gillan had come to love them too. He would sit listening, with his knees tucked up to his chest, and imagine being a brave warrior or a knight saving a princess from a monster.

But now all that had gone. Since the death of their master, the children had few duties to carry out and spent much of each day shut away in this room. That was not always a bad thing. Sir Torquin had a foul temper at the best of times and since the death of his son had been prone to lashing out at any servants who came within reach. At least up here Gillan and Levine would be safe from his rages.

"Gillan?" Levine had turned from the window and was watching him expectantly. "What are they saying?"

"Nothing," he said, "I can't make anything out."

Levine was unconvinced. She was older than Gillan and knew how much he wanted to look after her. But she also had a greater understanding of the ways of adults and she knew that something was going on downstairs. Her old master's parents had no need for two extra staff and were bound to sell them on eventually. But she knew that as long as she and Gillan were together, everything would be all right.

The pair of them had been in service to Nathaniel Arbiter's household for more than a year. It meant they virtually belonged to him, living under his roof and working six days a week as servants to the Knight. Their one day off, a Sunday, was when they got to see their parents. Gillan's father was a blacksmith and his mother took in washing, while Levine's parents worked in a bakery. For both families, sending their children to work in service was a way to give them a better start in life, a way to escape the poverty that dogged them at home. Nathaniel Arbiter had been one of the city's more progressive employers, even sparing time for the two children to be taught to read and write. It was unlikely they would find a new home with anyone quite so enlightened.

Gillan lifted his head from the floorboards and went back to his bed by the wall. He lifted a small box from the floor and took off the lid. Inside were several rough sheets of paper with drawings on. They were sketches and scribblings he had jotted down after listening to Nathaniel Arbiter's stories. There were castles with high towers, knights on horseback and swords with magnificent shining blades. Even seeing Nathaniel being devoured by the Lezard had not dimmed his fascination for such things.

He considered doing a drawing of the giant beast, which was now attacking anything that moved along the Great Track that led to the city's western bar. If he looked out of the attic window he could see the smoke from fires that had been lit along the city wall to keep the Lezard at bay. No one dared move beyond the gates for fear of death.

Suddenly he heard voices being raised again. He jumped back to the floor and pressed his ear to the boards and listened as hard as he could. Then his body went cold and he let out a short, hard gasp as he heard the words he had been dreading. "It is decided," Sir Torquin said, "the estate is to be divided. The male servants will stay here and the females shall be sold. It happens at the month's end."

Gillan sat up and looked at Levine, who was still gazing out of the window with a distant expression on her face. Their worst nightmare had come to pass; they were to be split up. He wondered how he would ever keep his promise to protect her. Even if they ran away, Sir Torquin was sure to send men to bring them back. Then he looked over Levine's shoulder at the rising towers of smoke in the distance, past which no one travelled.

And he knew what to do.

Chapter Twenty Four

A Woman Scorned

Sarah stared out of the window. The tap was running and she had the iron held up at an angle to catch the thin stream of water that ran from the spout. She was supposed to fill the steam compartment by using the special plastic jug that the iron had come with but she could never be bothered.

Her attention was focused on a small bird that she could see in the back garden. It was hopping about the lawn looking for worms and seemed quite frantic. She tried to work out if it was in any way a metaphor for the way her life was at that moment; if it summed up how she felt about Alex and their paths through a difficult and demanding universe. But she decided it was just a hungry sparrow. With skinny legs.

The sensation of cold water running over her fingers brought her out of the garden and back into the kitchen. She twisted the tap to stem the flow and moved across to the ironing board. A small mountain of children's clothes was awaiting her attention and she sighed wearily at the sight of it. Socks lay on top of vests, which were piled on pants and t-shirts. The book had nothing to say about laundry.

The book. It sat on the worktop near the packet of biscuits that the children had been feasting on earlier. She kept it close at all times, for the sense of security it gave her and the way it would revive her spirits when she felt alone and abandoned. Within its covers lay secrets known only to her and the man who had brought it to her door. At first she had thought it was meant for Alex but then it had shown her the truth hidden in its dry old pages. It had spoken to her and revealed her part in this great scheme. It had shown her the reason for Alex's sudden departure and told her what she must do when he returned to her.

"The bearer of this power must have one to light the way, to guard his soul and cast away the shadows." That was the fancy way in which it had described her role in this tale and now she sat and waited for her cue. The book carried all this in its pages. It was a kind of guidebook and instruction manual, telling her everything she needed to know and giving answers to so many great questions. It was also a vessel for some of the most wonderful magic that had ever been created. But it still did not mention ironing.

* * *

"Step forward my friend," said Marshall and one of the shadows moved a little closer. It had the vague outline of a man but its head was shaped more like an oversized reptile. Its powerful limbs hung by its side and two black, pupil-less eyes regarded him with no sign of emotion. "You've been summoned to carry out my work. You know you are to kill the woman and her children. They are all his and must be slain. His bloodline will end here." The figure nodded slowly and silently. "She is unlikely to put up much of a struggle but first you will have to get into the house. There may be traps laid and she will be on her guard but I have thought of a way for you to get through."

Marshall grinned smugly and placed one hand to the reptile's head. The creature twitched and shook but did not pull back as his fingertips pressed into its flesh. Lights danced over its skin as the transformation took place and Marshall's smile grew even wider as he took in his handiwork. He had been so clever to think of this idea that he could hardly contain himself. It was almost art. For so long he had listened to Alex Preston talking about his wife and kids. For things to end like this, he thought, was pure poetry.

* * *

The three men walking up the street looked uncomfortable in their surroundings. It was the way they kept their eyes lowered as they made their way along the pavement, except for the times when they seemed to be sniffing the air around them in disgust. Several sets of curtains twitched as they went past. The lady at number twenty eight was indiscrete and stuck her head around the patterned lace to get a closer look. She thought she recognised one of the men but then he turned and fixed her in the eye. She suddenly felt very cold, as if she was standing in a draught, and fell back from the window. It was worse than when she was having one of her funny turns. She did not even have the strength to call for her husband, Clive, to come in from the garden to fetch a glass of water. Instead she slumped on the sofa and closed her eyes. But then cruel, ugly images reared up inside her head: hideous faces twisted in pain and scaly fingers reaching out for her. She snapped her eyes open again and sat staring at the net curtains. She would stay like that for the rest of the afternoon.

The men continued up the road until they reached one particular house. They looked to each other as if to confirm that this was the right address and then pushed open the gate and walked up the path. As two of them peered through the front window into a lounge where some children were playing; the third stepped up to the door.

In the kitchen, the sound of the bell was a welcome release from the ironing. Sarah walked to the hall and could see the messy outline of a man's head through the frosted glass of the front door. She reached for the latch and pulled it open.

"Oh my God."

Alex beamed at her from the step.

"I'm home," he said.

At that moment she felt as if someone had taken her life and turned it upside down. She had been waiting so long for this day to come, for her beloved Alex to return, and now it had happened. Everything around her seemed to move into slow motion. She moved back to let him into the hall and they embraced politely, almost stiffly. Then she saw he had two companions; Andrew Marshall from the office and Foxton Scarfe, the man who had helped show her...

"Is there a cup of tea going my dear?" Foxton said. "I'm parched."

Back in the kitchen she flicked the kettle on. This felt odd. She could see Foxton standing in the lounge, near Katie and Matthew, while Andrew Marshall lingered by the kitchen door. Alex came close to her. She still felt numb with shock and held her breath as he moved near. She found it hard to raise her eyes to look him in the face and instead flicked her gaze to the worktop. The book still lay next to the biscuit packet but now it was glowing. It did this from time to time but the light that shone from it was normally a warming blue colour. Now it was pulsing red. It had to mean...

"Sarah..."

Alex's voice was so warm and soothing. She lifted her head as he stepped closer. His lips moved to hers and he kissed her hard. She pulled back, uncomfortable at his sudden intimacy. He had said no more than a few words and none of those had mentioned her or the children. This felt wrong. Now the book went into overdrive. Its pages began flapping madly and it drew the attention of Andrew Marshall, standing just inside the kitchen. "Finish this," he said.

At once, Alex pulled back and his appearance began to change. His skin and features dissolved to reveal a lizard-like creature standing before her. A scaled hand reached for her throat. Sarah sprang back out of its reach, taking the beast by surprise and leaving it grasping at thin air. "I will kill you," it said in a coarse, matter of fact way, before reaching to its waist where a vicious looking knife hung from a belt.

"That's not going to happen," Sarah replied, edging further backwards.

"It must. The other has been driven from this land and now you and his offspring must perish." The lizard had drawn its knife and was coming towards her.

"Driven where?" she said, within reach of her goal. She needed just a second more.

"The land my Master will conquer when he has finished with this one. He has run there like the weak lamb that he is. And now his kin will suffer in his place."

The lizard darted forward, ready to slice Sarah's throat with its blade. As it did, it pushed aside the mountain of neatly folded clothes and sent them flying to the floor. "Don't mess with my housework!" shouted Sarah and she grabbed the iron. She turned her body so that it avoided the oncoming assault and then spun forwards to put herself in reach of the lizard's head. She rammed the iron into the side of its face and pressed the steam button. The creature bellowed in agony and pulled back. Dark blood poured from a gash in its skull and the flesh around it was scorched and blistered. It reached up to its face, dropping the blade on the kitchen floor.

"Call that a knife?" Sarah mocked and she pulled open the cutlery drawer. "This is what you need," she said and she took out the expensive French carving knife that Alex had so kindly bought her for her last birthday. The lizard let out a muffled cry as the blade slid into its neck and it crumpled to the ground with more dark blood pouring from the wound. Sarah stepped back and regarded Andrew Marshall. He too had undergone a change. He looked at her through jet black eyes and let out a low, rumbling growl that slid out from between his jagged teeth. The sound filled the room, making the windows vibrate and the cupboards rattle. This was his way of filling her with fear. It had worked with every human who had ever heard it, in their last few moments of life.

Sarah felt the noise hit her like a shockwave. The strength left her body and her legs began to sag and buckle beneath her. But just as she fell back under the force of the creature's growl the book sprang back to life. Its pages flipped over again, before settling on one in particular. Now Sarah heard words in her head; as she had so many times in recent weeks. "Stand steady and He will not touch you with His magic." Then she heard an incantation in one of the ancient languages that rested within the book's pages. The quiet voice filled her head and drowned out the assassin's blast of fear. She stood her ground.

The lizard grew angry. It had not expected its magic to be so easily beaten and it reached down to draw two blades from its belt. As it hurled them at Sarah she grabbed the nearest thing to her to block their flight. It happened in the blink of an eye. The reptile in the doorway saw only a vague blur as she raised the ironing board in the air and the knives embedded themselves in the patterned surface. Then she counter-attacked.

The board was spun in her hands so that the sharp metal edge, designed to hold her hot iron, pointed towards her assailant. She charged forwards with it raised level like a spear. The attack came with such force and speed that the lizard had no time to move out of the way. Instead it was struck in the upper chest and shoved backwards into the doorframe with a crack. Its head went back and it bellowed in agony.

Sarah released her grip on the ironing board, thinking the creature was crippled, or better still dead, but it was not. With one sweep of its arm it made a lunge for her. But she bent over and twisted her body so that it rolled across her back and hit the worktop. It pulled itself upright and saw that a small book lay within reach, with a flickering light leaking from its pages. "This cannot be…" it said and opened the front cover.

It stood entranced as the light spilled out and swirled around before its eyes. In the dark places where it dwelt there had never been such magic. The light moved upwards towards its face and the lizard caught a glimpse of the secrets the book contained. "So many wonders…" it said it a dry, rasping voice. But then there was a sudden, stabbing pain that ran through its head like a bolt of lightning. It let out a breath of foul air as the light dimmed and the book faded from view. Even the pain in the creature's skull dissolved to nothing as its scaly legs gave way and it slid to the floor.

Behind the dead beast, Sarah bent to retrieve the fondue fork that was protruding from the back of its head. The shaft was bent in the middle. "What a waste," she said and tossed it into the sink.

"Mummy!" The sound of a child's voice coming from the lounge made her spin on the spot. The third assassin was standing over Katie and Matthew, one hand reaching forwards to the little boy.

"We will at least have the children," he hissed and made a grab for Matthew's neck. Sarah held her breath. There was no way she could cover the distance in time and she had nothing on hand to use as a weapon. Even the book was silent. She began moving forwards but the lizard's hand was already upon her son.

Then there was a sound, so dim that she barely heard it. It sounded like words being whispered in the night. A spot of light appeared on the little boy's forehead. From it appeared a beautiful creature borne on glowing wings. It flew upwards, its body taking on new shapes as it grew before Sarah's eyes. It had a human face but she could not see if it was a man or a woman. Then the same light appeared on Katie's forehead and another of the creatures emerged.

They held hands around the lizard, which looked back and forth between them. Then, with a scream from the reptile, there was a flash of the purest white light and all three were gone. Sarah stood in amazement. The children were giggling happily. "I heard Daddy's voice," laughed Katie. "He promised me sweet dreams. Does that mean he's coming home soon?"

"I don't know sweetheart," said Sarah, hugging both children tightly. She thought of what the first assassin had said, about Alex being weak. But she knew from this that he had the strength to defend his family no matter where he was. Now she needed the courage to bring him back. This was the cue she had been waiting for.

She reached for the phone. "Annie it's me, Sarah. I know it's cheeky but I was wondering if I could drop the kids round with you for a while. There's a little job I need to do."

Chapter Twenty Five
Coming Together

Johan Banberg poured himself another glass of brandy and lit a fresh cigar. He felt a shiver of excitement at the way events were developing. The power of his Master was growing by the day, as fresh fires were lit by His disciples. In Theland, a land so touched by magic that it lived in every blade of grass and drop of rain, He could create chaos and darkness with ease. Disease, fear, hate and destruction were already spreading; acts of cruelty were becoming commonplace thanks to the work of the souls under His command.

In the Other Place, things were different. Johan had learned about this land from some of the books that lined the walls of his study. It had once been much like Theland. But then magic had left it, driven out by science and discovery. That was something that Johan envied, even though he was a religious leader. It meant power rested in the hands of men, not a God who appeared once in a blue moon. It meant progress and change. It meant wealth.

Johan had never found a passage there, despite his best efforts. There were tales of secret doorways that led between the two worlds but for years they had eluded him. When he had discovered that he had a visitor from the Other Place in his own gaol he had finally learned how to get through. But by then Johan had become part of a much bigger plan and the idea was a distraction. Instead, he took the man's soul and added it to his Master's collection. Then he sent him on his way. It meant he could wreak havoc in the Other Place by stirring up the evil that rested in human hearts. That would clear a path for Him to break free from his prison. Only when enough fires were lit would that be possible.

The trap that was laid for Thomas Peters had started out as part of another conspiracy, but Johan was only too happy to weave it into his grand scheme. His fellow Commissioners had only one aim: fuelling the population's desire for a Messiah and then crushing their hopes in the cruellest way possible. The aim had been to destroy the masses' appetite for a hero coming to lead them to a better life. They wanted to protect their own positions as rulers and to secure their place at the top of the tree. There was a prophesy, written in the very book that Johan had open on his desk before him, that a gentle stranger would appear who bore the greatest weapon of all: the truth. What the Commissioners had to do was make to make it impossible for him to draw even the smallest crowd. They wanted the people to follow them instead.

So they found Thomas Peters and used magic copied from one of Johan's books to convince him and others that he was The One. Then, when he had whipped up hysterical enthusiasm among the great unwashed, they switched that good magic for something far darker and sat back and watched. The results were as bloody and dramatic as they had hoped. Now no one would believe any talk of a Messiah. No one likes being suckered.

Behind all this was Banberg's other plan, the one that took precedence over everything. By cynically destroying people's belief in the Almighty he could make it so much easier for the real God, the one he worshipped in secret, to walk again as a man. When his Lord was King of both worlds Banberg would sit at His right hand and help rule over the two worlds for an eternity. People would not need faith because it would not matter. They would do as they were told.

Now things were beginning to move. The Monkton Stone, below his study in the secret chamber, had been growing more frantic of late. It meant that He was stirring and beginning the last journey back to the lands of men. Then the two worlds would know the real meaning of power.

* * *

The forest air was so fresh and clean that Sarah paused for a moment to draw in a slow, deep breath. It made her giddy. On the ground before her was a carpet of bluebells that looked so perfect she could hardly believe it was real. Above her, the branches of the trees created a green canopy through which trickled the purest light she had ever seen. She stepped forwards and found a narrow path that led away into the wood.

As she walked along she wondered how Alex must have felt when he came here. The Alex she had known when they first met would have stopped every few yards just to peer at a bird or a squirrel but over the years he had become much more withdrawn and cut off from the world. She hoped that this place had touched him like it touched her now.

She reached a part of the path where the ground rose and fell in great dips between the trees. After a few minutes she began to sense something moving away to her right, in the undergrowth. At first she thought it was just a bird or small animal but every time she turned away she could see a large shadow out of the corner of her eye. She quickened her pace but she could not escape it. The shadow was tracking her through the woods, always the same distance away on her right side. Her heart was beating faster and she felt minded to run but she knew that whatever it was would probably catch her. She had the book tucked in her shoulder bag and she laid one hand on its cover. At once her fear and panic subsided. She turned to face the last spot where she had seen the shadow move. There was definitely something there, standing a short distance away between two enormous trunks covered in moss.

She shouted, "The one who was here; the one who was so afraid. I've come to bring him home." This was her voice, echoing through the trees, but the words: they came from somewhere beyond her self. The moment she opened her mouth they appeared on her lips in a flash of inspiration. "I know you meant him no harm so please help me. Time is short and the shadows gather." Her hand went back to the book in her bag just as the shape in the trees began to move towards her. Her heart began to beat faster once again but a deep breath of the forest air made her feel stronger and braver, filling her head with its sweetness.

The movement in the undergrowth was getting nearer and nearer. Ferns and bushes twitched as the creature moved through them but she still could not see what it was. Then the bush nearest the path parted down the middle and...

"I know why you are here."

A man was standing before her. He was wearing clothes made of bits of leaf and bark with patches of animal fur woven in. He had a dark beard and soft eyes and his hair lay around his shoulders. A rough cloth bag hung at his waist and he rested on a spear. "I mean you no harm either Sarah. None who pass through this forest need fear me unless they carry malice," he said, dipping his head politely as he spoke.

"How do you know my name?" she asked, as respectfully as she could manage.

He smiled again. "The answer to that question would take us all day and you've already said that time is pressing. But I do know you and I know the man you seek. The first time he came here I tried to speak with him but the magic of these woods can overpower the unwary. At least you had your companion to steady your nerves." The man nodded towards her bag where one hand still rested on the book. "The one you're searching for was less well prepared. The ancient power that runs through these trees became too much for him the first time he came here. After that I decided that he should be left to find his own way. Perhaps that was a mistake."

"Who are you?" Sarah asked, much more directly.

"I am... the one who built this forest. I have been given many titles, some of them far grander than I deserve. But I am cut from the same tree as him."

"Alex?"

"He is part of what I am. And you know what that is."

Sarah's breathing had slowed to a near standstill. She could feel each lingering rise and fall of her chest as she stood before the stranger. She summoned up the courage to speak again. "Will you help me find him?"

"I know where he is. He has taken refuge with friends but it's a long way from here. I'll give you something to speed you on your way," he said. "There's already darkness spreading across this land and he is the only one who can stop it, so you must hurry." He reached into his bag and took out a flat, grey stone with lines running through it. "These can be found throughout Theland if you know where to look. You can use it to take you to your husband." Sarah reached forward and let him drop it into her upturned palm. "But you must be prepared for what lies in his path," he said, his voice becoming deeper. "Only if your faith in him is true will he succeed."

Sarah opened her mouth to speak, a question already forming on her lips, but the man stepped back into the undergrowth. "God's speed," he said with a smile and he turned and walked away. The forest closed in around him and within seconds he was gone.

She examined the stone in her hand. It was perfectly ordinary; just a small grey pebble with a pattern of pale veins running through it. But as she looked at it, the lines began to spread like tiny roots. When they reached the edge of the stone they kept going and left the surface, growing into the air like the branches of a tree. Sarah held the pebble at arm's length and watched as the fragile white veins spread outwards in all directions. They moved over each other again and again as if weaving a pattern. As she watched, a shape appeared in the mesh of interwoven white lines.

A door stood on the path in front of her, formed by the tightly knitted white threads. It seemed as solid as wood. Sarah stepped closer and could see a pattern running over its surface. She brushed her fingers over it, tracing the raised outline. She was sure she had seen this before and she reached into her bag for the proof. There, on the front of the book, was the same pattern running across the cover. Her hand reached for the door and pushed it gently. As it opened, there was the sound of waves washing over rocks and the smell of salt air. Sarah stepped through.

She was on a path, hemmed in by low bushes and small trees. It ran close to the edge of a cliff and away to her right she could see the sea shimmering under the blue sky. Seagulls wheeled overhead and there was a sailing ship moored a short distance offshore. She headed up the slope, just once looking behind her for the door. There was nothing there. She reached a bend in the path and saw a large house up ahead with a courtyard fronted by large metal gates. As she approached, a tall man with a beard stepped up and spoke, "Good morning Miss, may I help you?"

"It's Mrs actually," she said, "but you can call me Sarah. I'm looking for my husband."

The big man's jaw went slack and he stammered. "You? You're Sarah?" He fumbled at the gates and heaved them open. "Please, please come in," he said. He had suddenly gone very pale.

The man, whom she decided really was very tall indeed, led her across the courtyard and in through the front door of the house. Inside was a grand hallway with a high ceiling. A door on the right stood open and she could see into a large room with chairs and a sofa. There was a figure in one of the chairs that she recognised.

"Oh my God."

Alex looked up at the sound of her voice. The look of shock on his face spoke volumes. She was clearly the last person he had expected to see. His eyes were wide and staring and his jaw flopped in disbelief. "Sarah?"

"Nice of you to remember my name," she said as she walked into the room. "I presumed you'd forgotten it completely." Her voice began to waver. She dearly wanted to run over and throw her arms around him but at the same time she was furious at him for leaving her and the children; for putting them all through this. "I wondered where you'd been hiding."

"How did you get here? Why...?" He trailed off, the shock in his eyes replaced by confusion.

"The same way as you. Well mostly. I went to your office and got myself down into the basement. It's amazing what you can find down there."

"But..." he tried to speak but Sarah cut him short.

"I've come to bring you home. You should have done that yourself when you came back from this place last time. It's where you belong. Where I can keep an eye on you."

"You? Keep an eye on me?"

She wanted to slap him now. She really felt like dragging him from his chair and slapping his face. Hard. "Oh, that surprises you does it? Did you think I was sat at home waiting for you to come back and save me? I've managed quite well on my own thanks. I've even seen off three assassins that He sent to kill us!"

Alec looked stunned and even more confused. "Who's HE?"

Sarah walked right up to him and leaned in to his face. "You really don't know do you?" she said angrily. "You really have not the faintest idea of what's going on."

Alex seemed on the verge of tears. "I'm some kind of... thing," he said, "A demon or a devil or something. I've done these terrible things. I've..." His tears began to flow.

A female voice came from the doorway, "Alex, what's wrong?" Sarah turned to see a woman coming in to the room. She was young and pretty and Sarah felt a knot tighten in her stomach at the way she spoke Alex's name. "Who is this?" the woman said, walking up to Alex and placing a hand on his shoulder.

"I'm Sarah, his wife. And who are you?" Sarah said. At once the woman drew her hand back and spoke more softly.

"Oh I'm so sorry. My name's Rebecca and this is our house."

"Our house? You mean you and…?" Sarah pointed at Alex. The knot inside her twisted again.

"Oh no. No!" Rebecca cried. Then there was the sound of a door slamming and footsteps coming down the hall.

"Ten years at sea and I end up fighting a rose bush," said a tall, good looking man who walked into the room with a piece of cloth wrapped around a bloodied finger. He stopped short when he saw Sarah. "Oh, I'm sorry. I didn't know we had a visitor."

"This is Alex's wife," said the giant of a man, who was standing nervously at the back of the room.

"Oh my Lord," said the new arrival and he offered his injured hand, bandage and all, to Sarah. The other hand went around Rebecca's waist. "I'm Daniel Webber, Rebecca's betrothed."

* * *

A little later, Sarah and Alex were sitting on a wooden bench in the large garden at the rear of the house. "So what is this place?" she asked. She really wanted to grab Alex by the scruff and yell at him to come home but she forced herself to be patient.

"They found it empty a few weeks ago. The police here, they're like the Gestapo. They were chasing them and they found their way here."

"It's not exactly a fortress is it?" Sarah said, looking across the garden to where Rebecca and Daniel were working to clear a thick, overgrown rosebush from the side of a high wall. "It wouldn't hold the police out for long, surely?"

"I know," said Alex. "But they said that something magical was protecting it. They said it was me."

"They were probably right," said Sarah, remembering the creatures who had saved Katie and Matthew. "You've been doing things you've not even been aware of. Without even knowing, you've been reaching out to take care of the ones you love. That's how they were able to protect themselves here. And you've done the same for people you don't even know. You're a good man."

"But I'm not. That's the point. I've killed people. Lots of people. Foxton said I was an angel but I'm not. I'm more like a devil."

"Foxton said you're an angel? Well then he did lie. But you're certainly not a devil. You're..." she paused. This was not how she had imagined their reunion would be. Alex was supposed to already know the truth. That had been Foxton's job. She did not know how to explain something like this to him. For her it had meant simply...

"Hold on," she said and she reached into her bag. "This will help you. That's why it was given to me to look after. This is how it was meant to be after all..." She was thinking out loud and Alex looked even more baffled. Then a book was dumped in his lap; a small hardback book with a patterned cover. "Open it," she said. He did as he was told.

"A cup of tea Alex?"

Foxton was sitting opposite him in a leather armchair, pouring from a delicate china teapot. He was wearing a dark blue quilted gown and his face was clean shaven for the first time in Alex's memory. Behind him was a wall covered in paintings and photographs. Shelves were stacked with ornaments, trophies and what appeared to be the contents of an antique shop.

"Where are we?"

"This is the place you said I should go to. The house you said I should find to retire to. I've actually had it quite a while; two or three hundred years in fact, but I don't spend much time here. Well, until now. Anyway: Bourbon Cream or Digestive?" A tea cup with a Chinese pattern on the side was offered and accepted, along with a biscuit. They sat back in their seats and took a few sips of their tea. After a few minutes Foxton said, "I'm so glad you popped by. I knew you would eventually. That wife of yours is a very clever lady. That's why I hadn't quite given up hope when we last parted."

Alex blushed. "I'm so sorry about that. I had no idea what I was doing." Foxton raised a hand in a gesture of forgiveness.

"Alex, my friend, it's of no importance now. I suspected that if you weren't going to find your own way home, what with everything spinning round in your head, then eventually home would come to fetch you. She's done a grand job."

"But why?" Alex asked. It sounded a daft question.

"It's all bound up in who you are. Yes, I did lie to you once, when I said you were an angel. Of course you're not. What a stupid idea my dear fellow. That's my job." Alex started to choke on his biscuit and reached for his drink. Foxton ignored him and went on. "What you are is something far more important. You're God." Alex's tea sprayed out of his mouth in a fine mist. "Would you like a hankie?" Foxton asked. Alex shook his head amid a flurry of coughs. "Well that's the thing you see Alex. If you react like this over afternoon tea in my parlour, how ever would you have coped out there in the world, surrounded by all the noise and shadows? I had to lie because you weren't ready. Or at least I thought you weren't."

"How can I be God?" Alex asked when he had his breath back.

"I did say this when we first met and it was the truth: forget everything you think you know or believe. There is no old man with a white beard. No fluffy clouds and harps. Forget anything you've ever read as well. Words on a page can hold great power but ultimately that's all they are: drops of ink." He poured another cup of tea. "But you are filled with the greatest and most wonderful magic ever. That's how they'd describe it here in Theland anyway. In your world, well I'm not sure any more. But I do know that there are dangers ahead, dark times that will threaten us all, even my sort. There will be a challenge that only a man can face and the one I serve had no choice but to place his power in another. He picked you."

"But you've seen the evil things I've done."

"Yes and I take the blame for not guiding you well enough and for leaving you like I did. The human soul is full of imperfections and that's what our enemy preys upon. When you stood alone in the desert to stop a war, He was controlling you, twisting you to act against your will. He is the one you must face at some point. This is about whether you'll do the right thing when that time comes. I've tried to prepare you as best I can, whispering in your ear and writing on bridges, but if one man isn't capable of doing that, then mankind as a whole is lost. Not worth keeping. That's why my Lord put his power in you. If you can't make the right choice then it proves mankind isn't worth the bother frankly."

"Not much pressure then," said Alex. He took another sip of tea to calm his nerves. "But I've already failed the test haven't I? I'm not up to the job."

Foxton sighed. "Were you always like this as a child? So stubborn?" He reached forwards and touched Alex's hand. "Come with me."

They were on a park bench. The room had gone and they were sitting in the park near Alex's house. "See her?" Foxton said, pointing at a woman in her early thirties on the other side of the duck pond, walking with a man of about the same age. "You sat here once and watched her. You knew she was alone and afraid and you made it right."

"I did?"

"Look."

As they watched, the man turned to the woman and took her hand. Then he leaned over and kissed her on the lips; nothing dramatic, just a gentle kiss of love that lasted no more than a few seconds. "It's a small thing," said Foxton, blinking repeatedly and reaching for a handkerchief from his pocket, "but I still get a lump in my throat when I see it." Alex regarded him with a look of disbelief. Then he had a thought.

"There was something else before this though," he said, "Probably the first thing I did. It's starting to make sense now."

They were at the side of a road. A man was standing a few feet away, staring at a car that was embedded in a metal post. He had sunglasses pushed up on the top of his head. "I did that," said Alex knowingly. "I'm not proud of it but that was my work. I remember it now. He annoyed me with his arrogance and selfishness and I made this happen. Now that's not very worthy is it?"

Foxton was laughing. "No it's not but then you do have a human heart and soul. You don't have to be perfect. And anyway..." he trailed off, giggling.

"What? What is it?"

"He's wearing sunglasses on a cloudy day. What a knob."

Then they were back in the parlour, finishing their tea. Alex had another question. "So my daydreams then: were they all part of this, a sign that I was something special?"

Foxton dunked his last biscuit in his drink. "Sorry Alex," he said with a smile, "That was just you. You're just a daft bugger at times." They talked some more, until the biscuit plate was empty and then Foxton said, "I must congratulate your wife on a job well done. Would you mind giving her a little note for me?" He passed Alex a slip of paper folded several times. "You'll be leaving me in a minute and I'm not sure when we'll see each other again. But you're not alone any more. He gave you his power knowing it would challenge you, knowing it could destroy a human soul so easily. But he gave you something to help you; the love of another to guide you; to show you the true path."

Alex blushed and looked away for a moment before speaking again. "But why now? I've lived with this all my life, been blissfully unaware. So why is it all happening now?" he asked.

"Because it has to Alex. I've always known that one day you might have to face a challenge, to make a choice that only a human could make. But it's coming sooner than we thought. So things were brought forward. You remember me saying how something stopped me seeing your death in time to prevent it? Well now I know what that was. It was you. With a little help from another."

Alex frowned.

"The one who put the power in you. He's always one stop ahead of me. He put those Militiamen on the road near the tall tree..."

"He sent them to kill me? Nice."

"No. You could have escaped. You could have stayed on the wagon and let the children walk away on their own. Or you could have run away from the Militia, maybe even given up your friends and saved yourself. But you didn't. You did what you thought was right. It was a kind of first test. I can see that now. A dry run. A choice. And because you had that choice, I could not predict what would happen next. And you still do. You still have a choice. I should have made it clearer from the start. This isn't one of those films where the hero is destined to save the planet."

"Nice of you to have such confidence in me."

"What I mean is, it's your choice. He may have picked you, but you get to choose in the end. It's what makes you human, different to him."

"I get it. I think."

"But your death on the road happened for a reason, make no mistake about that. It happened when it did because we need you. Something dark is drawing close."

"I've heard those words before. But what exactly is it that's coming?"

"The war in the desert, the spread of barbarity across the world, countries turning in on themselves and against each other; these are all signs. They point to the hand of our enemy. I've no doubt He's behind all this but there's also the whiff of Theland magic in the air. Your world, the Other Place, is no match for the kind of sorcery that Theland can conjure up. We need to find out who's been using it to stir up human hatred to boiling point."

There was a silence broken only by the sound of a clock ticking on one of the shelves. Then Alex sighed, "I know who it is."

In the garden he got up from the bench, feeling a sense of energy and power returning to his tired body. He passed Sarah the book and the folded slip of paper from Foxton. "It's time to go back," he said, "I need to find Marshall."

Chapter Twenty Six

Facing the Enemy

It had always been one of Alex's golden rules that pubs with car parks were best avoided. He made exceptions for nice country inns with good beer on tap but no city pub should have a car park. In his experience any urban boozer with cars littering the tarmac outside would serve you bad beer and probably throw in a punch in the face for good measure.

He took a deep breath and pulled open the doors of The Mitre. It was packed with people and music was playing at high volume. It was a terrible tune from his teenage years that he thought had long been forgotten. He could guess whose choice it was.

There, in the centre of the pub, was Marshall. He was holding court among some of the other drinkers. They were a rough looking bunch of stocky men with shaved heads and sunburn. All were holding pints and laughing at one of Marshall's jokes. This was a notoriously hard pub where few strangers ever dared tread but Marshall was basking in the attention he was receiving. He caught sight of Alex as he approached and nearly dropped his beer.

"What in God's name are you doing here?" he said. His companions stared at Alex with menace.

"Good choice of words," said Alex. "Actually, I've come for a little chat with you. Mind if we step outside?"

"I do actually," said Marshall with a nervous laugh. He was fumbling in his pocket for something. One of his companions, an enormous man with tattoos creeping up either side of his neck, stepped in front of Alex and leaned into his face.

"Our mate doesn't want to talk to you. Leave now or I'll break your legs."

"I think you should leave. After all, Dave, your wife's at home planning to leave you right this minute. She's packing the car and is taking the kids to her mum's house. She found out about the money you lost playing poker last month and she's been getting fed up with you for ages. You'll be seeing little Dale and Shaznay once a month if her lawyer gets his way."

The man stepped back and put his pint on the bar. "I'd best be off lads," he said in the quietest of voices. "See you around." Then he grabbed his jacket and left hurriedly.

"Now. Andrew. Mate. Where were we? Oh yeah..." Alex put a hand on Marshall's shoulder. "Outside. Now." He frog marched him across the bar and out through the door. The rest of the pub, excited at the prospect of a fight, followed suit. When they got into the car park they stopped in their tracks. They were floating over Hell.

The Mitre appeared to have been ripped from its normal resting place, just off Oakdale Road, and suspended over a vast fiery pit. The edge of the car park was a ragged line of torn tarmac and occasionally bits would crumble away and drop into the inferno. Huge jets of flame shot upwards from the burning depths and there was a constant rumbling from way below them. The drinkers, many still nursing their pints, had to balance themselves as the ground pitched from side to side like a boat on a stormy sea. A few dashed back inside for a fresh drink. One man wandered to the edge and peered down. "It goes on forever," he said to his friends between mouthfuls of beer. "There's nowt but fire and stuff and it goes on forever."

Marshall swung the first punch. He had never been in a fight before but he balled his hand into a fist and swung at Alex's nose. He missed his target and hit his cheek instead but it still made Alex cry out in pain. Marshall grinned at the sound. "You were supposed to be gone. You ran away and I made sure you had no one to come back to," he jeered.

Now Alex retaliated. He too had never been in a fight before but he managed to hit Marshall in the stomach and push him back against one of the parked cars. Immediately the lights started to flash and an alarm began whooping. Someone in the crowd shouted, "Oi! Mind the motor!" and Alex looked up and apologised.

Marshall saw his chance and lunged forwards, catching Alex off balance. The pair hit the ground together and started rolling about with fists flying, making the car park lurch to one side. As it did, more tarmac broke away and sent up a shower of white flames and sparks. "Aaargh!" shouted Marshall, "My hair!" Hot cinders had landed on his scalp and he began beating at his head wildly.

Alex jumped to his feet and ran to the rear of one of the cars, which had been hideously customised by its owner. As Marshall ran at him with hatred in his eyes he grabbed hold of the plastic spoiler that had been bolted to the rear of the vehicle and tore it off. With a single swing he hit Marshall on the side of the head with it and watched as he fell to the floor. Then he stood over him and shouted, "See what I can do?" Do you see the power I have? What made you think you should interfere in something that's none of your business?"

"It is my business mate," Marshall said as he wiped a trickle of blood from above one eye. "You don't have a monopoly on power. There's another far greater than you and far more deserving of a place on this earth. I answer to Him."

"What the hell are you talking about Marshall?" Alex said. The ground tipped again and he steadied himself as he stared down at the man he used to share an office with. He could feel the familiar rushing of the dark noise in his head but this time it did not scare him and he knew he had it under control. "What happened to you?"

"You left me Alex. You went your own way and I found a different path."

Alex knelt down and grabbed Marshall by the collar. "What

are you up to? You're messing in things you don't understand." As he spoke, Marshall reached into his jacket pocket and pulled out the piece of the Monkton Stone. It was glowing more brightly than ever and it burned his skin, even as he tried to dash it against the side of Alex's head. But Alex grabbed his wrist and twisted the stone free, taking it into his own hand.

He felt none of the heat that Marshall had. Instead, the stone glazed over as a thousand tiny cracks spread through it. In its last moment, before it crumbled into nothing but green dust, Alex saw some of the secrets it held. He saw Marshall losing his soul and he saw Johan Banberg, the Commissioner, standing back and watching with glee. "You poor sod," he said and he released his grip on Marshall's collar. "I never left you Marshall. I never did. I died so that you could get home safely and I came back to make sure you were all right. I did all that and I never even liked you."

Marshall was lying at his feet, half sobbing and half laughing. The blood from his cut ran down over his face, giving him a ghoulish appearance and he giggled hysterically. "It won't matter anyway, will it? Not when He comes. It's happening any day now. Then you'll be the poor sod. They all will."

Alex knelt down again and leaned over Marshall, who was beginning to twitch, now that the power of the Monkton Stone had left him. "Who's coming Marshall? Who's coming?"

"He is of course. Him. The devil. I've done what He and Johan told me to. I've lit the fires of hatred in human hearts and now they'll guide His way. He's taking human form and He'll be here anytime. Can't you feel it in the shadows Alex? There's nothing you can do, except maybe go to hell yourself and beg Him to be gentle with you."

Marshall collapsed into a spasm of laughter and lay back on the ground. The destruction of the piece of the Monkton Stone had left him empty. He twitched and shook like a dying animal.

Alex stood up and regarded what was left of his old colleague. This was not Andrew Marshall: he had died the moment his soul had been snatched away, but it was still a pitiful sight. "I'll do the right thing by you," Alex said. "I can promise you that."

He walked over to the edge of the car park and looked down. Below him was a world of flame that went on forever. Waves of fire crashed over each other and the air was crackling with the heat. He stepped off the edge and was gone.

* * *

"It's good to see you again Alex."

"I know you don't mean that. You hoped I was gone for good, or at least out of your way for a while."

"That's true. But it seems I underestimated your allies. That was my mistake but I'll remember it for next time."

"There won't be a next time." Alex walked beneath the branches of the tall tree and out onto the open road.

The man sitting on the grass a few yards away smiled as he approached. "It's too late though my friend. Can't you see what's happening?" He pointed out over the fields at the dark bottomed clouds that were gathering on the horizon. "The wheels are already turning. It's all coming together nicely." He sat on the grass verge and gestured for Alex to join him but the invitation was ignored. He went on, "Oh to be able to breathe the air again Alex. Maybe you can show me some good places to eat or perhaps a nice little coffee shop. I can't remember when I last actually tasted anything. But I'm forgetting. I'll be destroying you won't I? Sorry about that."

"And what makes you think that'll happen?" said Alex. "Last time I was here you only saw half of me, like a shadow. But now I know who I am, so you get it all. I won't let you walk the earth for a single minute."

"But you've seen for yourself how much hatred there is out there. What makes you think you can stop me?"

"Because people will listen to me. People will follow…"

"You're obsessed with people following you aren't you? Didn't that fool Peters in Theland teach you anything? Fools follow. Who wants to be admired by an army of halfwits?

The beauty of it is; I don't need to stir up legions of devoted followers, all trotting along to worship me once a day or once a week. You lot do my work for me without thinking. You even do my business, the fun stuff like death and destruction, in the name of God. No one's ever launched a bloody crusade in my name or burned some poor soul on a pyre to defend my honour but I still get to reap the benefits. I can't lose."

"So if things are going so well for you, why do you need to come to earth?" Alex said, "Why not stay here and carry on admiring your handiwork?"

"Do you know what I feel when I see acts of great cruelty being carried out by others Alex? Nothing. Nothing at all. Just complete indifference. I'm bored by it all and that's why I want to stir things up a bit. I want to be a bit more hands on. Anyway, you're a fine one to talk. If you'll pardon my pun; God only knows why he put his power in you. I think he's just so vain he wanted to see how one of the little people lives."

"It was for a reason: to stop you doing this. You knew that, the last time we met and you must have been desperate because you tried to bring me over to your side before I woke up and realised who I was."

"And do you know who you are?"

"I'm the most powerful person of all. I'm the key to your demise. I'm Alex Preston."

The man's eyes narrowed and his mouth moved nervously. "And how does that threaten me?"

"Because he did know what he was doing when he put this power inside me. That's what really scares you. I'm an ordinary man but I do know right from wrong. I know that I have a dark side; it's called being human. But I just get over it and get on with life. I don't prance about in the shadows dressed in black. This place isn't even real. You don't really hang around on a dusty road because there's no such place. This is just like one of my old daydreams. He knew I'd see through you."

The man was looking strangely at Alex. For the first time he seemed afraid. "You can never destroy me. You must know that. I'll be around as long as you are." He got to his feet. "And I'm sure we can make a deal. There are two worlds up there, as you know. Why don't we come to a gentleman's agreement? You can keep the Other Place, with your charming wife and children, and I'll take Theland. My magic is already running through the place like cancer anyway. There need be no unpleasantness. No pain. Just a simple handshake and we're done. Then you can get on with living like a God. Or just God. Whatever." He held his hand out to Alex.

"You know I won't accept. I will not let you walk as a man."

The hand was withdrawn. "Yes, I guessed you'd say that. But I had to try. Still, it's unlikely you'll find an easy way. However powerful you are, you're still a human and full of flaws. You might find it easy to protect your world but Theland, like I said, is almost mine already. I'll think of you as I make them suffer, especially that tiresome angel and the village girl." He went to walk away. "I think we're done here now."

But Alex had not finished. "You had Marshall start your little fires of hate in my world but I can put them out. And don't worry about Theland. There are plenty of seeds of good planted there. I know where they are and I can bring them to life. You think you've been clever but you haven't. This has all been part of someone else's plan to draw you out and then knock you down." He stepped forwards and landed on a punch on the man's jaw that sent him spinning to the ground. "How many centuries has it been? How many years have I waited to give you a slap? Call me petty, but it's been worth the wait." He stepped back. "Now we're done."

Then there was just one figure by the dusty road. A thin man in black was picking himself up off the ground and rubbing at his bruised jaw.

* * *

The ducks were swimming in circles and ignoring the lumps of bread that Matthew was throwing at them. Katie grew impatient

272

and grabbed a chunk of loaf from her brother's hand and hurled it at one of the birds, hitting it on the head. It squawked its displeasure and flapped away across the pond. As Alex watched the piece of bread sink below the surface he caught sight of the reflection of the sky in the water. The clouds were even darker than they had been when he and the children had arrived to feed the birds. They were casting vast shadows over the park and the sun seemed to be shrinking back away from them.

It had been a week since he had discovered his enemy's plan and each day the sky grew darker. He had not expected their confrontation to yield anything more than a few insults and he had been right. It seemed that His plan to walk again was moving ahead and now Alex had to find a way to stop it. So far he had come up with nothing.

When all the bread was gone he walked home with the kids. Every house they passed, every street they went down and every face they saw seemed perfectly normal. But Alex wondered how long it would be before His presence was felt. It could not be allowed to happen. Back at home he walked into the kitchen where Sarah was making tea. He felt frustrated at not knowing what to do; at finding himself without a way forward. As he put his arms around her and gave her a hug, her warmth drove away some of the coldness that had spread over him in recent days.

"Are you still reading that?" he said, pointing to the book that lay on the worktop. "I'd have thought you had it off by heart."

Sarah moved nervously to pick it up but Alex's hand was already on it and she drew back as he walked into the lounge, flicking through the pages. Several times over the last week he had been tempted to lift the cover and see if another great secret was revealed: how to defeat his enemy. But he had held back and now he was disappointed. There was no great light show, no blinding flash of magical inspiration. It was just a book, full of untidy black writing and inky drawings. Then he stopped.

Sarah caught the look on his face and realised that it was

over. She began to talk, to explain why she had kept the truth from him, but he did not hear her. "This is it," he said, "the answer was in here all along. It's like 'In Emergency Break Glass'. There's a way to release all the power I have in one go." Then he saw she was crying. "It'll be OK. I promise it'll be OK."

"Don't say things you know aren't true," she sobbed. "If you do what it says in there, then there's no coming back. You can't be resurrected from this Alex. I'll lose you forever."

"But if I don't then you'll all be lost," he said. "I can't let that happen can I?" She said nothing; she just buried her head deeper into his shoulder and sobbed. After a while they pulled apart and he opened the book again, studying one of the pages intently. He did not notice the way Sarah was watching him; nervous and edgy. She kept glancing from him to the book and back again. "I don't have time to read it all," he said, "but it's something that will roll back all His evil, at least to a point where he can't set foot on earth. It's called the Cirrus. By summoning it, I can set the power free from within me. In a single moment I can put things right."

"But you'll die. It's a means of destroying yourself. It says that at the top of the page." She pointed at the book. "It's the only thing that can kill you."

"You've read this already?"

She took a deep breath. "Yes I've read it. I'm sorry I…"

"It doesn't matter," Alex said with a smile. "What matters is that I put this right. I have to do this." He tucked the book under his arm and went to the mantelpiece where Sarah's pebble rested. "I'll need this," he said, "I just hope it works away from Theland." Tears were streaming down Sarah's face as she watched Alex kiss the children and give them one last hug. "At least there'll be no more goodbyes after this," he whispered as he pecked Matthew on the cheek. Katie giggled as he tickled her and she promised to be a good girl for her mummy. Then it was time to go.

"If I stay then you'll never be safe," he said as he held his wife for the last time. "But if I get this done then I promise you'll never be in danger. I'll watch over you every day, no matter where you are." She was still crying and he was struggling to keep control. He meant every word he said but the words still seemed empty and pointless. He was saying goodbye forever. He wanted to kiss her but her face was curled tightly, as if she was in great pain, so he pulled her closer for a moment.

"Take your coat with you," Sarah said as he headed for the door, "I don't want you getting cold." Then with a final wave and a smile he was gone and the front door closed with a thump.

* * *

Sarah stood in the kitchen, staring into space. She had not meant to do this thing but she just could not help herself. She knew her role was to be Alex's conscience and guide but that did not stop her being his wife. No woman would want to send her husband to his death, not when there was something she could do to save him. Now they would face whatever He, the shadowy enemy Alex had gone to destroy, could throw at them. In life or death, they would be together.

Her hand rested on a piece of paper, torn down one side. It was a page from the book, the last page in the chapter about the Cirrus. She had read it one night while Alex was away in Theland, when she had not expected him to return. It did not mean much to her then but once he was back she knew what a danger it was. Once the Cirrus was summoned, at a particular place and time, it would seek Alex out and crush him. In doing so, the power within him would be released in a single burst, able to cross all barriers that stood before it and enter into the hearts of men. It was a doomsday device with her husband's name on it.

So she had torn the last page out. Without it, the book would not work. She knew that Alex was bound to find the chapter eventually, as it seemed he was being drawn down a certain path with no way back, but she would do all she could to save him. That was her proper role.

And yet.

She went to her handbag and pulled out a small piece of notepaper, folded in half three times. Foxton's tidy handwriting ran across it in blue ink.

"Faith is not for the weak. Believe and be true."

"Damn you Foxton. No one likes a smart arse." She screwed it up and threw it across the room. She knew what she had done was wrong but there way no turning back. There was nothing she could do to...

The doorbell.

She stopped her empty tirade and went to the front door. A man she had never seen before was standing on the step. For a moment she suspected another assassination attempt and braced herself. But then he spoke. "Sarah, I'm here to help you. I've come to give you a lift...." He seemed a little out of sorts, as if he thought he was dreaming. He kept looking back down the street, to where a grey coloured car was parked with the engine running. "I've come to return a favour to your husband. My name is Peter Allen."

Chapter Twenty Seven

The Cirrus

The helicopter banked to one side as the top of the hill loomed up out of the dark. It circled the peak and through the window Sarah could make out two figures, one standing and one kneeling. "I'll have to find somewhere to put down!" shouted the pilot and he pulled the aircraft back. About half way down one side of the hill the ground levelled out briefly. It left just enough room to land. Before the blades had stopped turning Sarah had pulled the door open and was running up the slope.

The grass was slippery and she fell over several times as her feet lost grip on the wet ground. She resorted to clawing at the earth to help regain her balance. It meant her passage up the hill took several minutes and she was heavily out of breath by the time she reached the top and began sprinting towards the two figures.

Alex was staring off into the night, as if desperate to spot something out in the darkness. There was a look on his face: calm, contented, focused. It was so different to the panic and fear that he had carried with him for months and months. He looked like the Alex she had known years before. The one she had first fallen in love with a decade ago.

Andrew Marshall was kneeling on the ground in front of him. He had his arms wrapped around himself and his chin lolled against his chest. "You're keeping your promise to him then," Sarah said as she approached the pair. "I guess at least this way his misery will be over."

Alex turned at the sound of her voice. "Is there anything you won't do to stop me?" he said. "And I thought you hated flying."

"I do. But that's a government helicopter don't you know?" Sarah said. "It landed in the middle of the park to pick me up, so I'm getting my taxpayer's money's-worth. Anyway, I brought you something." She took the piece of paper from her back pocket and passed it to him. She could see the penny drop as he realised what it was.

"I've been wondering why it doesn't seem to be working," he said and he bent to the floor and picked up the book that lay at his feet. Opening it to the back, he slid the page inside. Immediately, the book spoke.

"The time has come." A pillar of light spread from its pages. It reached up into the dark sky like a beacon, illuminating the tiny drops of rain that fell on them as a fine mist.

"It's started," said Alex.

Even now, Sarah had not given up. "Why can't you just come home with me… come back to us all?" She felt the air growing colder around her and there was a mist forming on the ground.

"Because this is the only way to put things right. Without this you'll never be safe. None of you. This is my choice. It's what I have chosen."

"But you're choosing death."

"No, I'm not. I'm choosing life. Life for you and the children and for millions of others who need me to make the right decision. People who'll never even know my name. And no one's making me. This is what I've chosen to do." She felt tears begin to burn her eyes. She knew this was the end but she could not imagine a world without Alex. She threw her arms around him. By holding this moment in her mind it was as if she could keep him safe forever. He whispered in her ear, "The shadows have gone. For the first time in ages there's nothing in the way and I know how much I love you. All of you."

She choked on her tears as she spluttered back to him, "But

why did it have to take all this, you bloody idiot? Aren't you scared?"

"Yes," he said. "Terrified. But I love you more. All of you. And you've got to go now. You've got to get away from here. I don't know what will happen when..." He was staring at something over her shoulder; something out in the night. She turned to look but there was nothing but rain and darkness. Then she saw it too.

A cloud was sliding across the sky towards them. It rolled over and over within itself as it moved above the earth. It seemed to be reaching out towards the hilltop. "That's it," said Alex and he pushed her back. "Now you really have to go. Please."

"But I love you," she cried.

"I know. But you have to go." He looked down to where the helicopter sat on the grass. "All of you." The cloud was moving nearer and for the first time she was afraid. It was clawing its away through the air towards them, its moon shadow forming a huge black pool on the fields and farmhouses far below.

Sarah took a last look at Alex, who mouthed something to her. Then her legs took her down the hill as fast as they could. Half way to the helicopter she began shouting and waving her arms. The pilot understood and immediately the blades began turning, slowly winding their way up to speed with a moan that grew into a high whine. She threw herself in through the open door and Peter Allen hauled it shut behind her. Then the helicopter rose into the air. Its nose dipped as it pulled away from the hill and headed out over open countryside. Sarah strained to look back out of the window.

The Cirrus had stopped at the hill, directly over the two men. As the helicopter rose higher Sarah could see for the first time how large it really was, stretching upwards for several miles. Every bit of its surface seemed to be moving; twisting and tumbling inwards in a spiral.

On the hill top Alex looked up at the huge shape over him. It was the most amazing thing he had ever seen, a glistening tower of white cloud reaching forever upwards. He heard the helicopter retreating and Marshall's desperate whimpering at his feet but he could not take his eyes off the Cirrus.

Now there was no dark noise, no fearful shadow. At last he understood the greatest magic of all, the thing that so many ordinary men and women had laid down their lives for in the past; the purest, strongest magic that could snuff out the fire of evil in men's hearts, no matter how fiercely it burned. It was what he felt when he looked at Sarah and their beautiful, beautiful children and he knew that however great his fear, this magic was even greater. It was a magic that, when shared, would last forever; even death could only kneel before it. This is what Alex Preston stood for.

The swirling within the Cirrus stopped and now it hung in space. The air beneath it was still and cool and Alex looked up in awe. At that last moment, when he knew there was truly no way back, a smile crossed his lips. "This is for you Thomas Peters."

Then the Cirrus fell.

There were two shock waves. The first started with an almighty bang that caught the helicopter and threw it through the air like a toy. It was like a bomb had been dropped on the top of the hill, sending out ripples of energy. The pilot fought to keep control as his dials and instruments went into a frenzy and the machine rose and fell as forces pulled at its metal skin. There was a scream from the engine as the aircraft was hurled forwards by the blast.

Up ahead, standing proud of a grassy ridge, was a rocky outcrop. It was so large that it was a famous local landmark and now the helicopter was hurtling towards it, carried by a tide of energy. The pilot desperately tried to get the machine to respond, so that he could pull it away from the vast grey shape that was speeding towards them, but it was impossible. At the last second he raised his arms across his face and screamed in terror. Sarah closed her eyes and thought of her beloved Alex, mouthing "I love you" at her through the rain.

But then the second shockwave hit. It was like a wall of

blue light that spread out in all directions from the spot where Alex had been standing. It made no sound as it zipped through the air, lighting up the darkness and pushing back the heavy rain. For a moment it made the hilltop look like a lighthouse, piercing the gloom. Then it left the hill behind and travelled out into the world.

The first thing it met was a helicopter about to shatter into a thousand pieces as it struck a giant rock. And for a second or two, just long enough for it to matter, the rock was not there. It had stood in that spot for a million years or more but for the time it took for the small aircraft to pass safely by, the rock simply disappeared.

The wall of blue light went on.

Across the world, people saw the glowing move past them; felt it move through them. Those that were asleep suddenly awoke as it blazed through windows and lit up the night. Hearts filled with hatred were soothed by its touch. Those full of fear were calmed and made brave. One by one the fires that had been lit to guide the way of mankind's great beguiler were snuffed out. A great wave of peace rode around the surface of the earth, through cities and towns and across fields and deserts. There was nothing that could stand in its way as it swept over the planet. In a world so unaccustomed to magic its power was instantaneous. The Dark King would not walk as a man in this land. Not ever.

Then the wall of light reached a doorway to a world full of secrets and legends, ancient kings and loyal oaths; a land for lost souls where magic lived and breathed; a place where dreamers could believe and find peace. The doorway opened and it went through.

Chapter Twenty Eight
Marvellous Things

Nicholas hobbled across the centre of the village, the heavy bucket banging painfully against the side of his leg. Water spilled from the lip each time he swung a limb forward and splashed over his feet. He got to the house and pushed his way through the door. He raised the bucket to the table and plonked it down. "It's all right my boy," he said as he lifted a small wooden cup from a shelf, "a drink of water'll make you feel better."

The boy on the bed lay perfectly still. Only the tiniest movement came from his chest to give away that he was still breathing. His skin was grey and damp and his eyes stared sleepily at the ceiling. Nicholas knew that it was not long now before he slipped away but he was determined to make Edward's last moments as comfortable as possible.

He poured a cupful of water and took it to the bed. He raised his grandson's head from the pillow and brought the cup to his lips. The boy coughed as he swallowed the liquid then lay back. Nicholas brushed Edward's hair away from his forehead and stroked the child's skin. He had so wanted to see his grandson grow into a young man, even though the odds were always against it. He never imagined he would have to watch the child die before him. He brought his chair to the side of the bed and sat there, his head resting in his hands, as the boy dozed and death crept closer.

Deep in the forest something magical happened. There was a slight tremor as a door opened and a blue light burst through, growing and spreading until it formed a wall of colour that raced through the trees. It rolled down the pathways and tracks and rose up into the highest branches of the woodland canopy. A lone figure stood watching it, a man dressed in the colours of the forest, and he lowered his gaze respectfully as it went by.

It reached the stream that ran through the wood. This was the source of the mighty River Arwent. As the light touched the water, bubbles began to appear. There were just a few at first but then more and more broke on the surface. The stream began to swirl and boil, steam rising into the chill forest air. As the action of the water became more violent it turned into froth and rose up and over the banks in a fury, spilling onto the ground as a flood.

In one tiny part of the great forest was a shaded glen where not even weeds would grow. The earth lay in a raised heap and still bore the marks of shovels. The boiling water ran into the glen from between the trees and swirled on the ground. It was more furious than ever; becoming a bed of seething white foam that bubbled and boiled. Then it sank into the soil and disappeared.

In his house, Nicholas was asleep in his chair. He was dreaming that he was walking in the forest with a man dressed as a hunter. The man turned to him with a smile and said, "You kept your oath to the end. Your faith was unbreakable. Now I have the power to put things right." With a jolt, Nicholas awoke. The inside of the tiny room was being bathed in a beautiful blue light. The heavy sadness that had borne down on him was replaced by a wonderful sense of peace and joy. Then the light faded and he was back in the gloom. He rested his head in his hands again until a sound broke the silence.

There was a knock at the door. He opened his eyes and hauled himself to his feet then shuffled over and pulled it open.

"Nicholas."

A sea of faces. He held back tears of joy as he took them all in. Beautiful faces. Men, women, children. He knew them all by name. He had known them all through their lives and through death. Now they walked from the forest where the great magic had washed over them and they came to his door. "You kept the houses for us Nicholas," said one man. "You kept faith in us, even in death." The Village had returned to life.

Then from behind him came another voice. It was clear and strong and wonderful and made him weep with joy. Such a voice.

"Grandfather."

* * *

The bell rang out across Appledore. People jumped from their beds and pulled on coats and boots at the sound. They fetched lanterns and candles and ran from their houses. Minister Toms led a party to the village gate where a lamp was already burning. "Be quick," he said, "the more lights, the better. We'll drive him back again." He had a heavy, sick feeling in his stomach. He knew that each time Avery Tavistock and his ghouls paid them a visit the lights had less effect. The clever object that Alex had given him had stopped working a while ago and now they were back to relying on more traditional methods of defence.

"Light as many as possible," he called out. "Fires, lanterns, all we have." He knew he did not have to spell things out to the villagers. They had been haunted by Tavistock and his wretched band of followers for so many years that it had become a way of life.

And death. They had lost many of their friends and loved ones to Tavistock. At first no one knew how to defend themselves from the former Minister and his undead flock. And even when they had learned of his hatred for light there were times when an individual might not be quick enough to strike a fire and would be set upon by the beasts. Then on Avery's next visit there would be an extra member of his group.

In recent months they had found that their lights had less and less effect on the ghouls. It was as if they had found a way to suck the life out of the candles and lanterns that ringed Appledore at night. The only way the people had found to truly defend the village was to stand together, protecting the weakest amongst them. This is how they had survived so long in Appledore: terrified by the monsters in the dark but too afraid to leave the village and venture into the world beyond their valley where nightmares walked in the daylight.

"At least one of us got away," the Minister said to himself, as he helped light the fires. He thought of Rebecca each and every day and prayed that she had found what she was so desperately looking for.

"They're coming Minister," a cry went out.

In the darkness beyond the gate, shapes were moving. They came to the outer limits of the pools of light then stopped. They were just visible in the flickering of the torches. Rags of clothing hung from bodies of wasted flesh. Bones jutted from skin that was grey and dead. Many of them were barefoot, with open wounds on their feet and legs. The only thing keeping them going was the evil inside them, driving them on to seek fresh meat. "Good evening Minister," said a familiar voice.

"Avery, how long must this go on?"

"Only as long as you want Minister," Avery Tavistock said as he stepped forwards, dangerously close to the gate. "If you open the gate and dim the lights it will soon be over."

"But then it would just be beginning," the Minister snarled back. "Then we would be trapped in the same hell as you."

"Hell's not so bad when you get used to it," Avery said, "and how about you Minister? Aren't you trapped in your own little hell? Too scared to leave and face the world outside but equally terrified of the nasty monsters at the gate."

"We're in a better place than you Tavistock."

"Not for long I'm afraid, not for long," Avery said and he stepped forward into the pool of light. With a wave of his hand the lights went out. All of them. Every lantern, torch and candle was snuffed out and as darkness dropped on the villagers they began screaming with terror.

"To your houses," shouted Minister Toms. "Run home and lock yourself in your houses." As people began to scatter, with only the moonlight to guide them, the undead mob charged at the gate.

"Prepare to feast well my friends," Tavistock cried in the dark. "The man of God is mine. Once I am done with him you may eat your fill." He wanted to finish with Toms before the real fun could begin. Even now, the man was a potential threat.

The Minister sprinted for the church with Avery hot on his trail. He hoped that shutting himself in the chapel would buy him enough time to formulate a plan. It might also give some of the other villagers a chance to escape. He flew through the doors, slammed them shut behind him and turned the key in the lock. He ran down the aisle and lit two of the heavy candles standing near the altar. Then he began searching for the extra lanterns he kept stored away behind one of the pews.

"It's a little late for that I'm afraid Minister." Avery's voice was close. "You forgot; I built his place. I know every way in." He was inside the church. The candles flickered but stayed lit.

"We've done you no wrong Avery Tavistock, so why do you prey on us?" Minister Toms shouted into the shadows. "These are innocent people."

"Innocence means nothing. My Mary was innocent but it did nothing to save her." Avery moved out of the dark and stood in the aisle, just in reach of the candlelight. "There's just one thing I need to know Toms, before I finish with you. Why did you stay? I could always tell that you wanted to leave here, that you wanted to pack your bags and see the outside world. So why didn't you? Why not move on and save yourself?"

The Minister's heart was beating like a hammer. There was no way out. He had no plan of escape. "You're right, I could have left. I didn't stay because I was afraid but because I chose to. Because it's my duty to stay with my people and you would have devoured them all by now if I'd left."

Avery walked the last few yards to the altar. The candles seemed to wither as he drew closer but still did not go out. "Well you'll pay for that choice with your last breath," he said and he stepped right up to Toms. The weak light still burned his skin but he wanted to see the look in the Minister's eyes in the moment before death. He was disappointed: it was not one of terror, but of calm defiance. "Strong to the end," he said and with a single sweep of his hand the lights went out.

As he reached for the man's throat there was a tremor that made some of the stained glass windows rattle. Then the inside of the church was filled with a blue light that swept in from the wall behind the altar and moved off down the aisle. He felt a moment of panic as it passed over him but then nothing more: no pain and no burning. The light just moved away and vanished into the wall at the other end of the church. He turned back to the Minister and laid his hands on the man's skin. This would taste so sweet.

There was a movement out of the corner of his eye. A flickering white dot. A candle, a small white candle was burning by the southern wall of the church. He spun round. There was another by the northern wall. Then another and another. The whole church was filling with candles; brilliant, white, burning candles. He tried to snuff them out but they did not even flicker. They were only small and their flames were so delicate. But there were so many of them. Dozens. Scores. Hundreds. They sat on the floor, rested on the sills beneath the windows and lay in rows on the pews. The altar was lined with them and they ran in vast lines up and down the aisle.

Thousands and thousands of candles had filled the church and their brilliant light burst through the windows in every direction. Outside in the village the ghouls wailed as it tore through the flesh and burned them to ashes. Some tried to hide behind trees or in the shadows of buildings but the light would not let them escape. It shone into every dark corner and found them where they cowered. They were wiped from the face of the earth as the brightness from the church blazed through the night.

At the altar, Avery felt it overwhelm him. He began to dissolve into the burning white glow from the candles, fading almost to nothing. Then a shape appeared in the blanket of light that surrounded him. A beautiful young woman with long brown hair stood before him with her hand outstretched. A garland of flowers hung from her neck and she carried the scent of blossom. "My Mary," he cried.

As he took her hand, she smiled and drew him near. "My love," she whispered, "come home."

As the light finally engulfed him, Avery Tavistock turned to the man whose courage had kept him at bay for so many years. "Bless you brother," he said. Then he was gone.

Chapter Twenty Nine

Love is Stronger

"The end will come soon my dear," the Guardian croaked and he lay his head back down on the grass. Elisabeth nuzzled closer to him for warmth and drew her coat up around her neck.

"Don't say that," she whispered and she pressed one hand against his side. His scales were hard and dry and he felt cold to the touch. "We'll be all right. I promise we'll be all right."

On the plains south of Archangel there was little natural protection from the elements. The wind coming in across the tall grass whined and moaned. A face that was not protected from its touch by a cloak or scarf would soon be raw with cold. This was a desolate place with only an occasional tree to break up the monotony of the landscape. This was where they lay.

The Bishop had finally grown bored with his pet monster and had cast him out into the wilderness. First the crowds in the Plaza had dwindled as people found new attractions in the city. A crippled beast at the top of a stone tower was far less exciting than seeing a man fight a bear or a troop of dwarves throw knives at each other. The Guardian of Archangel should have been majestic and proud but this creature was tired and pathetic. On a good day the audience would simply drift away to seek other pleasures but on a bad day they would boo and hiss and even throw fruit at the Tower guards; none of which made Bishop Gerard happy. He was even less pleased when the Guardian failed to live up to his name.

The Mercenaries of Brampton, the men whom the Bishop had hired to return the Guardian to Archangel, had begun robbing merchants heading out of the city. The payment they had been promised for capturing the great beast had never materialised, so they had decided to take what they were owed from groups of traders heading home from the Archangel markets. The Bishop was furious and immediately put a price on their heads, which only escalated things further. Now the Mercenaries had promised to raise an army and sack the city.

While all this was going on, the Guardian did nothing. He was supposed to have flown over the city rooftops and scared away any attackers, as he had done in ancient times. But he was old and tired and had no strength left to fly. Also, the Bishop had taken the extreme step of blinding him as a way of preventing him from escaping. Bishop Gerard had never expected the city to actually come under threat and had not thought about the possible consequences of his actions. But it meant the Guardian was all but useless.

As the assaults on the merchants' wagon trains took place he lay on the top of the tower, half asleep. When the Bishop heard the first reports of the Mercenaries' actions he had stormed up to the roof and delivered a hard kick to the Guardian's ribs. The next time it happened he had struck him several times with his staff. Upon the third attack he had ordered that the beast should be taken from the Tower and disposed of. This was how the Guardian came to be lying on the southern plains, unprotected against the elements. The Bishop's men had trussed him up and winched him from the roof then strung him behind several pack horses and dragged him a mile out into the wilderness. Then he was dumped on the cold, hard ground and left to die.

But he was not alone. Elisabeth, the gentle soul who had cared for him since his return to Archangel, had hidden herself in a wagon that accompanied the men. When they untied the horses she had slipped away and hidden in the grass. The moment they were out of sight she came out of hiding and ran to her beloved Samuel. He was angry at first and told her to return home but she was too stubborn for him and he said she could stay for just one night.

That had been two days ago and despite his pleadings she would still not abandon him. He was weaker than ever now and could hardly move. "You have remained my true friend," he said to her before dawn on the third day, "but you must leave here and go back to your parents. Now that I am gone you can leave the Tower and your life can return to normal."

"My life can never be normal again," she said. "The things you've told me about the way the world used to be have opened my eyes. I can never go back to being who I was. I'd rather die here with you." She moved in closer to his enormous body for shelter. "I want to ride over the city on your shoulders. I want to hear the people call your name. These are what I want to…" The earth beneath them was shaking. "Samuel? What is that?" she said.

He raised his head from the ground and tried pitifully to see something, anything, with his ruined eye. There were definite vibrations coming from the ground and there was a sound like thunder that was moving in from the south west. Elisabeth turned to look and gasped.

"Riders!" she cried, "Hundreds of riders making for the city!" There was a wall of horsemen heading in the direction of Archangel, swords drawn at the ready.

"It's the army the Mercenaries spoke of," the Guardian said, "they're going to burn the city. I should have…"

"Mother and father!" Elisabeth shouted, "and my brother Benjamin. I must warn them. The city will be asleep. I have to warn them all!"

"There isn't time child. We are too far away."

"But I cannot leave them. I have to warn the people."

"No child, it is I who must try," he said and he managed to raise himself from the ground. Some strength returned to his limbs and he was able to push himself up to a kneeling position. But the abuse at the Tower had taken its toll and he collapsed again on to the stony ground. "I have failed you my child," he wept.

"No you haven't Samuel. No you haven't," Elisabeth said and she pressed herself against him. "I love you. And it's up to me to do this." Then she was away, running through the grass as fast as she could. The horses were a good distance behind her and she was sure she stood a chance of getting to the city before them. She at least had to try.

The lead horseman spotted the small figure running away across the open plain and he readied his sword. The Bishop would pay for his betrayal with the blood of the people and this would be a good place to start. He dug his heels into his horse's side and charged onwards.

The sun was rising on the western horizon but on this morning there was no warming red glow to mark the new day. Instead a wave of blue light was breaking over the distant hills. It rolled down into the valleys and over the forests and rivers that stood in its way. Then it pushed on across the flat lands that reached out around the city of Archangel. The Mercenaries watched it approach but did not slow their gallop. They merely tightened the grip on their swords and charged onwards. They rode through the wall of light unharmed and headed on to the city.

The Guardian lay on the ground and wept. This was not how it was meant to be. He was of a proud race, a magical race. They had been the holy envoys, able to cross between worlds and domains carrying the word of God. They were the Lord's watchmen and messengers, his eyes and ears. And now their race was reduced to this. He had been humbled by men and broken in two. The Guardian had served them for centuries but was treated as nothing more than a trophy. He meant nothing to them.

But then he had met this sweet soul, the only one to call him by her real name. Through her love for him, she had restored a tiny part of the magic and majesty that once flowed through his veins. While the others bent him to their will, she reminded him who he really was. His race had once been worshipped like kings but he felt honoured and humbled to have known her. The people looked on him as their Guardian but it was she who was willing to die to save them. He heard the horsemen thunder past and he cried out with sorrow.

Then the blue light reached him. It poured over his skin and wrapped itself around his wings. His scales grew hard and his limbs began to freeze as he slowly turned to stone. He managed to curl into a ball as the light worked its way over his body, encasing him in rock. Then it moved on.

The leader of the Mercenaries brought his sword arm out to the side. The blade was held at the perfect height for striking a running man in the back. But as he neared the sprinting figure he noticed how small it was and lowered the weapon slightly. He did not want to miss his prey. He had only a hundred yards to go.

On the plain behind him a large rock rested on the grass. Its surface was rough and scored and the crease that ran over its top resembled a giant scar. It started to twitch and shake and small pieces began to fall off the sides. Then the scar cracked open and something started to emerge. First a head covered with scales, then two arms rippling with muscle, then a vast body carried on two giant legs and finally a long silver tail. Its skin shone like a river and as it moved, the air around it seemed to shimmer. With one flex of its back, two great wings spread out on either side. Then it turned to look towards the city with a single, glinting eye and it gave a shout that carried across the plain, "I am Samuel. My name is Samuel."

The sword moved in a graceful arc to cut the girl down. The rider had realised this was a child in the last few yards but that meant nothing to him. He had a score to settle. But as the blade swung at her, a giant hand swooped from the sky to snatch her to safety. The swordsman looked up and saw a magnificent beast hanging above him. Ripples of silver ran through its scales and two huge wings stretched out on either side, beating a steady rhythm through the air.

He thrust his weapon upwards, to stab into the belly of the creature. But his blade glanced from the animal's skin and spun from his grip. He did not have time to curse before the monster flicked its tail and swept him from his horse. Only as he tumbled earthwards did he see the beast in full. This was the same creature that he had fetched back from the northern forest, broken and in shackles. But now it glided above him on wings of steel. The light from the pale morning sun moved over it like a cloak.

Then he crashed to the ground and the world went dark.

Samuel lifted Elisabeth onto his back and turned to fly away from the city. "But we must help them!" she cried. "My parents are there, and my brother. Please don't let them die."

"But I'm not their Guardian any more," he said.

"No," said Elisabeth, in tears, "but you are my friend."

Samuel had defended the city for centuries after a promise had been made. He had acted out of a sense of duty. But they had destroyed all honour he had and then had thrown him out to die. Now he had a choice: he could fly back north and spend his life in the peace of a forest, alone, or he could repay the love that one little girl had shown him. And if one ordinary child was capable of showing such love, then maybe others within the city walls had souls like hers. If the city burned then he would never find out.

He flew out in a circle so that he was gliding directly across the advancing lines of horsemen. By swinging his tail from side to side he sent a dozen riders tumbling to the floor. Others were thrown from their horses as the animals went into a panic. But there were scores more still galloping for the city and they would be upon it long before he could despatch them all.

Then he sensed Them. He felt Their presence for the first time in so many years. They were inside him; in his head and within his heart. They were not dead as men would understand death to be. The spark of love that Elisabeth had ignited in him had guided their souls to this place.

"My brothers and sisters," he sighed.

With that, his rebirth was complete. "My name is Samuel," he cried again. "And I am The Messenger."

He hovered in the air and looked down on the army that was nearing the city; at the men filled with hate and greed. The rise and fall of his wings slowed to a gentle, pulsing rhythm but he did not fall from the sky.

A beat.

It began as a low humming but as his wings moved through the cold morning air it began to grow.

A beat.

Like the droning of pipes, it carried out across the open plain. A wall of sound.

A beat.

It washed over the armed riders and swirled around between the lines of horses. It was something no one had heard in Theland for a millennium: a single note that sounded like a chorus of a thousand voices. It rose higher and higher until each man was forced to slow his mount and slide to the ground. The Mercenaries stood by their horses and stared up into the sky. Some shed tears as the sound swelled inside them. A mother's soothing lullaby. An infant's cry as it takes its first breath of life. A lover's gentle whisper in the darkness. The sound was all these things. It was a song of love. A promise of undying devotion carried by the last Messenger of God.

They sheathed their swords. No one would die today.

Samuel watched them remount and ride away. Then with Elisabeth astride his shoulders he glided over the city walls and flew low across the rooftops. People stood in the streets to stare up at them as they swept overheard. As he passed over a large open plaza he dropped even lower and landed on the roof of the Tower that stood at one end. Elisabeth slid from his back and he stood upright, taller than ever. He surveyed the crowd that had gathered at the foot of the Tower and the many hundreds of people who had crammed on to roof tops and balconies to watch him.

"Listen to me, people of Archangel," he cried. "Know my

name. It was given to me by one far greater than any man here. I am Samuel. My name is Samuel, the Messenger of the Lord. The Guardian of Archangel is no more. My debt has been repaid."

"You will suffer for such insolence!" boomed a voice from below. Bishop Gerard was striding out into the plaza, his face purple with rage. He waved his staff in the air above his head. "You are the Guardian. You have only the name we gave you. You will do as I tell you!"

"I will do what's right," shouted Samuel back. "The real enemies of Archangel are not beyond the city walls, but in the cold hearts of men like you." And he reached down with his great silver tail and snatched the staff from the Bishop's grasp. He took it in his own hands and snapped it in two. Then came a sound that he had never thought to hear from the people of the city. Applause.

The crowd in the plaza and the hundreds watching from rooftops and windows began to clap and cheer. Many had tears in their eyes as they roared and stamped their feet in approval. In the half lit moments before dawn they had each been woken by a glorious blue light that had crept into every room in every home in the city. The magic it brought touched their hearts. All but the Bishop's.

"It is over," said Samuel, looking down at Gerard, alone and adrift in the sea of smiling, cheering people.

"Where will you go now?" said Elisabeth.

Samuel looked down at her. "Well I know a place where the chicken broth is good."

*　*　*

She waited. Far above the stench of men she flew in great circles and waited. The fires they had lit on the city walls sent smoke high into the air, keeping her from swooping down to take what she wanted from within the winding streets. But she only had to wait for a few sad souls to stray too far or for a fat merchant to risk it all for a few bags of gold and she would have her fill.

The Lezard was growing fiercer by the day. One hundred

heads now sprouted from her torso and they each knew how to tear a bull in half or devour a horse in a single gulp. Though they shared one body, she was their mother and they were her offspring. Like children, they would sometimes fight with each other over food, ripping at flesh and bone in a game of tug of war until little was left of their poor victim. But they all shared one thing amongst themselves: their hatred of men. So she circled above the stinking city and they each scoured the earth below for fresh meat. It had been a day since their last meal and they were hungry.

Then one of the heads let out a cruel, cawing sound that signalled that prey had been found. Far below her two tiny forms were moving over the ground just outside the city, where few dared tread these days. This would not feed her for long but her empty belly cried out for food. She circled lower.

"Come Levine, we have to hurry," shouted Gillan as he turned back to urge her on. Away from the Great Track the ground was soft and boggy and it made the going slow.

"I'm doing the best I can," she said, pulling one foot out of the wet ground. "Why can't we just stick to the path anyway?"

"Because someone might see us!" he snapped back.

"But who?" she said. "There's no one out here. No one's mad enough to come this way. Except us."

"And that's why we're doing it," he said, "because they'd never think to look for us here. But you still can't be too careful, so it's best to keep off the path." He stepped forward and his leg sank up to the knee in a muddy puddle. Levine began to laugh.

They walked on for another minute until Levine told him to stop. "Can't you feel that?" she said. He looked at her, puzzled. "Something made me shiver. It felt like…"

"Over there!" he shouted, pointing at something closer to the Great Track. She followed his gaze and saw two objects poking from the ground. They looked like sticks. "It's Nathaniel's sword," he said, running towards them, "and the Archbishop's wand."

"It's called a crook," Levine said as she drew alongside him, staring at what was protruding from the damp soil. "They've been here since the day..." Her voice trailed off.

"What's wrong?" he asked. She had gone pale and was shivering. Then he heard the sound. It was like a roaring river, coming from far above. He raised his head and saw the one hundred snarling heads of the Lezard descending on them. "Run!" he screamed and they headed in different directions over the boggy ground. He felt a great wind build up around him and threw himself to the floor just as the creature swept past. Its teeth missed him by inches. Then the wind died down and he realised the Lezard was moving away from him. Towards Levine. He screamed at her to lie down on the ground but she could not hear him above the sound of the monster's downdraft. The Lezard was almost upon her and some of its heads were already snapping at her cloak.

Then the sky on the western horizon lit up. A wall of blue light stretched from north to south, hundreds of feet high. It rolled across the land towards them and the Lezard looked up as it drew near, giving Levine enough time to drop down into a ditch. Gillan watched the wave of light sweep past him. Ten yards behind him were the Knight's sword and the Archbishop's crook, standing upright in the mud. The light wrapped itself around them and he had to cover his eyes from the glare as they burst into flames. Steam rose from the damp ground as a great ball of fire encircled the two weapons. It was like looking into a blacksmith's forge as the metal buckled from the heat. He peered through a gap in his fingers as the sword and crook melted together, the tools of might and magic forming one single shape that lay on the ground. Then the fire went out.

"Gillan! Help me!" He turned at the sound of Levine's voice and saw her cowering in the ditch as two of the Lezard's heads snapped at her. "Please Gillan. Please." Her cries were growing more desperate. He lingered for a moment, watching the Lezard tear at the ground on either side of her. He had to protect her; he had sworn to do so. Then he turned and ran away.

The Lezard mother watched as her two youngest offspring

dug out their prey. This was a small morsel but killing it would be good practice for her babies. And the flesh would taste so sweet. She would let them play with it first before she finished it off.

"Hey, you, turn around and fight." She wheeled round at the sound of a human voice, young and shrill, that called to her. Behind her on the grass stood a boy with fair hair, holding a small sword. "I said turn and fight."

Gillan held the weapon out in front of him. He had run back to the spot when Nathaniel's sword and the Archbishop's crook had stood. They were nowhere to be seen, but lying on the scorched grass was a small sword made of plain steel. Unlike Nathaniel's broadsword, the only decoration it carried was an intricate pattern that wound its way around the hilt. He had picked it up and it felt as light as a feather as if it was made for a child. Now he held it out to challenge the Lezard.

She found this amusing. A boy with a toy sword was asking her to fight. She sent her very youngest head to deal with him and it approached with a mean hiss. It sniffed the air around Gillan and eyed him smugly. He raised the sword just as it was deciding which side to attack from and...

He sliced the head clean off. The blade cut through it like butter and the head rolled onto the grass and sank into the mud. The Lezard mother gave a scream and sent two more heads to despatch him. They came in from left and right to tear him in two. He dealt with them both, flicking the sword first one way and then the next. She went into a fury. More and more of her children dived at Gillan but the sword simply sliced and cut them, one by one. "I will protect Levine. I will protect her," he said and the sword responded by filling him with its magic. As a dozen heads flew in at once he spun on the spot and the blade somehow reached them all. The Lezard's blood formed pools on the waterlogged ground.

The mother withdrew. She lifted into the air in a swirling cloud of grass and mud and took to the skies. She would regroup and attack again from above. But Gillan would not let her escape. In the drawings under his bed the dragons were defeated and the Lezard would be too. The earth around his feet began to shake and a crack formed in the ground that encircled him. It began to rise into the air: a column of earth pushing upwards with Gillan standing on top of it. It went higher and higher, until he was no longer visible from the ground.

The Lezard saw him rise on the pillar of soil and rock and threw in her most vicious attack so far. A score of heads fell upon Gillan but the sword in his hand stayed true and he sent them all spinning to the earth far below. A shimmering light had formed around him and he seemed less like a boy and more like a man: a tall, striking man with white clothes and flowing blonde hair. The blade of the sword began to flame and it reached out like a burning whip to strike at the Lezard's heads. They were all attacking him at once now but he cut through each neck in turn with the blazing weapon.

On the ground, people were streaming out of the city bar. They craned their necks to look up at the column of earth rising into the heavens. There was such a blinding white light at the top that it seemed as if a second sun was burning there. They could see the Lezard fighting with someone on the pillar and the beast's screams were so loud that many pressed their hands over their ears to block out the din.

As the Lezard's heads attacked him, Gillan killed them all. He twisted and spun and the flaming sword arced back and forth and one by one he cut each head from its neck. Then there was just one left – the Mother. She drew in what strength she had left and prepared to strike. It seemed to her that this boy, this White Knight, was weakening and she waited for her moment to knock him from his pillar. Then she saw him lower his sword and she fell upon him.

"Look! Look!" One man saw it first and he pointed upwards so that others could see. The light at the top of the ragged column of earth had gone out and a tiny shape was falling from it. It spun over and over as it dropped towards them through the air, a small dark dot that grew larger with each turn. Then it hit the ground and lay still. Her head. The oldest head of all sat in a puddle of mud with its mouth gaping open.

The crowd looked skywards again. The body of the Lezard, its wings still flapping, hung in the air. Then it began a slow, spiralling descent to earth that gradually gathered pace. "It'll crush us!" someone shouted and people began running away in all directions. Only one figure remained at the base of the giant tower – a girl with tears in her eyes. Then the Lezard's body came crashing down with such force that it was partially buried in the mud.

The earth shook and the pillar began to sink back into the ground with a deep rumble. It moved slowly and the crowd kept their distance until it had finally dropped into place. When they surged forward there were gasps of shock at what they saw.

A small boy lay on the wet grass with a child's sword by his side. His face was battered and bruised and his arms were scored with bloody cuts. He did not seem to be breathing. A weeping girl knelt over him and held his hand. "Thank you Gillan," she whispered, "My brave little knight. Thank you."

* * *

Johan Banberg stood before the Monkton Stone in his secret chamber, his Black Chapel. He peered into the heart of the gem but it was no use. It had been a week since he had last had any contact with Andrew Marshall and he was growing worried. The small piece of the stone that he had given him must have stopped working. This was unexpected and he felt a tiny flutter of panic. His Master would be furious if anything happened to ruin His plans.

But Johan wanted this to succeed as much as He did. He dreamed of the day when he could sit at His right hand and rule over this land. Commissioner Banberg had given years of faithful service to his Dark Lord: stealing souls to act as servants in the living world and the next, plotting to spread His message across Theland and even killing colleagues to protect His great plan. If things went well then Johan would be rewarded.

He stared into the Monkton Stone, the ancient relic that had been corrupted by evil, and looked for some sign of Marshall. But there was nothing. Then, as he was about to leave the chamber, there was a slight tremor. "That's more like it," he said cheerily and he stepped back into place. But there was no swirling mist or green fire. Instead, the room was bathed in a wave of blue light. It swamped the walls with its colour and sent the jewel into a frenzy. Sparks flew from it and thousands of cracks began to score themselves over its surface. There was a sound like breaking glass. "Oh no! No!" he cried and he desperately tried to hold the Stone together as pieces began to fall from it. His skin was shredded as the gem started to disintegrate within his grasp.

Then the screaming started. There were voices, so many voices, and they filled his head with their noise. He knew who they were; they were the souls he had stolen to work as slaves for his Master. As the Monkton Stone fell apart, so they were being set free. He could see them now as dots of light, moving out of the crumbling remains of the green gem on the plinth. They swarmed around him like insects and he shrieked and swatted at them with his bloodied fists. Their torture was over but his was about to begin.

He ran from the chamber and fled up the stairs, slipping more than once in his panic. If he could just get to the top and shut the door, then he was sure he could escape. He could feel dead hands clawing at him as he scrambled up the cold stone steps. They snatched at his purple robe and he frantically tore it from his shoulders, letting it disappear behind him into the darkness as he ran for his life. Finally he made it up into the study and hauled the secret door closed behind him. He was free. He would pack a bag and leave the house immediately.

But first he needed a steadying drink and a cigar. He went to his desk and poured a large brandy. His hands were shaking so violently that much of it spilled down the sides of the glass. Then he went looking for something to light his cigar. As he was rummaging in his drawer he heard a voice say, "Need a match mate?" and he looked up to see the stolen soul of Andrew Marshall standing before him.

Then he screamed.

* * *

The shockwave rolled on. There were more places where it flashed through, changing destinies and bringing dreams to life, laying waste to nightmares and shining its light into the darkest corners of worlds. Then it came to the last barrier of all, the high dark wall through which nothing can be seen or heard, no matter how hard we try. The shimmering, burning wave of blue light came to the edge of life itself; to the border post with death. And it crossed over and went on.

On a cold, noisy train rattling its way down a track on a dark October night, a woman sat with her young child on her knee and an elderly couple held hands. Their lives were drawing towards a point of conclusion, towards the place where they would cross over to the other side of that high wall.

Then a pale blue light passed through the carriage, moving like a breeze on a summer's day. Each of the passengers felt something touch their face; brushing their skin so gently for one moment in time that the world beyond the dark windows ceased to exist. It was familiar and comforting and stirred in each of them a feeling of such peace and calm that if their lives were to end at that moment they would feel no fear or pain.

But life did not end. Because a man four miles down the track made the right decision. Because he chose to press a button on the panel in front of him. After too many hours at work his thoughts may have been disjointed and his vision blurred but when the warm blue light entered his signal box he felt his body lifted with a breaking wave of energy. He looked up and saw the flashing light. He switched the points.

And the trains passed by.

Chapter Thirty

Just the Ticket

"Mummy, I'm hungry."

Katie was looking forlornly towards the vending machine further down the platform. Sarah's first reaction was to tell her to wait until lunchtime but she could not face a tantrum in public so she rummaged in her purse for some change. She went to the machine and bought a packet of chocolate biscuits then slumped back down on the bench.

Life seemed surprisingly calm. The book had stopped working, at least in terms of flashing lights and magic. Now it was just a rather tatty looking hardback with a pretty pattern on the front cover. Her only visitor in the last week was Annie who had brought the children back after their sudden sleepover. Matthew was still sulking at her for not taking him for a ride in the helicopter.

She had tried telling Annie that Alex was dead but the words would not come. Her friend had guessed that something had happened and promised to be around when she needed someone to talk to.

And that was it. That was her life. She could not yet face explaining to the children that their father was gone for good but she knew that she would have to eventually. She looked at them now and a lump formed in her throat at the prospect. She would not wish that on her worst enemy.

Which reminded her: the world seemed to be getting back to normal now that He was back in his rightful place. People were still being unpleasant to each other, even unspeakably so in some cases. But the kind of violent hysteria that had been building for weeks and weeks had vanished on the night that...

She tore open the biscuit wrapper for Matthew.

There had been this feeling the day after; a sense that things could be better, if people only tried. Things could still go horribly wrong with the world but if they did, then mankind would only have itself to blame. Meddling hands had been slapped and sent on their way.

She pulled the train ticket from her pocket and peered at it for the third time in five minutes. It was the one that had fallen out of the book when it was first delivered to her door and its date and destination had been an inky blur. Earlier that day, when she was cleaning out her bedside drawers in a freak moment of tidiness, she had found it again and this time the print was perfectly clear. It was an advance booking for today and would bring her to this station. Her social diary was a bit blank at the moment so she and the kids had headed off. Now they were on a platform bench eating chocolate and wondering what to do next.

* * *

In the pages of a small, hardbound book lie the words:

The one who stands alone and faces the oldest enemy, the shadow that lies within all hearts, must have a choice. Without it they are all lost. It must not be because he Is but because he Has.

Chosen.

He will have found the greatest treasure of all. And from the love of others may come his salvation.

* * *

The man sits in his parlour drinking tea. He has dreamed of this moment for so long, of relaxing in his tidy little house surrounded by books, and reflect on the past. But he is already

305

bored and lonely and sits there each day watching the hours escape. Then there is a knock at the door.

There is a house near the sea where a young woman is working in the garden. She cuts away at the overgrown roses that cover the wall, taking care to avoid their jagged teeth. The work has taken weeks but now is nearly finished. Then she will see what lies behind the thorns. She pulls away the last of the branches and steps back. There is a stone archway and beneath it stands a door. She opens it and walks through.

The tall man has a new home high on a hill. He will farm this land one day, grazing sheep in the fields, but first he has to rebuild the house. In an upstairs room he strips away the peeling paper on the wall and behind it he finds a door. It springs open at his touch.

On a moonlit hillside a man stands beneath a cloud of heavenly proportions. He gazes up at it in wonder. There is a brilliant flash and he feels himself drifting, floating upwards towards the stars. He looks down and sees ripples of blue spreading out like waves on a pond.

He hears a voice calling, "Alex." Someone is with him. They stand together in a room with four closed doors.

"Did I do all right?" the man asks.

"Oh yes," the other says. "In the end you did what I could never do, you gave up everything you had for the sake of love. You were never less than human and yet you knew when to choose one path from another. You showed that love and dreams can overcome hate and fear."

"It's nice to be of some use."

They talk a while and time passes. Then three of the doors open and the others are there, the ones from the land of magic: the angel, the shepherd and the leader of men. They hold him close and he feels their love wrap itself around him. Then they go to the fourth doorway and lead him through.

* * *

On the station platform Sarah watched the trains come and go. People hurried past without even glancing down. Just one person, a young mother carrying a baby, turned to look at her: a lonely figure on a bench, lost in her own thoughts. The woman smiled and walked on. Then Matthew started complaining that he was hungry again. Sarah opened the second packet from the snack machine and bent down in front him.

"Say biscuit."

"Daddy."

Her heart ached. "No, not Daddy. Say biscuit."

"Daddy."

"Biscuit."

"Daddy." He was pointing over her shoulder. Something had caught his eye and was making him smile. She turned and saw a familiar pair of legs behind her, then a torso, then some shoulders and then...

"Alex?" She stood up and looked at him. This had happened once before and it had been a cruel trick. The assassins had played on her weaknesses and could be doing it again. His lips hovered over hers for a moment and she braced herself. Then they moved upwards and kissed her softly on the tip of her nose.

"Sorry I'm late."

The End

1757584